tiger *season*

Gojan Nikolich

Black Rose Writing | Texas

ISBN: 978-1-68513-500-3
LIBRARY OF CONGRESS CONTROL NUMBER: 2024947559
PUBLISHED BY BLACK ROSE WRITING
www.blackrosewriting.com

Printed in the United States of America
Suggested Retail Price (SRP) $24.95

Tiger Season is printed in Garamond Premier Pro

*As a planet-friendly publisher, Black Rose Writing does its best to eliminate unnecessary waste to reduce paper usage and energy costs, while never compromising the reading experience. As a result, the final word count vs. page count may not meet common expectations.

IN MEMORY

Captain D.B., US Army, SOF

tiger
season

PROLOGUE

They poked him. All day they poked his nether cheeks beneath the sheets and they poked his wrist, and then they stabbed his feet.

Tubes ran tangled across the bed, up the wall to the machines. A hose curled from the hole in his throat. It felt so familiar. And still, nothing really hurt. The nurses came and went in their rubber shoes. His insensible self seemed small and worthless, like it could fit into the palm of his hand. He felt a lonesome anguish, a growing wish to remain on earth at least one more day before his brain broke like an egg and spilled its nonsense everywhere.

This is how he now lay dying, though his nose seemed to work better each day. They said the ears were the last to go, but they were wrong. He could smell everything, though he had the sense that he might now also be insane.

From the dark behind his closed lids he could remember how this had all started. How the distant river looked, like someone had dragged a fork through white frosting on a chocolate cake. How the wind blew snow from the ice. In the old Korea storybooks they called the Imjin River *The Water Dragon* and on that freezing night so long ago Eddie Profar had heard it roar.

In this new timeless and benumbed world he sensed that everyone who'd ever lived was as old as the first oceans. As ancient as those volcano stones that were now dust in which all must one day be buried. It had passed so quickly, this conspiracy of time devised by unseen laughing clockmakers, the tricksters. In the end, we were all just one memory away from oblivion.

He'd long forgotten what her beautiful face looked like, the touch of her hand. And as he waited to die, he wondered if his own grizzled self now resembled some fairytale forest sorcerer who'd come to cast a magic spell on thee.

He wished he'd written his own obituary. God knows what a mess they would make of it now.

Edward J. Profar was from Duluth. The J was for Johannes. Dutch, they claimed.

From the house where he grew up he could smell the lake and see the Ferry Bridge when they turned on the lights for the ore freighters who'd sound their moaning horns in the fog as if they were in pain.

Nobody explained the details of his death or how they got him here. Who'd found him. He guessed there wasn't time.

At the end, there were people in the little room. His brother, cousins. Certain friends. Unknown others, each of whom had their own odor. He didn't understand why anyone would bring kids to watch somebody die. This cheered him up, the visiting children who had better things to think of than death.

Profar was good with horses. He could shoot a rifle, though he'd stopped hunting long ago. He enjoyed gardening and fishing, but he never ate the fish. He once won an expensive casting reel and a tackle box filled with lures and hooks from a TV sports show in Chicago. Rapalas and bright red Daredevils in fancy boxes. They showed his name in big letters on the screen, and for a while he was a hero at school.

He once won a medal in the Army. He did not like people in general and did a good job of pretending that he did. He tried to be polite. Don't go out of your way to hurt anybody on purpose and mind your own business, is what he always said.

When singing carolers in costume showed up at his door one snowy Christmas Eve he peeked through the curtains and turned off the lights. He felt the same about Halloween, Thanksgiving, New Year's Eve and Valentine's Day. All the greeting card company holidays. He disliked professional sports but for baseball, and his favorite team was the Twins. Harmon Killebrew autographed his Little League cap.

He once helped his uncle count the wolves and moose on Isle Royale in Lake Superior. They took the ferry and lived in those deep wet woods all summer.

He remembered going to the Sears and Roebuck downtown with his father on Saturdays and touching all the tools, walking up and down the aisles, examining saws and hammers. Clawing through sacks of bolts and screws. For hours they'd walk around like inspectors of all Indisputable Non-Bullshit Things that were useful and true. In the car on the way home they'd talk about what they'd seen at the store. Hacksaws and crimpers and pipe benders. Glorious drill bits of every shape. Awls and axes. His dad would smoke cigarettes in the car with the window open, sleet blowing off the lake. His father died when he was a boy.

He called his cars 'automobiles' and drove them until they disintegrated. Until the wheels fell off. He had much on his mind most of his life but kept these things to himself. He had no mottos and distrusted those who did. He disliked slogans, rallying cries and sayings and was suspicious of anyone with charisma. He was not at all a quiet man and believed that one day everyone on Earth would be a hologram managed by their murdering makers and that when the world said 'for the sake of the greater good,' it usually meant 'what's good for the fewest.'

Rock music drifted from the ceiling speakers, something bouncy and hopeful. He peed warmly into the tube that emptied into the bag on the floor. He no longer had to eat food through his mouth. This was full-service dying.

He'd played guitar when he was young, so now Profar's hypersensitive tuning fork mind raced off with another memory. He thought: bands in my generation practiced in freezing garages. We dreamed of three-chord hits that would make us famous just like The Singer Zimmerman from Duluth. We named our bands *Ozzie and the Harlots of Harriet* and the *Insane Calliope Gymnasts of Armageddon* and went to sleep humming *Louie Louie*. Our disappointed parents worked nights in factories and shoveled Mesabi iron ore. We played As Loud as Possible on decrepit Sears Silvertone guitars while singing like desperate music beggars into plastic microphones purchased at flea markets. We played and played furiously like mentally ill and armless jugglers, and said: this is living, man this is living.

Those were the days, Eddie thought. His brain now seemed so finely tuned, like a cat whisker. If he could only open his eyes.

He peed into the tube. On this day he was bursting with a clarity of remembrance he had not expected. One squeak of a chair could set things off. Any smell, of course.

His ear itched, so he riffed on the rainforest of hair that had been sprouting there for years. He thought perhaps that angels, both fallen and those legally licensed to fly, had been commanded by God to go forth and seek each and every old man and cause his hindmost twin cheek parts to vanish and become droopy and jejune in such a pendulous manner as to render them athletically useless and without their previously celebrated allure. And God further said: "And then shalt thou fill their ears with hair to grow and dangle with wildering fury as do the weeds from Nebuchadnezzar's Babylon garden. Amen."

And so he fell asleep wondering if the nurse ever trimmed the hair in his ears.

He woke to the murmur of their voices in the room. He wondered if his visitors spoke of him or the weather, and realized that this is how it would be at the funeral service where he was the guest of honor. People whispering as they sat and stared at his coffin.

Some days he was filled with hope, a sense of sweet kinship with every living thing in the world. When the death-watchers were gone, their smells lingering, and the nurse came with her loud starchy pants and wiped him with the wet cloth and pulled out his pee tube and lifted him with the rubber bed cradle, he wanted to give up and just disappear. He'd had his turn and now it was time to move on.

In the morning he felt air blowing on his face from the floor vent. The sunlight was warm on his legs when they opened the curtains and cleaned him like he was a baby. Coffee smells drifted into the room. He sensed the rumble of the nurse's wheeled medicine cart, the cups with their pills rattling. Someone pulled socks onto his feet and rubbed him with a cloth. He listened to the children, their busy voices like chirping birds. He'd forgotten what was killing him. The truth will set you free, but only after it has had its way with you.

Two nurses laughed and their voices reminded him of every woman he had ever touched. A dog barked outside and he remembered all the dogs he'd ever loved. He heard the rumble of a car and so he thought of every car he had ever owned. His head was revved up. He was almost dead, though his brain burned fiercely like a stubborn ember in an ebbing fire. He thought that while everything now seemed to end at his numb feet, it would soon end at his knees. Then his chin. Then it would just end. Life never asks for permission to surprise you.

Each of his visitors whispered their farewells with careful enunciation, like they were speaking to a moron.

"Eddie. Hey, pal. How. Are. *Yooou.*"

The snot tube wiggled inside his nose as he listened to someone tap their phone. He now heard his visitors speak suddenly in grave and somber tones. There had been a change in the vibe in the room. After a long silence, during which their feet shuffled, someone took a deep and thoughtful breath. Another sighed and wept. He smelled the doctor standing at the end of the bed. A sobbing woman stepped up and held his hand tightly.

It seemed like they'd all finally agreed on something.

The day remained timeless, without beginning or end. When everyone was gone, the nurse who smelled like hairspray pulled at the tube before it had a chance to empty and Eddie felt embarrassed as he lay there naked and she wiped him and changed his gown and slid the tube back in.

The medicine cart came rattling. Something icy stung his wrist and this reminded him of that freezing winter in Korea, and he thought once more about the women in their plastic flip-flops washing clothes in the village courtyard so very long ago. And he thought again about her.

He took a deep breath to slow his racing heart. The hospital room now smelled like a cat.

PART ONE

Winter 1968
Republic of South Korea

"My Pezhetairoi, upon the conduct of each depends the fate of all."
– Alexander of Macedon
356-323 BC

CHAPTER 1

In the blue light of the full moon, Eddie Profar's steaming breath lifted from his mouth and hung as frosty smoke in the thirty-below air, if air is what you could call it.

Such awful cold turns to stinging heat when breathed through frozen nose holes. His eyes burned as he squinted at the sky, slung the M14 rifle barrel-down across his shoulder on its leather strap and stepped through the plywood door of Guard Post Robideaux. He stomped the powdery snow from his feet and his boots squeaked on the floor. He thought: not a single sweet swinging piece of me will ever be warm again.

He was a Minnesota boy and thought he knew cold and ice, but after these few months in Korea he did not. This was not like fishing in winter on a North Woods lake or playing hockey at night in the park with the girls clapping their mittens from the sideline benches. The popping sound when you walked on this peculiar snow was different, like stepping on glass marbles in a Styrofoam cup. Gunfire and the rattle of the metal safety latch on his weapon sounded different here. Rifle shots had no resonance. The noise was like coins dropped on a wood floor. Leather boots cracked if left outside and your rising breath froze white on your eyebrows. Everything familiar seemed chemically transformed in this icy world that sat on the very edge of the middle of nowhere.

He looked through the window of the twenty-by-twenty shack that was a box sitting on four peg legs like a barstool above the valley. From here you could look downriver for miles. The seven dipper stars he'd seen so often in his other life seemed skewed overhead and altogether foreign, like fireflies frozen against the black night sky, the entire world caught silent and hanging immobile as if nothing might ever come alive again.

It was 2 a.m. So cold and getting colder by the hour. He felt suspended and numb within his own foggy breath. As if the sun would never return.

Back home, there was not this heavy wet wind howling across the sea from Siberia. Down all the way from the Gobi Desert, he'd heard. The icy wastes of Mongolia. He could not imagine fighting a war in such godawful weather. He could not imagine ten thousand crazy shouting Chinese soldiers running toward you in the dark in such weather. They blew trumpets and whistles when they attacked at night and slept in their quilted white parkas during the day, dissolved into the snow like ghosts. Themselves wholly apiece of the winter rocks. In this relentless cold, they did such a thing. Even the whiskered Mongol invaders in their droopy hats and leather shoulder capes, charging on ponies down from Manchuria a thousand years ago through these same mountains along the Ch'orwon invasion route, waited sensibly for the warmth of summer to attack.

Profar wondered how many soldiers like him had died on this exact icebound spot during the war that had ended fifteen years ago with an uneasy truce that still held warrant on such a cold and miserable night.

It was now 2:33 a.m. at Guard Post Robideaux, a plywood shack with its single slanted window overlooking a chemically denuded hill on the southern bank of the Imjin River.

Every metallic sound seemed amplified in the desolate stillness, where Profar now studied the snow outside with his spotting scope. He could see his breath drifting past the lens. The valley beyond the distant wire barrier fence formed an oxbow, and he could clearly see a row of perimeter lights on that side of the DMZ, where a soldier from the North was at this moment likely also looking toward him. Also freezing his ass off. Another bewildered son of a bitch wrapped in green wool sitting with a weapon on his lap looking across a two-mile-wide expanse of one million buried land mines.

He heard a hollow pop and thought it might be another of those midget DMZ deer that sometimes stepped on a mine. It seemed like shots had been fired. Maybe tree sap cracking in the cold. They're usually not that loud, he thought. Exploding mines made an altogether different sound. There came another burst of popcorn popping and he now thought it might be rifle fire. A pistol sounds muted out here at night when it's this cold. It was easy to tell the difference between one of their long guns and a side arm. The North Koreans used the old Czech thirty-threes, sometimes grandpa's M1 Garand. Mostly, when they snuck across the river, it was the AKS with that folding stock they carried. Profar knew exactly what each weapon sounded like.

Don't make me go out there again, he thought.

Profar rubbed his two-finger trigger mittens together. He held his arms outstretched above the hot diesel stove like somebody invoking a magic spell. There was a laminated sheet of paper tacked to the wall next to a girlie poster. Somebody had also taped up a Fillmore West show flyer hawking a concert date for Jefferson Airplane and Quicksilver Messenger Service:

RULES OF ENGAGEMENT FOR THE INDIVIDUAL SOLDIER.

(1) Daylight: Challenge all unidentified individuals.
If they attempt to escape or evade, shoot them.

(2) In or on the Imjin River at night: Shoot ALL unidentified individuals.

(3) Challenge anyone in the Civilian Easement Zone during curfew:
If they attempt to escape or evade, shoot them.

That week, the entire garrison had been placed on full alert after a US Navy freighter was captured in the Sea of Japan. The North Koreans said the USS Viator was on a spy mission. The Americans claimed the vessel was gathering scientific information about the stars. The ship carried a crew of eighty-three, not counting six officers, all of whom were taken to a prison camp near Pyongyang. Two sailors died. They showed a picture of the sour-looking crew on the front page of *Stars & Stripes.* Company First Sergeant Ralph Cobb mustered everybody on the parade field to announce the new 24/7 alert that included cancellation of any scheduled leave time or R&R until further notice, weekend passes to the village red-light entertainment district outside the camp gate excluded.

"As we speak, they're being tortured," Cobb said and pointed to a photo on an easel that showed the handcuffed USS Viator crew being marched off their vessel like men headed for the gallows.

The "Viator Incident," as it was being referred to in the newspapers, happened days after thirty-six North Korean commandos infiltrated the DMZ in the middle of a snow storm, later killing two dozen ROK soldiers while they tried to assassinate the South Korean President at his home in Seoul. On top of that, there was serious intel chatter about something big ready to happen in Vietnam, which forced the transfer of troops from Profar's own battalion on a midnight flight to Ton Son Nhut Air Base in Saigon. Things were cooking along the Demilitarized Zone.

Following the Viator's capture, an hour after Profar and his guard post partner, Private First Class Yevgeny Lee, had finished their pre-dawn breakfast of chipped beef on toast and scrambled eggs, a geyser of dirt lifted above the camp mess hall. This was followed by another explosion that sent the building's rooftop swamp cooler flying across the street through the front door of the USO recreation hall. Those who could, escaped the chow hall attack by jumping through the front window. From inside the burning structure came the shouts of the wounded. It happened in the middle of the night, so there had been only a few soldiers inside, three five-man ambush squads headed to their dawn patrols along the barrier fence and a detachment of MPs who had just completed their curfew patrol in the village.

The second blast was followed by a barrage of small arms fire and the sound of splintering wood, along with the rattle of a .50 cal machine gun raking the trees where the assault was thought to have come from. Two gun jeeps fishtailed to a sliding stop in front of the burning mess hall and they too began to return fire toward where the North Korean infiltrators were cornered against a row of shipping containers that were being used as kitchen storage sheds. The firefight lasted only minutes. Medics in an armored ambulance dragged the wounded and dead from the damaged building. By the time reinforcements arrived, the North Korean bodies had already been arranged on a canvas tarp in the middle of the street, weapons displayed next to each corpse like booty from a smuggling bust.

While Profar stood warming himself next to the diesel stove, there came the sound of stomping feet on the guard post steps. PFC Yevgeny Lee barged through the door and shook more snow from his boots and quickly stepped to the heater. He dropped his mittens on the floor and held his bare hands near the hot stove pipe and gave a dramatic full-body shiver.

Profar nodded at the pouch of twenty-round M14 magazines strapped to the front of Lee's pistol belt.

"You can't see that?"

Lee moved even closer and danced up against the heater.

"Your ammo," Profar said. "Want to blow us up?"

"Mother Eddie, you worry too much about everything."

Lee peeled off his quilted field cap and tossed it over his shoulder. "No wonder they made you the General's driver. You're like an old hen."

"I take Yardley to Panmunjom twice a week, is all," Profar said. "The rest of the time I babysit your sorry ass. Don't make it sound like it's a cushy job."

"Listen to the commanding General's personal chauffeur," Lee said. He gave an eye roll.

Lee unzipped his parka and picked up his rucksack from the bench near the door. He took out a small drawstring bag and pulled out his pipe and held it to the light. He fished a Korean language magazine from the rucksack and showed it to Profar.

"I'm brushing up on my Hangul," he said.

"I thought you talked the lingo just fine."

"Not the reading part," Lee said. "My folks talked Korean at home so I can speak it okay, but I need work on the reading part." He opened the magazine. "It's a soap opera rag. I strive for literary self-improvement."

He jerked a matchbook from his pocket and lit the pipe. PFC Lee took a wheezy draw and studied the glowing ash in the bowl and leaned with his elbows on his knees as he flipped through the magazine. The front cover showed a man and a woman in a passionate embrace. Lee's dope smoke filled the shack. Profar gave him another look.

"Relax," Lee said. "Where is our fearless leader this week?"

"Yongsan. For that thing with the Navy boat. Brass came on a bus from Seoul yesterday, all dressed in their goody suits."

"Hand me that," Lee said.

Profar took the coffee thermos from the wire hanger fastened to the side of the stove. Lee filled the bottle lid and sipped with his eyes closed.

"When you go back out," Lee said. "Check where they cut the fence last week. Tell me those jackasses didn't just twist some wire together instead of stringing new Number Nine. Shit just breaks again. They know that."

"Did they move the dozer?" Profar said.

"Slid off that hill on the ice just like we said."

"Not our business, I suppose," Profar said. "What are you reading?"

"Some Korean TV show," Lee said. "I think I figured out the plot. As far as I can tell, Mr. Kim wants to have sex with Miss Lee and there's a second Mr. Kim who's having a mental breakdown about his job. Miss Soo, who has ulterior motives involving a family inheritance, wants to help Mr. Kim Number Two but first she has to take the train to Busan to visit her dying relative, they call her *Imo*, who is a prosperous farmer's wife and Miss Soo, whose first name is Hee, is convinced she's sick because the village Mudang, who is a witch, invoked a hex on her while she was milking the cows."

"A lot to keep track of," Profar said.

Lee held up the back cover that showed two lovers pawing madly at each other. They were kneeling on the floor. The woman wore a traditional puffy Hanbok dress.

"There's some kind of romance down in Busan, too, but I can't figure out between who or why. I think it involves either Ming Chi-Yeong the lovely seamstress or Min the embezzling bank teller or maybe the sex worker who lives near the US Navy base who goes by the professional name of Katy, but her real name is Sook Han. Katy, who likes anybody in uniform, is in love with a Chief Petty Officer who's promised to take her home to Clear Lake, Iowa, of all places...but it's all been a lie, and so Katy is heartbroken and decides to poison her pimp and build her own bawdyhouse empire."

"Sounds like a Madame Butterfly ripoff," Profar said.

"Doesn't it always?" Lee said.

"You said Clear Lake? She could see where Buddy Holly crashed."

"Yeah, and the Big Bopper. Didn't think of that."

Lee took a long, contemplative puff and studied his pipe. "There's a backstory that was introduced in Episode Three about a beautiful abalone sea diver they call Haenyeo who has gorgeous legs and she lives in Jeju, a tourist island that looks like Florida with mountains. I'm familiar with the place. This Jeju water goddess has magical powers and she shows off a rubber wetsuit like nobody's business and she can hold her breath for three minutes. Think of it, Eddie. She can hold her breath for three minutes. She also communicates with the fishes."

Lee flipped through the magazine. "That's where it gets confusing," he said. "In the next episode there's a handsome stud in Seoul who's been diagnosed with a flesh eating disease that can consume your entire face in seventy-two hours. I have to read that part again because something just doesn't sound right. I need a Korean dictionary. There's a lot of slang. I'm not too good with the slang over here."

Profar had hardly listened. He was used to Lee's crazy word jags, especially when he started talking about reincarnation. That was a very big deal with him. Yevgeny Lee said he'd lived other lives going back thousands of years.

Profar wiped frost off the window with his parka sleeve. Outside, across the river and up a snowy hillside, the twisting north side barrier fence looked like a twinkling holiday decoration. The lights hung from coils of razor wire. He saw the dark space between two mountains where the broad Imjin River looped out of sight.

He thought about home. He felt sorry for all the walleye he had ever caught while ice fishing. You're eating, minding your own business at the bottom of the lake and some schmo yanks you flopping naked through a hole and just like that you're stiff and dead with your eyes open after the worst moment of your short fishy life. He wondered about the fish he'd murdered while drinking beer, sitting in a garden chair and bundled up in a shack not much smaller than the one he was in now.

Lee's weed smoke drifted to the bare ceiling. You could think of the oddest things when it was this cold outside. There was nothing else to do when you came back from patrol except the paperwork and then you'd sit and just think. And watch the river. And think some more. It was why they smoked. To make time go by. It was hard to worry about anything but your freezing feet, though Profar wondered about Lee as he watched him pack his pipe and take another hit and curl himself up in his baggy parka on the bench, the magazine held up to his face like he was cramming for a school exam. He hoped Lee's head would clear by the time the morning patrol squad arrived for the shift change. Sometimes First Sergeant Cobb himself would wander by unannounced in the middle of the night and if he did that now, they would both be in deep shit. Like a lot of NCOs, Cobb spent his time away from the camp barracks in his rented hooch in the village with his Korean girlfriend. It was only a short drive from the guard post.

"What if he shows up?" Profar said.

Lee shrugged. "Cobb? I hate that lifer Army gung-ho horseshit he always talks. What is he, fifty? Should have made Sergeant Major by now. Shows how full of it he is."

"The guys seem to like him," Profar said. "You're not a fan because he's a hard ass and told you to tuck in your shirt, remember?"

"Thinks he's the king of the DMZ," Lee said. "Carries around that crazy grease gun he brought from Vietnam. Who does that? Nobody uses an M3 anymore."

Profar took the clipboard from the wall. There were weapons manuals stacked in the corner on the floor. One of them said: *Supplemental Pamphlet 413-1, Use and Maintenance of the M16 Rifle.* The new M16s hadn't arrived and nobody liked the idea, anyway. The sixteen was a lower caliber weapon and a bad choice for long-range confrontations. Seemed junky and plastic, a glorified .22. Worked better on full automatic than the M14, he'd heard. Maybe it was good for the jungle, but not in Korea. He hoped he could continue using the M14 for the rest of his tour. He liked the heavy wood stock. He didn't feel like learning how to take apart and clean something new.

He looked at the clock above the door and signed the clipboard. They'd both walk another route along the cliff above the river before 5 a.m., and then it was quits. By this time Lee was usually too ripped to do his own paperwork, so Profar scribbled his partner's initials and wrote down the time. He stepped to the window and twisted the focus ring on the swiveled spotting scope that sat on a monopod bolted to the floor.

Something out on the empty ice moved like a brief shift of bright color against the snow.

He rubbed his eyes. He blinked and squinted, looked again. Maybe it was one of those goofy midget deer that stayed on the river all winter, oblivious to the stupid cold.

Snow blew against the shack like sand. Lee had a coughing fit, smoke exploding from his nose as he lay choking on the bench, the pipe and his hand resting on his chest. He'd set aside the soap opera magazine and was staring dreamily at the ceiling. His lips were moving like he was singing to himself.

Profar hunched closer to the stove and pulled the fur parka hood across his face. The shack was leaky and another gust of wind came off the river and shook the corrugated metal roof. Profar looked again. Nothing but white on white out there along with the blurry lights of the northern demarkation barrier. Lee's eyes were watering and he had a goofy grin on his face as he lay on the bench and took another hit. He sat up like he'd suddenly remembered something and started fiddling with the radio that hung on the wall. Music began to play.

Profar thought he'd be famous by now, playing in a rock band and signing autographs, his music career on autopilot. A future filled with girls and money. That's what he thought about as he stood looking out the window, annoyed that Lee was getting hammered so close to the end of their rotation. It was his third pipe of the night. He'd already walked his route along the fence all jacked up, so who knows what could have happened had he actually run into trouble. It was always just dope and girls with Lee, if you didn't count the stories about being a reincarnated soldier from Alexander the Great's army in 332 BC. Or walking through the snow in Russia with Napoleon. Profar couldn't remember, but the Romans and ancient Greeks were also part of the deal. Lee had once jabbered on about fighting barbarians in some German forest two thousand years ago.

"Something's out there," Profar said as he focused the scope.

Lee was flat on his back with the burning pipe in his hand and he was snoring.

CHAPTER 2

In Duluth, that year when everybody got drafted, they'd parked on Third Avenue and smoked Marlboros in front of Bob Dylan's birthplace house. They weren't kids anymore, but close to it. Profar had lost his 2-S deferment when he registered too late to start his sophomore semester at school.

Margolis was the oldest. He was the leader of the band because he had the best equipment. He owned a new cherry-red Gibson SG that made everybody jealous. Had a fancy case for it and always played with new strings. Profar's crummy Silvertone had the worst fretboard action in the world and Jimmy Lewis used a cheap, off-brand bass with a warped neck and a bent tuning peg. The other Jimmy, Jimmy Agronski the drummer, banged a black pearl Slingerland kit that he'd bought used and it looked like it had been dragged down the street behind a truck.

You could roll down Third right into the harbor, that's how close Dylan's place was to Lake Superior. They all sat and talked about music, and the big deal was that the house was nothing special. Just another old thing with a pointy roof on a street lined with other homes with the same pointy wooden roof and tiny fenced yard. The same front steps everywhere. It made you think you too could be somebody special and didn't need to grow up in a mansion to get famous.

In the car, with the music cranked up loud on the AM station out of Minneapolis, they smoked and smoked with the windows open and out of the blue Lewis wanted to know what everybody would do if they could travel back in time and change something. Alter the future. Rig their destiny.

"The Beatles," Agronsky said. "I'd go to Hamburg in Germany when they wore those leather jackets and tried to look like tough greasers. Maybe they were a year from being famous. Just right before things caught fire and everybody on the planet knew their names. That's where I'd go."

"What's the point?" Margolis said.

"The point?" Agronsky sucked on the last of his smoke and tossed the butt out the window. "I'll tell you what the point is. That's when they dumped Pete Best on drums and got Ringo. I'd make sure Ringo never auditioned, that's what I'd do. I know it's sounds sleazy. Maybe I'd mess with his drums, break his bass pedal. Nothing too nasty. I'd just figure out a way to go instead of him. I'd be their drummer now and I'd be a Beatle instead of sitting here with you jackass losers in a cold car on a cold day in freezing Duluth, MinneWhatsItsPlace. That's what the point would be."

"You're a dipshit," Margolis said. "I bet you wouldn't do it. Screw Ringo like that."

"Would," Agronsky said.

"Wouldn't. What if Lennon didn't like the way you played?"

"He would. I got a feeling he would," Agronsky said. "We got similar personalities. They'd all like me a lot and that would be all she wrote, and Ringo would just be Dick Starkey today, another guy from whatever that town was that they came from in England. A crummy place just like this dump. Anybody got anything to eat?"

They were in Agronsky's dad's red Pontiac station wagon, the one the band used to haul gear to gigs each weekend. Later, they drove seventy-five miles to Hibbing to see where Dylan actually grew up. It was the week everybody had gotten their draft notice in the mail. The Week of Hopeless Sorrow and Despair, is what they officially called it. The postponement of their promising rock and roll music careers.

Dylan's Hibbing house was also ordinary. Bigger, but basically a square box with a little garage. Pruned hedges under the front window, a green garden hose attached to a faucet next to a driveway where a Karmann Ghia sat propped on cinder blocks. They sat parked across the street for a long time smoking and smoking and passing around a bag of potato chips and drinking beer, except for Agronsky, who slammed cokes one after the other and had to walk down the street to pee at a gas station. Margolis said that if a little short skinny kid like Dylan could be famous and come from a crummy place like that, there was definitely a chance for the four of them. They too could become immortal legends, for they also lived in square little domiciles in the middle of Arctic North Woods Nowhere, Minnesota.

After driving past Dylan's high school it was agreed that when everybody got out of the Army in two years that they would start up the band again and resume the business of becoming legendary, just like Bob. Meanwhile, they would just have to do their duty and defend civilization from the stinking communist hordes.

By the time they drove the two hours home, the inspiration for making music history was gone. All they talked about was the Army and who would be sent to Vietnam and who might land a cushy tour with the Fräuleins in Germany. Japan would be okay. Nobody wanted to get sent to Alaska. It got colder than Minnesota up there.

Profar worked for another week picking auto parts off a shelf at the NAPA warehouse before he gave his notice. The others did the same, quitting their jobs at the burger place and the Ben Franklin store and at the Conoco gas station. Getting famous didn't seem important anymore after they watched Walter Cronkite one night on TV telling everybody how 300 soldiers had been killed in just one week in Vietnam at a place whose name nobody knew how to pronounce.

Profar got shipped to Korea. Margolis and Agronsky went straight from Fort Lewis, Washington to Vietnam, where the two of them died somewhere in the Central Highlands three weeks after their Pan Am charter flight landed at Tan Son Nhut Air Base. Agronsky had been one hell of a drummer and Margolis had the sweet voice of an angel. Margolis had been the first one to grow sideburns, and all the girls loved him. He lost track of Lewis after AIT school and the last he'd heard was that he'd landed a breezy job driving a supply truck at the Army garrison in Wiesbaden, Germany.

Hunched into his white patrol parka, Profar stood next to the stove and thought again about yanking up fish from the bottom of a lake and he felt sorry for every walleye and northern pike and bluegill he'd ever caught. He tried to think about girls but it was the poor fish and the freezing cold and his dead friends and Bob Dylan's crummy house that occupied him now. He closed his eyes and tried to concentrate, but it only made things worse. He undressed the girls in his head. He tried to feel their warm soft skin on his face but it was still the freezing cold that was more important than women. The Korean cold on a winter night at the DMZ was absolute. He thought of the doomed fish flopping on the ice and the way they gave you the side-eye look as he piled them stiff in the cooler for the trip home.

While Yevgeny Lee snored on the bench, this was all Eddie Profar could think about.

They'd seen strange things on the Imjin. The animals in the mined buffer zone sometimes got blown up. The red head-headed storks, the tiny deer, wild boars and every kind of bird lived here. The big cranes flying back and forth all winter, standing on their storky long legs in the hot springs. It was a wildlife paradise, an accidental zoo behind barbed wire that was two miles wide and 150 miles long. Before Profar joined him at Robideaux, Lee had been walking the DMZ fence since spring and he was on an ambush patrol during Christmas week when they caught a squad of North Korean infiltrators crawling across the ice a mile upriver from the guard post. The firefight lasted two hours, during which the North Koreans mysteriously disappeared. They just vanished into the dead bushes and trees that grew along the river. Nobody knew how that could happen. When they were finally spotted, it took two circling Hueys with their door guns to finally kill them all. That's how it was: days and days of boredom and then things would just explode.

They'd been on alert for six weeks and things only got worse after the North Koreans captured the USS Viator. Civilians anywhere near the barrier fence or this stretch of the river were on special dusk to dawn curfew and they'd doubled the MP patrols through the government-monitored village GI night club district outside the camp. Everybody was on edge. Flak jackets were mandatory. Everybody carried a side arm. They loosened the regs for checking out ammo and weapons.

Profar wiped the frosted window and swiveled the scope. He studied the brightly illuminated coils of razor wire at the bottom of the cliff. Something jittered out on the featureless ice halfway across the river and when he heard another pop, this one louder than before, even Lee in his stupefied state sat up and rubbed his face.

"The hell," he said. "What was that?"

They watched from the window and when it began to snow heavily Profar stood with his back to the stove and asked Lee if he sometimes felt that out here it was like they were the only people on earth.

"When you think of it," he said and pointed. "There's a half million Northies over there waiting for somebody to give them the word. And over here, another half million ROK guys along with forty-thousand of us doing the same thing. A million people with guns waiting for somebody to do something stupid. Waiting for an excuse to start shooting."

They remained silent. Lee's pipe glowed from within the cowl of his parka hood. Profar tried to focus the scope on what he thought was another moving smudge on the river, but it was snowing sideways now. The wind shook the shack.

"I'd go out there if it wasn't blowing like this," he said. "Could be a dumb deer, but I know I saw something."

"Deer don't walk around when it's like this," Lee said. "It's too easy to get ambushed or lost. They got bears out there. You're jumpy. You should smoke something, Edward."

Profar warmed his hands beneath his armpits. He stooped close enough to the stove to smell the singed fur on his parka hood. He wobbled the metal fuel plunger and the hut filled with an oily stink. There was never an in-between with the stove; it was either freezing or blazing hot inside the shack. He was convinced that he would never be warm again. Lee let loose with a violent cough and inhaled and blew a giant cloud across the room.

Profar squinted through the scope and thought: one day I'll break like a piece of ice myself and they'll ship the thawed chunks back home. The white marble tombstone at the veterans cemetery will say: *Eddie Profar, Specialist 4, US Army. He won no medals and was not a hero. He froze in Korea.*

Lee, recently busted to PFC for catching the clap for the second time, folded up his legs like he was about to meditate. He reached for the radio on the wall. There was music from Pyongyang, a brassy military tune with stray background voices chanting slogans in Chinese.

"You can always get the Bolshevik shows this time of night," Lee said. "Listen. It's her."

A woman came on who spoke slightly accented British English in a pleasant voice that sounded like she had a stuffy nose. Lee twisted the dial, but the woman faded away just as she was starting to gush about the glorious protector and gallant leader, His Wonderful Perfectness, the Big Daddy Himself, Kim Il-Sung.

He finally found the loudest of two Armed Forces Network signals and suddenly Ginger Baker was pounding out his double-footed bass beat to *White Room.* The lady with the sniffles briefly returned and then it was another woman with a husky voice singing something slow and moody in Korean. Lee wistfully studied the bowl of the pipe.

"I want that woman to sit naked on the edge of my bed and sing to me," he said. "Maybe I'm in Fiji, on an island. Palm trees outside. There's a breeze, I can hear the beach surf and she hands me a rum drink. She's jay-bird naked with long hair and singing to me like this is just another day in paradise and the only human being in the world that matters to her is me. Half Russian, half Korean Yevgeny Lee, that's who she loves like none other."

He offered the pipe to Profar, who wiped the wet stem on his shirt and smoked.

"Turn that thing up," Lee said and looked past the M60 tripod that stood in the corner by the window on its steel floor plate and he flipped his hand casually at the heater.

"I already did," Profar said and glanced at the wall clock. "If you juice it too much, it floods. We don't have much time left. Put your hat on if you're cold."

Lee pulled the furry ear flaps down on his cap and sat holding his knees. Profar handed back the pipe.

"We should go to Jeju on R&R," Lee said. He stared at the window dreamily like he was still thinking of the naked Fiji singer.

"Forget Bangkok. Everybody goes to Bangkok. It's just another version of this place but with more lights and the girls are too expensive, anyway. It's warm in Jeju. Like Miami. My folks went there when I was a kid to visit the relatives. It was their first trip since the war and my dad's sister was a teacher on the island. She married a fisherman and they lived in a house next to the ocean. All the roofs were tied down with rope because it gets so windy. There's women on that island, Eddie. And I mean goddess women, tall goddesses. Palm trees. Not many people. You can wear shorts instead of these Eskimo clothes. There's something different about the girls on Jeju. Maybe it's all that fresh salt air and maybe because they never saw snow. You could fish all you want. I know you like to fish, Eddie. There's an Air Force radar station. We could catch the mail shuttle easy from Seoul. Cobb would let us go, what do you think?"

Profar had already stood and was looking through the scope. He shoved aside the M60 on its pintle swivel, but decided he wouldn't crank open the window just yet.

"Something's out there."

"You're hammered, Eddie," Lee said.

"I can still see stuff," Profar said.

Condensation from the heater had formed a halo on the window and Lee wiped the glass and the scope with his mitten.

"I don't know how animals live in this," Lee said. "Those red-headed birds with the long legs, maybe that's what you saw. They're like five feet tall."

"I know what birds look like."

"So, if it's a Northie we'll call it in," Lee said. "Let the ROKs handle it. I don't feel like running into some bad ass out there at night when it's cold like this. Let it go, Eddie. Put it in the report and sign your name and let the daytime guys take care of it. I'm not walking out there in the dark in that snow."

Profar looked at the clock. "I have to go out in an hour, anyway," he said. "I'll head to Fletcher's shack and we can take a look together. He's on until noon and he can tell the ROKs."

"You do that," Lee said. "Jesus, my face is hot and I can't feel my feet. What a joke."

They stood in silence and listened to the rattle of the stove's burn pan as it ignited and flared. The burst of flames filled the round glass window and the glow lit the shack like flickers from a campfire. They handed the pipe back and forth and smoked.

"You know where I'd like to be now?" Lee said.

"The naked singer."

"No, I'd like to be in the Ville with one of the ladies."

"They won't go near you," Profar said. "Word's out that your willie is ready to fall off. I never knew anybody who caught the clap twice. You should be in a medical journal."

"When's your DEROS?"

"Five months and I'm gone," Profar said.

"I'm three. That's the sad part," Lee said. "Place is crawling with girls and I'm out of business. Closed up shop. Doc says I'm fixed, but you're right. The ladies don't think so and they don't take risks. They get sick and it's off to that weird-ass government penicillin clinic."

"You're a medical liability, Romeo."

"You know what the girls call me?" Lee said. "*Helelleh*. It means something like, 'he who is stoned all the time.'"

"Well."

Lee said, "The mamasan calls me 'half moon.' It's a nice way of saying I'm a half breed, but I don't mind. The old lady likes me ever since I scored that electric rice cooker from the PX."

Profar said, "I don't think they run into many people who talk the lingo."

"I grew up in Chicago on Lawrence Avenue," Lee said. "The folks owned a little grocery store. I played little league and was a Cub Scout. I guess sometimes I don't know what I am. We ended up talking Korean at the house instead of Russian."

Profar shook the unmelted snow from his boots. The shack groaned as another gusting wind rolled up from the river. Snow blew across the sand bag wall that encircled the guard post.

Lee spoke softly: "Yeah, I'd like to be at the hooch with one of them. Maybe with that Jia. She's a beauty."

"Somebody was talking about her the other day," Profar said. "She's got a yeobo."

"Remo from the Quartermaster's office," Lee said. "Remo's her yeobo. When I got here she was still goosing drinks. The top earner. Came here from Itaewon where she was a brigadier's girl, but he got sent stateside and so she went back to work in the Ville. Some of these big time club girls get transferred around like they're with IBM. Like it's a corporation, which it is, and this is just another career move."

"Remo?" Profar said.

"I hate that guy, too," Lee said. "She's always worked as a yeobo. Mostly the brass, Colonels and staff officers. Upper tier. None of this 'hey you wanna drinky-drinky GI' stuff like they do with you and me. I don't think she ever gave an enlisted guy the time of day. Remo gets here with his money and he charms that pimp Choi and the rest is history. Didn't see her for a long while until last week when somebody said Remo hasn't been to town. He just disappeared. Usually he's at the club handing out trinkets and kissing ass with the mamasan. I heard he was getting cold feet. I guess he'd told Jia he would take her back home after his hitch was over. Promised to pay for marriage school classes, the whole bit. Had everything lined up with the visa and paying off her debt to the pimp."

"Get married?" Profar said.

"That's the rumor."

"She believed him?" Profar said.

"They all believe it, Edward," Lee said. "They all want a ticket to paradise in the USA."

"Remo is a prick."

"And dumb as a mop," Lee said. "Jia is smart, so it was surprising that she fell for it. Choi had her at one of his other clubs until she went to the 8th Army red-light district in Seoul and attracted the big money. Remo paid top tier cash, plus extra gravy for the pimp. Those marriage classes aren't cheap and you have to have connections to get on the list. He gave her clothes from the PX. Once a girl goes to those classes and starts seeing pictures of life back home she can just about taste Thanksgiving dinner with the in-laws in America."

"He actually promised her?"

Lee ignored Profar. Once he started talking you couldn't really interrupt. "Talk is, that he's paying a fortune for the yeobo fee. Right up there with what the big boys—Colonels and Generals, embassy staff, shell out in Yongsan. Nobody makes that kind of money in a *kijichon* camp out in the boonies. She's big league *kisaeng* material. Like the old time courtesans back in the day. A Korean geisha, you could say."

"And you know this, how?" Profar said.

"The girls, they talk to me," Lee said. "I'm the only GI they ever met who can speak the lingo. They can't resist gossiping. They told me Remo takes her to the big city once a month for a shopping spree. And I'm not talking about cheap PX shit. I mean the Tokyo stores in Seoul."

"I didn't know Remo was loaded," Profar said. "I've seen him buy rounds at the club. The mamasan thinks he's god's gift."

"Daddy owns car dealerships in Arizona," Lee said. "Sends his boy blue jeans and Remo black markets those for top dollar. He sells Kodak film he skims from his job at the Quartermaster. Cosmetics go to Choi, who marks that shit up for his girls and makes them go into more debt just so they can have lipstick and eyeliner. Remo's no better than some Korean slicky boy who steals socks and razor blades. This system here is sleazy. The whole US Army on this side of the ocean is one big pimp outfit."

"Romance is expensive," Profar said. "Look what you paid."

Lee handed over the pipe. "Once you get a look at her, you'll see what I mean. Just you wait. She casts a magic spell."

The snow began to pile up on the window sill. The mounted radio antenna outside bowed in the wind and the coils of concertina wire that lay across the top row of sand bags shook. Two Chinooks from the base at Kimpo had sprayed defoliant that week, and where the sand bags were soaked it was slushy and black and the snow would not freeze or gather there. During the day when it was sunny, the stinking chemical would make you vaguely nauseous and Profar had shoveled dirt over the wet spots. The reek clung to his clothes and at the barracks laundry room everything lately smelled like the defoliant they'd shipped in barrels from Vietnam. It was a sweet, sickening odor that reminded Profar of rotting corn silage at his grandparents' farm.

Profar knew they shouldn't get stoned this far along at night. He still had to walk his final patrol along the fence and that would mean calling in on the field radio. You needed time to settle down and clear your head, but Lee always pushed things to the next level.

CHAPTER 3

Yevgeny Lee believed he'd lived dozens of previous lives and once worked as a librettist for Mozart in Vienna. He claimed he served as a Caporal-fourrier with Napoleon's Grande Armée at the Battle of Borodino during the fateful winter of 1812. And marched with Alexander's troops from Macedon until the boy wonder's sudden death in Babylon which Lee, of course, witnessed.

You could never tell when he'd suddenly recollect one of his many lives, and Profar had lost track of his friend's multiple incarnations. Half the time he didn't know what General or what ruler he was talking about. Conversations about Lee's former lives almost always happened when they were stoned at the guard post or drinking sweet carbonated Oscar wine at their rented hooch in the Ville.

"It's a bitch," Lee said. "Not being allowed to die just once."

"How come you didn't get promoted?" Profar said.

"Promoted."

"You were with Napoleon and these famous people and here you are freezing your ass off in the middle of nowhere. Why didn't each life get better? Doesn't it make sense that you'd learn stuff and life would get better the next time around? It's bullshit. How come you always die young?"

"You have a point, Edward," he said. "I never get past thirty."

Profar touched the stove pipe. It was shiny where other cold hands had rubbed it over the years. He tried to ignore Lee as he repeated his story about getting arrested at his shabby Moscow apartment in 1905 by the Tsar's secret police and being dragged shoeless to a train bound for Siberia, where he ate frozen dirt and drank water from a filthy pail for many years before suffocating while trying to escape buried in a manure wagon.

Lee shook his head. "In a shit wagon. That's how I died."

"I rest my case. You never upgraded," Profar said. "Seems like it would make sense to have each life better than the one before."

Lee sighed and said the winter sunsets outside the prison window in Tobolsk were amazing.

Profar studied the brightly illuminated ice at the bottom of the cliff outside the shack where the fence took a sharp turn, intersecting the Imjin River where the shore was cross-hatched with more hanging lights that looked like a madman had organized somebody's front yard Christmas display. From this distance and when it was windy, the lights shook and seemed to blink on and off.

Lee studied the flames in the stove and kept jabbering. Once he got started there was no stopping him unless you literally walked out of the room, and it was too damn cold for that.

Profar thought about the girl Jia at the club and tried to imagine somebody like her living in Phoenix in the desert with Remo, maybe working at his dad's car dealership. Jia learning how to play golf in Scottsdale. Jia driving the kids to school in her station wagon. Jia the former hooker baking cookies for the PTA.

"They had these dirty shitters, holes in the cement floor with a wood plug that you pulled off with a rope," Lee said. "It was godawful filthy, that plug, because everybody was sick all the time so you can imagine what was going on. Just a mess. I got used to the smell, but the bastard in the room with me, a printer from Ukraine who got arrested for publishing the wrong kind of Marxist pamphlets and kept making speeches about the glorious Decembrists, he never put the plug back and it was just the worst smell. Like somebody died. I'd cover my nose with a rag and try to sleep. The stink burned my eyes and made me want to faint, you couldn't get away from it. The prison guard Kirilov would yell at us about it. This room mate I had, Pavlo Ignatovich, always had stomach problems, which isn't a good thing in a place like that with no real toilet. No running water. Just a wood bucket they filled when the guard felt like it and then the water would freeze. We all had stomach problems, lice, you name it, but you have to be civilized about it. In the end, good manners is all we have left."

Lee wore a dumbstruck look, like something had just occurred to him. "They made me chop down trees. No gloves, no boots. Sawing and chopping down trees in that awful cold. I'd been arrested in summer so that's all I had, summer clothes and whatever I could scrape up when somebody died. You can imagine. If you got hurt, maybe twisted your ankle, you were useless to them and they took you to the forest, and boom, a bullet to the back of the neck. If you broke a toe or cut yourself, they took you to the woods. Boom. Almost everybody I met when I got there was dead when I left. I remembered that, just now."

Lee looked out the window. "That's why Korea just gets to me. I could never tolerate the cold after Tobolsk. Fifty lousy degrees now and my hands get numb. Edward, I know you don't believe any of this. But I wish I could just forget the past. I'm tired of remembering so much. My head is ready to explode."

Profar stared at the flimsy door where he thought he'd heard something outside on the steps. Maybe snow sliding off the roof.

"Stop with the bullshit just a minute," he said and whispered, "Hear that?"

Lee ignored him. "The wind would blow through the camp at night. Like somebody was groaning. Yeah, Tobolsk was almost as cold as this place."

"That roomie with the shits. Did you drive him nuts?" Profar said. "With the same crazy stories, did you? Probably why he had diarrhea."

Lee spoke sadly about the wife he had left behind on the mainland during his seven years in Siberia. His eyes got moist and he seemed to be on the edge of a sob. Though he could never really say if Lee was bullshitting about all those former lives, the memory about his wife seemed genuine.

"That's what we called home, the *mainland*. She was very pretty, my wife," Lee said. "Dark eyes and the best hair. I missed her. I suppose it was good we never had kids. I never saw her again, of course. Her letters just stopped coming, or maybe the camp guards took them. I never knew. I can't really remember her face now. By the time I died, I'd forgotten what she looked like and what her voice sounded like, and that was the saddest thing. Forgetting her face, how she smelled and the sound of her laugh. The way it felt to hold her hand. I do know she was very beautiful, though. That part you never forget. They never let me take personal things from home. No pictures, no socks. No hat. In my summer clothes they dragged me away like I was a dog."

Lee looked outside and said the DMZ barrier lights reminded him of the barbed wire that encircled the prison camp in Siberia.

Profar finally jerked up his hands. "Eugene. Okay. Please."

"I was once a Roman centurion, you know," Lee said. "The Battle of Teutoburg Forest was the end of me. They nailed our heads to the trees."

Lee always remembered the details, you had to give him that. Right down to the clumsy way the short Gladius sword banged against his hip when he marched in sandals in the mud of Germania in 9 AD. As a bullshitter, he was scientifically precise. The best bullshitters always are. The food he ate, what the weather was like. How he wiped his ass with a rag wrapped around the end of a stick when they marched along the Danube River through the Black Forest. Lee would forget to sign his duty log on the guard post clip board, or walk around with his boots unlaced but he was careful in his recollection of what he wore when he marched with Alexander the Great, nibbling on figs in the desert on the way to Babylon. He was almost always a soldier in each of his previous lives except for those stints as Mozart's pal and as a Russian revolutionary. Never a baker or simple farmer, always an infantry warrior.

This is what happens when you can get weed for two bucks a bag from the old lady at the shoe repair shop in the village, Profar thought. Dope here was cheaper than Marlboros and easier to buy.

Both soldiers took tandem hits on the pipe. Profar's Timex dial glowed in the dark.

"It's not what you think, this dying and coming back," Lee said after holding his breath for the longest time. "First, you might do your encore as a baby but you don't know you came back until you're already well into another life, maybe into your twenties, in which case you could drop dead any day and so have to start the hassle all over again without having any sense of what happened. It's very confusing. You could be thirty years old or you could be a teenager before you figure things out. It's messed up, the whole system. All the lives overlap. It's very crazy the way I remember things. I wasn't at all comfortable with any of this until after the Civil War."

"You were in the Civil War?"

"British. With Cromwell in 1644," Lee said and closed his eyes in serious contemplation as if he was about to launch into another reverie of soul rebirthing.

Instead, he stood and looked out the window. "Did you see that?"

"We should go look," Profar said.

"In the dark. No way," Lee said. "Wait."

"Wait for what?"

"A few hours and it'll be light. Let the other guys do it. Let Fletcher take care of it. We'll call on the radio just before we leave."

"We're supposed to check," Profar said. "It might be Northies. What if they get through? It's our fault if they get through."

"We're high," Lee said.

"You had more than me," Profar said and reached for his rifle where it stood leaning barrel-down next to the door. He checked the magazine for ammo and slapped the upright clip with his palm and in three strides he was already across the room and zipping up his parka.

"We've got weapons. We can take on anything out there."

"Well, that's something to worry about, too," Lee said. "I'm not comforted with that."

"I promise I won't shoot you."

"We didn't really see anything yet," Lee said. "Let's wait."

"I'm going," Profar said.

CHAPTER 4

The summer his father died Profar was thirteen and they sent him to work with his uncle on Isle Royale.

They took the ferry from Grand Portage. Standing on the deck, looking out across the lake at the Minnesota shoreline, Profar thought how strange it was that he was headed off somewhere with a guy who looked a lot like his dead dad. When he glanced at his uncle quickly it almost seemed comforting that he had the same chin and nose, though he was a bit taller and skinnier. Maybe that's why they'd done it, his mom and his aunt. To make him forget, but not quite all the way. Grownups were tricky like that.

His uncle was a Michigan wildlife warden and the purpose of the trip to the island was to do an annual biological survey. Plant trees, count the beaver ponds and make repairs to a boat dock that was used by the pontoon planes to bring tourists from Rock Harbor on the south side of the lake. He remembered spending days in a semi-conscious state of insanity from the swarming black flies and mosquitos. They wore bug nets under their caps while they worked.

The thick pine and birch forest was green and endless and always wet that entire summer, the air cold and blowy off the water, more like deepest Canada than Michigan. It was the first true wilderness Profar had ever seen. Like living in the pages of a Jack London story, he thought. They studied the remains of dead moose that lay dry and white like fake chalk carvings in the grass. Profar was allowed to sort the bones on a picnic table at the ranger cabin that was ancient and broken like some barely habitable frontier pioneer ruin. Giant brass hinges on the door. Old shake roof covered with moss and a chimney made from beach stones. There was an outhouse with a phone book hanging from a peg. Profar thought it was paradise.

His uncle, who began to look less and less like his father as the summer progressed, showed him how the moose bones had been gnawed and cracked so the wolves could reach the marrow. Profar learned to judge the age of the animals whose remains were scattered everywhere like they'd been dropped from the sky. The long skulls with their rows of big square teeth on detached, grinning jaws. The eye sockets and the ear holes where flesh clung to the bone like jerked meat. During the day they tracked the animals. At night he listened to the wolves howl, the birch trees outside rubbing against the cabin in the wind that blew constantly off the lake, and he thought about his father and how they'd hunted that winter during Christmas vacation. The last winter they'd spent together. How they'd hunted every winter he could remember before that and how they'd been planning to drive north with the boat that summer to Red Lake in Ontario to fish for muskie and walleye. But just like that, he was gone.

His father showed him how to track. He would set ice cubes in the grass, four or five rows, each cube a certain number of hours or days apart. At the end of the week, they would sit and it would be explained how and why the ice had dissolved the way it did. What temperature had been required to melt it. What time the sun had risen and set that week, the direction of the wind. He learned from his father exactly how ice would react in the sun and how it would break down in the grass on a cloudy day. Or not.

"You have to read the book," his father said and pointed at the rabbit track and brushed his finger against its powdery ridges. He examined the crumbled snow.

"And this is the book right here. If you want to read the track you have to know what the weather was," he said. "If it snowed. If it rained. Was it wet snow? Was it windy and which way did the wind blow? The book tells you that. Right here. And up there, in the sky."

At Robideaux Guard Post, Profar and Lee now stepped outside bundled in their parkas.

They carried their weapons unslung. Profar heard Lee's crunching footsteps behind him as they noticed a long fracture in the ice near shore.

They avoided this. Every few meters one of them would test the thickness of the ice with the heel of his boot. All was quiet, every sound deadened. The sky had cleared, yet a solid wall of white hung above the northern shore where it was still snowing. Lee swept the beam of the gooseneck flashlight back and forth as he held it against the wooden fore stock of the rifle. One of those spike-horned deer lifted its head from behind a bush and stared at both men, chewing. It stomped one hind foot and bounded off into the darkness. Profar saw the three-toed forward facing footmarks of the red-headed cranes that lived here in winter, a long trail of deep tracks like tiny post holes headed toward the hot springs. There was the faint smell of sulfur, a low fog clinging to a row of bare bushes.

Profar thought this all looked like an old Asian scroll painting with its exotic vertical calligraphy drawn on rice paper: the sky with its cartoon moon like a diorama, the stars out, the black hills in silhouette. He turned and saw the guard post shack with its string of lights like smeared paint spots above the little fortress of sand bags. It all seemed so serene, not dangerous-looking at all.

The ice cracked. They stopped and looked at each other. Profar knew what could happen out here. They'd forgotten to bring the radio, which was a bad sign that indicated, yes…they were indeed stoned. They were not at their sharpest. On top of that, the cold could make you feel confused. Being hammered and freezing was a bad combination. It was a marvel at how humans survived in such a narrow, precarious temperature band. Only seven degrees of body heat between you and complete amnesia. Below ninety-degrees and you stop shivering, which is when the real trouble begins. A dog had more sense on how to escape the cold.

Profar held his burning eyes closed for a few seconds, knowing that corneal frostbite was a real thing. Spit will freeze when it leaves your lips at fifty below. Take your mittens off to light a fire in that temperature, and your fingers instantly go numb. No fire, no life. The end. It wasn't that bad yet, but it felt like it.

There was a loud crack and they both stepped carefully. Profar knew the dangers of layered ice. It could be two inches thick and a foot of water beneath that, and then another band of thinner ice through which you could fall and be swept away with the current. It was all so beautifully dangerous.

Lee slung the M14 and arched his back and unbuttoned the flap on his quilted field pants and started peeing. He held the flashlight under his chin and let out a groan. He twisted his hips and drew a half-circle in the snow. His stream sparkled in the light.

"Don't get frostbite," Profar said.

"I'm still on penicillin. It's like dick antifreeze."

Lee bounced up and down once and buttoned up. He shivered and pulled on his mittens and rubbed his hands.

Music started blasting from the row of giant North Korean propaganda speakers a mile away. It was January and they were still playing Christmas tunes. *Silent Night.* Profar felt homesick.

"Bolsheviks," Lee said and snapped his suspenders, zipped his parka. "That would be an easy shot with the right gear. We could take it out. A fifty might do it."

"Go ahead, start a war," Profar said.

"They keep playing that crap and I will. Last night it was Bing Crosby."

At night the woman with the slight British accent would sometimes ask what was it like to be so far from home and wasn't it a shame that the capitalist American running dogs had come uninvited to occupy her poor nation. Everybody called her the Wicked Bitch of the North, but once she started talking it was almost soothing to hear a female voice when you were alone on duty in the dark. While you were walking along the fence in the snow, checking for breaks in the wire. You could close your eyes and pretend she was saying something romantic. Even the guys on ambush patrol, the special quick response scout teams called out when there was a report of infiltrators, would stop and listen and say nothing. After a while you learned how to ignore the nonsense she was actually talking. Didn't matter what she said or if she happened to recite somebody's social security number or described a soldier's home town. She once spelled out the full name of a buck Sergeant at camp who everybody knew because he ran one of the scout squads. She proceeded to give details about his neighborhood back home. She knew how long he'd been in-country and reminded the Sergeant that he had two beautiful kids and a good job waiting for him if he ever decided to stop serving the evil colonial devils and war maniacs of the United States Army.

One night, the Sergeant started firing his M60 at the loud speakers. Though the rounds barely made it to one thousand meters, the North Koreans filed an official United Nations complaint that they discussed at the Joint Security Area at Panmunjom. That was the first week Profar had begun driving the CG, General Yardley. The old man busted the Sergeant to E4 and had him reassigned him to Vietnam. The Wicked Bitch of the North continued to call out the Sergeant's name before she finally had the bright idea to recite Sunday football scores. She then counted down the Top 40 AM radio hits, which was a proven trick to make you crazy with homesickness.

The Americans had their own speakers, a half dozen arrays of eighteen-inch Panasonics stacked into thirty-foot towers, each cluster spaced a hundred meters apart to ensure maximum coverage. On a clear night they could be heard twenty miles away. Wagner's *Götterdämmerung* was a favorite to crank up at midnight. *Sgt. Pepper's Lonely Hearts Club Band*— the entire album played non-stop, was a daytime staple, especially around 5 p.m. when the North Korean guards at Panmunjom changed shifts. Recorded as a continuous loop by the DJs at the AFN radio station in Seoul, the speakers also blasted full-volume Rolling Stones music and cuts from *West Side Story* and Carol Channing belting out *Hello Dolly*, the most annoying song Profar had ever heard. The AFN programmers often interspersed their music with a long silence that would be interrupted by a sudden high-volume loop of the *Twilight Zone* soundtrack, with Rod Serling's voice booming: "You're traveling through another dimension, a dimension not only of sight and sound, but of mind."

Profar's favorite stunt was when they overwhelmed one of the Bitch's soliloquies with the screeching soundtrack from the naked shower murder scene in *Psycho*. The one where Janet Leigh gets stabbed. When that happened, soldiers working the DMZ fence that night usually stopped what they were doing and took out their K-Bar knives and made exaggerated pantomime slashing motions with their arms. The guys at AFN were heroes to everybody just for their work with the loud speakers. Lately, somebody in Seoul had gotten the genius idea that Bugs Bunny cartoon dialogue excerpts would be an artful touch, as well as full-volume conversations and arguments between Fred Flintstone and Barney Rubble. All, of course, at 140 decibels, enough to blow the eardrums out of your skull at close range.

That fall, Profar had escorted Richie Kraus, the editor of the *Warrior*, the division newspaper, to take photos of the propaganda speaker towers. Kraus was setting up his tripod for the shot when he walked up to the lowest row of speakers that sat on a metal shelf that was bolted to the side of a cliff.

The long, deep scratch marks on the green camo paint went up ten feet. Snagged in the heavy wire mesh cage that protected the speakers were long orange hairs that hung in clumps like something had rubbed with such force that one of the exposed eighteen-inch speakers had shifted off its bracket.

"What the hell?" Kraus said as he examined a tuft of hair. "Something climbed up."

"Nothing climbed up, look." Profar dropped to one knee and examined the shallow hole at the base of the cliff.

"It stood right here and just reached up. It didn't have to jump."

"Maybe it's a joke," Kraus said. "I know you guys get bored and play gags."

"Nope," Profar said and pointed to the hairball clinging to the mesh grate. "Something big was here."

"Something?" Kraus said.

"It," Profar said. "Since we don't know what did this, it's an *it*. An animal, for sure. Maybe a bear. You taking your picture or what? Maybe birds flew into it."

"Hairy birds? An orange bear?"

"Yeah, big hairy birds," Profar said. "Take your pictures. I got enough to think about out here."

Profar and Lee swept their light beams across the ice. Profar looked sideways at the trees because he could see movement better that way in the dark. For an instant, he thought he saw two shapes sitting in the snow, but after he blinked they were gone.

At the river oxbow you could see both the North Korean and the American perimeter fences. The black shapes of other guard post towers with their drooping lights. They had to be careful now. The closer you got to the fence on shore, the closer the mines were. They followed a few animal tracks and when Lee came upon the patch of disturbed snow he stopped and held up his arm. It would be easy to get lost here. Everything was white on white. The only references were the rows of fence lights, and those started moving if you looked too long. Clouds floated away and Profar saw the stars and the boxy silhouette of Robideaux sitting on the cliff behind them. It looked like a child's treehouse, the vapor lamps casting a pale glow across the river ice.

Lee shook his light toward what Profar thought was a frozen tree stump on the ice.

"Edward," he said gravely and stooped. "Looky what we got here."

The torso, one arm and shoulder completely absent, was enclosed within a pair of torn wool field pants and a shirt of a style they'd both seen before. The shirt had been ripped into tassels from behind with such force that the canvas trouser belt loops were missing from their metal rivets. Profar squatted while Lee stood guard with his rifle at-the-ready. In the bitter windless cold, there was the metallic smell of blood.

In the joined beams of both flashlights there were other body parts and oddly shaped pieces, everything scattered randomly. Four rifles lay where they'd been dropped. They stood back-to-back with their M14s aimed at the darkness. Lee said it looked like somebody had chewed and spit out a cherry pie. With the sky now clear, the bright moon appeared and the snow was covered with an enormous spray of red compote. Long, deep furrows showed where the other bodies may have been dragged away.

"It took them south," Profar said.

"It," Lee said. "What do you mean, *it*?"

"You know what I mean."

"You're the lumberjack North Woods hunter boy," Lee said. "Tell me what I'm looking at. Is this real?"

A slight breeze blew and with it came a heavy, musky stink.

"Do you smell popcorn?" Lee said.

"That's stupid," Profar said. "It's not popcorn."

Their clothing lay scattered like dropped laundry: a detached parka hood and one lone mitten next to a green undershirt. Other fabric that had frozen into a ball seemed as if it might have first been chewed. An orphan shirt sleeve and a piece of collar cloth that showed the ghost stitching of a North Korean rank badge lay beside an AK47. The other body pieces were strewn like abandoned doll parts. It was hard to tell if it all came from one body. Profar checked his magazine and it seemed full. He touched his ammo pouch.

"Do they wear their unit patch on the left?" Profar said.

"The NoKos? I never bothered to look," Lee said. "Seems like they take off their patches when they sneak over. The jackets, I recognize those from when Cobb made us look when they shot those guys last month. There's just one of them here, I think."

Profar pointed his light. "There were three more."

"But they're gone,"

Profar jittered the flashlight: "Dragged off. Look. This is where it stopped to eat."

"You said that again. What does *it* mean?"

"I don't know," Profar said. "I know bear tracks and wolf tracks. I saw lion tracks in Colorado once."

Profar stepped from the body to where the round pug marks continued. He studied the deep parallel forepaw impressions where the animal had come to a sliding stop in the powdery snow. There was a deep rut where it sat and stretched those forepaws to lay and feed. The snow hadn't melted at all in this temperature. A meter further on, he saw the black frozen blood spatter and a strip of macerated fabric that looked like it had been spit out. There wasn't really much blood except for the chewed parts and the chunky gouts. It was much too cold for anything to bleed for very long.

The concentric circle of running boot marks flared outward from where it seemed the first North Korean soldier had been attacked, the one that now lay in pieces on the ice. All else was a confused mess of heel and toe impressions and the unmistakable prints of an animal that had alternately leaped in jumping-jack fashion to attack what had certainly been at least four men.

"The old timers say they're still out there, you know," Lee said. The bright bore of his light barely reached across the river.

"Say it." Profar said.

"They hunted them when the Japanese were around," Lee said. "The wild pigs and deer. Everything eats those pine nuts. It's a nature preserve since the war. Like a zoo."

They both stopped and looked across the ice.

"It killed these guys," Lee said. "All that stuff to eat out here and it goes after people?"

Profar held his mittened hand above one of the tracks. "Six inches," he said. "Something isn't right with that hind leg. It's favoring the right hind leg."

"And you know this, how?"

"I know," Profar said. "It's hurt."

For some reason, their rifles had been tossed aside. A knife with its handle wrapped like a US military K-bar lay beside a pistol and a mitten. A few meters ahead there was a quilted vest that would have been worn beneath the soldier's reversible parka. The vest was torn with the cotton stuffing tumbling across the ice in the slight breeze. It was as if the infiltrators had shed their clothing while they ran, but of course they had not. Profar guessed that they'd been toyed with, caught and released and caught again, like a cat playing with a mouse.

"It stopped snowing a half hour ago," Profar said. "And just a little when we came out here. So this just happened. Maybe twenty minutes ago."

"No shell casings," Lee said. He walked a circle and jittered the light.

"They would have melted into the ice, anyway," Profar said as he picked up the .45 and removed the seven-round magazine and with some effort pulled back the barrel slide. A single snub-nosed round popped from the weapon.

"Chambered. Never fired," Profar said. "I didn't know they carried these. It's American stuff."

"They didn't have time to fire, but they had all the time in the world to run around and get their jackets ripped off. That's crazy."

"It was a game," Profar said.

Lee picked up the two-handled canvas tote filled with a disassembled light machine gun and its tripod, something that would have been carried by two men because of its weight. In the bag were wire bore brushes and cleaning patches, a bottle of solvent labeled in English. There were Chinese characters stenciled on the sack. From a discarded shoulder satchel Lee pulled out an old style fragmentation grenade with a hard steel tip, like something from the war. He shined the light on the big seventy-round AK47 barrel magazine. He took the bundle of cloth maps and documents from the satchel and slipped it into his parka liner pocket.

"Soviet crap. Maybe I can read it," he said and tapped the pocket as Profar handed him the .45. Lee sniffed the barrel and snapped open the receiver.

"Cobb has pictures of this antique shit hanging on his office wall. Jesus. The safety is still on. All I smell is the oil. It was never fired."

"Maybe we shouldn't touch anything," Profar said as he turned and sniffed. Now he smelled nothing at all.

"This isn't a detective movie," Lee said. "I'd like to know everything before we follow those tracks. If there's more guys up ahead, they'll be jumpy. Maybe they have other weapons. Or maybe there's more coming from behind us. We don't know, do we? I sure wish I wasn't high."

"Eugene," Profar said. "They dropped all their shit and ran. They didn't have time to fire. They don't have any weapons. We're not getting attacked by any North Koreans tonight. Everybody here is dead."

Profar was on his hands and knees, the rifle swung onto his back. He studied the tracks with his cheek almost touching the snow.

"They got dragged away. One by one."

The tracks told Profar that the animal had circled as if doing a final survey of its work. It then stopped at the first body and fed on parts of each calf and some ass cheek, trouser fabric and all. The parka hood had been torn away at the neck and what remained of the torso lay some distance from the other pieces. The violence seemed overly abundant, perhaps a bit of pure rage involved. Most animals just want to stop their food from moving. Beyond that, it's a waste of energy to get angry. This thing took it up a notch. He wondered what was wrong with the animal's hind leg.

The Korean soldier lay looking up at the stars, his expressionless frosted face without a scratch on it. Profar had stopped looking over his shoulder because he knew exactly where the tracks were now headed. They were aimed toward their own guard post. From the fabric of a torn coat sleeve he took a piece of fur and examined it in the light. The DMZ American propaganda speakers suddenly kicked in. Steppenwolf singing *Born to be Wild* crackled to life and echoed up and down the river.

Profar and Lee stared at each other.

"They won't look you in the face, you know," Profar said. "That's what I read once."

"What?"

"Tigers," Profar said. "They grab you from behind by the neck because they don't like to look you in the face."

"Okay," Lee said. "Now that we have that out of the way."

Another dropped blade lay next to someone's chewed leg. Why did they have time to pull out their knives but had no time to shoot?

He sniffed the spot where the spray of urine had melted the snow like somebody had waved a dribbling garden hose.

Lee had walked ahead. His voice sounded muffled. "Be careful, Eddie. Remember what Cobb said. Out here at night it won't be like stabbing a straw dummy in boot camp. It's up close and personal with these people. They don't send their worst soldiers to cross the river."

"This wasn't a routine infiltration," Profar said. "They were carrying too much shit. And that thing followed them for a long time. All the way from the North. It waited until they got to the middle, away from the lights. While it was snowing, when nobody could see. It knew."

They squatted back-to-back in the snow, their breaths steaming. The wind came up and carried off a scrap of clothing. The tracks lay shadowed within a pool of moonlight. Enormous round pug marks, four toes on the hind feet. No claw impressions. The length of a four-foot stride was about the same as a six-foot-tall human strolling along with a normal gait. The spray of the flicked snow in front of each forepaw showed the direction from which it had walked and how fast it had traveled. Where the animal paused, the tiny sprinkles were loose and foreshortened, the leading hind paw still carrying the blood of one of the victims.

Blood freezes at about one degree colder than water. If the attack had happened in daylight, the sun would have caused some melting, no matter what the temperature. A twelve-hour track feels stiff and firm. He studied the brightly lit snow and pulled off his mitten and with his skin burning in the cold he touched the edge of the bloody rear track lightly with a bare finger and the snow crumbled away. An older track grows larger as it collapses and freezes. These were tightly defined, like they'd been impressed with a cookie cutter. The front paw was wider than the hind print, and so Profar had a good guess of where the animal had left its feet for the attack. The four-pug paw marks were placed precisely in the track of the forward stride, the perfect walk of a cat. Not a bear or anything else of that size. Bears waddle. Cats do not. He put the mitten on and stretched his hand across the cleanest track and measured again. Six inches.

"They only jump once," Lee said.

"What?"

"Tigers," Lee said. "My mom's family is from Primorye. In Siberia. They know tigers. Her grandpa said they only jump once when they attack. Said the poachers would never go out with less than six armed men when they hunted or checked their traps. Two men in the group always walked backwards when they followed the track of a tiger. They're like assassins, you know. Sneaky assassins."

Lee waved his light beam toward the guard post.

"Right here in these hills, they used to hunt them. I bet there's old papasans in the village who remember."

"We don't need more shit to spook us," Profar said. "How the hell do tigers get here?"

"You read books, Eddie?"

"You read any?"

"Lots."

"Name one. Name something you read. Soap opera magazines don't count," Profar said.

Lee wiggled his light across the ice. "I'll get back to you."

"Why are you whispering?" Profar said.

"It'd be no trick at all for that thing to walk down from Russia," Lee said. "Maybe it would take a month, tops. There's everything you want to eat out there. All those pine nuts. Everything here eats pine nuts. It could live just on those little deer."

"Why are you whispering?"

"Maybe we should call this in," Lee said.

"So they find out we've been smoking weed? Besides, we already waited too long. We should have brought the radio."

"They won't know."

"They'll smell the shack. They'll smell us. Everybody knows what stoned looks like."

"What if this is all a trick?"

"You smell that?" Profar said and pointed at another dark explosion of frozen urine in the snow. "So, he stopped right there and took a leak. Marked his real estate. Walked in a big circle and he sat down again. Like he had all the time in the world. Christ, he just sat and looked at the shit he'd just done like we're doing right now."

"How do you know it's a he?"

"I don't. The tracks were awfully big. A cat with feet like that could mean it's a he. I'm guessing four, five-hundred pounds."

"Quite a kitty," Lee said.

They walked with their boots crunching loudly and Profar held up his arm and waved at another deep rut in the snow.

"It was dragging something. There's blood here. And it picked up something else. The drag marks change shape over there."

"Don't look at me," Lee said. "You're the one who wants to keep going. I say we get our asses back to the shack and call Cobb or the ROK duty liaison and let them handle it."

"If we call it in, they'll ask why we didn't make the report right away," Profar said. "We're too deep into this now. The police are gonna want in on this. I don't feel like being in the middle of that circus. They'll just blame us for something. We're just grunts."

"We're already in the middle," Lee said.

Profar followed the track. "It walked back again in a circle to this spot, like it maybe was worried about that body that was still out there. Like it was deciding whether to protect its food."

"Are you still high?" Lee said.

"Clear as a bell," Profar said. "I know what I see."

"I think we're both whacky," Lee said. "We're not scared enough. A normal person would be shitting his pants and here we are like it's just another night. Eddie, we should call it in right now."

"We have weapons, don't worry," Profar said.

"These guys had guns, too," Lee said.

Profar walked away. There were more drag marks, like somebody hauling a heavy sack through the snow. More pieces of fabric lay scattered next to the diminishing trail. After a while there was no blood at all.

"Is this even real?" Lee said. "I don't think it is. I'm walking around in the dark in the snow following a giant tiger and everything just seems fine. That's not right."

"Whatever we find, somebody's blaming this on us," Profar said. "The Army works like that. When they can't explain something or find it in a manual, they just lock the closest guy up. Article Fifteen, minimum. They'll look at our paperwork and match up the times and they'll say we should have engaged the enemy or some bogus John Wayne horseshit like that. You know how they are. They won't bring the tiger into it. It doesn't fit any regs so they won't mention it. We're screwed whatever we do."

Profar tried to distinguish their own meandering boot prints. "I'll cover you. Go ahead. I don't want that thing circling behind us."

The prints followed the south shore cliffs where lights lit the path leading to the guard post. They walked past this trail and through a dense row of shrubs that shed snow as they made their way along the base of the cliff. They twisted through the heavy branches and swept the trail ahead with their beams. Nobody ever patrolled this area. Profar could hear a flock of unseen cranes making a fuss from the far side of the river. Lee raised his arm and made a fist. He pointed ahead with his light and walked over and picked up the belt with its two canvas ammo pouches attached, the tips of the brass AK47 rounds shining in the light. There were long shreds of cloth hanging from the belt and Lee said he guessed it was somebody's pants and belt loop pieces just like the last guy. He tossed the belt aside and that's when they both smelled the odor. It reeked to high heaven. They raised their weapons and aimed.

"You see what I see?" Profar said.

"It took a sloppy piss," Lee said.

"This time, it was in a hurry."

The rut of repeating tracks ended in a patch of packed snow. The drag marks led up the sandstone cliff into a pile of boulders and pine trees that looked like they'd been clinging to life among the rocks for hundreds of years. They had to squeeze sideways as they followed the trail.

It was Lee who saw the cave opening and jiggled his light.

They grabbed roots as handholds up the frozen dirt path. Profar saw the scrabbling claw marks, but he said nothing. It wouldn't matter now. It could have jumped them from any direction, they were so exposed and helpless. There would have been no room to turn and fire a shot. He felt strangely calm about this whole mess. Maybe Lee was right. They were still high. When they reached the top, Profar saw the torn canvas tarp hanging crossed with branches and sticks like something used to shroud an artillery piece or a tank. It had been hanging here for a very long time and it was meant to hide something.

"So it wouldn't be seen from overhead," he said aloud.

It looked like a cave and it was completely invisible until you were at the very top of the trail. A routine patrol would have never walked this route. They would have followed the illuminated fence at the top of the cliff. They were not that far from the guard post, maybe a ten-minute walk. There were shovel and pick ax marks on the cliff walls and rebar driven into the rock. Profar kicked the snow from a broken wooden box that was covered with stenciled Chinese characters and numbers. He brushed dirt from a stack of identical boxes lined up just feet inside the entrance.

They stepped inside with both flashlights shining in a joined beam and their rifles aimed at shoulder height into the darkness.

"Maybe this isn't real," Lee said. "Maybe we smoked bad shit and this is some trippy mess we got ourselves into."

Now the cave looked like a tunnel, a twenty-foot wide cylinder that sloped toward a black endpoint, where it turned sharply. Hanging from u-bolts made from rebar on the wall were eighteen-inch sheet metal ventilation pipes. Above that, empty light sockets in rusted wire baskets that were connected by unfastened electrical conduit that hung in loops from the ceiling. A work in progress. Everything was covered with dirt and looked like nothing here had been touched in years.

Profar said he thought the rebar had been there for a very long time, the pipes also old and rusting from the constant moisture. Everything was dripping wet as they splashed through puddles, walking back-to-back, their rifles raised.

"They never finished it," Profar said.

"Who is they?" Lee said and took out his compass from his belt pack.

"That won't work in here," Profar said and shined his beam across the floor and up at the limestone walls and ceiling. There were stubby pieces of metal imbedded everywhere.

Lee said. "Smell that?"

One of the ventilation pipes bent ninety degrees toward the ceiling. Profar walked to the pile of snow on the floor and when he looked up there was a perfect circular opening cut into the stone. He saw stars. He felt the steady downdraft of much colder air. Snow drifted down through the hole.

It was wet and clammy, the dripping rock walls shinning. There were boards pegged to the ground with stakes, as if someone might have begun to build a walkway. Pick axes and shovels, the metal parts coated as if sprayed with rust, were leaned against a row of wheeled carts with open padlocks hanging from their lids. It was so much warmer inside the tunnel. They pulled off their hoods and took off their mittens. The sloping grade got muddier and wetter the further they walked and then they saw more tracks.

"We should come here with Cobb," Profar said.

"Now you want to tell Cobb?"

Profar shined his beam on a set of forepaw prints.

"I don't know if we should go all the way in," Profar said. They both stared ahead into the darkness. "We should come back with more gear."

"We got weapons, Eddie," Lee said. "Don't you want to know where it is? Where it took the other bodies?"

"No. I really don't want to know," Profar said.

Lee watched his flashlight beam disappear into the dark reaches of the tunnel. He picked up a rock and tossed it and listened to it bounce and echo. After a long silence the rock splashed into water.

They turned quickly and went outside. It was snowing again. There was absolutely no wind and their voices were muffled as they stood at the tunnel entrance.

"Maybe you're right," Lee said. "Maybe we should just tell Cobb and beg for mercy."

Profar shined his light at the trail. "Is that your boot?"

"You know it is," Lee said.

The five distinct pug marks of a forefoot were thinly covered in snow, the snow that had just begun to fall. Next to it, where another paw had scuffed the ground, was the mark showing where it had lifted and paused the other foot in mid-air, as if the animal had stopped to observe the trail. Or maybe change its mind about something.

"That track. It's right on top of yours," Profar said. "Just now, while we were inside, it was out here waiting."

CHAPTER 5

Sergeant E5 Manny Perez, recently returned to the garrison from a TDY hitch as a combat emergency medical tech with an artillery unit in Vietnam, rubbed his eyes and yawned loudly. He'd been assigned to the local civilian clinic in addition to his day job as a platoon field medic and he was dog tired.

Perez had worked his extra shift so often lately that he sometimes bunked in one of the 1950s Quonset huts located behind the building where he gave penicillin shots and dispensed antibiotics to the club girls who were brought there as part of a government treatment program managed by the Korean National Police. Perez trained the civilian staff on how to administer the US Army-supplied penicillin, but he was also there to make sure the clinic's drug inventory wasn't pilfered for the local black market. Korea's formal *kijichon* system of licensed prostitution accounted for a big chunk of the country's economy. Keeping bar girls healthy and STD-free was a key component of the Korea-US Mutual Defense Treaty. For Perez, although the hours were tiring, it was easy and predictable duty. As a New Mexico boy from Las Cruces, he hated winter in Korea but it was better than one hundred degrees in a steaming jungle with people shooting at you.

The Soyosan Health Center was operationally controlled by the US. Its sole purpose was to address the sexual health of American GIs, after it was discovered that the venereal disease rate among Korea's American military personnel was far higher than at similar installations in Japan and Europe. The nerds at 8th Army headquarters had revealed that half of all post-armistice troops stationed in the Republic of Korea had been infected with one or more flavors of venereal disease during their thirteen-month tours.

KNP officers were instructed to seek out licensed hospitality and entertainment workers who might be VD carriers—"infection vectors," they were called in the reports, so they could be treated before being allowed to return to their clubs. There were rumors that other monkey business went on at the clinic, but it existed officially to make sure all the village "entertainment hostesses" were examined at least once a month.

The clinic, an ugly concrete building surrounded by barbed wire and accessed through a police checkpoint, was commonly known as the Zoo. You could see it easily from the MSR. They called it the Zoo because its zombie residents were usually so pumped full of meds that they stood at the barred windows in their blue hospital gowns like dazed and captive animals. There had been an alarming number of penicillin overdoses lately, not to mention the smuggled barbiturates and opioids, so the division CG had ordered his own medics and nurses to help with staffing. The Zoo was also where the local pimps sent pregnant girls for abortions.

Perez was filling out paperwork and writing up his inventory requests when one of the Army nurses walked in waving a pink telephone message slip.

"Your company NCO wants you at the G2 office, pronto," she said. "Been spying for the Kremlin again? How come the spooks want to talk to you?"

"Was it Cobb who called?"

"Didn't say. I'm the humble messenger," the nurse said. "I would think Major Grissom would have called from the clinic, but this came straight from the Head Shed. He said *on the double* and then he said *lickity split*. He said *giddyup*."

"That's Cobb," Perez said. "He said *giddyup*?"

"With gusto," the nurse said. She gave a sloppy mock salute and crossed her eyes.

Perez had been hand-drawing a supply room organization chart. He had the poster board tacked to the wall and was separating the clinic's weekly needs into their proper categories: electronic, diagnostic, surgical, durable medical equipment (DME), acute care, and storage and transport.

"Aren't you the boy genius," the nurse said as she studied the chart.

"They run a loose ship here," Perez said. "The head doc is actually a pharmacist. He keeps it all in his head about what supplies they need. It doesn't help that the cops really run this place and they don't care about standard medical procedures. I found a crate of Doxycycline that was two years old, and they were wondering why they had all those chlamydia cases here last month. They just want to keep the conveyor belt moving. It's all about needles in the ass and quotas. What's a division G2 want with me, anyway?"

The nurse watched as Perez circled each supply category with his red marker. He stepped back and studied his creation.

"You'll know in about fifteen minutes." The nurse said there was only one "a" in durable.

"They're in a hurry. Said to wait outside for your ride and to bring a full field kit."

Perez was jamming supplies into a canvas rucksack when the two MPs outside laid on their horn and revved the engine of their patrol jeep.

The vehicle was topless with a canvas roof stretched across struts that wobbled as Perez hunched forward against the cold. They raced down the MSR, past the roadside billboard that proclaimed, "Danger! This is a Venereal Disease Zone." The sign was often the target of obscene midnight graffiti. Smiling soldiers had their photos taken next to the sign. It was like taking your picture in front of Mount Rushmore.

At division headquarters, a Lieutenant Colonel wearing a Panmunjom Joint Security Area armband escorted Perez into Major General Darin J. Yardley's office. The two-star was standing next to his desk in his shirtsleeves, his tie undone, gnawing on a cigar like he'd been waiting anxiously for Perez to arrive. The Sergeant stiffened up and saluted. He told Perez to take off his parka and make himself at home. The medic was wearing his rumpled hospital scrubs, a package of surgical gauze hanging from his pocket. He sat on the sofa.

Yardley held up a coffee pot. "Cream, sugar?"

The General puttered at the buffet next to a cabinet filled with booze and seltzer water, bottles of wine slanted in a wooden rack. Little statues and framed award plaques inside the cabinet.

Perez thought Yardley looked like a father working up courage to spill the beans to his kid about the birds and the bees. He seemed fidgety. On the wall there were pictures of the General posed with other soldiers. Famous people. Men in suits standing in front of an American flag. Yardley as a younger man dressed in civies smiling from the front steps of the US Capitol in Washington, DC. A TV actor who Perez recognized from a USO show was shaking Yardley's hand, both men caught in the middle of a boisterous laugh.

"Black is okay, sir," Perez said. "Thank you, sir."

"That your gear?" Yardley looked at the rucksack. "Don't worry, you're not in trouble. Relax."

"Yes, sir," Perez said. "I didn't have time to get my full kit. Not sure what you wanted me to bring, sir. I was just told to come ASAP."

There were framed pictures of children on the desk, empty in and out boxes, the division's ceremonial flag tacked on the wall, along with rows of framed certificates and award ribbons arranged in a curving half circle above a giant map of Korea.

"Is somebody hurt, sir?" Perez said and looked around.

Yardley said, "Nobody got hurt and this is no big deal."

The General tugged at his necktie. He poured coffee and put the pot on a table coaster and pointed at the office kitchenette.

"I probably took you from lunch," Yardley said.

"I ate, sir. Thank you, sir."

Yardley quizzed him about his hometown. He asked how long he'd been in the Army and if he'd enlisted for a regular three-year hitch or was drafted. Perez's assumed Yardley would have already known these things, but he answered. When the General asked him what he wanted to do after he was discharged, Perez answered: "Go to school and be a nurse. They need male nurses these days."

"Why doin't you go the full route?" Yardley said. "Medical school. Be a doc."

"My family doesn't have that kind of money," Perez said. "The GI bill won't go that far. And I like the nursing part better. I have to finish college when I get out and I'll be too old for med school, even if I had the money and could get in. Which I don't. My dad's a grammar school teacher. I've got four brothers."

"Nothing wrong with that," Yardley said. "My old man raised six kids on a miner's wage in Minnesota. Iron ore. I wouldn't see him for weeks at a time. My mother worked, too."

"Yes, sir."

"Well, excellent," Yardley slapped his knee. "So, let's get to it."

The General pointed at the stitched black-and-white cloth badge below Perez's right jacket pocket.

"You're a scout, I see."

"Yes, sir."

"How many missions?"

"About thirty," Perez said. "Last month they took me off the patrol roster and I'm at the camp clinic, mostly. Sometimes at the dispensary. Whatever they need. The MPs call when something happens in the Ville. My tour is up pretty soon."

"I know that part," Yardley said. "About you being short. You did your last deployment with the Fourth, correct? In Vietnam."

"TDY, yes sir. That's okay, though. I like my unit. I like the guys here. Gets a little cold, though. I grew up in the desert."

"You like your unit, that's good. I suppose you want to know why I sent for you," Yardley said.

He eyed the door, crossed the room and turned on the Panasonic stereo next to the giant TEAC reel-to-reel tape player. He turned on music. Folk music.

"Now, this is just between you and me," the General said. "Do you love your country?"

"Yes, sir. Everybody loves their country."

"Not everybody. I looked at your file," Yardley said. "There's other people in your MOS I could have chosen. Career men. You're the best sixty-eight-whiskey in this outfit, I'm told. All good things in your two-oh-one file. Nobody comes close. Your CO told me himself, along with Sergeant Cobb, who I've known for years, they spoke highly of you. Said you were a man who could be trusted."

"Thanks, sir. That's very nice to hear. Yes, sir."

"You don't have to thank me. What I'm about to ask you to do, it's important that it stays between us," Yardley said. "This is like a sacred promise from one soldier to another on the field of battle. Nothing is more important than that, understand? We have a bond from now on, you and me. A soldier's ever-lasting covenant."

"Yes, sir. Of course. I still don't understand, sir."

Yardley took the cold cigar from the ashtray and flicked his Zippo lighter. He examined the burning ash and took a puff.

"For now, let's call it a special medical requirement," he said. "But it's also a practical matter, something that might save a life. Many lives."

Perez suddenly thought he knew what was going on.

"If you're sick, sir. You know, embarrassed," he said. Perez was nervous now.

"Something maybe embarrassing. You maybe don't want anybody to know about it. I'm not a doctor. A doctor would be the person you should see. I can't really do much except give you the penicillin and tell you how to clean it up...you know, clean it, but that's not the right way to do it. A doctor would tell you more. He'd tell you the proper way to do it. I really can't help you with that sort of thing, sir. I think the General, if you don't mind me saying, should go see a doctor."

Yardley dropped his chin and stared at Perez and took a puff. "What the hell are you jabbering about?"

"The clap, sir," Perez said. "If you have the clap...I don't even know how to diagnose which kind you'd have. There's a bunch of STDs. It takes testing..."

Yardley flicked the ash. "I don't have the damn crabs, Perez," he said.

The General stood, unfastened his vertical weave belt and pushed aside the empty black leather .45 pistol holster that was embossed with the division insignia. He now wore a big, shit-eating grin and shook his head.

Perez wondered why he didn't just take the short chopper ride to Seoul and have any doctor treat him and the whole deal would be swept under a rug, no questions asked. It wasn't the first time that an officer had picked up the crawlies or the pecker drips in the village and tried to keep it secret. He'd heard about people using mercury, of all things, just so they didn't have to tell anybody. There was still Salvarsan out there on the street from when the Japanese were here and using arsenic for gonorrhea. They had people at 8th Army who just took care of staff officers and upper level government workers who picked up something at one of the clubs. The embassy people went there all the time. It was the cost of doing business in Korea.

Yardley pushed himself away from the desk. Perez could see the elastic waist band of his green boxer shorts. His gut spilled over the open belt buckle and the General couldn't stop grinning.

"The clap," he said. "Shit, Perez, I just want you to strap one of those plastic piss bags on me."

"Sir?"

The General pointed at his crotch with both hands. "I need you to put one of those tubes in me so I can take a leak while I'm sitting in a chair. Like now. Into a bag or whatever they use. Like in the hospital. If I was sitting in this chair and I was dressed and I had to go see somebody about a dog. One of those. Can you do that? Soldier, I just asked you a damn simple-ass question."

"You're not sick?"

Yardley bit down on the cigar. He made his bulldog face.

"You got ears, Perez? I'm not sick," he said. "Now can you do that? Strap one of those bags on me and show how to put it in and take it out? On second thought, I don't want to do that. You'll be doing that for me."

He looked at his watch. Perez stared as the General's trousers that were now bunched at his ankles. The initials DJY were embroidered on his knee-high socks.

"In two hours I have a meeting with our little friends at the JSA. Panmunjom. I can't be late. Those pricks keep track of everything, so I can't be late. Stop looking at me that way, Perez."

"I still don't know why you would need a catheter if you have crabs, sir," Perez said. "It's really a simple treatment. A catheter won't help at all. In fact, it would irritate things down there. They can give you medicine. If you had it less than a year you only need one shot, sir. Benzathine works like magic these days. Like magic."

"Jesus Christ all mighty, Perez. Do I have to say it again?" Yardley said. "I'm healthier than a god damn horse, and if you can't do this I'll get somebody else. I thought I picked the right man, Sergeant Perez. You have a chance to do something for your country and from your record—the two ARCOMs for valor in combat, Christ, you know how to do your job. Now open that bag of tricks and stick a tube up my whizzle so I can piss in one of those plastic bags. Actually, soldier, today you're going up to Panmunjom with me in case the thing falls out. I already told your CO that you've been assigned to me as part of my security detail, so get used to it. This will be the easiest thing you've ever done in Uncle Sam's Army. I know what kind of hours you've been working over at that hooker repair shop, so this should be a piece of cake. I'll explain things on the way to the JSA."

"Sir, if I do that I'm not so sure I have the right gear with me," Perez said. "There's different catheters. Different sizes. I don't mean to ask, but how's your prostate, sir? I'd need to know that. A doc would ask you that, too. Are you having any trouble urinating, sir? Like at night. Getting out of bed lots of times. Maybe a doctor..."

"Now, shut up with the doctor stuff, Perez. I don't have time to tell you again that I don't need to see a doctor. My ass apple is in perfect condition. I got a first class ass apple, understand?" Yardley said. "And not a word of this to anybody. Christ, I thought I picked the right man. You ask too many questions."

Yardley hiked up his pants and knotted his necktie. He put on his Class A jacket and took his dress cap from the coat rack. He handed Perez an elastic Military Police arm band with Korean lettering on it and unlocked his desk drawer.

"I also want you to carry this. You're now part of my security detail."

Perez strapped on the .45 shoulder holster and followed Yardley out the door into a waiting gun jeep with a blue two-star pennant flagstaff made from a lead pipe mounted on the right side of the hood.

Eddie Profar was on duty that day as the General's driver and he nodded at Perez and gave him a surprised look.

"I think you men know each other," Yardley said and took the back seat.

Profar drove through the front gate where two other vehicles, each with a three-man security team and a .50 cal mounted on the rear seat floorboard, began to escort them down the MSR.

Perez looked at Profar. "You look like shit," he said.

Profar yawned and his breath blew sideways in the bitter cold. He leaned and spoke softly.

"Long night, brother. Long night."

CHAPTER 6

The highway was icy and windblown and the plastic window zippers had frozen on the jeep, causing the old man to cuss all the way back from Panmunjom. The General shouted and said that Korea was indeed the coldest place ever engineered by God Almighty Himself.

"And we're from the North Woods, aren't we Profar?"

"Yes, sir," Profar said as he hunched over the wheel and hoped his feet wouldn't go numb before they got back to camp. He lifted his boot off the clutch pedal and held it up against the useless heater vent.

Manny Perez sat in the rear seat with his face tucked into his parka. Profar still didn't know why the old man had needed a medic that day. All Perez did during the entire meeting was sit with his medical kit on his lap. Asking too many questions never got you far in the Army, so Profar had kept his mouth shut.

"And we know what it's like to be cold," the General said. "Isn't that right?"

"Yes, sir. We sure do."

"Not even Duluth gets this cold, I'll tell you that," the General said.

Profar's lips were numb. "Yes, sir."

***

After he dropped off the jeep at the motor pool, he took a nap at the hooch and walked to the club and took his usual spot at the end of the bar closest to the kitchen, where you could observe the entire gallery of leering red light rangers who came to troll for dates at the Ville's largest officially sanctioned cathouse.

With its promise of medically risk-free, economical and convenient companionship, the bar was a temptation not to be withstood by most soldiers stationed along this stretch of the Military Supply Route that connected the DMZ with 8th Army headquarters in Seoul forty miles away.

At the club he ordered OB beer and sat peeling off the wet paper label with his fingernail. He looked around. There was always a pleasant vibe at this time of night, before things got loud and rowdy. He watched the stage where the house band drummer sat twisting the lugs on his Ludwig snare, tuning it until it seemed he'd found the right punchy sound and he stomped the pedals and pulled his cymbals closer until it seemed that all was perfect and correct. It was a Korean cover band and they all wore odd short black waist jackets of the kind you might find on a Spanish toreador in a bull ring.

Profar sipped and covered the open bottle with his cork coaster to make sure nobody would take it away. He slipped out the door, where he waited outside the alley byeonso. It was snowing again, everything muffled as if a blanket had been dropped over the darkened world. Faint music drifted up the alley. Another GI leaned against the outhouse as he lit his cigarette and nodded at Profar from behind the glow of his cupped hands. The soldier wore his blue jeans bloused with an elastic band above his boots as if he'd been reluctant to abandon his Army uniform. His zipped satin jacket was decorated with a stitched golden dragon whose tail coiled down one sleeve, the standard evening garb for carousing GIs. His Army dog tags swung freely outside the jacket. Somebody opened a door and the alley was suddenly filled with loud rock music. A few buildings further down an old papasan with a shovel chipped ice from the paving stones behind the Lucky Five Saloon, another club that appealed to older NCOs and officers. It was a subdued and quiet place where they played folk music and even the girls were older and more seasoned. The Water Dragon Club catered to the lower ranks and was the biggest brothel in the Ville with the most girls on the payroll.

The village entertainment district was open for business each night except Sundays until the 1 a.m. curfew. Profar could hear laughing from inside one of the girly shacks arranged uniformly along the alley like giant gym lockers. Each narrow room had its own single window and a similarly latched doorway and while Profar waited, he watched two girls lead a stumbling soldier by both hands into one of the numbered units. Another smiling GI, his business completed, emerged drunkenly from a different door and he walked in short, mincing steps down the slippery alley, his jacket at half-mast as he tried to light his cigarette in the falling snow.

A girl who Profar recognized wobbled from the byeonso on her high heels. She hitched up her sequined skirt and stood on one leg to adjust her slipping shoe and smiled warmly as she took a long drag on her cigarette. The light from the bare swinging ceiling bulb in the dark and stinking shed cast her shape in a glowing nimbus, giving the girl's silhouette a ghostly aspect, like some saintly figurine lit by candles in a church. Goddess of the holy privy, he thought. Our Lady of the Latrines. They were all like lovely butterflies sprung fully formed from their cocoons, these farmers' daughters and former orphans turned painted courtesans of the night. He loved to study them as they walked and danced and spoke their innocent pidgin English.

"Sorry, sorry," she said and made a fake sad face. Her hair was bobbed. She wagged her hand back and forth and pinched her nose.

"Tummy taksan sicky. I no feel good. Sorry, sorry."

Profar shrugged. He smiled as the girl looked him up and down and walked away, spike heels clacking on the alley stones. He turned sideways through the narrow doorway and pulled on the rope that lit a second ceiling light. A broken space heater lay on its side in the corner in a pile of trash. An awful smell everywhere. There was ice on the cement floor and he was careful not to slip as he stood and aimed between the two stacked brick handholds. He'd never gotten the hang of squat toilets. A wood wall peg held sheets of newsprint paper, and in the strange orange glow of the two swinging lights the room and his own stooped shape looked like the cartoon sketch of a torture chamber. A place where you were dragged to confess state secrets.

The music outside, the persistent thump of a bass guitar from the Water Dragon's house band, grew louder and already someone was shouting drunkenly from one of the alley shacks. This was followed by a chorus of angry female screams as more Korean voices joined the argument. He recognized the colorful profanity. A door slammed and a woman shouted and there was the band singing a Rolling Stones tune about time being on our side.

Profar walked to the front club entrance. Everything was lit with blazing colored neon. He hiked up his collar and breathed the fresh icy air. More girls were reporting for duty, walking in pairs and threes like dutiful shift workers headed for their factory piecework jobs. All that was missing was their lunch pails. They stood in line while some were randomly asked for their medical ID cards by a KNP patrol officer in civies. Other girls from other clubs walked past shivering in their short furry jackets and vests, costume jewelry rattling as they high-stepped across banks of shoveled snow in their high heels, unsmiling and all business as they reported for another night of love in the Ville.

Inside, the ornamented bar girls of the Water Dragon Club coalesced onto the dance floor in their spiky footwear and satin skirts like creatures wholly natural to the world. Luminous temptresses to boys just arrived from their Indiana farms and city suburbs. And this left the GIs open-mouthed in wonder as they watched the girls teasingly sashay and shuffle. Nothing like this back home. Nothing even came close. This was like being one of Captain Cook's sex-starved sailors welcomed by half-naked Tahitian hula girls after months at sea. It was something they'd never expected in their wildest dreams. The GIs stood dressed in their checkered PX shirts and off-brand blue jeans, gawking and pointing, lighting their smokes and paying for diluted overpriced drinks at the standup tables that encircled the dance floor, above which a glitter ball spun lazily and lit the world in happy red, white and blue polka dots.

Eddie Profar shoved his way through the crowd to the bar and picked up his warm beer and drank. He scooped a handful of peanuts. He turned and leaned on the bar top and watched the girls dance, squirming and preening, others barely shuffling their feet as they displayed themselves to the ogling gallery of GIs. This was the nightly warm-up. They were like baseball pitchers getting loose in a bullpen. Batting practice, Profar thought as they broke away one by one and approached their chosen soldier and lifted a beckoning finger. The glitter ball spun, the air in the overheated room already blue with cigarette smoke. He liked to study them. He liked to watch while the girls commiserated with one another in whispers and cryptic hand signals, then walked off to tug at someone's sleeve. In the flickering light their shapes made them seen like something from a dream, unearthly in their improbable grace and manner. Unaccountable, exotic creatures that could exist only in this enchanted room.

Yevgeny Lee arrived carrying on a loud conversation in Korean over his shoulder with one of the server girls whose only task was to make sure customers kept ordering drinks. Loitering at the Water Dragon Club without a glass or bottle in your hand was not allowed. He ordered Oscar wine. Mrs. Yoshida, the madame who managed the club for the boss pimp Mr. Choi, walked up with a loaded tray and unscrewed the cap on Lee's bottle with a practiced flourish. She pulled a plastic change purse from her baggy smock and took Lee's coins. Lee said something and Mrs. Yoshida frowned and shook her head and walked away.

The band stopped playing. There was a sudden murmur in the room as a strikingly beautiful woman walked across the dance floor.

"That her?" Profar said.

He pointed with his bottle. He took a swig and shook out a cigarette and lay the pack and his lighter on the bar top. Everybody at the bar was smoking and everyone now seemed to turn where they stood or sat as they paid attention to the dance floor. A few cat calls, somebody whistled. And as if on cue the band began playing a slow and moody tune. The glitter ball lights changed colors.

She paused alone beneath the glow of spinning dots and stood looking over her shoulder at someone unseen, one arm lifting slowly to brush her long dark hair across her bare and perfectly formed shoulder. Like that graceful flourish ballet dancers do with their bowed arms just before they glide across a stage, Profar thought. A practiced, artful gesture. She had a lovely and delicate cat face and she moved like a cat, slightly bouncy-assed with a stately gait, very bosomy and much taller than any other girl in the club. Jia seemed ethereally light on those beautiful long legs, as if she might at any moment turn to magic smoke and rise and dissolve into the ceiling.

For many of the GIs that night this was something they'd not witnessed before, and so they stood silent and watched open-mouthed as the famous Kim Jia-Soon seemed to drift on air across the Water Dragon dance floor.

Something inside Profar at that moment changed forever. He took a long, deep breath and sighed.

"She doesn't go by Wendy or Cindy or Lisa, like the other girls. Just Jia," Lee said. "Nobody else does that. They all have their cheesy American nicknames. Even the old lady refers to her formally as Kim Jia-Soon. You're looking at a true old time *ginyeo* courtesan, like they had back in the day when there were kings and princesses. It's like she's a high-class geisha, only better. I wouldn't be surprised if she dresses up and does a tea ceremony before she sends you into paradise. Sits there naked and fills her tea cups and takes you to heaven. Yes, sir. What a sight, brother Edward. I never get tired of looking at her. She's out of my pay grade, though. And yours, too. What you see out there costs a fortune. Me and you are allowed only to observe and appreciate, dear Eddie. No touchy, as they say. Only looky. We have to order off a different menu."

"And she's Remo's girl?" Profar said.

Lee gave an exaggerated shrug. "What a shame."

Jia's demeanor, as she danced alone with eyes closed, was relaxed and effortless, a gentle swaying with her head tilted. The small tiger tattoo on the underside of her forearm showed plainly in the scarlet light as she briefly lifted her arms and spun once on those high heels, trance-like, the slightest of smiles breaking across her lovely porcelain face. As if she knew she'd made her point with such calculating brevity, she stopped the teasing dance and strolled off the dance floor. The other girls parted in obvious deference as a row of GIs stopped talking and leaned in her direction, pointing and nodding as if they'd just now been furnished their first close look at a true female in its consummate form. The other girls acknowledged her with shy consideration, stepping politely away as Jia crossed the room and sidestepped a trio of other soldiers who'd reached out to touch her, perhaps to see if she was real and not some seductive hallucination. She glanced at them with indifference and stepped behind the bar and picked up a serving tray and two glasses. She lifted a bottle of Seagrams off the mirrored backbar and measured two fingers and poured the liquor into one glass. She mixed in ginger and the lemon juice and dropped in a stir stick with her other hand and added the ice, all in a single motion. She filled the other glass with soda water. She turned and smiled politely at Yevgeny Lee like a good hostess. Lee lifted his Oscar bottle and hollered something in Korean that made Jia burst into laughter. Her smile was luminous and Profar shook his head.

"Dear Lord," he said.

Lee drank. "Met her the first month I came here," he said. "The old lady needed a translator for some legal paperwork and I was the designated hitter. Mamasan doesn't trust the Katusas who work for the Americans. Calls them houseboys. She came right out and asked if I was halfbreed, but she used the Korean slang word. I should have been pissed, but I understand. I asked her if she was the mamasan, and it was a mistake to use that word. That's not something you ask an older woman in this country. She was offended, but I reminded her she'd called me part-Korean alley rat and she busted a smile and waved me away with her hand. We've been pals ever since. Jia is her favorite, of course. Because Jia makes money for everybody. Jia is the star here. The rainmaker, the MVP. The most expensive yeobo up and down the whole MSR. I guess you've noticed she's also the prettiest damn girl in town."

"You talk with her?" Profar said. "About what?"

"Things," Lee said. "Before that lucky bastard Remo got her she was hooked up with a brigadier at 8th Army HQ. That's the company she keeps. Guys like you and me don't have a chance, but for some reason she likes to gab with me."

"Remo's a stupid Spec 4," Profar said. "He's a box kicker at the Quartermaster's office."

"Remo's a plenty cash-rich stupid Spec. 4," Lee said. "There's a difference."

Jia replenished her drink tray a half dozen times in the next fifteen minutes. She walked back and forth along the edge of the crowded dance floor, parading herself beneath the spinning glitter ball, taunting and flashing that flirty smile, the silver hem of her rising skirt sparkling against those long and beautifully sculpted legs with each stride. Profar could not keep his eyes off her. His heart raced and his mouth was dry.

"She'll do that all night," Lee said. He took a long swallow of the sugary wine that all the GIs drank. Soju liquor tasted better but it got you drunk too quickly.

"She'll get guys to buy a drink," Lee said. "When they ask her for something more she'll flirt for a bit and make a polite excuse and refer them to another girl. She gets them horny and worked up and then disappears and does the same thing with another guy. She's the money magnet. That's how she keeps the ship afloat for Choi, along with what she earns from being somebody's yeobo. The other girls like her because she never steals their hooch business. She makes them quick, efficient money. They've got strict rules for everything in this place. If a GI wants something more than a short time quicky, he pays the mamasan a bar penalty fine so the girl can miss the next day's work. That's the deal. That way he can spend the night in her hooch and she can have a rest the next day. If she doesn't make her quota each night, the girl has to pay the pimp a bar fine as well. Every hour gets sold here, every minute has its price. The clock never stops running."

"So she lives in the Ville?" Profar said.

"Don't get any ideas, Romeo," Lee said. "Unless you have the cold cash and lots of it, don't get any bright ideas. She's dangerous. You're asking for trouble."

Lee took a cigar from his shirt and with his pocket knife sliced off the tip and turned the cigar in his fingers before he reached across the bar top for Profar's lighter.

Profar watched him smoke. Lee had a small head and small delicate hands and the giant fat cigar looked ridiculous.

"When did that start?"

Lee took a long draw and snapped the Zippo shut. Like he'd practiced the move or had seen it in a movie. He blew smoke at the kitchen doors behind the bar and nodded.

"The mamasan," he said. "Mrs. Yoshida found a box of Padróns in an officer's hooch that Choi rents outside of town at the old Methodist missionary house. Used to be an orphanage but Choi turned it into rental property. The officer had to ship out in a hurry, so he left a shitload of stuff behind. These things aren't cheap."

He ordered another OB and this time he poured it into a glass. He chewed his peanuts.

"Hey, Edward?" Lee said and released a cloud of smoke sideways from his mouth. He waved away the smoke with one hand.

"I was wondering again the other day why I never make it past thirty."

"Are we starting?" Profar said.

"I always seem to eat dirt too soon," Lee said. He looked like he was about to whistle. He tried to blow a smoke ring, but it didn't work.

"I hope you don't talk this reincarnation stuff with everybody," Profar said. "The wrong person might think you're batshit crazy."

"I'd like just once to end up as an old guy," Lee said. "Have grandkids, maybe stay married for a long time to the same woman. Just once. Live a ripe and fruitful life. I'm in some kind of rut lately."

He studied the glowing cigar ash. One of the girls came and offered him a food menu and Lee shook his head.

"A rut," Profar said as he watched Jia flirt with a tall handsome soldier in uniform. The two of them stood at the table and talked. He had a thoughtful look on his face as he pointed to the unit patch on his sleeve. Jia nodded politely but you could see she didn't give a shit about the man's insignia or his rank. He leaned and spoke into her ear and rested his hand on her bare shoulder, one finger sliding under the delicate black strap of her blouse. He wore a bright gold wedding ring. Jia batted her eyes, shook her hair, and handed the officer his drink and paper napkin with the club's dragon logo and gave him a sultry gaze and walked off. She offered him an extra, heavenly wiggle and batted her eyes at him, just to make sure he'd seen it. He leered and drank and stared at her with his mouth open.

They'd both been watching this and Lee said, "He thinks she'll come back. She won't. He thinks he charmed her. He didn't. He just paid two hours' salary for a cocktail that's half water and another girl will come by soon and close the deal. By that time Jia is gone. She's gotten him all hot and sweaty so he'll walk off with the second girl and that's all she wrote. A smooth operation, don't you think? Mr. Choi has got to be printing money these days. He's got fifty girls under contract, I hear. And they all owe him money. They'll never get out of debt. It's legalized slavery, no worse than what the Japanese did in this country when they kidnapped women and handed them over to their soldiers like toys."

"You think she owes Choi money?"

Lee said, "That vampire? They all owe him."

Something fluttered inside Profar's chest as he watched Jia stand behind the bar next to the cash register where Mrs. Yoshida was counting money. Profar wondered if life would always be so interesting as it was at that moment. Would the surprises come as often? He sensed that some profound truth may have been revealed that night, though he didn't have a clue as to what it was. Or what it promised. Knowledge and wisdom deferred, perhaps, though his youth convinced him that what he now saw would remain there forever, frozen in place like a picture. Instead, he was only gazing out the window of a moving train and trying to grasp the scenery with his hand.

Lee spoke with the cigar clenched in his teeth. "You'll be happy to know that she's our neighbor. Choi just moved her to the regular hooches. Jia's in the corner unit with the big door. You can stare at her all day long. It won't be long before she hooks up with somebody. But forget about getting her attention, Eddie. She can smell poverty a mile away."

The club was packed. Two off-duty KNP officers stood at the door and gave everybody the once-over. An MP watched a GI hand over his pocket knife to one of the policemen. They were frisking another soldier up against the wall.

"You do the talking tomorrow, when we see Cobb about the tunnel," Lee said.

"I don't like him, either," Profar said.

"I'll just say something stupid," Lee said. "He's a dick, you know. In the Big Book of Dicks his name is on page one. He's just looking for an excuse to bust my balls again."

Lee wandered off and started talking with two girls. Mrs. Yoshida brought another OB and more peanuts and that's what Profar did for the next hour: got buzzed and sleepy and watched whores dance and thought about home and the plans he'd made before Korea. He thought about

Margolis and how when they were kids he'd drawn his best friend's cartoon face on an anatomically impossible flying donkey on a schoolyard wall in 1960, his name spray painted in yellow letters three feet tall: MARGOLIS IS A DUMBASS, it said. His friend swung a right hook the next day and chipped Profar's front tooth. Profar raised his beer in a phantom toast to the memory. He missed Margolis. He missed everything.

He thought about what they would say to First Sergeant Cobb. They might both already be knee-deep with a bunch of Army regs and rules waiting for them. He could see trouble piling up ahead. The only thing left to do was to spill what they knew and hope Cobb would take the whole episode off their shoulders. Profar wondered if the tiger might kill again, maybe one of their own guys. That's what bothered him now. You could just shoot the North Koreans, but he didn't think it would that easy to shoot a hungry tiger in the dark.

Somebody stepped through the back door carrying boxes and Profar felt the gust of freezing air wash across the room. The alley behind the club twisted through the village like a lab rat maze, in some spots not wide enough for two people to squeeze through. There were dead ends everywhere—walkways to nowhere that led to someone's mysteriously padlocked door. The adjoining brothel buildings in the village were a crazy jumble of shacks and slanted tile roofs patched with corrugated metal, everything lit with swinging bare bulbs and whatever illumination that came from the tiny windows where the ladies did their work.

Profar tried to ignore the girl with a pageboy haircut who came and tugged at his sleeve.

"You no like me?" she said and stood and flapped her eyes. She recited the script: "Quicky cheap five dolla' short time I make-a-you smile taksan number one happy time. Best you ebah hab."

"I like you okay," he said.

She glanced at the fake wedding ring he wore whenever he went to the club. The girl looked over at Mrs. Yoshida, who waved her hand as if telling the girl to step away.

The pimp Mr. Choi was standing behind the mamasan in his white tailored shirt. He wore a gold wristwatch and casually sorted through a bundle of receipts and made notes on the papers and bundled everything together with a rubber band. Jewelry sparkled from his neck. He stacked the receipts. He lit a cigarette and studied the dance floor. One of the girls came and stood shyly with her head bowed while Choi seemed to lecture her, angrily shaking one of the receipt bundles in her face. The girl gave Choi a few short bows, almost curtsied. The mamasan watched and disappeared through the swinging rubber kitchen doors. The girl wiped her eye and remained standing with her hands crossed long after Choi had picked up his papers and walked away.

Profar wondered if the tiger had lived its entire life in the DMZ and if it was now numb to the sound of the patrolling helicopters and occasional gunfire from the troops who took pot shots at the animals during winter on the Imjin River. He wondered if it ignored the loud music and maniacal propaganda announcements that screeched loudly at night from the giant speakers on both sides of the buffer zone. He wondered if it had a mate and where it had come from.

He left his half empty glass on the bar top and when one of the girls came by with his tab he pointed at Lee's Oscar and said he would pay for him too.

"Gamsahamnida," he said. The girl smiled and took the change as her tip. She thanked him in perfect English and put the money into a jar next to the cash register. She tossed her hair and walked off, all business.

Profar thought he could not live with himself if that animal killed somebody else.

CHAPTER 7

At the hooch Lee spoke with a certain reverence. He said Profar couldn't possibly understand how Koreans felt about tigers. For thousands of years, it was told in stories that when a tiger got old and had survived a lifetime of troubles and danger that it gained wisdom and that was when it would turn white and become sacred. It then became the tiger's duty to keep an eye on the peoples' rulers. And if you killed a tiger without good reason, its spirit would inhabit another tiger who would seek vengeance. Like people, tigers were heroes and they were sometimes fools, Lee said. If you were eaten by a tiger you would be transformed into a *Changgwi*, a lost soul unable to enter the afterlife.

Lee told Profar that he was a casserole-eating honky Lutheran wasp from Norwegian Minnesota and he didn't understand shit about how other people in the world lived and what they believed.

"I bet you Vikings have legends," Lee said. "Legends about smoked fish and polar bears."

"I'm Dutch," Profar said.

"Same honky flavor, the Dutch. Just a bunch of big loud blond freckled people," Lee said. "Mr. Ed, you'll never understand. In this part of the world the tiger is about strength and protection. My dad told me fairy tales when I was a kid and they almost always had a tiger in them. It spooked me when I first went on patrol, even before we saw those tracks. I just never told you."

"Why are you telling me this now?" Profar said.

"Because it stinks that we had to find that tunnel," Lee said. "I wish Fletcher or some other chump saw it first. I don't have a good feeling at all about any of this."

Profar had known Lee since they both drew rotating patrol duty that summer. Lee was more seasoned, Profar the newbie who split duties as General Yardley's driver and shifts at the Robideaux GP. The General was from Duluth and had fished the lakes around Bemidji.

Lee now looked like he might launch into one of his stories.

"Human beings only make myths out of their worst fears," he said. "What scares us is what ends up a legend and what shows up in storybooks. Nobody ever heard about a dangerous duck with magic powers. A bunny rabbit doesn't inspire a good yarn."

Yevgeny Lee's parents met after World War Two while they were students in the Komsomol. His communist Russian mother was studying forestry science and hailed from the Primorye maritime region in Siberia. After his parents hooked up while working on the same logging crew out on the Taiga, Lee's mother tried to get a job as a teacher in Pyongyang. Her background, loyal communist or not, native Soviet Russian or not, made that impossible in North Korea because of her low *songbun* social status as a foreigner. She scrubbed floors and cleaned bathrooms at the Pyongyang railway station while Lee's father served his three-year obligation as a soldier in the DPRK military. He came home on weekends.

"Mom had me strapped to her back when she worked at the station," Lee said. "By the time dad's hitch was finished, he was already sour on the great wise and supreme leader Kim Il-Sung and my parents began to read things they were not supposed to be read. They went to secret basement meetings and listened to forbidden western music. They read foreign newspapers that mom found in the trash at the train station and smuggled home under her dress. The Japanese were long gone by then and though life was tough under the communists, they headed south to Seoul before the war started in 1950. Travel across the 38th parallel wasn't a big deal. They took a train south as far as they could go on the mainland and then a ferry to Jeju Island, where dad had a cousin who worked as a fisherman. When war broke out that June and the whole country was filled with refugees and even the government and that old dictator Syngman Rhee was running away, they found room on a US Navy transport ship that gave them a ride up the coast to Busan. When the Americans got trapped in Busan, that's where they stayed for the rest of the war. Lived in refugee shacks by the pier. My mom said she heard Russian T-34 tanks firing from the other side of the Nakdong River the night the reds finally retreated north when their supply lines got busted up. Then the Incheon landing happened and soon the Americans were fighting all the way up on the Yalu River. Pushing the reds north. MacArthur said he wanted to bomb China, so the folks got a bad vibe and headed to Seoul where my dad's folks lived

"They were like gypsies, moving from one place to another. Mom said they owned one suitcase. Everybody knew they had to get to the port near Seoul to get out of the country. In fifty-three when the truce got signed they caught a Red Cross freighter out of Incheon. It was a merchant marine ship leased by the United Nations to carry car tires from Long Beach to Korea. Three thousand refugees were crowded together like cattle headed for market. Mom said everything smelled like rubber. When they got to the US the folks had their only suitcase stolen. Dad had cash sewn into his jacket, a hundred bucks in worthless pre-war Korean money, their life savings. That's how they started. Nobodies with nothing. Fast-forward five years and they owned a little grocery store on Lawrence Avenue in Chicago and my mom and me were riding the El train to Lake Michigan on weekends for a picnic in Grant Park. I was on a Little League team. Just another American kid with a baseball mitt who worshipped Mickey Mantel and Ernie Banks. Things happened that fast. When I got drafted, they of course sent my ass to Korea."

"What did they think when you got sent to the Zone?" Profar said.

"Started bawling, that's what," Lee said. "Mom said my dad rolled around on the living room rug like a dog. All that work, all that time spent escaping and walking and living in tents and their little Yevgeny gets sent back so he can get shot by the same commies they'd run away from. It was just too much. Mom called the Army "those miserable sons of bitches," and it sounds worse when you say it in Russian. Nobody swears better than a Russian. They gave me names of relatives in Seoul, but I never got anywhere trying to find them. People died or they hopped on a boat and just disappeared into the world. Everybody else got trapped up North and now that's where they're stuck forever. Koreans don't take it well when their families get split up. Weird, freaky mojo happens. The whole dynamic changes. It's like a physical thing when the clan structure is damaged, when the chronological order of ancestors is out of whack. It's a terrible head game. The whole ancestor thing is off balance and I think it affects them physically. I told my mom, 'It's better than going to Vietnam,' and that helped a bit, me not being sent off to some jungle, where there were actually more commies shooting at you. Now it's a family joke that I'm freezing off my ass in minus thirty degrees. That kind of cold means nothing to somebody who grew up in Siberia."

"You staying here tonight?" Profar said.

"I had too much Oscar. I suppose I will."

Profar crossed the courtyard into the alley and walked the shortcut along the river behind another complex of nightclubs. The shallow water never seemed to freeze, the air filled with an oily smell that came from a standpipe from which flowed gray and sudsy sewage that trickled into the river.

The older village buildings stood here in a long row behind a common stone wall topped with embedded broken glass bottles and barbed wire. In the morning on Sunday the girls stood leaning over their porch railings in their plastic flip-flops, tea cups lifted to their faces, as they laughed from behind their tousled hair and shouted gibberish to one another. Laundry hung from clotheslines and each hooch seemed to have a clay kimchee pot flower planter standing outside. There were garden chairs and little cafe tables. The girls slept most of the morning on their day off and when they came outside they shuffled hurriedly from doorway to doorway as if they were afraid to be touched by daylight. They looked much younger without their makeup and heavy mascara, baby-cheeked and shorter in their sandals and house slippers, dressed in baggy cotton shifts like the farm girls most of them were. It smelled different here during the day: like laundered clothing and cooked cabbage and the sour sewer stink that lifted off the dirty river.

The Army landfill was only a mile away and when they burned trash a smoky haze hung over the village rooftops.

At a bend in the river there was a market on weekends with boxes filled with eels and piles of stacked cabbage and potatoes everywhere. The stalls stood empty now, but some chickens still flapped inside their wire cages. In the freezing cold, a bundled up old woman sat on a stool and carefully stacked her turnips in rows inside a cardboard box top as if they were fancy truffles. She wiped them clean one by one and when a gust of wind came along and blew her inventory down she stacked them all over again. She nodded at Profar and pointed at her bounty but he shrugged politely and walked on toward the camp. A farmer in a winter cap walked leading his ox and cart through a field alongside the MSR. He turned toward a little house with a thatched roof where smoke drifted up from a clay chimney. Profar smelled food cooking.

He crossed the highway to the MP shack and lifted his pass. An open police jeep was parked at the gate with a soldier slumped in the rear seat with his hands cuffed behind his back. When Profar turned, there was a Korean man smiling at him from behind a cloud of woodsmoke beneath the big venereal disease warning sign outside the camp entrance. The man stood on the sidewalk frying gobs of meat on a trash can lid, poking things with a stick, sprinkling salt and spices from the palm of his hand. A pile of bread buns warming on a metal tray. In the cold his breath steamed. He wore a torn quilted jacket and bowed smiling at the passing GIs who were stumbling home from their night in the Ville. The cook folded a tabloid page of the *Warrior* newspaper into a cone and filled it with the meat and tossed in some fried hot peppers and handed over a bun. Profar gave him a single Korean coin and nodded as he ate the smoking food and walked away. It tasted good. He wiped the grease from his chin with his coat sleeve.

The Quonset hut at camp was dark and silent. He stoked the diesel furnace. There were six stacked bunks in the hut. Cement floors and rows of green metal lockers at the end of which stood a steel case strapped with a padlocked chain. The case was bolted to the wall and this is where the weapons were kept. For more ammo you went behind the main barracks where an NCO recorded your weapon serial number and wrote down your name. It was a flawed system, though they'd been on hard alert now for as long as Profar could remember. There was a small kitchen at the end of the Quonset with two hotplates and an old fridge that Lee had finagled from somebody who owed him a favor at the mess hall. He was a known expert at kitchen appliance thievery. The concrete block shower and toilet were a hundred meters away outside next to the helicopter landing pad, where a mercury lamp on a pole blazed its light through the Quonset windows all night long. When they weren't on a shift at Robideaux or at the hooch in the Ville he and Lee would get stoned and play frisbee at night and watch the Hueys land in a hurricane of blowing snow. Frisbee games at night in the snow while stoned out of your mind. One of these nights somebody in a chopper would finally get annoyed enough to shoot them both.

There were three more remote huts at this end of camp that housed the platoon that rotated along two DMZ guard posts and a radar station. The Second Lieutenant, who Profar never saw, lived in his own room next to the kitchen. Everybody took orders from one of the two E5 buck Sergeants who ran things and were in charge of the duty sheets. First Sergeant Cobb was everybody's boss and now Profar didn't look forward to talking to him at all.

That night he lay on his cot and thought about Jia and the way she'd moved across the dance floor.

"This is dangerous," he said out loud and stared at the girlie posters taped to the curved metal ceiling above his bed. He wasn't thinking about the tiger anymore.

CHAPTER 8

Mrs. Yoshida didn't talk much. She smiled and nodded and bowed. Occasionally, she chuckled. Though she seemed to understand English, the mamasan mostly spoke Korean with Lee, who seemed to have sparked a motherly instinct in the older woman. She lectured him about the sloppy manner in which he left his shoes and boots outside the hooch. She said no good Korean man would ever toss things around like that. Like a round-eye, she said.

Mrs. Yoshida was always busy. Lee and Profar rented the smallest of three hooch rooms reserved for GIs in a courtyard encircled by a brick wall topped with broken bottles stuck nose-down in cement. Their single-window unit had a sliding door and room for not much more than two mattresses, a table and a cheap armoire. There was no plumbing.

Profar had recently written his fifteen-year-old bother in Minnesota that he and his friend Gene lived in a party pad in a whorehouse. The next letter he received from home was from his mother, who scolded Eddie and asked that he never again mention his association with people in "such a terrible place," or that he might have taken advantage of its services.

"I worry about you, Edward," she wrote. "Since your father's death I've always feared that the absence of his guidance might have left a void which would be filled with bad judgement and disreputable people. Now I have to concern myself with your influence on your brother, who might be enchanted by your tasteless letter, which I must say, was inappropriately graphic. Frankly, I was embarrassed. Your youth and inexperience in life can serve as an excuse for only so long before your decisions begin to hold you accountable. Please don't continue to disappoint me, Edward."

His brother wrote: "The pictures of the dead guys in the snow that you sent? Lucky mom didn't see most of them because you put them in the ammo pouch you sent me. Mom went off her rocker, just started yelling like she was going nutty. Were you there when they got shot? Did you shoot them? Tell me, Eddie. Here's the address for Greg Andriessen's brother. He just got out of the Army. Send stuff to him and that way mom won't know anything. She's super pissed. Do you have pictures of the girls? Tell me their names. What kind of gun do you have? Do they let you walk around with a gun all day? How many girls live in that place? Do you have a girlfriend? What does she look like? My friends think it's neat that you live with hookers. How is that even possible?"

His mother wrote: "Son, please do not make the unfortunate sight of dead people sound like an adventure. The photos you sent were in very poor taste and are disgusting. Your casual talk about death and violence concerns me. It reflects a person of rude and thoughtless character, a heartless person, which I know you are not. The dark and sinful side of life is not worth investigation, for it neither instructs or enlightens and will cause you harm in ways that you don't now realize. I shall put your photos aside as a courtesy, should you want to use them as a reflective reminder in the years to come when you yourself might have a family and more insight into the good and the bad in life. I would rather burn these disgusting photos, of course, for they are sickening, but they are not mine to destroy."

Lee told Profar that the mysterious mamasan was a wealthy woman whose police and political connections went far beyond what you might expect of a simple village business woman.

"Don't let the peasant act fool you," he said. "The smock and the ratty sweater. That lady is a powerhouse. She doesn't take shit from Choi, who understands she runs the place and knows the Korean cops and who needs to get paid off at the provincial courthouse. I hear she signs his name to checks. She's got relatives in the KNP, so that's in the bag. She's half Korean and the Japanese side of her family lost everything in the war, but she still had contacts. Choi's sex factory, not to mention the clubs and investments, they all need the old lady's local connections. She has the keys to his office. This all doesn't work without mamasan pulling the strings."

"You're making this up," Profit said. "Just like the reincarnation thing."

"You break my heart with your doubts," Lee said. "Kraus, at the newspaper? He told me stuff."

"The *Warrior*? The division rag?"

"Richie Kraus can't print what he knows. He's a Chicago boy, like me. Worked for the *City News Bureau.* They keep killing his stories. He said the mamasan's parents were with Syngman Rhee's people and when that fell apart they switched loyalties. Now she's got connections with Park Chung Hee's crowd. I told her about my dad and mom and she asked where they were from and said some of her family used to be Trotskyites who went south, just so nobody would kill them. She knows all the battles in the war and the American units who fought them and who won and who lost. Hates the Kims up North, of course. She might look like a scrub lady, but she's got smarts. Choi struts around like he's the boss, but it's the mamasan who runs the railroad. The girls call her *halmoni,* their granny. If you have to be a hooker in Korea, you might as well work at the River Dragon Club."

Profar sat on the hooch steps in his parka. He felt the warmth under his feet from the *ondol* ducts. Mrs. Yoshida was dressed in her cardigan and the baggy skirt, squatting as she fed kindling into a glowing fire that channeled heat beneath the floors of the connected hooches. She kept shoving wood into the brick oven and Profar put his palm on the porch and felt everything get warmer. It was freezing outside but it was nice to sit and watch the girls come and go while the millionaire Mrs. Yoshida did her chores in her poor-lady clothes and knitted cap.

In winter Profar sometimes slept on a straw floor matt that captured the rising heat. It was too warm if you stayed in the same spot too long, especially if it was early evening when the *ondol* charcoal cylinder bricks were red hot.

Mamasan squatted in her fuzzy boots and pushed in more wood. The glow flickered on her face. She crossed the courtyard and came back carrying the charcoal with her iron tongs. She pushed the cylinder that was the size of a coffee can deep into the furnace and stepped away and grabbed a pail filled with chopped ice. She pushed the bucket into the hearth with the tongs and after a few minutes the steam from the melting ice began to flow out. She adjusted the oven damper so moisture would draft through the *ondol* pipes. Mrs. Yoshida wrapped herself in her sweater and went inside and closed the door.

Inside his hooch, Profar boiled noodles and drank a cold beer he'd taken from a hanging bag on the porch. He listened as the girls headed off to work. When he took his shoes from the porch one of them waved and smiled.

Mrs. Yoshida stepped outside with a towel in her hand and shouted. The girl laughed as if dismissing some silly instruction. The mamasan lifted her arms as if pretending to be shocked. For the first time, he saw her smile and noticed the perfect white Hollywood teeth against her brown face.

He carried the steaming noodles outside and watched the old lady stand by her window. She combed her hair in front of a wall mirror with long thoughtful strokes, and then she shook her head and combed again. An old barrel washing machine stood on the porch with its hand crank clothes ringer, laundry powder in a box next to it. The mamasan twisted her gray hair into a bun with a rubber band and removed those blazing white teeth and set them aside on a shelf next to the mirror. She examined her face, turning side to side, and rinsed her mouth and put the dentures back in. The lights went off and she stepped out dressed in her winter jacket and boots and walked quickly into the alley. He heard the byeonso door slam shut.

Lee was at work at Robideaux that night and Profar had the day off, so he stayed in the hooch reading and drinking wine. Next door, somebody was playing practice riffs on a bass guitar. A woman's voice shouted "...you taksan crayzu!" And from another hooch across the alley came hysterical laughing and the sound of Jimi Hendrix playing *The Star Spangled Banner* through a cheap stereo speaker. Somebody began to sing drunkenly in the alley and when Profar opened his door he saw a half dozen somber-looking bar girls standing outside one of the hooches, their arms folded. One of the girls kept walking back and forth and looking down at her shoes and the mamasan was also now standing in the courtyard talking to a Korean policeman who held a military field radio to his ear.

Flashing hazard lights filled the courtyard as the Army ambulance came to a skidding halt in the alley. Somebody shouted in English for the drunk to stop singing. Profar heard scuffling feet and watched Manny Perez the medic follow two soldiers bearing an empty stretcher into the hooch next door. Mamasan stood smoking, one hand holding the other elbow. The other doors opened one by one.

An American in civies with a plastic ID card clipped to his jacket collar—CID, Profar guessed, followed an MP into the hooch. The mamasan hushed a few of the girls who were jabbering loudly. More people walked into the courtyard.

Profar didn't know the soldiers who shared the next door hooch. They were from an upriver artillery outfit. The mamasan was always warning them for making a ruckus, leaving booze bottles in the courtyard. One day she caught one of them urinating off their porch. She asked Lee to write a note that she pinned to their door that said if they didn't behave they'd lose their rent deposit and also be banned permanently from the Water Dragon Club.

Profar looked inside the room. In Perez's flashlight beam there was something big sprawled across the floor. The MP found the light switch and there was an audible groan as everybody stepped outside and took a deep breath. The MP fanned his face with one hand and bent over like he might upchuck. It was as if someone had cooked a foul-smelling meal. Profar was familiar with the sweetly farty odor and so was Perez and they glanced at each other before going back inside. It was stifling hot and a faint chemical smell drifted from the overheated *ondol* flue. Perez tossed the MP a paper mask and pulled on his own and looked at Profar and shrugged. Profar put his sleeve to his face and stepped away as the CID guy shoved past and started writing in his notepad. The smell didn't seem to bother him at all. The MP stood with his arms folded and watched while Perez dropped his rucksack and started pulling out a stethoscope but changed his mind and instead put on a pair of white cotton gloves. The CID inspector stood and watched.

The dead man lay with his chin pressed to the floor. He was looking straight ahead. His hips were raised, knees pulled forward, as if there had been uncertainty and a lack of conviction about something. A surrender. His boxer shorts hung at half mast, arms spread away from his naked hips as if in some gesture of practiced supplication. A pronated adoration, perhaps. As if to mark the end of some difficult pilgrimage to a shrine. A final spiritual arrival.

Everything on him was swollen, his arms grotesquely tight within their sleeves, the sausage fingers like chubby party balloon digits, the nails black like they'd been painted. His slicked hair was combed and parted like he'd just stood in front of a mirror and when Perez tried to move his legs the man's dog tags rattled to the floor.

Perez nodded at the MP when Profar dropped to his knee and took a closer look.

He said. "He's with me. We work together."

Profar said, "I don't know his name but he comes every weekend with his buddies. There's four of them."

The CID guy brought out a Leica and started snapping pictures. He asked Perez to turn the body over and unbuttoned his long coat and pulled out his own rubber gloves. Profar saw the holstered .38 and the badge on its lanyard.

"He's the third this week," he said and bent low for another picture.

"When they're down like this on a hot floor for a long time they get slow-cooked," Perez said to nobody in particular. "Like meat in a stew pot."

His voice sounded muffled inside the mask "He's worse than most. I'm guessing a few days he's been here, maybe more. Surprised nobody noticed sooner. They have their own smell."

The CID guy stooped and aimed his camera. "The old lady says she got suspicious yesterday," he said. "One of her employees told the police, but they never followed up."

"I don't know how the rats didn't find this," Profar said and looked up at the ceiling. "They can chew their way in, easy."

Perez looked at the stain that had dried into a sticky pool on the rug next to the bed, on which lay a green Army sleeping bag, no sheets, no pillow. Empty beer bottles stood on the nightstand and military-issue condoms in their wrappers lay next to an ashtray overflowing with cigarette butts.

"If they've been boozing it takes a couple of days to die, but their kidneys keep working and when they swell up everything just comes out." Perez said.

"They hardly ever take a crap, I don't know why. But they pee big time. This is nothing. Sometimes it's gallons."

Perez reached to the table made from a painted ammo crate. He read the label on the empty pill bottle and handed it to the CID inspector.

"A club girl came to the gate and said she thought somebody might be sick because she knew the guy and he was always tossing his cookies when he got drunk," the inspector said. "Said her boss, the lady out there, got mad once because he'd hurled all over his front steps and never cleaned it up. They've seen this before. It's nothing new."

Perez explained that several thousand Seconal pills recently shipped from the Yongsan pharmacy never made it to the camp dispensary.

"Stuff is all over the Ville," he said. "Half of what they send us disappears and that means it's out on the street. "

Perez signed the CID paperwork. Everybody stepped outside while the inspector and the MP walked off and talked. The cold night air smelled clean and fresh.

"The spooks use reds when they interrogate infiltrators," Perez said and turned to make sure nobody was listening. "They learned it from the KNP. When the ROKs catch somebody coming across the river they just get them stoned on Seconal and then beat the shit out of them until they get their information. It's cheap and quick. They use the stuff over at the clinic to keep the girls calmed down."

Perez and the MP tried to peel the body from the floor. Perez used a mason's trowel as if such a specialized tool was just another necessity in his medical kit. He worked the blade under the soldier's stomach like a spatula and when the MP gave a tug, a piece of wet shirt fabric along with a patch of skin remained on the floor. The room filled up with that candy fart smell and Profar turned and ducked outside again. He looked back through the open door. Perez and the MP kept lifting, their faces turned away from the corpse. Now the cooked soggy underpants tore away and stayed stuck to the floor and Perez shuffled sideways on his knees to avoid the liquid that had pooled there. Something vaguely pink, an opaque mucous jelly. The CID investigator came back and this time he groaned and turned on his heels and stepped outside again.

The name on the military Class A shirt hanging from a hook on the wall said *Sorrenson* and he was a Corporal. He wore his previous deployment patch on his right sleeve and so Profar guessed he had been in Vietnam. He looked old for an artillery E-4. There was a toolbox on the floor next to the mattress. A Vargas *Playboy* poster was tacked to the wall above the disheveled bed. There was a blacklight on the Panasonic stereo speaker cabinet and pairs of civilian shoes sat next to the doorway. Nothing seemed unusual. Sorrenson had a hot plate and cardboard box filled with noodle packets and a few bottles of unopened Oscar stood in the corner where the wine would stay cool. A stack of bootleg knock-off rock albums, their titles written crudely in Chinese, sat in an egg crate next to the stereo.

They finally unstuck the horribly bloated body and rolled it onto the stretcher. Sorrenson had already been overweight and his puffed up arms and legs made the body look enormous. His face was ballooned like a frowning fat man mask, something out of a cartoon. Perez took the sleeping bag off the bed and tried to cover him. More of the clear fluid dripped from the bottom of the stretcher as the MP twisted his end through the narrow doorway and into the courtyard. Perez gasped. The CID man shooed everyone aside who had gathered in the alley next to the open ambulance door. The flashing red lights made the falling snow look like colored confetti. The snow that gathered on Sorrenson's cold dead face did not melt.

Mrs. Yoshida headed across the courtyard with a bucket and mop. One of the KNP officers shouted for her to stay out of the room until the evidence work was completed. She tossed her head and mumbled something in that guttural, gurgling Korean manner that indicates nothing at all nice is being said. She shuffled off in her oversized boots and pointed with the mop and told all the girls to get back to work. She was still muttering to herself as she slammed her door shut.

Profar locked up. He turned on the porch light and walked to the Water Dragon Club. He sat at his usual place at the bar and watched one of the girls stoop and sweep the empty dance floor with a whisk broom. Her skirt slid up her leg, the black straps on her spiked heels wrapped tightly across her ankles. She swept the paper scraps into the dust pan and turned and saw that Profar was watching her. She blew a theatrical kiss across her palm, which he pretended to catch in mid-air and hold to his heart with an exaggerated flourish. The girl laughed and put her hand to her mouth. She stood wiping her forehead with the back of the same hand and then mouthed a pouty romantic whisper. Her sequined green skirt was fluorescent in the light and her costume necklace sparkled. He didn't know her name, but he had certainly seen her before. He'd seen most of them before. She wasn't wearing much makeup, which seemed unusual. Choi liked his girls to pile on the makeup.

They'd turned off the glitter ball and the club appeared shabby and worn, the floor scuffed with shoe marks. The white ceiling had a grimy nicotine cast. Her name was Tammy or Julie or Kitty, Profar didn't remember. These homesick castaways, he thought. Orphans and runaways who wrote lies home to their families about their jobs as supposed tourist hospitality workers and restaurant cooks. Entertainment assistants, maids at the military camp. They would carry each other's letters out of the Ville to be postmarked in Seoul or Munsan or Suwan. Never from one of the camp towns, where everybody knew what was going on. There was a tender, vulnerable sorrow to their beauty as they spoke their pidgin English and peddled themselves and their diluted cocktails. Even in such sordid surroundings they seemed strangely innocent. There was an inexplicable, ardent grace about them that Profar, in his naivety, found utterly charming.

He went outside. Another storm was brewing and they were tossing snowballs at each other like frolicking schoolgirls, their giggles muffled by the falling snow. Profar stood and watched. He lit a cigarette and smoked. He could look at them all night.

Jia stepped around the corner wrapped in a hooded shawl and sweatpants, her hands stuffed into her pockets. Her hair dangled messily across her cheek. No makeup. She was gorgeous.

"Eddie, you no see Remo?" she said without smiling.

Profar shrugged. She'd called him Eddie. She knew his name.

Nobody had seen Remo in the Ville for weeks. The other girls had already asked about him and Profar avoided saying anything. Lee had told him that Jia was running out of money and was being pressured by Choi for the tardy yeobo payments.

"You tell me true?" she said. "Nobody tell me true what happen. They say today at marriage school at USO that he no pay for long time. I only have month left to finish marriage school. Tell me true, please?"

"I just don't know," Profar lied. "We're not really friends. He doesn't tell me anything. I didn't know about the school."

"No school, no paperwork for marry," she said. "Remo promise me."

She was carrying a grocery bag that she'd set down on the sidewalk. "Why he lie, Eddie? I go to school like he tell me and he say he pay for everything and now he no see me no more. My boss he angry. Why he lie?"

"If I see him I'll tell him," Profar said and picked up her bag because it was starting to get covered with snow.

"Don't say I am mad, okay? I not mad," she said. "I just want to know why he not come to see me and explain."

Beneath the glow of the street lamp the snow fell aslant as if it came from anywhere but the sky.

"Helelleh, he say you good man," she said. There was a slight smile.

Her hooded face seemed like a face in a museum painting as she timidly bowed her head and thanked him for picking up the bag. She touched his shoulder and let her hand linger before she turned and walked away.

That night he lay on the warm floor listening to the tapping steps of the rats as they raced back and forth across the metal roof of the hooch. When he closed his eyes he heard the freight train pass through the village, the locomotive wheels clanking. The iron steamer sounded its lonesome horn and hooted three times. Profar pretended he was in Duluth in his bedroom, half a world away.

In the morning he walked to the old stone war bunker on the hill above the river, a bombed-out shell since fifty-two. What remained standing were two leaning walls decorated with graffiti that looked like faded petroglyphs. Some of the Chinese scribbling was overwritten with Korean script, other phrases crossed out and replaced with vulgar English profanities and crude drawings. Inside the ruins were charred stone campfire rings. Rusted pots and pieces of clothing lay scattered as if this had been a refugee hideout during those years when the valley had been filled with those fleeing south during the war. A child's toy, pieces of a ceramic doll and a basket packed with dirt sat in a pile of ashes in the corner. It was on military property now and encircled with barbed wire that had been cut away long ago. He wondered what strange soldiering and drunken nonsense had taken place here. Strange stripes on the walls showed the scars of bullets that now remained as red rust. If these ruins were alive, what they could tell him about time?

He headed to camp. The path along the highway ran past frozen fields and the oldest part of the village where the farmer's huts each had a smoking clay chimney. Thatched roofs lashed with rice rope. The snow kept falling. Behind him, he saw the Ville's glowing neon shop signs. Tethered farm oxen in their yokes stared as he passed. An old papasan wearing a tall hat and ear muffs sat on his steps with a cane propped between his knees. He took a pull on his pipe and watched as Profar lifted his hand in greeting. The papasan blew his smoke. He stared at Profar and stood and quickly went inside.

Profar pulled up his collar and leaned into the blowing snow. A deuce-and-a-half sped past. Soldiers draped in ponchos and duty gear sat shoulder to shoulder beneath the truck's flapping canvas cover. They seemed like hard and tired old men with their gaunt faces. You could tell who'd been in Korea for a while and who walked patrol on the fence and who was a clerk at camp. At this point in their tours, most GIs were weary of the bar girls and the constant drinking and the cheap dope. It got old after a while and all you wanted to do was to go home.

CHAPTER 9

First Sergeant Ralph Cobb had been with Ahn Sun-Kyung for six months. She called herself Debbie. It was an opportune and mutually agreeable arrangement.

She made the best Galbitang beef soup and always had his coffee waiting for him in his favorite mug at the table by the window overlooking the MSR. Cobb liked to sit and read his *Stars and Stripes* while he watched the passing traffic. He could tell when somebody was speeding.

When they first met at the Lucky Brooklyn Club, another low-key bar that catered to older career NCOs, Cobb wasted no time asking Manny Perez to have Debbie checked out at the clinic. Debbie's English was passable and she was an excellent cook and housekeeper. Somebody at the Provost Marshall's office with a connection at the Ville KNP station pulled her file and found she'd already had a long stint as a housekeeper at 8th Army headquarters in Yongsan. She seemed to have no family connections anywhere. Cobb had engaged the services of a yeobo during his previous Korea deployment, so he knew the routine. According to Cobb's PMO source, Debbie had been a bar girl in her younger years, just another western princess *Yang-gong-ju*, but that was all behind her now.

Cobb felt comfortable bringing work home from the office. He stayed at his little hideout three or four nights a week. As far as he could tell, Debbie couldn't read or write English and she seemed to have no interest in what the Sergeant's duties were at work. This was a business arrangement with romance tossed in when it suited First Sergeant Cobb.

With his square head and matching square jaw, Cobb looked like he'd jumped off an Army recruiting poster. He had big raw hands and stood ramrod straight and he walked with a confident gait. His fatigues were always crisply starched. On his right shoulder he wore the four-leaf clover 4th Infantry Division patch from his most recent combat deployment in Vietnam. He had applied for a stateside post, but here he was back in the Land of the Frozen Chosen. And now these two joker ground pounders said they had "discovered something" near the Robideaux GP overlook, a known location for spotting infiltrators. He thought the soldiers might be playing a game. Cobb didn't like games. He liked regulations and the military chain of command and the notion that an enlisted soldier should do what he was told to do, without question. These boys had refused to put their concerns on paper. They had not filed an official report through proper channels. They should have gone through their own platoon Sergeant instead of jumping the chain of command. He thought that they may have stumbled on some crackerjack black market booty and were now looking for a commendation letter.

Debbie—he never called her by her full Korean name, stepped up behind Cobb and playfully squeezed his shoulder. She asked if he wanted another coffee. A space heater blew hot air across the kitchen floor. Cobb patted her hand.

"A man can never be too awake."

She took his mug and added the customary heavy wallop of sugar. She poured the coffee and brought over a plate of his favorite sticky Korean sweet rice cookies. She kissed his cheek and left the room.

There was a story in the paper about a Lieutenant who'd stepped on a mine while supervising a training operation near the river. They'd choppered him to the 121st Evacuation Hospital in Seoul, where Cobb himself had been treated in 1952 when he served with the 7th Cavalry. The brigadier himself had pinned the Purple Heart and the Bronze Star on Cobb's hospital pajamas. The Sergeant felt a sense of historical continuity as he read the newspaper, as if his career had come full circle. As if he had always been part of something bigger than himself, on a mission grand and noble, something called the United States Army, where people like him were doers of good and protectors of the righteous.

Another article described the capture of two infiltrators not far from where a squad of North Koreans in wet suits were encountered that autumn upriver from the Robideaux GP. Those particular NoKos were carrying Czech-made machine guns and an impressive collection of detailed maps that showed the location of every US and ROK military asset along the MSR. The infiltrators were killed in a firefight after they were spotted floating across a thawed stretch of the Imjin behind a raft made from deadfall trees, one of the standard tricks in the North Korean playbook.

Cobb laughed. "Nobody ever gets across that way."

A photo caption explained that no Military Armistice Commission meeting had been called to discuss the incident, but that the battalion's high alert status was being continued until further notice.

Cobb knew that there had already been a UN meeting at Panmunjom, although the official report had been disguised as a personnel staffing session and so could be legitimately omitted from the Public Information Office media report for that week. The *Stars & Stripes* reporters never dug deeper than what they were spoon fed by the PIO. Cobb was surprised that there were no updates about the capture of the USS *Viator*, since he knew that negotiations had stalled and that the division CG, General Yardley, was getting frustrated. The politicians in Seoul were starting to get antsy. Cobb hated when civilians interfered with Army business.

"Come here *jagiya*," Cobb said when Ahn Sun-Kyun poured more coffee. He pulled her close and rose from his chair and gave her a smooch on the cheek. She squirmed playfully and patted his cheek.

"You do take good care of me, dearie," he said.

"You numba' one yeobo," she said. "You go work late tonight?"

"I'll be back in time to eat."

In an off-handed manner, he told Ahn Sun-Kyung that a couple of his boys had discovered something sketchy up on the river near one of the guard posts he supervised and that he was meeting with them before heading to the DMZ himself to check things out. He said it was all routine.

"It's probably nothing," he said. "Those boys are always seeing stuff at night up there. They get jumpy. They spook each other."

"What they find?"

"Maybe buried pirate treasure," Cobb said

She slapped his shoulder. "You lie."

"They claim they saw a cave or something. Not a thousand meters from their GP. I'm sure it's nothing."

He was about to make another joke about the possible buried treasure but when he turned, Debbie had already walked off. He heard her on the porch, moving things around.

Cobb tried the crossword puzzle and gave up. He drank his coffee and tipped the dregs into the kitchen sink. He washed the mug and wiped it dry and placed it upside down on the little terrycloth hand towel next to the sink.

He checked the time again and shouted that he was headed to his meeting at the camp, but she did not answer.

CHAPTER 10

Lee was asleep when Profar returned from driving Yardley to the parade field, where the General reviewed a platoon of marching United Nations soldiers from the Netherlands, Sweden and Turkey. The Turks wore feather plumes in their hats and they all had mustaches. The Swedes wore white pants with matching tasseled epaulets, like high school band majorettes. The Dutch in their tight jackets looked like old school car mechanics.

The CG did this each month: walked back and forth across the field where the troops played touch football on Saturdays, holding a perfect salute while a band played somebody's national anthem and then everybody presented arms and did more fancy strutting until the show ended and Profar drove Yardley to the division HQ. A couple hours work and he was done for the day.

Lee emerged from the mummy sack sleeping bag and scratched his foot and yawned.

"Time is it?"

"Cobb says he wants to see us at the chow hall."

"You told him?"

"I said we needed to talk," Profar said.

Lee pulled up his socks and plugged in their hot plate and filled a pot with water from the jug by the door. He unscrewed the Sanka jar and took a spoon from where it stood in a glass and wiped it on his tee shirt.

"But you do the talking. I don't get along with him," he said.

"You're the champ of gab," Profar said.

"Not with GI Joe."

The pot whistled. Lee filled his mug and lit a cigarette and kicked open the sliding door with his foot. In the morning, the room was overheated and stuffy because of the *ondol.* You couldn't open the window because the warped sash had been painted shut, so Lee stood there in his boxers and smoked.

Two girls were sitting on stools in the courtyard next to the communal laundry tub, the soapy water steaming. They had towels over their shoulders and wore sweatpants under their bath robes. One of them raised her hand and waved.

She pointed and said, "Helelleh."

A row of socks hung frozen on the sagging wash line and from across the courtyard Korean music played softly.

"I'm afraid my decadent ways have branded me forever with these fine people," Lee said and raised his hand. "They don't know my real name anymore."

He closed the door halfway and pulled on his pants and boots and tried to rub away a stain on his fatigue shirt with his thumb.

"Cobb sees this, he'll shit," Lee said.

"Maybe he'll buy lunch."

"The food's free," Lee said. "Which reminds me."

"Not now, Eugene."

Lee took a drag and launched into another story about when he'd fought with Alexander in 323 BC and how terrible the food was for a soldier marching a thousand miles through the Persian desert, eating jerked meat and olives and drinking from a goatskin bag.

He went on about the other lives he'd lived. Profar wondered if Lee's acquaintances in these other worlds had tolerated such crazy memory riffs. Lee changed the topic to the French Revolution and the madness of Robespierre and the emergence of Napoleon.

"Both were psychopaths, you know," Lee said as he searched for his wallet.

Profar thought he'd soon have to write down the timeline of Lee's previous lives. Maybe he'd catch him in a lie. Did he really have carbuncles as an Illyrian peasant in the Balkans who'd been sent to the silver mines of

Srebrenica as a Roman slave? Why had he died so few times between the barbarian invasion of Rome and the day the cannons fired at Fort Sumter in Charleston Harbor?

Lee claimed there was often a long lull between re-births. At one point it was better to shrug and let him go at it. If nothing else, Lee usually never told the same story twice.

"Let me stop you right there," Profar said. "How come you're always a soldier? You're never a farmer."

"Maybe there's a plan," Lee said. "Maybe it all repeats until the plan is fulfilled. Amor Fati, my friend."

"What?"

"It means 'love your fate.' I don't ask questions."

Lee said he once lived in a Black Forest village in Germany. "I remember a place built in 764 on the ruins of a Roman garrison that once guarded the Danube River frontier during the reign of Emperor Nero," he said. He looked like he might cry.

"There was a medieval church and on a shelf in the vestry there were ledgers that recorded a thousand years of village births, including those in my mother's family going back to when they purchased a farm house with sixteenth century Thalers. A Thaler was a coin whose name is the source of the word 'dollar' and is pronounced almost the same. I bet you didn't know that, Edward. I was also a soldier in that life."

Lee carried on about an endless war between Catholics and Protestants that erased a third of the town's citizens.

"It was worse than the Black Death, Eddie. At least you could blame the Plague on a flea. The forest at the edge of town was fertilized by the blood of thousands. Roman legionnaires, bubonic plague, all those psycho kings and rulers. History only shrugs at that stuff. It doesn't care what we do or how we feel."

"You ever think of visiting those places now?" Profar said. Reluctantly, he was drawn into Lee's monologue. "To see if it changed?"

"It would be unbearable, Edward. I have enough trouble with the memories I have. More would drive me mad."

"We're sitting watching prostitutes do their laundry," Profar said. "We live in a whorehouse, ever think of that?"

Lee said, "I love to watch them. They put up a bigger VD sign out by the MP gate. You think that was Yardley's idea?"

"He made me stop last week and take a picture of it for the newspaper," Profar said. "Said he wanted to make a speech about the sign."

"A speech about pecker cooties?"

"I didn't ask," Profar said.

Profar regretted sending his brother the photo of himself standing in front of the VD sign.

"Keep in mind, son," his mother had written in her letter: "One day you will owe your future wife a sound and healthy body and mind. I would ask that your little brother not see such things or learn that they exist, for its influence on him is certainly harmful. I'm very worried about you, Edward."

The mamasan knocked on the door and stepped inside unannounced and looked at the pizza cartons and the empty OB bottles. Dirty paper plates everywhere. The overflowing ashtrays and the full trash bag in the corner.

"You clean up? Me no clean."

They nodded like apologetic school boys caught in some playground mischief. The deal at the hooch was the rent money paid on time each month and Mrs. Yoshida would tidy things up to a point but any true housekeeping was their problem.

"If I clean, you pay more money," she said and straightened the trash bag so it wouldn't spill. She looked around the room and shook her head. "I tell you this before. This numba' ten. Not good," she said and stepped outside, where she snapped a few curt words at the girls who were doing their laundry.

It was Lee who'd scored the hooch. Their place came with a black-and-white TV that had been left behind by the previous tenant. Profar had rigged up the Zenith antenna to catch the Armed Forces Network signal out of Munsan. The network carried re-runs of the *Days of Our Lives* soap opera, depending on the weather. The girls were hypnotized by the show's tales of divorce and romantic intrigue, the miscarriages and rapes and corrupt lawyers and the crooks and thieves and experimental cosmetic surgeries that had gone wrong. Best of all were the long and dramatic hospital bed scenes. The girls loved the return to the living by characters who'd been thought dead. They would squeal hysterically at the TV screen, rising from where they sat in the courtyard on cushions, when someone on the show cheated or lied or did both. They adored the TV commercials. If Lee was awake on a Sunday morning, they would shout for him to translate ads for Revlon makeup and eye shadow sticks and Max Factor eye crayons, and Cover Girl eye shadow pots. Lee once claimed that a certain product was actually a hormonal sex enhancer commonly used by American women so they could please their husbands. He was immediately covered with tossed cushions.

The girls were curious about the clothes they saw on TV. Lee and Profar would be consulted about whether all American men wore business suits and neckties while they were at home in the middle of the day, or if wives were expected to wear dresses and makeup while they were making dinner. Why was everyone a lawyer or a doctor? Was there really a town in America called Oakdale?

The network would often string together three or four *Days of Our Lives* re-runs, making such a marathon the major entertainment event of the weekend. Mrs. Yoshida sometimes watched and shouted her two cents from her porch, from which she'd serve tea and sesame seed and honey cookies.

Korean music now drifted from the Panasonic four-track stereo inside Mrs. Yoshida's apartment. A great, sweeping operatic orchestra arrangement with violins and cellos and the deep roll of kettledrums.

"*Arirang*," Lee said and smiled. "The music. It means 'my beloved one' and it's about a boy trying to cross a river to court a beautiful young maiden, but the water is too high and he can't get there. So they both sing a song to express their sorrow and yearning. It's the official Korean folk anthem, the one thing the commies and South Koreans agree on. My dad listened to it all the time and it would make him homesick. It was the only time I ever saw him cry."

But Profar wasn't listening. He was leaning against the wall with his arms crossed and staring off at nothing.

"Let's say I believe you," he said. "About being in Alexander the Great's Army, marching...

"To Egypt," Lee said.

"Wherever. India. Columbus, Ohio. Let me finish. That time you said you were with Alexander sitting in his tent, looking at maps, drinking wine from some bag made from a goat..."

"That was 332 BC. In Egypt," Lee said.

"Let me talk, okay? Do people get smarter with each life? Is it like you're practicing for the next one and you don't make the same mistakes? I mean, what's the purpose if you don't learn something in each life? Who would want to be a dumbass for a thousand years?"

Lee didn't answer. They sat in silence and listened to mamasan's woeful song about the two lovers and the raging river that divided them. One of the girls outside stood looking up at the sky with her arms folded.

"You think Jia has to go back to work now?" Profar said.

"Once the yeobo money dries up, she has to pull her weight. Choi isn't running a lonely hearts club. She's not young compared to the other ones. These girls don't have a retirement plan. Remo was her last shot."

The music stopped. After a while, the mamasan started it up again from the beginning and the richly sobbing orchestra violins of *Arirang* and its story of lost and forbidden love once more drifted sadly across the courtyard.

CHAPTER 11

Lee sat chain-smoking on the mess hall steps and waited while Profar made his stop at the Quartermaster's warehouse next door. They had a few minutes before the meeting with Cobb and he'd made Jia a promise.

Remo looked surprised when he saw Profar standing in front of the wire screen at the front counter. Profar launched into his list of questions.

"I don't see where it's your business," Remo said. He put his pencil behind his ear and looked around to see if anybody was listening.

"Yeah. I told her we might get hitched. That's nothing new, you know that," he said.

"You did more than tell her," Profar said. "She thinks she's going to the states."

Remo shrugged and wrote something in a ledger book. He turned and rolled a sheet of paper into his Underwood typewriter. On the wall behind him there were hanging clipboards and posters and inventory lists highlighted with colored circles and checkmarks. Remo's name and rank were spelled in a gaudy Germanic font on a plate on a shelf crammed with stacks of Army clothing.

"If you don't love her, don't lie to her," Profar said.

"Christ, Profar," Remo said. "You some kind of guardian angel? A marriage counselor? I told her I'd do that, yeah. But maybe I changed my mind. I don't have to tell that pimp anything. She's a hooker, Profar. I don't care what Choi thought I was going to do. She's a whore who works in a whorehouse. Why do you care? You trying to get down her pants? Why didn't you just say it? She's all yours. Have at it, pal."

Remo looked around. "Look, the visa request didn't go through. There was a hitch," he said. "Choi has a thing for her, anyway. I can tell. He'd never let her go. I can tell he's got a thing."

"So, don't be a candy ass. Tell her the truth."

"There's something in her record," Remo said. "There's a police file. It came up in the paperwork. It was petty stuff, but enough to blow any chance of a visa. Somehow, they found out. You know how many bar workers are waiting in line to get married to a GI?"

"You were playing with her," Profar said. "You strung her along. There's guys who would make it work. It seems like she'd make it work. This was her last chance."

"You're serious," Remo said. "You don't know anything."

"You're a pussy."

"Maybe you could do it, Eddie," Remo said. "Take her home with you. See how that works out."

Remo stared at his folded hands. "Choi wanted ten grand."

A line of soldiers began to form and Remo stepped to the wall and gathered an armload of fatigue shirts and socks and dropped everything into a laundry sack and handed it to a newly arrived soldier with a fresh buzzcut and a dazed look.

"Ten grand, Eddie," he said.

***

It was Meatloaf Monday. The line at the mess hall buffet counter wasn't very long, so Lee suddenly didn't mind this meeting at all.

The Sergeant's trousers were predictably starched, his black boots shined to a mirror glow and when Profar walked in and saw him sitting at the cafe table he pointed at Lee's mouth.

"He doesn't like that, remember?"

Lee looked around for a place to spit his wad of Copenhagen Long Cut and pulled a tissue from his pocket.

"What a schmo," he said.

"He's the guy who decides if we get in trouble, remember?"

"Eddie, you think if we weren't high that night we would have called it in?"

"Yeah," Profar said. "You know we would have. We were hammered."

"We're not telling him we were high, right?"

"Roger that," Profar said. "He probably knows. Let me do the talking."

Lee again spit into the tissue.

"And don't start yakking about Napoleon, okay?"

Lee had a strange gleam in his eye. "You're the chosen one, Eddie. I don't say that stuff to just anybody. Just you."

Cobb was shaking open the pages of the *Warrior* and creasing the sports section where a photo showed the winner of the new 8th Army welterweight boxing championship, a guy from the brigade transportation platoon. Cobb wore reading glasses low on his nose and his closely cropped thick hair was pepper gray. Profar noticed the jeweled sports team ring on his right hand.

The Sergeant nodded at two empty chairs. "So, what's this all about and why all the hush-hush?" he said. "Am I going to hear something to complicate my day?"

Lee turned to the buffet counter where GIs were standing with their trays, waiting for the cook to bring another load of steaming meatloaf. Everything smelled real good and Lee glared at Profar as if he were attempting telepathy. His eyebrows lifted and Profar nodded.

Profar cleared his throat. He began with an explanation of the noises they'd heard that night. The suspicious shots. He told Cobb the animal tracks seemed fresh and that at first it was thought this was just another North Korean infiltration. That the animal was the least of it. Maybe it was their own guys from the previous night's patrol. Maybe tracks that were days old. They felt they should investigate before calling in a report, like the regs said.

"It could have been anything," Profar said. "By the time we saw the dead Northie it was too late. We both figured it was too late to call on the radio."

He described the scattered clothing, the weapons they'd found. He didn't mention the maps he'd taken from the dead soldier. He wanted to hold something back. He described the tracks. And then, at the very last, he said they'd found a tunnel.

Cobb suddenly put down his knife and fork and started fidgeting in his chair, squirming as he turned and looked to see if anybody was sitting at the one of the nearby tables. He'd seemed inattentive until Profar mentioned the tunnel.

"Say again?" he said in a low voice.

"We thought it was an animal cave," Profar said. "We were sure that's where it dragged the other bodies. But now we think it's a tunnel."

Cobb stopped chewing and placed his fork so it lay parallel to the knife. He took a napkin from the dispenser and wiped his chin and sat back in his chair and once more looked around.

"I'm all ears," he said.

"You can tell it's been there awhile, the tunnel," Profar said. "We think there's other bodies. We didn't want to walk all the way in. The tunnel goes on and on."

"So it was killing North Koreans," Cobb said. "This thing you think was a tiger."

"It *was* a tiger," Profar said. "It killed the other Northies who tried to get across. Maybe they'd been coming across for a while and the tiger knew it and he just waited. It was an easy meal. I think it's hurt. The tiger."

"And how would you know that?"

"Because I know, Sarge," Profar said. "I know what tracks look like when there's something wrong with the animal."

"They wouldn't know anybody was missing, the North Koreans," Cobb said. "When they get sent over they don't exactly contact the home office."

"That's what PFC Lee thinks, too," Profar said. When Cobb looked at him, Lee grinned but said nothing.

"Why didn't you just make a report? That's SOP. It's been days now. This doesn't make you boys look good. You didn't take along your field radio?"

"We thought nobody would believe us," Profar said. "It was my idea to wait."

Cobb looked at Lee, who gave another wise-ass grin. "You boys were shit-faced, weren't you?" he said.

Lee now spoke, "Maybe a little, Sarge. That part was my idea. But we know what we saw. It's a tunnel. There's a whole part of it that's flooded and it goes on forever. They used it for storage or they had bigger plans. Maybe the tiger made them quit."

"You were stinko and thought you saw tiger tracks and you imagined you saw this tunnel. And assumed you saw dead bodies. You expect me to believe this?"

"There's more," Profar took just one of the maps from his pocket. He knew he would have to show Cobb something.

Cobb put his reading glasses on and said the handwritten notations were in Russian Cyrillic script. He said the artillery scales seemed to indicate distances between various military installations along the MSR and that each guard post, including Robideaux, was marked with a red square.

"We noticed that, Sarge," Profar said. "Private Lee knows some Russian. The GPs are all marked, even the new one they built this summer. Are we in trouble?"

"How do I explain this to the CO?" Cobb said.

Without asking, he put the map in the briefcase on the floor and said nothing more about it.

He stood and stepped to the coffee machine. He tore a sugar packet with his teeth and did the same with the creamer and he sat down and stirred the coffee with his finger. The mess hall was filled with a heavy dampness. Steam lifted from hot food bins. Cooks were shouting in the kitchen, banging pots. The place got suddenly noisy with clattering silverware and the sound of the trays sliding along the pipes of the serving shelf.

"You're taking me there today," Cobb said. "You on duty tonight?"

"We start at three," Profar said and looked at his watch.

"Who's up after you, Fletcher's crew?" Cobb said. They nodded and said the overnight rifle squad of six would rotate on patrol between Robideaux and the other two GPs along that stretch of the river. Maybe there would be a full patrol out on the ice.

"Meet me in front of the HQ shed on your way up. There's still enough daylight. I have to stop at my place in the Ville, but you can follow. It's supposed to snow, but I don't want to wait."

"This is a big deal, right?" Profar said.

"Could be," Cobb said. "If it's a tunnel and not just some stupid bat cave or something the locals use to store black market shit, then it's the first one that's been found. We always suspected they would try to dig under our noses. Been looking forever. So, yeah, a big stinking deal if it's true. But this thing about the tiger, that complicates things."

"Guys hear that and they'll be freaked, is that what you mean?" Lee said.

Cobb nodded. "The last thing I want is my men thinking there's some giant man eater walking around in the dark. And I don't want you boys saying a word about that thing to anybody, understood? Not until I figure out a way to break it to the CO, who'll take it all the way to the top. The time lapse complicates things. It should have been reported right away. In fact, I don't think I'm saying anything about the tiger right now. Forget the tiger. What a god damn mess. This is all between you and me until I tell you different, so get out of here. I'll see you later."

Cobb took his jacket off the back of the chair. He smoothed his buzzed haircut with one hand. He squared his cap.

"The old man is up to his neck at the JSA with that Navy ship business. I have to think about who should hear this first. That is, if it turns out to be what you say it is. Be in front of my building at fourteen-hundred. I want to do this in daylight, and we all know why."

CHAPTER 12

They pulled up in their patrol jeep at the three-story concrete block building that housed most of the regiment's enlisted troops and NCOs. Rock music blasted from inside the barracks and frozen GI laundry swung stiffly from some of the open casement windows. The admin office was on the top floor and that's where Cobb had his desk.

The Sergeant stood outside leaning against his vehicle, writing in a small notebook. He pointed with his pen and got behind the wheel of an identical two-seater and waved for Profar and Lee to follow. Bolted to floor of Cobb's vehicle next to the tiny jump seat stood an empty M60 tripod.

It was freezing outside, overcast, and looked like it was about to snow. Profar sat hunched close to the windshield with his arms crossed against the dashboard, his rifle upright between his knees. The vehicle's useless plastic side windows were scrolled up beneath the canvas top. Lee drove with his parka hood cinched beneath his chin, the drawstring pulled so tight that you could hardly see his face. He lifted his hand when the MP raised the front gate and they turned onto the highway toward the DMZ. The road was ice-packed and Cobb's jeep fishtailed. They were both wearing ballistic nylon and ceramic vests beneath their parkas and with all those layers it was still miserably cold in the exposed vehicle. Cobb raced ahead, dressed in a short jacket and wearing a fur cap with the earflaps flying in the wind. The cold didn't seem to bother him at all.

They followed the Sergeant to the two-story apartment building at the edge of the Ville. When Ahn Sun-Kyung came down the front steps she seemed surprised that Lee and Profar were there and when Lee nodded and greeted her in Korean she stared at him coldly.

They spoke for a while and she handed the Sergeant his coffee thermos and Cobb kissed her on the cheek and patted her shoulder like they were an old married couple and she was sending him off to work. He gave her his briefcase.

Ahn Sun-Kyung eyed Profar and Lee grimly as if they were trespassers. She studied their vehicle's stenciled six digit white ID hood number. That was when Profar noticed that their jeep and Cobb's were twins, similarly topless winter torture chambers, the only different being the empty weapon tripod on the Sergeant's vehicle.

Cobb drove off and waved over his shoulder but Sun-Ko Hee barely acknowledged the goodbye. She headed quickly up the outside stairway to their apartment, the briefcase in her hand.

The Sergeant pulled over and shouted: "I'm taking the old dirt service road along the river. It's faster. That's where those Katusas in the deuce got shot up last month, so keep your eyes and ears open."

Everybody had been tense since the boat capture. Profar knew they both should have been wearing their vests on the night they found the tunnel. Another mistake, the kind that happens when you're loaded and not paying attention. The jeep they now drove had armored fender guards and steel shield plates bolted to the undercarriage. A six-foot sharpened steel v-bar was mounted on the front bumper, angled forward, away from the windshield in case somebody strung an ambush wire across the road. In summer, most everyone drove with the windshield folded down against the hood. Why Cobb wanted to take such a route to the GP they didn't know. They'd received a report that this stretch along the river would be sprayed with defoliant that summer, but the stack of fifty-gallon drums from Tan Son Nhut air base in Vietnam was still sitting alongside the helicopter landing pad at camp. There were more barrels stored under tarpaulins alongside the MSR, but so far nothing at all had been sprayed where it might do any good.

They parked behind the Robideaux shack uphill from the outhouse and Profar waved at two soldiers walking up the patrol path alongside the river cliffs. One of them was carrying his PRC radio pack, the tall antenna wobbling as he disappeared around a turn on the illuminated trail. The fence here twisted into the distance for miles, its razor wire coils shining in the light like a giant Slinky toy. In the distance were the snow-covered mountains of North Korea, everything on that side of the river cast in a warm late afternoon glow.

Cobb's .45 pistol showed inside his unzipped jacket. He wore the weapon on a shoulder holster over his flak vest. He snapped open the dashboard bracket that held his M3, something the old timers called a grease gun. The weapon hadn't been used much since the 1950s and Cobb liked to carry it during his inspection visits. He said he'd brought the short-barreled thirty-round M3 back from Vietnam as an official war trophy and now carried it for sentimental reasons. He said he liked the feel of it in his hand. He said he had good memories of carrying it during both of his wars. Everybody called it Cobb's mob gun and he'd carved his initials in the pistol-style stock and carried the weapon across his back on a worn canvas strap that still had the old school brass buckles. Something out of a museum exhibit. The M3 had been replaced for a while by the M14, soon to be nudged aside by the new M16, which would finally make the clumsy M3 obsolete. The sixteen, not widely used yet in Korea, was also two pounds lighter than the M3. Cobb said he favored his antique because it looked bad-ass. He called the M16 a glorified .22 that had no stopping power. He bemoaned the Army's new light weaponry and said he was saddened by the demise of the reliable M14, a rifle suited for long range combat.

They used the stone steps to the guard post, where another gravel footpath continued along the edge of the cliff above the river. Profar pushed aside the snowy bushes with his rifle while Lee followed, occasionally turning with his binoculars. The Imjin was dotted with shrub islands and frozen deadfall trees.

The river was lined with balconies of sandstone and black granite, the rubble of collapsed cliffs. They'd trudged along for fifteen minutes when Profar pointed to a boulder the size of a school bus. It seemed different in the dusky light. The tunnel entrance looked like it had been gouged by a giant ice cream scooper, its edges hung with dead kudzu. They stopped and stood shaking the snow from their boots.

It was warmer inside, a familiar clammy dampness. They waved their lights.

"Where are those tracks?" Cobb said.

"Inside," Profar said. "We didn't go too far."

"How much happy weed did you boys have?" Cobb said as he picked up a soggy cardboard box containing a spool of copper wire. He pointed to the safety symbol stamped onto the lid. He dropped the box and kicked a wooden crate.

"Detonators," he said. "That alphabet style is old school."

A fully laced boot lay in the mud. Lee reached for it and jerked away. Inside was a sock and inside the sock was a foot.

"Old *Chicom* canvas," Cobb said.

The tunnel bowed. Cobb wobbled his light at the chiseled ceiling.

"They curved the tunnel to absorb the sound. There's a blast pattern." He jittered the light again across the row of drilled holes.

"That was fourteen gauge copper back there. Blasting wire. Those holes are drilled at an angle to concentrate the blast so nobody sees smoke or dust from the outside. I bet nobody could hear anything anyway when those loudspeakers kicked in."

"You calling the engineers?" Lee said.

"I have to think about that," Cobb said. "Debbie says the reds are too stupid to dig a tunnel."

Profar said, "Your yeobo knows about this?"

"Says it's always been just gossip. Says anything you'd find is from the Japanese. I talk to her about things sometimes."

Lee gave Profar a look.

"These had time to rust up," Cobb said. "It's like they stopped in the middle of the whole project years ago."

Profar's beam lit another row of crates.

"The tiger knew about this place," Lee said.

Cobb walked off and stood at the edge of a large hole filled with water. An iron ladder came up from the hole.

"This is where it comes from under the river. It flooded."

"What happens now?" Lee said.

"Nobody tells anybody anything," Cobb said. "I have to think about this."

They found torn clothing, an ammo pouch with the canvas loops sliced off. Profar felt the blowing cold draft from the ceiling. At his feet lay the sheetmetal duct work. There were brackets on the wall that were meant to hold the pipe.

"That's an air intake," Cobb said. "Maybe they used this part for storage."

"This is as far as we walked," Profar said. "We didn't want to press our luck."

Cobb shined his light. "Here we are, boys," he said.

The bodies lay face-down, side by side, a startling funerary arrangement illuminated by the beams of the three flashlights.

Cobb said. "Why would it take off their boots? I don't see any tracks."

"Water's been coming through that hole," Profar said. "Everything washed away. I don't think it's been back to eat."

"To eat," Cobb said.

One of the soldiers had a perfect oval bald spot on the back of his head.

"Like he was scalped," Lee said.

"They have that tongue," Profar said. "Cats do. Like sandpaper."

"Why would it just lick off the hair?" Lee said.

Profar stepped to the steel mesh that had been mortared to the wall. The pale hairs were snagged in the mesh at a height beyond Profar's reach. Below that, the vague forepaw impressions showed like discs in the soft clay, the tip of each pug mark the size of a quarter.

"It sat and looked at the bodies and marked its real estate," Profar said.

"I smell it," Lee said.

"What are you two talking about?" Cobb said.

"I think we should leave now," Lee said.

"It sat, but didn't eat anything," Profar said.

Cobb walked with his .45 pointed at the ground.

"I don't know how to shoot a tiger," Lee said.

"I heard that," Cobb said. "You aim your weapon and fire. We're United States Army infantry soldiers. We've got a machine gun, two M14s and three forty-fives between us. I'm not concerned with a damn kitty cat."

Cobb grabbed his back and stretched. "This is all I need to see."

He pointed out more shelves and storage boxes. Ordnance lockers made from poured concrete. Rolls of unused electrical conduit sat next to a wheeled cart. Everything wet and covered with mud, water dripping everywhere.

"I'm sure the plan was to use this as storage," Cobb said. "A couple hundred troops could live here, easy. If that flooded hole is part of something else, who knows how far along this was before they decided to chuck the whole project and stop. Something made them stop. Maybe they started another tunnel somewhere else."

Cobb looked at the bodies and shook his head and walked quickly toward the tunnel entrance.

"Maybe your cat made them stop," he said.

Lee whispered to Profar: "Did you hear him say he told his yeobo?"

"Maybe we didn't hear it right," Profar said.

"He told her," Lee said.

Profar had seen the scratch marks on the sides of the ventilation pipe. The tiger had tried to crawl out of the tunnel through the hole.

Lee dropped to his knee. He turned his face and pulled a wad of papers from the dead soldier's pocket. He nodded at Profar.

They found Cobb outside, staring down at his feet.

"Is this it?"

The crumbled forepaw prints showed in the hardened snow. Profar could make out the wiry hairs on each of the ten pug marks.

"Time to skedaddle," Cobb said. "I've seen enough."

By the time they returned to the guard post it was dark. A low-flying Huey was making its way south toward camp. Cobb leaned his M3 against the bench. He unzipped his flak jacket and stood with his back to the hot diesel stove. He studied the shack.

"This place looks like a dorm room," he said and pointed to the *Playboy* poster on the wall.

"I repeat, this thing is between us, understood? Right now the North Koreans don't even know that their people didn't make it across. I think you would have told me if you'd found a radio. I'm guessing they didn't carry one. They know we'd pick up the chatter. And nothing about that animal, understand?" Cobb said. "I know how these Koreans feel about tigers. Am I right Lee?"

"If somebody gets killed by a tiger they turn into a ghost that leads other victims to the tiger," Lee said. "You have to burn a body like that and cover the gravestone with a special clay pot. Otherwise, you're screwed."

Cobb looked out the window. "Point is, this gets out and it's trouble."

The Sergeant spoke with gravity as he looked through the mounted spotting scope. "We came through here at the end of the war and nothing looks the same anymore," he said. He began to talk about the Battle of Osan in 1950 when the Han River defense line collapsed, sending his battalion into retreat after an embarrassing six-hour battle. It was the first ground conflict of the war.

"We were at Juke Pass and it was awful," Cobb said. "We finally had enough troops that MacArthur sent from Japan so we could make a stand down south. The North Koreans had already advanced, chasing the refugees all the way to the Nakdong River. We established a perimeter and if it wasn't for that everything would have gone to hell. MacArthur would have gotten his ass handed to him and he would have taken old Harry Truman with him. Busan was the key to everything. The North Koreans outdistanced their supply lines. We fought all summer. After Osan it was night and day and I was proud as hell of our boys. If it wasn't for Busan, MacArthur couldn't have done what he did at Incheon. Those poor Koreans, what they suffered."

They followed Cobb outside. The Sergeant pointed over his shoulder.

"To think this all started not far down the road at Uijonbu. All these years, and that little town still has dirt streets and we're still here with guns in our hands."

He stepped into the Jeep, cranked the engine and turned on the amber headlamps. Cold air blew fiercely from the heater as Cobb zipped his insufficient jacket.

He shouted: "The implications of what you found could be international, do you understand?" he said.

"I'm getting ready to rotate home in three months," Cobb said. "This is the last thing I need. Now, in the morning, I want you to go out there and see if anything else is on the ice. Clothes, equipment, anything. Bring it back. I don't want somebody stumbling on another body. Patrol the service road tonight."

Cobb put the jeep into gear and fish-tailed down the dark road.

"I don't trust him," Lee said. "Now he's got the ball and we don't have jack shit to say about anything."

Inside the shack Profar signed the duty log and checked his watch. Lee sat with rifle parts in his lap, wiping them with an oiled cloth. He squinted into the empty chamber and released the handle and watched the bolt snap forward.

"I suppose we have to go out," Profar said. "He'll find out if we don't check that road."

"Nothing's out there," Lee said.

"He said to look," Profar said and took off his flak jacket and tossed it on the bench. "I hate this thing. I wore it for Cobb."

Profar stepped to the window. More lights began to blink to life along the far side of the buffer zone.

"The Northies have more lights, ever notice?" Lee said.

"I never counted," Profar said. He shook the last cigarette from his pack and went to the stove and wiggled the primer.

"I did," Lee said. "Got bored once, so I counted. When I was a kid my dad and me would look down on Lake Shore Drive from the Oak Street bridge. For no reason, we'd count the cars. He said it was easier if you did it in threes. I counted those North Korean lights the same way, in threes, and now whenever I look over there I think about my dad."

Lee said his grandparents on his mother's side had been gulag prisoners who stayed in Siberia after they were released because they didn't have permission to work in any major city in the Soviet Union.

"If you didn't have the right papers, you didn't exist," Lee said. "In the Army they can make somebody disappear with the right signature on the right piece of paper. It's all about the paperwork."

Lee examined his ammo pouch and he checked the magazine in the M14.

"Even after the war, all that Bolshevik poison stayed in their blood and when Stalin died my mom said she cried. This was the guy who'd sent her own parents into hell, but there she was all weepy about that son of a bitch. They didn't like the Chinese and they didn't like Syngman Rhee and they actually didn't think much of the United States, but that was where the future was. They were lucky that everything they owned, every scrap of paper with their name on it, got destroyed in the war. They could start from scratch. Dad said with all the Koreans coming to America they'd have to buy their cabbages and peppers and noodles from somebody, so he opened his store.

"I remember stacking shelves in the storage room. I'd take the two-wheeler and unload cases of Coke and Pepsi off the truck. I was thirteen and should have been doing my homework. Mom was afraid the cops would catch me working in the store. She was always afraid of anything that had to do with the government.

"Mom enjoyed vodka with her kimchee. She really didn't like to eat the stuff, but dad did. We spoke Korean because dad was the man and a good family followed the ways of the guy of the house. Mom taught me enough Russian to understand things when she invited people from the old country over for dinner. She went to the local Orthodox Church for a while, but it didn't stick.

"Those two never had much in common except for Marx and Engels," Lee said. "When that wore off, they became very close friends who held hands. Maybe that's the way it's supposed to be. You know what mom told me once? She said, if you enjoy life too much it will pass too quickly."

CHAPTER 13

They took extra ammo. Lee slapped the snow off the M60 with his mittens and shook the hanging belt to make sure it would feed cleanly in a loop from the box on the floor behind the driver's seat, which is where Profar sat with his arm hooked around the gun post.

Lee commented on the squawking cranes flying unseen above the hot springs. He said it sounded like the big birds were arguing. Snow now fell softly in heavy flakes. It had gotten much colder.

Lee struck a match and lit a cigarette. Another bright row of lights came on and the Imjin ice appeared as a spotless white sheet before them.

Profar swung the M60 out of the way. He turned on the field radio beneath the dash. He watched the red light blink and heard a brief burst of static. He called out the hood number of their vehicle on the secure channel and reported their position and estimated return to the GP. He spoke his code for that night.

"I used to think a fifty was better," he said.

"That's a whole different animal, the fifty," Lee said. "Longer range, but the sucker weighs a ton. And you need three guys minimum to fire the thing. The sixty fires faster. It's better at close range, which is what you need here. The MPs use the fifty, but they like to show off."

"Let's get this over with," Profar said. "We still have to walk our routes."

Lee switched on the jeep's low beam amber lights. They were wearing their steel pots, Lee with his vest on, and each man carried the required .45 and M14. An old school Remington shotgun with a twenty-inch barrel stood clipped upright behind the driver's seat, where Profar sat with his arm holding the swivel handle of the machine gun. His head was turtled into his parka. There was a spotlight mounted on the M60 post and he switched it on and slowly swept the beam back and forth. Lee snapped the blackout headlights on and off to see how far they would reach. Not far. These were hooded amber lamps that prevented the jeep from being spotted from a distance. The lights did a poor job of illuminating the icy switchback that led down into the valley from the Robideaux Guard Post. The road was a known ambush spot.

"He wants us to take it all the way to the ROK sector," Profar said, reading from the notecard he pulled from his pocket. "Two klicks, maybe."

The nightly DMZ propaganda lineup from North Korea kicked in with a burst of static. It was a man's voice. Then the US speakers came on with twice the volume. Tonight's selection began with Howlin' Wolf singing *Riding in the Moonlight*, and Lee drummed his mittened hands on the steering wheel as he drove up an incline to an overlook. A gust of snow blew up from the river and both soldiers bowed their heads and waited for it to pass.

"Perez said there's a party tomorrow at his place," Profar shouted.

"We should go," Lee said. "There's always nurses."

"We should try that town up the road next week and see the New Year parade," Profar said. "All that dragon costume shit. Might be interesting. I'd like to see that."

"Why don't they do that in the Ville?" Lee said.

"Bad for business," Profar said. "They don't want everybody standing outside and not buying drinks."

"You think it's still out there?"

"It's not stopping because we found those guys," Profar said. "No reason for it to go anywhere else. All the easy eating is right here."

Profar saw the lights of a village, a circle of thatched roofs piled with snow. Burning oil lamps flickered through the little windows. They drove past a numbered sign with an arrow pointing ahead to the next GP where the night ambush patrols usually began. That guard post was larger than Robideaux and was made of poured concrete and had an indoor toilet with running water. There was a shower, bunks with mattresses and a heater that worked.

Another sign in Korean script warned of the civilian curfew. In the bright lights the hills north of the river were bare and white. The M60 rattled on its mount as they drove. Lee leaned over the wheel. In his winter goggles he looked like an old time aviator. Profar squinted through the sheets of blowing snow.

The squatting human shape appeared suddenly in the dim glow of the jeep's yellow headlamps like something contrived without reason, a wholly unexpected phantom flicker of movement that seemed out of place in the middle of the snowy road. Not real, a ghostly figment. Profar blinked and hardly had time to reach for the M60 post.

The man in the road wore a white parka and white boots and he quickly jumped to his feet. He stood and faced the oncoming jeep, arms defiantly at his side, as if he was angered by the unexpected interruption.

Lee shouted and jerked the wheel.

The jeep tipped and wobbled violently for the longest time before it bounced back on its four wheels and began to slide broadside on the icy road. The heavy M60 gun barrel with its load of hanging brass spun and slammed into Profar's shoulder, nearly knocking him out of his seat. When he opened his eyes the man who'd been standing in the road was tumbling toward him across the hood, head over heels in a wild somersault. The jutting metal hood deflector snagged and ripped his parka, spinning him around in mid-air. His hip slammed into the right headlamp and his torso jackknifed. His head snapped back and then bounced face-first off the windshield. A bright splatter of blood raced instantly across the glass and quickly froze into a spidered red blotch. During all of this, he'd heard hardly a sound but for Lee's crazed shouting. Everything that happened from this point seemed strangely mute, as if someone had closed the door to a noisy room. The man on the hood was yanked into the darkness as if he'd been pulled away by a rope. In its speed and silence, everything seemed even more violent and frightening.

And then came the thunderous explosion that lifted the jeep into the air and sent it tumbling off the cliff.

Lee had luckily swerved away from the land mine when he tried to avoid the man's flying body. The peripheral explosion, a broadside blast, lifted a wall of ice and dirt chunks above the road as the airborne jeep flipped end over end, finally sliding over the cliff and onto a frozen rice paddy. Everything happened so quickly, with time for Profar to catch his breath and only that. He thought he might float suspended in the dark night forever, his legs flailing, arms spread improbably like useless wings, so tranquil, and at an altitude that made him believe he might never touch earth again. Catapulted, he felt snow sting his face as he soared through the air. When he opened his mouth to gasp his throat seized up from the awful cold. And then came the walloping crash as the jeep exploded in flames at the bottom of the cliff.

He felt as if this surely meant the end of everything. It was what oblivion looked like. Instead, Profar reached up and tried to hold onto his cap as if that might now be the secret to saving his life.

There was no pain at all, only an appreciation for the solid ground on which he'd suddenly landed.

A heavy numbness filled his belly, as if a bad case of gas might be brewing. His legs felt too hot and when he realized he was face down in the snow he also understood that his boots had been torn from his feet. As he lay in his socks he reached around and found a stick imbedded in his back like a target arrow. When he tried to remove it, an odd itching commenced and he felt warm blood dribbling across his groin. Nothing on his adrenaline-riddled body hurt at all.

The burning jeep lay upside down with its tires spinning, the entire front end peeled away, the engine block bulging from beneath the crumpled hood. Oily black smoke poured out. The headlamps sent a bore of light across the snow. He saw Lee's legs scrabbling beneath the jeep and his garbled screaming stopped when the vehicle shuddered and broke through the ice of the shallow rice paddy. Profar crawled over and Lee frantically took hold of his arm and pulled himself free, one hand cupped to the side of his bleeding face.

Lee began screaming. "My ear, oh Eddie! Help me find my ear!"

Profar tried to stand, but his legs melted away as he collapsed and curled up in the snow.

"Eddie. Help me find it, for god's sake, you just gotta help me find it," Lee kept repeating as he staggered off toward the shine of the jeep's headlights.

Profar tried to breathe, but he could not. His swollen belly felt hard and hot. When he tried to loosen his belt his freezing fingers would not move and the pain slid to his crotch with a sudden intensity. His chest burned. When he tried to stand, the sloshing heat in his gut expanded. He heard a whistling when he finally took a deep breath. Now he only wished he could faint.

Lee hollered, "Eddie? Did you find it? There's a hole in my head, Eddie."

Profar felt an odd trickling inside his belly, like a dripping faucet. He wondered if he'd wet his pants. And then he remembered that people had their rigs blown off in a land mine explosion just like this, and so he grabbed his crotch and checked.

Again, Lee's voice: "Eddie? My ear."

Profar wondered if the Indians would return and shoot him with another arrow. And then he realized they were both spooned together on the ground as if keeping each other warm while the Huey medevac helicopter with its flashing lights began to land in a storm of blowing snow.

CHAPTER 14

He woke with a tube tickling his nose and a thicker plastic hose in his throat and another tube that snaked from his crotch to a hanging bag that swung from a hook near the floor. Everything was tangled and the sheets were yanked halfway off and he was cold.

There were lights blinking everywhere. Something beeped from the wall like an alarm. His toes were tented beneath the sheet and his arms seemed glued to the bed. A cold numbness on his face, like he'd been dipped in ice. There was the smell of disinfectant in the gauze that held the tube in his nose. He wished he could scratch with the hand at his side that now weighed a thousand pounds. He wondered if they'd taken out the arrow. He'd have to ask someone why there were Indians with bows and arrows on the DMZ.

Immobile shapes similar to his own lay draped nearby beneath their white sheets. Contraptions on wheels moved past the bed.

His chest was wrapped in gauze. A tube bowed from his belly and stood upright between his legs. Beyond his swollen cheek he saw a blurred suture thread rise and fall as he breathed. He tried to move his hand but it was taped to a platter that itself was fastened to the bed.

He saw someone's gold collar rank pin and when the Major's grim face leaned across the bed Profar tried to speak but got dizzy from the pain in his throat.

"You're one lucky soldier," the doctor said. "Three fractured ribs, the collapsed lung. The ruptured spleen was the biggest problem. There's the lacerated liver, of course. No small thing there. You almost bled out. There's the other things, of course. But that can wait while we take care of the bigger problems. I'll have them take out the brachial tube tomorrow. Don't try to talk right now. I'm surprised you're awake."

He tried to move his mouth.

"Don't talk," the doctor said. "I know it's uncomfortable."

The nurse changed one of the IV bags and Profar closed his eyes. When he woke, someone's voice from a ceiling speaker drifted down the hallway and the nurse came again and reached past his face. Her arms smelled soapy. He could sense the heat lifting from her skin as she fussed with the plastic clip taped to his burning throat. He fell instantly in love with her smell and with her beautiful bare freckled arm and when he tried to turn and see her face she held his head firmly in place with her hand.

"Please don't do that," she said. Her low whispery voice was sweet and he loved her more than ever.

He lost track of the days and nights and he woke in a different room with many more colored flashing lights. His tongue had more room inside his mouth. They'd lifted his leg into a sling above the bed. He smelled seawater and thought he heard a ship sounding its horn.

In the morning the nurse with the scented arms lifted his gown. She was a freckled blond Second Lieutenant and she cleaned the stitches that ran from his chest to his crotch, and so he felt embarrassed. The raspy sound of his own voice surprised him when he asked how long he had been in the hospital.

She squeezed the dripping sponge into the bedpan and peeled away the tape that fastened one of the tubes to the side of his belly. It seemed like they'd shaved him down there. She wore a wedding ring and the dark hollow of her lovely throat with its throbbing vein funneled past the buttons of her starched white uniform.

"They brought you both from Seoul. Two weeks ago," she said. "They ran out of beds. You're in Busan. Your friend, I forgot his name."

"Lee," Profar said.

"He's in another ward. Burns and lacerations, mostly. Not as bad as you," she said.

"I don't remember anything," Profar said, but she was already walking away in her white stockings.

He heard the Hueys land outside that night. They wheeled in more patients and soon the room was filled with the sounds of men groaning. The next week they let him use the toilet, but he got dizzy and vomited. The freckled nurse said he had a fever. The doctor came and looked at his yellow eyes and nodded.

They moved him to isolation, and in the weeks to come the long incision on his belly infected and they had to stitch him up again while they tried to get his Hepatitis under control. His ribs would not heal. The fever lingered for another week, sending him into shivering fits. He grew a rash where they'd left a drain hole in his side that made him feel like he'd go mad from the itching. He lay in a tiny room where no one spoke to him. Another nurse with the thickest eyebrows he'd ever seen wore a mask and brought him books from the hospital library that she wiped with disinfectant.

When they finally removed the tape around his chest he could count his ribs and see the red knot beneath his arm where the bone had not healed correctly. Such a mess, he thought. No matter what they fed him, he could not gain weight. The freckled nurse put milkshakes and mashed potatoes and chocolate cake on his meal orders.

When Lee visited, a giant gauze bandage hung from the side of his shaved head. He walked with a crutch, the cast on his foot showing through the slit they'd cut in his pajamas.

"Edward," he said softly. "You look like absolute shit."

"You've not aged well yourself."

"Have you met Gloria, the nurse?"

"Freckles?"

"I love a woman with freckles," Lee said. "She told me you had the liver cooties. They had you in a special room, where they put the lepers. They made me wash my hands before I came in here."

"What day is it?"

"You've been here six weeks," Lee said. "They sprung me last month, but I fell on my ass at the Quonset and broke my foot and they sent me down here again. The hospital in Yongsan is filled up with wounded Marines from Vietnam. They told me not to touch you. I said I wouldn't touch you even if you were healthy."

Profar lay with the sheet rolled to his feet. By this time he had only one tube in his wrist and he pointed at the long blue welt on his belly. Lee whistled.

"Damn good needle work," he said. Lee peeled away the gauze square to show the red hole where his ear had once been.

"There goes the male modeling career," Profar said.

Lee said, "They're making me a plastic ear."

"A nice conversation starter," Profar said. "Where are you?"

"Another week of rehab in the ortho ward," Lee said. "Me and some Air Force guy who keeps complaining there's no air conditioning."

Next day, Nurse Freckles wheeled him to Lee's room, where somebody else lay smoking in bed, listening to music through a pair of giant ear phones. His arm and bare leg were covered in a checkerboard of red skin grafts. He'd been on a heavy lift C-124 cargo flight from the radar station on Jeju Island when it caught fire during landing at Kimpo. He'd been in rehab in Busan for three months.

"Say high to Levinson," Lee said from where he sat on his bed fiddling with a transistor radio. "He got overcooked."

Levinson took off the earphones. "I heard about you guys and the amazing flying DMZ jeep," he said.

"Eddie, they said it was ninety feet off that cliff," Lee said. "Even the chopper medics were impressed. Said the jeep looked like something had chewed it and spit it out."

"How'd they know to come get us?" Profar said.

Lee grinned at Levinson, who nodded knowingly. "Seems like somebody, maybe a farmer from that little village, crawled under that damn jeep and called on the radio. Eddie, it was twenty below. It was snowing and some son of a bitch bothered to go under there, you believe that? The pilot said he saw a man run off when he landed. Said the guy probably was afraid of getting into trouble because he was out past curfew. I don't know why somebody was out there in the middle of the night in that cold-ass weather."

"I'm never playing poker with you guys," Levinson said. "That's some kind of mojo."

Levinson slid off the bed sideways like an old man and teetered in his slippers for a moment, trying to keep his balance. The grafts on his legs were puffy and smeared with Vaseline. He said he was headed to the mess hall. He nodded to Profar and Lee and took his cane and waddled from the room.

Profar wheeled himself closer to Lee's bed and looked at the open doorway to make sure nobody was listening.

"I've been thinking about Cobb and what we told him," he said. "I got a theory."

"He's dead. Cobb is dead," Lee said. "They wouldn't let me visit until they took you out of isolation. Otherwise, I would have said something. They said you couldn't use the phone."

"Cobb?" Profar said.

"I called up Manny Perez when we were both still banged up because I figured he'd know about the ambush. He used to work at 44th M.A.S.H. and he has friends at the evac hospital where they took us in Seoul. It was Manny who told me about the chopper and the farmer because all the medics were talking about it. That same night we hit the mine? Well, they shot up Fletcher's guard post. Six infiltrators got across and the ambush squad tracked them almost all the way to the village, near where we got ambushed. It was a busy night."

Lee winced and pressed his hand against the bandage on his head. "Jesus, this thing still hurts," he said. "Now I got that ringing. It's like cicadas having sex and fighting with angry owls next to a jet engine. All day, all night."

He closed the door to the room and spoke softly.

"And so I tell Manny about us patrolling the road that night. Like how did somebody know we were going to drive that way? It couldn't have been an accident. I didn't say how Cobb told us to go out on the ice and see if there was anything left from those dead Koreans. I just said we'd talked to Cobb that night. I just said he was on one of his surprise GP inspections. That's when Manny gives me this wise ass look and says Cobb's yeobo did him in. Killed him. Said she was a NoKo spy all this time. Said he was with the CID when they did the on-scene investigation at Cobb's apartment and there was nothing left of him at all. Said the explosion blew off the roof of the building where they lived. They found Cobb's dog tags and one of his boots in the middle of the street three hundred meters away."

"What happened to the yeobo?"

"Zip. A ghost. Gone like smoke," Lee said. "If she didn't head north they'll find that bitch sooner or later. There's reward money and the KNP is embarrassed because she's had a top grade medical and security clearance for years. Cobb had her checked at the clinic and he ran his own security screen. She had everybody fooled. They said she shot him with that stupid gun, the M3."

They sat silent for a long time. Profar's chest was sore and he tried not to take deep breaths. Lee tried to scratch under his leg cast and he rubbed the side of his bandaged head and then he stared at Profar.

"He was driving the same kind of jeep that night," Profar said. "Except for the M60, they both looked the same."

"And she knew he was headed to Robideaux," Lee said.

"Why would he tell her about the tunnel?"

"Why do guys think with their dick?" Lee said. "He didn't need to really say much. She could have figured it out. Hell, he took those papers with him. She could have found that. She could have looked in that briefcase he carried."

"What's that got to do with us?" Profar said.

"She knew that we knew and now it's only us who know about the tunnel, that's what," Lee said. "They thought it would be him driving down that road, not us."

Lee started to say something when Levinson came carrying his food in a paper sack

"They got that soup again?" Lee said.

"Smells like feet. Yeah," Levinson said and blew on his spoon.

The radiator was crackling. It was smothering hot in the room and the window was open and now the sounds drifted up off the busy street. The hospital was in the middle of town near the main market square. The harbor and its long wharf lined with tall cargo cranes stood at the end of the alley and this is what you could see from the window. Lee pushed Profar's wheelchair into the hallway. It was noisy, nurses shoving carts and carrying their trays, orderlies with brooms and mops and the clattering of dishes coming from the mess hall.

"So, let's say we're the only people who know about the tunnel," Lee whispered. "We should tell somebody, huh?"

"No," Profar said. "They won't believe us now. It's way too late. They won't even believe we told Cobb or the story you just told me about his yeobo. They'll only know that we waited too long. You know how the Army works. Everybody starts covering their ass and before you know, it's us locked up in the stockade. Nobody listens to a Spec 4 and a guy who's been busted to PFC who's had the clap twice."

"Thanks, pal. That hurts," Lee said.

"It's Cobb's fault. We were ready to do the right thing and he mucked it up and didn't know enough to keep his mouth shut."

"Perez said everybody at the battalion office is tied up with that captured ship. That's all they can talk about. How did we get into this mess?"

"As long as we shut up, we're not in any mess," Profar said.

"You think Cobb mentioned our names to her?"

"He didn't have sense to shut up about the cave, so what do you think? Remember how she looked at us?" Profar said. "Funny how that road was just patrolled, but when we drove back there's suddenly a guy trying to bury a mine."

"Perez told me the guy we saw, he was clean," Lee said. "His paper work checked out. Probably a spy, too."

"So, when Cobb gets home that night, his yeobo is surprised. She can't let anybody know about the tunnel, even if it's been abandoned. So she gets rid of him and boogies out of town."

Lee was released that week. Levinson's third skin graft didn't take and they sent him to another hospital in Okinawa. For the rest of his stay in Busan, Profar guzzled milkshakes and candy bars and tried to gain weight. He'd sit on a bench in the little park near the hospital entrance and watch the traffic. He'd find a chair in the mess hall and nurse his coffee all morning, studying the patients as they came and went, trying to guess what was wrong with them. Some wounded special forces guys from Vietnam were pulled off the Navy hospital ship docked in the harbor. They had mostly leg wounds and those on crutches or wheelchairs would fill up the day room, where they played cards or watched sitcom re-runs and two-day-old news broadcasts on the black-and-white TV. He read paperbacks and old magazines from the hospital library. He re-read Hemingway's Nick Adams fishing stories because they reminded him of his dad and their trips to the North Woods, where he'd watched men with poles rake cranberries from a pond on the Chippewa reservation at Red Lake.

Three weeks and ten pounds later they handed him a one-way train ticket to Seoul. That afternoon he was laying in bed watching the ceiling fan turn when he heard boots shuffle into the room.

"Get up, you malingering useless no-good piece of draft bait."

Lee looked him up and down. "You don't look much better than the last time. They fattened your ass up a little."

"How did you get here?"

"Weekend pass. Hitched a ride with the mail shuttle, some little fixed-wing suicide Piper Cub that flies down here twice a week." Lee looked at the stack of papers on the bed stand. "They finally give you a medical back home?"

"Nope," Profar said. "Back to work."

"With your shit? There's got to be some doc who signs off on a discharge. Jesus."

"They gave you a pass to come all the way down here?"

"New company Top signed it," Lee said. "By the way, this thing with Cobb. It's turned into a big deal. The old man made a formal UN accusation that it was an assassination planned out of Pyongyang. A TV crew from Tokyo tried to take pictures, but the MPs chased them off."

"I've been thinking," Profar said.

Lee shook his head: "I was hoping you wouldn't do that."

"Maybe there's more tunnels."

"Look, Eddie. Nobody's going back to that place. Let's forget about the whole thing. This is too big for guys like us. It won't take much right now to make the world catch fire. Do we really want to get in the middle of that? Everything's rigged and neither one of us is pulling the strings."

Profar almost felt relieved. He was tired of thinking about the tunnel. He held up his train ticket.

"Headed back on Tuesday," he said.

"They gave your bunk at camp to some new guy," Lee said.

"My bunk."

"At the Quonset. They reckoned you were out of commission. For a while, everybody thought we were dead. Kraus almost ran a story in the paper, but he checked and found out we were still among the living."

Lee pointed at his head. "You didn't even notice," he said.

"The ear. You got a new ear?"

"Watch this."

Lee twisted the oval metal clasp and the plastic ear came away in his hand. He held it up proudly. It was smooth and waxy, not quite the same color as his real ear.

"If I had these doctors when we were at Borodino with Napoleon, it would have changed the history of Europe. We lost more guys to disease than to bullets and..."

"Don't start." Profard handed back the prosthetic ear.

"Once I can grow my hair long you won't notice," Lee said. "Hey, you feel like some real food instead of mess hall mush?"

"As long as you don't talk about Caesar or the Roman Empire, yeah. Maybe you should ask Nurse Freckles for a date," Profar said. "She likes you. I saw her checking you out."

"Must be the ear," Lee said. "I'm totally irresistible now."

CHAPTER 15

Lee took him to a hole-in-the wall noodle shop in an alley behind a trinket store filled with fake US Navy souvenirs and bootleg American rock and roll albums.

The shop sold the usual logoed satin jackets, *Playboy* centerfold posters and tie-dyed hippie tee shirts. If you said the right words and didn't look like a police narc, they'd take you to a side room and sell you a hundred grams of top quality black Thai hash for five bucks.

The five-table restaurant was two streets off the main harbor highway and far enough from the railroad station so that it catered mostly to locals. There was no sign on the door, just a plate hanging from the pagoda roof with a single Hangul character etched into the metal. You had a sense the place had been there long before the American military arrived. Long before any modern war. Long before the Japanese occupiers. The tall ceramic stove in the corner looked like it was two hundred years old. One of the stove tiles was embossed with a Joseon Dynasty battle flag. Staring down with benevolence from the plaster ceiling was a badly painted portrait of Confucius holding up two fingers like a Boy Scout reciting the oath of honor. Or a fat bald hippie flashing a peace sign.

Lee ordered the food. There was no menu. The owner, a chubby guy in a tee shirt and white apron, laced his fingers across his belly and gave a little bow and studied them both. He lifted one eyebrow and regarded Lee with some suspicion, perhaps surprised to see an Asian soldier dressed in a US Army uniform. Profar noticed the man staring at the combat infantry badge stitched above Lee's left pocket, as if he recognized it.

Lee turned to Profar, "I'll go easy on the peppers and spicy stuff. Last thing you need is to get the shits."

He lifted his chin at the owner. "This joint doesn't look like it's got a byeonso worth the risk of admission."

Lee started to gab with the man. He must have told a joke because the owner gave out a belly laugh and tossed up his hands as if Lee had just said the most outrageous thing. He showed his missing front tooth and grinned.

"I told him I was mixed," Lee said. "Just to get that part out of the way. I don't think he has much contact with Americanos. Maybe I used the wrong word. I guess I told him I was half crazy instead of half-Korean. He got a kick out of it."

The man took a pencil from behind his ear and wrote the order on a notepad. He turned and disappeared behind a plywood wall that seemed to have been built to hide the little kitchen from view. A woman's voice chattered from behind the wall and Profar could hear the man mumbling the order and there was the scrape of a spatula on a sizzling grill. It began to smell real good and a cloud of cooking smoke drifted out from behind the wall. They were the only customers in the restaurant. Profar looked around and there seemed to be no cash register where you paid your bill, only a cigar box sitting on a counter where they sold cigarettes and Korean candies and chewing gum.

After all these weeks of watery mess hall soup and bland meatloaf and Wonder Bread and margarine sandwiches, this all seemed exotic. The smell was fabulous and Profar tried to breathe deeply, though his ribs still ached. The man and the woman started arguing in the kitchen, but in a kidding and easy manner that had nothing to do with understanding the language. Like an old grousing married couple seeing who could get the other's goat. They both started laughing as a pot rattled on the stovetop.

"Wow," Lee said when the smiling woman brought out two giant trays with platters piled high with grilled meat and steaming squash and thinly slices cucumbers. Little bowls with sauces, one of them heaped with chopped red chili peppers. There were arranged chrysanthemum leaves spread over a bed of diced onions. A ring of yellow peppers surrounded a pile of steamed eggplant. A plate of stir-fried radishes smoking in a dark paste.

"I told him to give us mild food. Just a light dinner," Lee said and pointed to what Profar thought were bean sprouts. "That's *muchim*. Stay away from that. It'll burn your face off."

Lee explained in great detail what they were about to eat and what significance the order of its consumption might have on the success of the meal. In the center of one of the trays sat a square container piled with beef *bulgogi*. There were hunks of pork belly that Lee said looked like it had been dusted with more pepper than he thought Profar could stomach.

"Jesus," he said and took some cabbage with his sticks. "Maybe go easy on the kimchee. This wasn't a good idea, pal. This dinner might just kill you. They'll be insulted if we don't try some of it."

The owner asked about drinks. Profar ordered beer and Lee shook his hand.

"You had the Hep, remember? You said they told you no booze for a year."

"Okay, mom."

"Yeah, I'm your momma," Lee said and told the waiter to bring a Pepsi and a ginger ale. They ate. Profar chewed in the manner of someone who'd just come from the dentist. His stomach growled, but the food was perfect. He heard the man pouring water on the sizzling grill to clean it. The woman walked out wiping her hands on her apron and she sat behind the counter and started reading a newspaper. When she smiled she too had a missing tooth, just like her husband.

"I've been wondering," Profar said. "How old do you think Jia is. And whatever happened to Remo?"

"You still in your love stupor?" Lee said. "I haven't heard about Remo, but she asked about you."

Profar stabbed a piece of meat and dipped it into one of the sauces. He scooped the rice.

He tried not to sound surprised. "She asked about me?"

"Yeah, lover boy. She did."

Lee held up the sliced barbecue beef and dipped it into the red pepper paste. He swallowed and ate more rice and said something to the woman, who quickly brought them two cups of syrupy tea.

"Drink that," he said. "Helps the stomach. Tastes weird, but it works. Yeah, she did ask about you. The girls all knew. The grapevine, of course. For a few days they thought we were pushing up daisies. Even the mamasan wanted to know. When I got back I told them you were a prick and pricks are like cockroaches and they never die and that you had fortunately not succumbed to your injuries and were well on the road to a full recovery, though a tragic side effect might linger."

"Side effect," Profar said.

"I told them it was your dipstick. Shrapnel, I said. The doctors tried their best, but unfortunately they could not save it."

"So she asked about me."

"You just blushed, Eddie," Lee said. "Christ, don't tell me you're still smitten. There's no future with her. Now eat your kimchee. Nothing more healthy for a man than cabbage that's been rotting underground in a clay jar for two months."

Lee poured sugar into his tea and sipped. "Remo hasn't left camp," he said. "Hasn't paid Choi a dime and she's still earning her keep making GIs buy drinks. But I hear the Pimpster is out of patience. She's getting close to her shelf life."

"How do you know all this?" Profar said. "And don't call her a whore."

"The little brother thing kicked in and she likes to talk to me," Lee said. "She won't shut up."

"She feels sorry for you," Profar said. "You being half crazy and all."

Lee pointed at one of the trays. "Try that. It's good for your brain."

They ate in silence. Lee spoke about Jia's life during the war.

"She was a little girl when it started. She didn't want to say much about those days, but nothing went well. My folks lived through that, so I've heard all the stories. We both can't understand what kind of life she's lived."

"How did she hook up with the pimp?" Profar said.

The woman put down her newspaper. She cleared away one of the trays. Lee leaned and scratched his stomach and smothered a burp with his fist. He hailed the owner and spun his finger in a circle above the leftover food and said he wanted a bag. Three white paperboard containers with wire handles quickly appeared and Lee and Profar started spooning their food into the boxes. Lee tossed a piece of beef into his mouth and chewed as he talked.

"Things happened to her before that," he said. "It was chaos in those days. Refugees everywhere, the whole country destroyed. It was a wasteland. She met some religious folks who were trying to start their first church in Korea, the Rapturous Holy Covenant of Whatever. I don't remember the name. She said they seemed like good folks because they helped bury dead refugees they found on the road. Gave them a Christian service, but did it in the traditional Korean way. Coins over the eyes, old school stuff. The body bound from head to foot. They did their best to put the people to rest with honor. Said they could baptize the dead retroactively to make sure their spirits weren't in limbo. This impressed Jia. Confucius had never thought of something like that."

The owner handed Lee the bill and nodded at the leftovers. He seemed disappointed that they hadn't eaten everything. Lee said something and rubbed his full stomach and tapped his wristwatch. He examined the check, took out his wallet. Profar tried to pay. Lee raised his middle finger.

"That's when Mr. Choi Il-Seong, our pimp, comes into the picture," Lee said with a flourish of his outstretched hands. "I'll tell you that unpleasant story later."

Lee paid the bill with a wad of small denomination MPCs, which he knew would be appreciated, and then set aside the generous tip beneath his empty glass. He tapped the stack of Korean currency with his finger and snapped a brief head bow and thanked the man for the fine meal.

They had a short conversation in which the restaurant owner said he recognized Lee's unit shoulder patch and the embroidered black CIB and asked what had brought them so far south to Busan. He was used to seeing US Navy sailors, he said. Lee gave him the abbreviated version of their ambush up on the DMZ months before and the man nodded gravely as he listened and leaned with both hands on the back of the table chair. His white towel tossed over his shoulder. His eyes moistened as he alternately stared at Lee and Profar. He turned and shouted and when his wife answered and stepped out wiping her hands on her apron all three of them laughed and looked at Profar.

"What?" Profar said.

The owner shook Profar's hand while his wife grinned and nodded in the manner of someone who has been told an epic tale of a grand and gallant adventure. She spoke some long and passionate Korean phrase and raised both her hands in astonishment.

Lee winked. "They're congratulating us. His wife says we've both 'been licked by the tiger.'"

"And this means what?"

"It's an old saying from way back. From one of the ancient legends. Means we're distinguished men of rare luck and good fortune. Men of destiny and noble accomplishment whose proud ancestors will smile down upon them for generations to come," Lee said. "She called us great warriors who cheated fate. It's a compliment, brother Edward. The highest of compliments."

CHAPTER 16

Next week, an orderly tossed a thick envelope on his cot and walked out of Profar's room without saying a word. His file and hospital discharge papers included a typed sheet of orders instructing him to report to the CO of his company within forty-eight hours.

They'd pulled out the eighty-two stitches on his belly that Monday and it itched like crazy. He was still bleeding as he shuffled like an old man down the hall carrying his laundry bag. He nodded to the desk clerk, who handed him a form to sign along with a roll of Korean currency wrapped in a rubber band. He stepped outside and stood blinking in the sunlight as if he'd just been sprung from prison and was confused about this sudden and unexpected freedom.

He felt woozy, light-headed. He sat on the bench near the hospital entrance and watched people come and go. It was almost warm outside, the cool spring breeze blowing off the harbor with its fish smell and the oily, gritty odor of the wharf. A ship's horn groaned and tooted twice as if it might be a signal for passengers to board. The mournful sound reminded him of home.

He tried to read his medical records with their cryptic chicken scratches and charts. There were details of his five-liter blood transfusion at the evacuation hospital in Seoul. Doctors' signatures and lists of meds and the careful record of the progress of his liver damage that seemed to have been caused by the bad blood they gave him during the medevac flight. There was something about a heart murmur they'd discovered, but it was labeled "innocent." There was a stretcher number for the flight to Busan that he didn't remember. X-rays for the back injury and instructions that he sleep on a thin mattress and bed board and do no heavy lifting for the next month. More endless temperature, pulse and respiration charts. Finally, like evidence in a coroner's inquest, a schematic sketch of the eight-inch frozen tree branch that had impaled him and caused his lung to collapse. He should have worn the flak jacket that night.

He watched the traffic. A man walked past holding a horse pulling a cart stacked with vegetables and Profar closed his eyes and listened to the wheels clatter on the street. He could smell onions and cabbage, the sweet manure odor of the horse. The scabby wound on his belly ached and itched at the same time and he tried not to scratch it. It kept bleeding, but there was no way he would now tell anyone. He was done with doctors and bed pans, though he had the feeling that it might be nice to go back inside to take a nap.

He was sore everywhere. Don't get me started on the rash, he thought. The pain in his back shot down one leg and when he sat too long the limb went completely numb. His meds were in the shaving kit at the bottom of the laundry bag and so he dug out one of the plastic bottles and tipped a capsule into his mouth and swallowed it dry. He didn't feel like walking, so he hailed a taxi for the ride to the train station.

The summer civies they'd given him didn't fit at all. Even with the weight gain, he looked like a shabby vagrant in his baggy pants and shirt. In the shop across the street from the station he bought a sweater and smaller trousers with a leather belt three notches too big for his waist that was embossed with images of the Korean flag. The clerk looked him over and asked if he had a jacket to wear. It was getting blustery outside, but when Profar saw the store's display of farm clothes and bib overalls and rubber work boots, he politely said no.

"Got nice GI jacket for you, ten dolla' only," the clerk said and ducked behind a curtain. He returned waving a zippered jacket with a dragon embroidered across the back. He had no idea what the Korean script on the sleeves said but the jacket seemed warm, so he handed over an MPC note. The man looked at the black loafers they'd issued Profar at the hospital.

"Got nice numba' one man shoe. Every size."

"I'm good," Profar said. He pointed to bags of what looked like cookies hanging from hooks on the wall. "What's that?"

"Choco," the man said and made a circle with his thumb and forefinger. "Little pies."

Profar paid for two bags with his Korean money and put the change in the pocket of the outlandish dragon jacket.

At the train station across from the bay he stood in line in front of a brass ticket cage at the information counter where a Korean girl wearing a bow tie and high white socks stamped his one-way ticket. She pointed to the boarding platform where an ancient locomotive sat with steam puffing from beneath its giant iron wheels. Men in overalls carrying cans of piston oil crawled between the black wheel sets. Workers were loading caged chickens and ducks. Bawling cows walked up a ramp into a boxcar.

Two ROK soldiers holding rifles studied him from where they stood beside one of the locomotive's boarding steps. Profar nodded, but they only stared in his direction as if he were invisible. He wondered what he looked like in the satin jacket, the long raw scar running up the side of his swollen cheek still showing its crosshatch of suture marks. Like a bad Frankenstein mask. The stubble on his shaved head had grown back unevenly and he thought he should have asked the shopkeeper for a cap. His ribs were wrapped beneath the shirt and so he leaned oddly as he walked as if he were carrying some invisible cargo. Or shambling along like a derelict ready to beg for coins. With the Army-issue green laundry sack slung over his shoulder, the baggy pants, the dumbass jacket and the penny loafers, he had the appearance of a lost and confused wayfarer in search of food and shelter for the night. He wished they'd just issued him Army fatigues when he was discharged from the hospital, but by the time he thought of going to the Quartermaster's office it was already too late. He hadn't been thinking straight about any of this.

He now hoped for sleep once he found his seat for the six-hour train ride to Seoul. He counted his MPCs. He counted his coins and the Korean bills. The rich smells of food rising from the people sitting along the train platform made him hungry. Some of them were eating from steaming bowls or cooking on their charcoal braziers like campers in the woods. He hoped there would be a military bus at the station in Seoul. He was pretty much broke but for the little money they'd given him at the hospital. He didn't know if he had enough for the taxi ride to Yongsan. There was no hitchhiking allowed in Korea anywhere and dressed in his civies and looking the way he did he'd certainly attract attention from the local police, who would arrest him and ask questions later. Damn Army, he thought. God damn Sergeant Cobb and his god damn little yeobo bolshevik commie North Korean assassin.

Profar leaned against a lamp post next to the locomotive and squinted at the inscribed lettering below the front face of the wheel rim. The wheel came to the top of his hip. He recognized the Japanese characters, though he had no idea what they meant. There was the date 1940 and above that the much larger words, "Friederich Krupp, Essen" stamped into the blackened iron. He watched a worker wearing leather gloves stand on one of the connecting rods attached to the engine crankshaft and jump lightly to the catwalk that led to the engine cab. There was a dull hiss and then the bright glow as somebody tossed coal into the firebox. He heard the scrape of shovels and smelled smoke. He stepped away and saw the wall of illuminated glass gauges. There were tools and short-shafted shovels leaning against a narrow ladder down which the same worker now clambered carrying an armful of rags. Profar felt a rumble beneath his shoes as something heavy clattered beneath the locomotive and lurched it forward. There came an announcement on the loud speaker and those who had been sitting on the platform began to gather their things and rise like the commencement of some grand mass pilgrimage.

Profar held the ticket in his mouth as the boarding passengers surged forward. It was chaos. If he fell, he knew he'd never get up. His back throbbed and he tried to shake the numbness from his leg. Children clung to their mothers' baggy skirts and a woman with a basket stacked with potatoes shook her finger at someone who may have been sitting in her third class train seat. All the good cushioned seats were soon occupied, so Profar tried to hold the laundry sack above his head as he shuffled sideways down the aisle. He tossed the bag to mark his spot on a wooden bench next to the window and sat there for a moment, wheezing and holding his belly with one hand. He thought of trying to find one of his pills but decided it was not worth the effort. He felt dizzy. You're like a miserable old cripple, he said out loud.

The uniformed conductor flourished his silver device from a holster, a chrome handled punch, and quickly snapped it against Profar's ticket with such speed that he hardly saw him return the thing to his belt like a gunslinger with a six-shooter. The conductor seemed to enjoy showing off this ticket validating skill as he walked jauntily down the length of the aisle clicking his punch and nodding at passengers. He wore a blue suit and a billed cap with a badge. When he walked past Profar toward the next rail car he brought two fingers to his forehead in a salute and said in clipped English, "Good day to you, sir."

A family of farmers sat across from him. They were dressed alike in the same style of baggy white work clothing, the men in loose frocks or vests and the women with their billowing long skirts fastened with plain white sashes that came up past their waists. They each studied him, unsmiling, as if there might somehow be a school quiz afterwards as to how he looked and what strange clothing this western stranger who'd dropped from the sky might have worn. The old papasan wore a tall black horsehair hat over his headband and his long, brushy chin beard came to the middle of his chest. He smiled through two bad front teeth and a little boy stepped up and tapped Profar's knee and quickly hopped back to the safety of his mother's lap like he was playing a game of tag. The whole bunch grinned broadly and started chattering at each other.

The train crawled along until it reached the edge of town and then there was a sudden clanking and forward jolt. Outside, he could see the wide bay and the wharf. Profar smelled the oily grit as a puff of black smoke floated past the open window. They began to gain speed and the heavily loaded train car yawed sideways on the tracks. He watched a farmer and his yoked ox walk across a field in a rising haze, as if man and animal were floating, not of this time or world, a pastoral fairy book scene that had been repeating itself at this very spot for thousands of years with the same ox and the same man. Nothing had changed but the farmer's rubber knee boots and the curved steel plow blade that lifted curling clods of black dirt as he walked. Profar turned in his seat and watched the farmer's progress until the train entered a tunnel and everything went black but for the green fluorescent glow of Profar's wristwatch. It was noon and he had six hours to go before he reached Seoul.

The countryside flowed past in that hurried and smeary fashion that made Profar think that life might be this way, too. Everything rushing with a speed you never comprehend until it's too late. Killing time until time kills you.

One of the farmers motioned at him with his cupped hand and one by one the others offered Profar food from wrapped parcels they'd been holding on their laps. A warm and steaming bowl draped in a towel appeared out of nowhere. He smelled the kimchee and something fishy and one of the smallest children dropped a bread roll onto the bench next to him. Everyone stared as if anticipating what it might look like when the stranger with the scar on his face finally ate. As if they were now to witness exactly how and with what acquired skill he would use his hands and mouth and if such a thing might be similar to their own way of consuming food. They must think I'm from the moon, Profar thought. Just landed here on a damn spaceship. Some ugly round-eyed scarface dressed like a silly clown.

He smiled and sniffed the bowl. He nodded as he chewed and swallowed and felt the spiced fermented cabbage burn its way down the back of his throat. His eyes watered. He tried not to gasp, thinking this might be impolite. He wiped his sweating face with his sleeve and tried to smile but his tingling lips had gone numb. The food was wonderful. Someone handed him a metal canteen cup, a US Army issue MRE utensil. Another of the five children, a smiling tiny elfish girl with a single long braid hanging across her shoulder, poured him water from a stoppered thermos and now they all glared at him intently as he gulped and wiped his mouth with the sleeve of his shirt. After watching for a while they seemed satisfied that Profar would not starve and so resumed their own conversations, handing food to each other across their grandfather's lap. The little girl lay curled up beside her mother and studied everything with her giant dark eyes.

When he was finished he handed back the cup and bowl and the towel. From his pocket he took out a handful of Korean coins and offered this to the old papasan.

"Go ahead," Profar said and held out the money. "I was about to pass out, I was so hungry."

The old man shrugged and laughed. He leaned and whispered something. He scratched his chin and shook his head and with both hands spread apart pretended to push away the money. When Profar tried to give it to one of the children, the boy cringed away and giggled as if someone had just tried to hand him a snake. He offered the money again, but nobody in that crew would take it. They just laughed and squirmed around on the bench and looked at each other in amusement. Profar nodded his thanks and pressed his palms together. He gave a slight bow. He rubbed his stomach dramatically and pretended to take a deep and satisfied breath to let them know the food he had eaten had indeed been tasty. This seemed to be the only payment they would accept.

Its took no effort to fall asleep. When he woke they were still hours south of Seoul, the train climbing toward mountains covered with sturdy young trees that had been planted after the war. They passed through villages with straw roofs lashed with ropes. After Gimcheon and Daejeon they slowed and began to stop at boarding platforms in the middle of nowhere. Just a shack with a tin sign and a bench to sit on. Men with their a-frame backpacks carrying firewood as they leaned on their walking sticks and trudged up a hill. Through the open window it was cooler and everything smelled of manure and wet planted fields and he heard unseen insects screeching from the trees that grew alongside the tracks.

He closed his eyes and found that if he breathed very slowly with a certain cadence that his ribs would not hurt as much. He thought about what Lee had told him at the restaurant about Jia. He remembered when he'd first seen her at the club, standing alone in a pool of light as if she'd been lowered from the sky just for him. He knew immediately that there was no retreat from this. She'd filled his entire heart in that instant. The whole magical thing was almost frightening in its speed. Nothing seemed real anymore and he already felt like he'd lost his bearings and stepped across an invisible line into uncharted territory.

Lee, looking very serious, had told him more while they sat having coffee that day in the hospital cafeteria.

"She's like Marco Polo, Eddie," he said. "She's led more lives and seen twice as much as ten normal people and even that's only half the story. She knows everything there is to know about this world. We're little boys, Eddie. We don't know a damn thing, you and me, about wars or starving or her kind of sadness and pain. It's kind of sexy, I know, her being so worldly and beautiful at the same time. But it's dangerous, my friend. Very risky. I hope you know what you're getting into. This won't be easy. Things like this can change the direction of somebody's life. Just one small move and everything is different from then on."

"She's had more lives than you?" Profar said.

"Don't be a wise ass," Lee said. "That's not what I meant. Just be careful."

At the next train platform the family that had fed him lunch stood and gathered their bundles. When Profar tried to thank them again he was ignored. They seemed busy keeping track of the bouncing happy children and making sure no parcels were left behind, and when he leaned out the window as the train got ready to depart he saw it was the old papasan who was allowed to first step onto the platform. He walked slowly. The old guy was stooped and moved carefully in his rope sandals as he tapped the ground with his cane. Everyone else stood aside with great deference and one of the grandchildren guided him by the hand to a bench and only then did the others in the clan get off the train. Leaning from the window as the train began to pull away, Profar once more raised his hand again in farewell but they never looked his way again.

He fell asleep. He woke as the locomotive whistled through a long tunnel and crossed a river. He saw men in small boats pushing upstream with their long poles. The next small station was nothing more than a walkway covered with wood planks next to a stone house with wicker doors surrounded by animal pens. A noisy chicken yard, endless green fields sloping up the side of a mountain.

Villagers stooped and cleaned something from a cemetery that was too large for such a small community, the gravestones identical, each row ascending up a grassy terrace that seemed recently landscaped. There were cars parked along the dirt road where children dressed in blue uniforms stepped off a school bus. The grave tenders, whole families carrying baskets and rakes and pails, the little children playing with brooms, wandered across the cemetery. There was a tunnel running through a viaduct, its walls pockmarked with holes and scarred where chunks of cement had fallen away. Where a crowd of people stared up at a metal plaque fastened to the wall. A tourist spot, he thought. The train continued on its way and when it reached Seoul it was dusk, the dark neighborhood streets teeming with people on bikes and motorcycles.

He found a bathroom and washed his face. He looked like a ghoul in the mirror, like some bony derelict who'd visited a blind barber. He felt stiff and sore and there were spots of blood on his undershirt where he'd scratched the itching belly scab. He found his meds. That might be a bad idea, he thought. Drinking from a sink faucet in a train station. He chewed the pills dry. The bandage on the leaking surgical drain hole at his side had purposely never been stitched and it now felt soggy and was beginning to peel away. They'd pulled out the long tube the week before and the scabby hole was just another thing that kept itching as it healed. His ribs ached terribly when he tried to take a deep breath and as he turned away from the byeonso squat toilet he pulled up his shirt and tried to adjust the gauze they'd wrapped around his chest, but that only made it worse. He splashed sulfur-smelling water on his face. As he walked through the crowded station he was careful not to bump into anyone. He felt something move and pleasantly loosen in his shoulder and so he shifted the laundry sack and stopped to rest on another wooden bench where he watched people for a while. He looked for a proper water fountain but decided it wasn't worth it to get up and so took out two more pills and chewed. He closed his eyes and listened as another train pulled into the station with a noisy burst of steam and clanking brakes. More loudspeaker announcements in Korean, the clatter of wooden luggage carts. He toyed with the idea of napping on the bench for a while, but they would only think he was a drunk GI hobo and somebody would call the MPs.

The military bus stop outside said YONGSAN in giant lettering with the silhouette drawing of the 8th Army logo behind it. Profar handed over his ID and unfolded the mimeographed official orders and he took a seat on the bus. Outside it was dark, a vapor lamp hanging from a post above the bus sign. The civilian Korean driver wrote his name on a clipboard and walked back and returned the laminated ID card, looking again at the photo and then cautiously down at Profar's face.

"You okay?" he said.

Profar nodded and eased himself against the laundry bag and closed his eyes.

It was raining when he arrived. The MP at the 8th Army gate told him about another bus that made stops along the MSR. He'd get to camp around midnight.

Profar bought a bowl of noodles from a man in a lean-to outside the gate and he tried to think about all that had happened to him in these last months and he got homesick. The hot broth felt good as he swallowed two more pills, this time the big Darvon capsules lovely Nurse Freckles had given him on the sly. She'd planted a sisterly kiss on his cheek and wished him luck. She'd squeezed his hand. He sat shivering in the bus stop shelter. With the Darvon, his ribs ached less and less until he had that dopey feeling of floating disconnected within his clothes.

He thought about summers on Isle Royale when he was a boy. The Grand Portage ferry looked like a giant floating bread box. The island, with its mossy rocks, was an exotic world of wet dripping birch trees and pines. Two hundred square miles of emptiness to themselves but for the few forest service employees. He would listen to the baritone howling of the wolves at night from his bed next to the window in his uncle's government cabin. The howling would come closer and closer until he could hear their thin, high yipping and everything would stop and there would be nothing from them for the rest of the night. The wolves vanished into the woods like spirits.

The wind blew constantly off Lake Superior and it would be cold enough to sleet in September as they searched for the chalky skull bones of moose that lay everywhere with their perfectly square teeth. The popped jaw hinges were covered with desiccated hide and flesh that he'd scrape and clean before they cataloged each piece and arranged everything outdoors on a long table. Counting Bullwinkles, his uncle called it, and they did this for wolf bones and otter bones and the bones of skunk and muskrat, the remains of foxes and bats and the beavers whose carcasses seemed to be all teeth. Everything like petrified dinosaur parts.

They once found the perfectly bare skeleton of a dead loon folded up on a tree branch, its eyeless white head tucked beneath one empty wing bone as if it had determined one day long ago that this was the quiet moment in which to close its eyes and die.

CHAPTER 17

He was the last passenger off the bus when it arrived at the main camp gate. A wet spring wind was blowing sideways. Profar pulled up his jacket collar and walked.

He'd thought of going to the hooch but he had no paperwork for a proper overnight pass, which meant sneaking through the MP gate in the morning would be complicated. He'd lost his ID and keys in the crash. It would not be a good idea to bother Mrs. Yoshida on a busy night and he didn't feel like dealing with the noise in the Ville.

He felt woozy, hungry. He counted the pills from Nurse Freckles and glanced at the illuminated VD sign outside the front gate, where two GIs were clowning around and taking each other's picture.

His pills rattled in this jacket pocket as he walked uphill from the gate. Music played from the main barracks and he decided it wasn't worth the longer hike to the Quonset hut.

The Korean houseboy with his mop and pail nodded as Profar, one hand on the banister, pulled himself up the barracks steps. He found an unmade bunk in an empty bay and sat down in the dark. He already had that disconnected, hovering feeling from the Darvon, like his head was floating above his shoulders, but he took out an aspirin anyway and chewed it dry. And he chewed another. He'd lost track of how many pills he'd taken that day. You're an idiot, he thought. They said your liver was already screwed up and you're doing this. He leaned against the cement block wall and gathered himself and wondered if it would be okay to just lay down and sleep. There was no footlocker or signs that this was someone's bunk. He heard snoring and from down the hallway came the splash of a toilet flushing.

Somebody clicked on the fluorescent ceiling light and Profar covered his eyes.

"Who are you?"

Profar saw the collar badge and polished boots, the stitched paratrooper jump wings below his left shirt pocket and the Ranger rocker patch on his shoulder. He smelled like hair tonic and carried a white shower towel over his shoulder. He had shaving cream on his neck.

"Profar. Okay to bunk here tonight?" He handed the Sergeant his orders.

"You don't look too good," the NCO said.

Profar tried to read the name tag.

"Bingham. I took over for Cobb. You know about Sergeant Cobb?"

"You're the new Top. Somebody said there was a new Top."

"Not my choice," Bingham said. "The last thing I wanted to do is work at division out in the boonies."

Bingham studied Profar's orders. "You've been around," he said. "Signal corps, a strange rotation up on the fence and then the old man's driver. How'd you get to be the CG's driver? This says they have you down for a pair of shifts each week at your old guard post and it's driving the General on the other days. Never heard of anything like that."

Profar shrugged. He didn't feel like explaining anything.

"He's from my home town, the General," Profar said. "Said all the years in the Army and he hadn't met anybody from there. Next thing I know he's got me on TDY driving him to the JSA."

"I was one of the staff NCOs when he was the G1 at Eighth," Bingham said. "When that happened to Cobb, Yardley said he wanted me here to help with the investigation. So, it was just you and another guy that got banged up? I'm surprised they just didn't ship you stateside with a medical and be done with it. You don't look like you're ready to go back on duty."

Profar rubbed his face. He yawned and held one hand to his side, where he felt a cramp coming. "Maybe they need to get their money's worth out of me."

"I draw up the rotation sheet," Bingham said. "They wanted to let your Lieutenant do it, but I bitched. Take some slack time. It says here you need to check with the dispensary before you go on duty. I'll sign whatever sick leave they give you. The old man asked about you, so you'll get your sweet driver gig back soon. Meanwhile, fatten up at the mess hall and get some sleep.

"Our beloved commander is on everybody's ass because of that Navy ship. Panmunjom has been smoking hot with newspaper people, *Stars and Stripes*, UPI and all the wire services out of Tokyo. Some congressional committee is grilling the Pentagon brass about how we could let our boys get captured by the Northies. They're looking for somebody to blame.

"Those sailors are probably getting banged up in Pyongyang," Bingham said. "There's some itchy trigger fingers up and down the fence. The ROKs are mad and we're mad and the brass at Yongsan is mad. And on top of that Cobb gets offed."

Bingham gave Profar another once-over. "After you rest up, come see me. Same office upstairs," he said. "Bring whatever papers the dispensary gives you. By the way, that pal of yours..."

"Lee," Profar said.

"He's a piece of work. I looked at his file. They put you both in for an ARCOM. For valor."

"For what?"

"Valor. For getting blown up. You were getting hazard pay when they blew you up."

"I don't need a medal," Profar said.

"You need it if Uncle Sam says you need it."

"We drove down a road. We didn't fire a shot," Profar said. "Some farmer saved our ass and called on the radio. They should give him a medal."

Profar started coughing. "They gave me a lot of meds. Maybe I took too many today."

"See me tomorrow," Bingham said and flipped the towel over his other shoulder and walked off.

Profar shuffled to the bathroom. The Korean janitor stared at him from behind his mop. There was a shape on the sofa next to the soda machine. The soldier moaned and lifted one arm across his face.

"Turn that light off."

The janitor tipped his thumb up and down in front of his mouth.

"Him taksan stinko," he said. "MPs bring him. New boss man Sergeant say he in trouble."

Remo pulled the blanket over his head.

"Profar?" he said. "I thought you were dead."

"I feel dead," Profar said.

The janitor started mopping and Remo sat up and lifted his legs off the floor. He had a coughing fit and found his pants and took a pack of cigarettes from a pocket. He sat smoking in his underwear. He smelled like sweat and beer. He started scratching his feet. One of his eyes was swollen shut and there was a shiny red knot on his forehead.

The janitor tipped the sudsy water across the floor and swung his mop. Profar stepped aside and Remo folded up his legs again.

Long story," Remo said. "In the Ville, somebody jumped me."

"I thought you were staying away from the Ville. You settle things with your girl?"

Remo looked away. "I was trying to get my stuff. My stereo. I still had a key."

Remo took a drag and blew smoke at the wet floor. "So, these two guys come at me from behind the shithouse. MPs said they were from another town. I shouldn't have been there alone but that's the time the girls are all at work. I didn't want to run into her. Those skanky sluts just stood there and laughed."

Remo touched the purple egg on his forehead and winced. "Don't look at me like that," he said. "You don't understand. I can't be involved anymore with her."

"It's your business, like you said."

"Damn straight." Remo blew more smoke at the ceiling and lay down. He pulled up the green blanket and turned to the wall.

Profar slept that night with no dreams. When he woke, Remo was snoring.

He thought God might listen better in the morning, so he asked for his ribs to please stop hurting. He tried to pray but he'd long forgotten what words to use.

In the bathroom, he studied the stitch marks that ran from his eye to his chin as if a drunk had tried to sew a sock. Everything was swollen. When he moved his jaw, the empty spot where some of his teeth used to be made the skin there stretch and hurt. His spongy cheek felt hot.

At the dispensary, the doctor flipped through Profar's file and wrote on his clipboard before he turned on his stool and dropped his hands into his lap.

"Damn," he said. "That's quite a tale. And they discharged you?"

"Yes, sir."

He scratched the rash on his neck. The doctor's unit patch said he'd been with the 82nd Airborne. He wore a jump badge. A physician who falls out of flying airplanes on purpose.

"You should leave that alone," the Captain said.

"Drives me nuts, sir," Profar said. "Everything itches or hurts or it's numb."

"That's from the Hep B," the doctor said and flipped through Profar's folder. "Your blood looks good for now. At least there's that. We'll need to take pictures of that liver to see if it started to repair itself."

He scooted over on his wheeled stool and put the stethoscope to Profar's chest. When he asked him to take a deep breath, Profar had a coughing fit.

"I suppose they already told you how lucky your were," he said. "All the non-displaced fractures, the ribs, that spleen, soft tissue injuries. Your lungs. The cracked teeth and the herniated L1. Your neck X-rays are a circus and the lacerated liver alone was pretty serious. That busted disc is something you need to watch. And the pneumothorax, the collapsed lung. They did some quick thinking aboard the medevac."

"My friend's a medic and he explained it," Profar said. "Sounds disgusting."

"Saved your life," the doctor said.

"My neck tingles," Profar said.

"That's the least of your problems," the doctor said. "How you got away with so few actual fractures and you're not paralyzed is beyond me. They gave you five units of blood. Twice. There were the repeated infections. Not to mention the hepatitis."

"From the transfusion," Profar said.

"Not uncommon."

"Can I have time off?"

"They should let you go home," the doctor said. "I'm recommending an early out. No promises. It might take a while for the paperwork. What's your duty now?"

"I drive the CG," Profar said.

"That's as rough as it should get," the Captain said. "I'm recommending no 11B duty. You shouldn't lift anything heavier than a few pounds."

The doctor signed a mimeographed form and handed it to Profar.

"And the other guy with you?"

"Lost his ear, sir. We both got lucky."

"If I'd read this file without you sitting in front of me I'd say they'd already shipped you home in a bag," the doctor said. "Somebody thinks you're a cat."

***

Later, in Bingham's office, he was introduced to a baby-faced JAG officer who was looking out the window when Profar walked in.

"This is First Lieutenant Andrews," Bingham said. Profar snapped a salute.

The Sergeant smiled. "You're not in trouble, Eddie," he said. "The Lieutenant has questions about Sergeant Cobb. You and Lee were the last people to speak to him, did you know that? Not counting his little sweetheart, and we know how that worked out. Why was he at the Robideaux GP that night? It's unusual for an NCO of Sergeant Cobb's rank to be in the field at a duty post on his day off. We're not sure how long he was there but we do know what time of the day his vehicle passed through the gate. The same time you and PFC Lee left the compound. Am I correct? They record the hood numbers."

The Lieutenant turned and stared out the window with both hands in his pockets.

"He would do that, Sarge. Just drop in out of the blue," Profar said. "He told us when he had trouble sleeping he liked to visit with his boys. That's the way he described, it. Visiting with his boys. I think he just wanted to catch people screwing around. He'd burn your ass if your sideburns were too long."

The Lieutenant lit a cigarette and took his time blowing smoke, like he was thinking of what to say. Profar had the feeling that no matter what he said nobody would believe him, anyway. The doc that morning had said they'd taken out a piece of his torn small intestine. He said his liver would grow back in time but that he'd be smart if he didn't drink a drop of booze. The hepatitis could come back with a vengeance if he wasn't careful.

Profar dropped the signed five-day medical leave form on Bingham's desk.

"So, did he indicate where he was headed after he left the GP?" the Lieutenant finally said. "And what did you all talk about? Seems like a long routine inspection visit. According to the log you signed, he stopped but never went inside. He also went to another GP. But we know he hung with you boys for an hour. Where did you go?"

"If that's Fletcher's post you're talking about, the Sergeant told us he was headed there. We wondered why he didn't just use the river road to get to camp. He went up the supply route. It was snowy. Would have been easier for him to use the river road like we did."

Bingham and the officer glared at him.

"PFC Lee called Fletcher to tell him he'd have a visitor soon. We wanted to give him a heads-up."

"How thoughtful of you," the Lieutenant said.

"Well," Bingham said. "He never visited anybody else that night. He drove past the other two GPs and used the longest way possible to drive to his apartment. It was easy to check because there was a deuce-and-a-half with mechanical problems at the side of the road and Sergeant Cobb stopped and called the motor pool on his field radio. He offered to drive them back, but they said the truck was filled with ordnance and they had to stay with the vehicle. They said this in their report so we know what time that happened. Seems everybody did their paperwork correctly that day except for you two men. You didn't mention Cobb on your duty log. The explosion at Sergeant Cobb's apartment happened that evening shortly after you both were injured. Specialist Profar? Let me ask you what the odds might be that this would all occur in such a tight time frame, could you tell me that?"

"I don't know what's strange about it," Profar said.

"Prior to the explosion, we now know that Sergeant Cobb was shot at close range with his own M3," the Lieutenant said. "You were familiar with Sergeant Cobb's M3? It's a peculiar piece of weaponry to carry."

"Everybody knew about the M3. We called it his mob gun. He had it with him at the GP."

Bingham started to speak but the Lieutenant interrupted.

"The explosion at Sergeant Cobb's off-base residence was made to look like a household accident. The Sergeant disliked traditional Korean charcoal floor heating and so he had installed a diesel stove. He considered charcoal briquettes to be unsafe. We know that the diesel fuel had purposely been spilled prior to ignition. The canisters on the porch were ignited separately. Quite a clumsy act of arson, actually. It wasn't enough to destroy the evidence of the prior shooting with the M3, which is what killed the Sergeant. They found a grenade inside a coffee mug in the kitchen that had failed to detonate. Why would he bring the M3 when he visited you?"

"I don't know, sir," Profar said.

The Lieutenant smiled. "Specialist Profar, you and Lee were using the river road to patrol the curfew sector because there had been a high level alert issued that day, isn't that true?"

"There's always an alert for that stretch, sir," Profar said. "We were told not to do a foot inspection because it was just the two of us. Sergeant Cobb gave the order. That's how we got the jeep from the motor pool. Usually we get a ride from somebody else, like one of the ambush squad leaders. It's a loose arrangement."

"We haven't seen anything of the sort. These orders."

"Verbal, sir," Profar said. "We saw Sergeant Cobb that morning at the mess hall and that's what he told us to do."

The Lieutenant glanced warily at Bingham and explained that General Yardley had issued a moratorium on off-base girlfriends. The yeobo days were over.

"There's some local money impact, of course," the Lieutenant said. "That business is a big deal. But the General feels what happened to Cobb has made the whole thing a security issue."

"Not to mention the other incidents we've been having up and down the river," Bingham said.

"Whole other story," the Lieutenant said.

"How so, sir? If I could ask," Profar said.

He wanted to spill everything about the tunnel and the tiger and the dead bodies, but he wanted to ask Lee about it first. He had a bad feeling that Bingham and the officer were trying to blame him for something.

"How so?" The Lieutenant took a long drag on his smoke and snubbed the cigarette in Bingham's ashtray.

"A war, that's how," he said. "It's getting hot up there. Nobody wants to lose face. That's how wars get started. Nobody wants to put their dick back in their pants up at Panmunjom and when two people start pissing at each other, somebody is bound to get wet."

Now Bingham stood and they both studied Profar as if he somehow held the secret to avoiding a global blowup. As if they might silently be asking for his humble guidance.

"Don't underestimate something stupid happening because of politics," Bingham said. "It was a teenager with a 9 mm Browning pistol who shot that Austrian guy and the next thing you know it's World War One and twenty-million people are dead. That's why we're talking to you about Cobb and that communist bitch who assassinated him. Between that and the damn boat and we got us a first class shit fire about to happen."

"A shit fire," the Lieutenant said and nodded at Profar.

Profar noticed the JAG insignia pins on the officer's shirt collar: the gold quill crossed above a sword. The laurel wreath, to indicate fealty and honor.

Lieutenant Anderson excused himself and Bingham and Profar saluted. They listened until the steel door in the barracks hallway slammed shut. Bingham looked out the window and watched the Lieutenant walk across the street.

"I didn't want to bring it up, but your friend Remo says something is cooking in the village. Unrest, is the way he described it."

"I don't know anything about that, Top," Profar said. "He said he's in trouble, that's all. I'm not really Remo's pal."

Bingham jammed his hands into his pockets and looked at the floor.

"For some reason you and that little loser PFC Lee seem to be well-liked around here. Now, don't shit me. There's a rumor that the business girls are up to something. Is that true?"

Profar shrugged and Bingham said, "I'm asking if there's a problem I need to know about. This is between you and me."

"I don't know what you want me to say," Profar said. "There's a general opinion that girls get the short end. Legally, I mean. Like when a GI gets drunk and lays lumps, nothing ever happens to the guy. The Korean cops turn the other way. I know how things work, Sarge. It's a joke. Guys rough up those girls all the time and nobody gives a shit. Everybody knows how things work in the Ville."

"Let me know if you hear anything else," Bingham said. "Remo has his hands full because of some other things he shouldn't be involved in."

Bingham wore a wedding band, but he wasn't married. Most guys wore a ring so the girls wouldn't bother you when you walked through the Ville. It wasn't that they respected that you were married, it was just that it might not be an efficient use of their time to hustle you.

"There's something else," Bingham said. "It seems Remo mouthed off at the cop shop while he was drunk. It was about Perez providing the old man with some unconventional specialized medical assistance."

"I don't know..."

"Come on, Eddie. The catheter Perez put in General Yardley so he wouldn't have to get up and take a leak during meetings at Panmunjom."

"Top, everybody knows about the tube," Profar said.

"Shit," Bingham said.

"Nobody cares, Sarge," Profar said. "They kind of like the old man for doing it. It's pretty creative, a dick tube. Drives the North Koreans crazy that he never has to go take a piss. Makes them lose face."

CHAPTER 18

He sensed that life's roulette wheel was purposely rigged beforehand by the same nameless planner who'd ordained someone to crawl beneath the crushed jeep to call for help that night on the radio.

Profar was never able to find out the farmer's name. Nobody could explain why he would have been alone and on foot in the middle of nowhere on such a bitter cold night. He was told that the pilot had seen someone run off when the medevac helicopter landed, likely fearing he would be punished for defying the civilian curfew that was strictly enforced in that area. They arrested the locals for walking around at night and they shot you if you took your stroll near the barrier fence or one of the guard posts. Walking along the MSR or any of its many service roads between midnight and sunrise was off-limits.

Lee promised it would be a waste of time, but Profar said he wanted to find the man who had saved their lives. So they went to the village that owned the rice paddy, but nobody would talk.

"I don't think we inspire trust," Lee said after explaining why they were there. "A Katusa translator would have been smarter."

It was daylight, sunny. The rice paddy was muddy with newly plowed furrows curving away on the river's floodplain as far Profar could see. The village stood on a hillside overlooking the field. Everything smelled of manure and the standing water was buggy, insects hopping and flying everywhere. Profar remembered seeing the little window lights of the village on the night they were blown up.

The nervous Koreans today stood in their rubber boots, leaning on hoes and rakes near where the jeep had crashed onto their property months before. You could tell they weren't happy about having their work interrupted. The gouged black soil at the bottom of the cliff from which they'd launched the jeep still showed the impressed shape of the vehicle's front bumper. The gash in the soil was deep. Bent metal and scraps of engine parts lay everywhere. There were broken bushes and small trees nearby that had been scorched black by the fire. A long raw scrape in the dirt marked where they'd towed the wrecked jeep up the embankment. Looking at it now, harmless terrain on a fine spring day, Profar wondered why he'd survived. What was the point of such luck? People stumbled down stairs and died.

Lee stood talking with an old farmer who must have had the knees of a teenager because he'd been lifting rocks from a dead squat into his a-frame backpack. He was sweating through his white headband and seemed jumpy. Profar felt he would surely know something about that night. The old man would not make eye contact, but kept glancing away while Lee explained that they had not come to get anyone in trouble and that they had brought humble gifts to show their appreciation and respect.

"They know about the curfew," Lee said. "They know how much trouble they can get into. There's been talk of closing down the whole village and moving it further south. That would be a disaster. These are valuable fields along the river. There's a thousand years of ancestors buried here, and now we show up and expect them to start yapping and risk everything."

The old man waved the other villagers closer and he summoned Lee.

"He wants to pow-wow," Lee said. The farmers stood in a circle.

The old man stood next to where his loaded a-frame sat with its woven basket propped upright on a walking stick. He grinned politely at Lee.

"Pops here, he says if one person in the community breaks the law, the family and the whole village are shamed," Lee said. "He said I should know that because I was Korean. To ask them to do otherwise was ignorant on my part, he said. Yeah, he actually said I was stupid. Said he would excuse me because I was a half-and-half. We won't get anything from these people.

Let's just do the polite GI Joe bow and say thanks and leave our stuff here. We brought gifts for the natives. Mission accomplished."

Profar hauled out the forty-pound sack of rice that he'd sweet-talked from a cook at the mess hall. Lee carried the two boxes of blue jeans from the jeep, new folded Levis with the tags still on them, and with great drama and a loud grunt dropped them next to the bag of rice. He took out a five-gallon jerrycan filled with kerosene heating oil and set it down at the old man's feet. He tried to tell a joke in Korean about how there would be American soldiers this winter who would freeze while him and his buddies would be cozy next to their stoves. Nobody smiled. They exchanged confused looks. One of the men stood examining a pair of jeans, opening and closing the zipper, and they passed this article of valuable clothing back and forth like some strange and bartered textile they'd never seen before. More bagged and boxed items came from the jeep: a fifty-count case of Ivory soap, a crate of C-rations, sugar packets and two giant cans of instant coffee. One of the villagers stood examining a package of instant noodles. The jeans had now been unboxed and the men were exchanging them according to proper waist size and trouser length.

The old man walked to the churned up patch of oily dirt. He kicked at what was left of the jeep's smashed radiator. He wore a thoughtful look and stroked his white beard. He squatted and touched the ground with the flat of his hand and stayed that way like some frontier water dowser searching for a well to dig. Like he was feeling around for inspirational vibration. He patted the spot several times and spoke slowly.

Lee's expression got oddly serious and he asked the papasan to repeat what he'd just said.

"Gramps claims they came in the morning after we crashed, him and his son," Lee said. "The jeep was still here. They'd seen it burning through the night and they were worried about the fuel spilling into their field. They get reimbursement money from Uncle Sam when things like that happen. Well, the old guy says there were tracks that had been covered by the snow, but you could still see them that morning because the top layer of the new snow had blown away."

Lee looked down at his feet. The old papasan was watching him as he translated.

"Eddie, those tracks were on top of where you and me had been walking around that night. You know, when I was looking for my ear? He said his own father had been a hunting guide for the Japanese, a *Chakho*. He knew exactly what kind of animal had made the tracks. Lately, everybody here has seen them. They know what kind of critters are out in the DMZ. When they lose a cow or a pig, they'll say it was a bear and they get money from the government. They always say it's a bear."

"Ask him where the tracks went," Profar said

The papasan walked a circle and studied the spot where the jeep had landed and pointed at several places where he said Lee and Profar had left their own meandering foot prints that night.

"The old man says he could see where we'd walked and fell down. Where we were curled up on the ground when the chopper picked us up. He says it must have been out there the whole time, the tiger," Lee said. "He thinks it sat in the dark watching everything. Says it didn't move when the Huey landed because that spot where it was sitting showed in the snow plain as day. The chopper came with all that noise and it just watched. When the medics put us in stretchers it must have been sitting a few dozen meters away, out in the dark. Could have come and got us easy, Eddie. While we were walking around, it could have killed us easy."

"You sure you heard him right?"

Lee's face tightened up. "I heard everything just fine, Eddie. Papasan thinks it brought us both good luck."

"We almost died," Profar said.

"That's just it, Eddie," Lee said. "The old man said nobody dies when the *Sansin* tiger spirit watches over you."

PART TWO

Summer, 1950
Gyeongsang Province

"The waters which you saw, where the harlot sits, are peoples, multitudes, nations, and tongues. And the ten horns which you saw on the beast, these will hate the harlot, make her desolate and naked, eat her flesh and burn her with fire."
– Revelation 17:15

CHAPTER 19

It was the lunar Year of the Tiger, the season of strength and power. The appointed time on the celestial calendar for bravery and resilience.

She would remember this day for the rest of her life.

The persimmon trees in the village orchard were still in blossom. The new duck pond had not been filled, and the broken stone cow pen next to their simple three-room house was in need of repair. When the soldiers from the North arrived on that summer day, Kim Jia-Soon's father was wearing his old barley straw hat. He always wore it at a jaunty tilt, and it was his daughter's favorite hat.

He was also wearing baggy white trousers rolled to his knees as he stood in his rubber boots and buttoned vest on the far side of the rice field on the path that led past the village ancestor stone. They'd stopped in front of the enormous rock that morning and bowed to the rows of temple jars and carved figurines as they always did before going to work in the fields. Her father carried the wooden *jige* a-frame carrier strapped to his shoulders with rice straw rope and it was loaded with stones headed for the cow pen wall. He crouched and slid his arms from the heavy backpack and stood and waved frantically to Jia with his wooden walking stick. She waved at him and jumped up and down, thinking he might be playing a game.

Her mother wore her hair twisted beneath a white headband that day, the long braids trailing down her back and swinging with a familiar motion when she walked. Jia could easily recognize her mother's rather swaggering and confident gate from a great distance. She seemed to hop when she walked with those long strides and her deeply creased beautiful eyes twinkled when she smiled. Jia had inherited her mother's tall, willowy figure and her father said that she walked with the same confident and graceful gait, like a differently aged twin.

Jia had looked up at the sky that morning, shielding the bright sun with her hand as the airplanes flew overhead in a V formation. Just like geese, she thought. Giant flying metal geese heading south. She'd never seen so many airplanes at one time or heard such a deep and threatening rumble from their distant engines, and it frightened her. The animals on their farm that day also seemed agitated and disturbed, as if they somehow sensed that their world was about to change forever.

Her father had been carrying the heavy stones back and forth from the field to the cow pen all morning. Jia could see the rocks stacked in the woven basket of the *jige* from where she stood waving as her father now motioned again with the stick, this time angrily. He wanted her and her mother to come to him right away.

There were thousands of people who'd suddenly started walking past the village. Jia had never seen so many strangers or heard the loud scraping sound of such a crowd of shuffling feet. There were hundreds of loaded wooden carts and bawling animals, everyone carrying roped bundles and suitcases on their shoulders as they tossed up a cloud that hung above the village rice ponds like a brown fog. The constant rising dust coated the leaves of the orchard trees and seemed to make their branches droop in sorrow.

At this time of year everything on the hillside above the village was green and lush. The pear trees had already begun to shed their sweet-smelling flowers. The cranes were standing tall in the rice ponds, red-headed and stately, their slender shapes starkly white as they stepped in their strange fidgety manner through the brown paddy water.

She'd worked all morning with her mother planting the last of the young summer rice shoots. Jia pulled up her baggy skirt and high-stepped through the muddy warm water and felt for weeds with her bare toes and pulled and tossed the weeds aside as she'd been taught to do. There was no wind, and in the muggy heat the fields smelled sweetly of manure, the water shimmering in the hazy sunshine. When Jia stooped to do her work she saw tiny shrimp and bugs squirming around her bare legs.

Jia's mother carried her sleeping baby brother, Ji-Yeong, wrapped in a blanket on her back as she worked. The child's head wobbled as she stooped among the rows of delicate new plants that bent and moved with the slightest breeze. Everything was so green and bright in the sun. She watched her younger brother Hyeon walk ahead and stomp the planted rice shoots into the mud with his feet, making sure they stood firm and straight. The village shaman, the old Mudang, had chosen all their names. As the eldest son, Hyeon's had been selected to match the number of strokes it took to write his name in Hangul so that it corresponded in certain multiples to the days in the month of his birth. It was Hyeon's name that was written prominently in the *jokbo,* the family genealogy book that was stored in a box made from persimmon wood. The *jokbo* preserved the generational order of all the Kim family ancestors, including the surnames of extended relatives and the given names of males, their death and burial dates and the description and location of their final resting place.

The road through the village was now teeming with more people who had walked from the North. Jia had no idea of where they'd come from or why they were all walking in the same direction. The airplanes had passed and the sky was filled with thunderheads. It was quiet but for the deep mutter of the approaching storm and the shuffling feet of those who were fleeing south on the road to Busan. Jia had never heard of Busan or been to a large city. She had never heard of the Americans or North Korean soldiers. She had never seen so many soldiers with rifles or watched a plane fly this low through the sky above their village. She had seen none of these things until that day when her family was told by two soldiers with rifles that they must abandon their home forever.

Jia's young life to this point had been one of strict and predictable social order, a world of rice and pickled cabbage stored in clay *onggi* urns. Two-wheeled ox carts, oil lamps and the authority of village shamans and soothsayers who could cast spells, good or bad, that would last a thousand years. It was a rigid world of esteemed elders and carefully orchestrated social manners, a life in which to be shunned or ignored by your family or community was worse than death. Where girls and boys played marbles with garden stones on the steps of the house that had been in the Kim family for dozens of generations. A millennium of barley straw hats and *jiges* carried on the backs of old men.

Jia had been taught that there was a world of sight as well as a parallel realm of unseen ancestors and spirits, and she viewed these coexisting realities with calm acceptance. She'd been taught that the dead inhabited the world of the living, and without their benevolent and silent protection, the living would be doomed.

When she and her family were told to leave their home, they'd only had time to pack what they could into burlap rice sacks and a single suitcase, much of it piled high onto her father's backpack. They did not know that a battalion of Russian-made T-34 tanks were leading a column of North Korean infantry troops south directly toward their village. Or that the same armor regiment had easily pushed aside the badly organized and under-supplied Americans, themselves now among the swarm of 400,000 refugees who were fleeing south from the border that separated the two Koreas. She did not realize that the American soldiers had been ordered to keep the refugees north of their own lines of defense and that anyone south of the retreating Korean troops would be suspected of being a communist spy.

On the fifth day away from their village she noticed the lice. They were smaller than a grain of rice and they crawled in wooly gray clumps along the seams of her dress. They seemed to like it under her arms, where it was moist and dark, and when she tried to scratch them away they wriggled off in single file to disappear into whatever dark nook was available in her clothing. The inflamed and itching red bites were on her hips and spread across her neck and behind her swollen ears. Her younger brother Hyeon couldn't stop scratching himself and baby Ji-Yeong's face was already scabby with bites. Her mother rubbed them all with vinegar and cooking oil and that's what the Kim family smelled like as they lay together with the others in the dark alongside the road in the summer heat, the tanks rumbling past each night, their iron treads clanking and covering everything in a layer of powdery red dirt. The vibration from the tanks and the trucks made their bundles shake and fall over and her brother Ji-Yeong would not stop crying. Jia also did not know that 40,000 more North Korean infantry regulars were only a few marching days away, headed south on the same miserably crowded road as the refugees. They too were coming with more tanks.

Jia did not know that by this time, the poorly supplied American and South Korean soldiers were retreating frantically and had been told to be wary of refugee women who might be hiding radios under their skirts. Or spy maps tucked into the swaddled blankets of their babies. Or hand-cranked devices that could signal their exact location to the communist troops. Jia knew none of this. She only knew that she had lice and that they itched terribly.

The baby Ji-Yeong got sick and began to vomit on the day they boarded the train at the station near the Nakdong River. Here they climbed ladders into an empty fifty-foot freight hopper coated with oily coal dust. In the sleepless heat at night Jia lay and studied the sky overhead and watched her worried mother rock her brother in her arms as the child grew feverish and his cough worsened. Larger airplanes began to fly overhead, floating across the starry sky like drifting fireflies. And in the distance, wholly separate from the thunder of another approaching summer storm, came the explosions, a deep and hollow thumping with the silent flare of yellow light that followed, as these new airplanes began to drop more bombs up and down the valley.

The train and its bulging cargo of people continued to move south. In the choking cloud of coal dust Jia covered her mouth with the hem of her skirt and scratched her ears and thought about the lice. She wished she could scrub herself with soap. She fondly remembered the cool, clean water that came from the village well and she started to itch.

By the time they reached the next train station to pick up more refugees Jia's hair was clotted with greasy coal dust, and when her baby brother began to choke from the constant locomotive smoke, her mother tipped him naked by his little feet and slapped his back until he could finally catch his breath. With her finger she pulled a snotty clot of black soot from his little mouth and then rocked her son until he fell asleep. For days they traveled like this, gathering up more refugees, until other soldiers wearing different uniforms finally stopped the train and told everyone to walk along the collapsed iron bridge that crossed the flooding river at Waegwan.

Jia watched the soldiers clamber hand-over-hand like gymnasts as they strapped boxes that looked like bird feeders to the bridge girders. They stacked bags of sand along the train tracks and wrapped them with wires whose loose ends dangled into the water. There were oared boats and men with goggles floated alongside them as they tethered the same wires and fuses to the stone bridge foundations. The people were screaming. The soldiers pointed their rifles and shouted that everyone should stop trying to cross the bridge or they would be shot. More planes flew low overhead, circling across the river before they continued south, where they once again began to drop their bombs.

Her father told her that the soldiers were destroying the bridge so the North Koreans could not cross and harm the people. He said they must now move quickly to reach the other side of the river before it was too late. The soldiers began firing their weapons. They warned everyone to stand away while the little boxes were detonated and the bridge began to collapse in pieces into the river. Some of the refugees refused to stop crawling across the twisted steel girders and when the smoke cleared Jia could see their shapes floating face-down, and they were not swimming or moving their arms. She saw a woman with a sewing machine tied to a bundle of clothing on her back, and when she stumbled from the bridge she quickly sank and some of what she'd been carrying floated away in the current. There was more gunfire as the soldiers tried to force the people to return to shore.

But the frantic refugees continued to crawl across the ruined bridge, balanced and teetering on their outstretched hands and knees as they made their way along the twisted iron struts like insects swarming madly along a burning log. People tried desperately to lead their animals across, but nearly every bawling cow and horse and pig lost its balance and fell. Chickens in sinking wood cages floated away. Someone tumbled off the sunken bridge holding a pair of ducks whose legs were tied with twine and they were quickly swept under. The sound of so many people moaning and screaming frightened Jia as she desperately tried to stay close to her parents as they crossed what was left of the collapsed iron bridge.

It began to rain. Jia followed her mother along a slippery iron truss, balancing both knees on the narrow beam. The little boy Hyeon followed on his hands and knees. Her mother carried the baby, her father leading them across with the overloaded and badly balanced *jige* swaying dangerously on his back, threatening to tip him over into the river fifty feet below. When Jia stopped and dared to look down she saw more people being swept away in the current. Heads bobbing, arms reaching. The screams, the hands splashing and lifting from the churning water.

After they reached shore and rested that night, Jia's father led them further along the train tracks south for two more days until they finally stopped at a railroad trestle and this is where they camped with another group of refugees who had escaped the fighting in Daegu. They stayed inside the viaduct tunnel, where Jia's father said they would be protected from the bombing. The seeping wet cement walls inside the tunnel dripped water on those who'd already been camped there all week. It was muggy inside, the humid air foul with cooking smells and the odor of animals who were penned alongside the stream that flowed through a culvert. Oil lamps made from food cans glowed like lanterns in the dark, the echoing voices of five hundred people murmuring in that small, claustrophobic space. Jia shyly lifted her skirt and relieved herself in a metal bucket that was handed from person to person down the length of the tunnel. It was impossible to stand and step outside. Her father warned that the airplanes were beginning to drop their bombs closer to the tunnel each day. He said he'd read a leaflet dropped by one of the airplanes that said they must remain north of the retreating military lines, but they were already too far south to walk back again. He said this worried him. He said the soldiers would not answer his questions, but only ordered him back inside the tunnel.

Jia listened to the distant explosions each day that week. They began to run out of water. Her mother used a rag to collect moisture from the dripping tunnel walls. She crept outside at night to walk upstream in the dark to scoop a few cups to boil for soup.

Swallows flew in and out of the tunnel at dusk. Firesmoke lifted and sorted itself into sheets across the ceiling, where Jia watched the tiny birds blink down from their daubed mud nests.

Her father unpacked the *jige* and said they must leave some of their things behind. It was too heavy to carry all they'd taken and he knew that they might soon have to cross another river. He said he'd heard that Busan was where the Americans had gathered and that it was the only safe place left in Korea. He sat and pulled one sandal from his dusty foot and pushed back his straw hat. He wiped his palm across his sweating forehead and said there were now soldiers with rifles standing at each end of the tunnel and that he hoped they might be protecting the refugees, but he wasn't sure. He told Jia that he was also now worried that they might not be allowed to leave. He said Jia was old enough to understand such things and that she must help her parents care for her brothers. He looked at Jia and Hyeon sternly and told them not to speak to strangers. He pointed at one soldier who was drinking from a metal flask and when he offered it to his friend the two men began to laugh wildly. They waved their rifles as if playing a game.

Her father shook his head. "A whiskey man," he said. "Don't go near the whiskey men, do you hear me? Be careful and don't speak to any soldier, even if he is Korean."

They ate cold rice off of scrap wood boards with their hands because they'd lost their bowls in the river. After Jia changed her brother's cloth diaper she asked why the baby had blood on his chin. He had stopped crying. Her mother wiped her eye and shook her head. Her parents walked away some distance and stood talking and touching Ji-Yeong's face as they fussed with his blanket. None of them could sleep in the miserable, stifling heat and when it rained that night the rising mist clung to the dripping tunnel walls and forced them to cover themselves in their filthy blankets.

Next morning, her father pointed to a man in a white shirt and neatly pressed trousers who stood smoking a cigarette. His name was Paek Ho-Sung, a school teacher from a nearby village in their province. He seemed frail and wore suspenders and round owl eyeglasses. He was always tidying up the space where he slept with his head on a small suitcase. Her father said the suitcase was filled with books and papers and that occasionally he had seen the teacher take a notebook from his pocket.

"He is studying. He's a teacher. They write things down all the time," he said, laughing. "There's always something new to learn in this world. Remember that."

Her father told Jia that someone had already accused the teacher of being a North Korean spy, because that would be the only reason anyone would write in a notebook during a time like this. Or carry books when there was certainly no opportunity to read.

"People like to make trouble," her father said. "It's best to mind your own business."

Jia listened to the approaching gunfire. Through the far end of the tunnel she watched an airplane fly low and shoot at something along the railroad tracks. She heard the explosion and the screaming.

"They want to see how many of us are here," her father said when Jia asked why there were so many airplanes flying past the tunnel. "They're counting us so they can help."

"They're not counting anything. They're shooting," her mother said angrily as she rocked the baby Ji-Yeong in her arms. Jia had never heard her mother speak to her father in such a way.

"How does that help us? Flying so close and shooting like that? Don't tell the child something that can't be true. We should leave here now and walk ahead on our own. We don't have to follow everyone like goats."

"Tomorrow, a new train will come to take us to Busan. You will see," Jia's father said.

"Nobody is coming tomorrow," her mother said. "Or the next day. There is no train. They've bombed the tracks. No more trains will come, do you understand? We are all animals to them. Nobody is coming to save us or to feed us. Nobody cares at all."

"I heard someone from Munsan-ri say that the government will help us," her father said.

Her mother snapped loudly at him.

"The government ran away, don't you know that? Open your eyes. I speak to people, too. They all say the same thing. Everyone is running away. Do you understand, nobody will help us if we just sit here," she said. "The government? Even the Americans are running away like rabbits."

When the planes were gone and the tunnel was quiet that night, she watched her exhausted mother slump against the wall and fuss with the baby's blanket. She kept touching the child's forehead with the back of her hand. She stared off into the distance in a way Jia had never seen before. Her mother looked over and studied her husband wistfully, as if she were trying to read his mind. As if she wished she could foretell their future. She glanced at Ji-Yeong and then over at Hyeon, who was helping his father pack what they'd sorted into the wooden a-frame. When her mother looked at Jia she lowered her eyes sorrowfully and slid her shoulder from her dress and tried to nurse the baby, but the infant jerked away and began to shiver. Ji-Yeong's deeply set eyes darted back and forth as if he were trying to recognize where he was in this world. His pudgy hands were balled up tightly and he fluttered them against his chest, where his tiny ribs flinched convulsively as he breathed. He gasped and punched wildly at the air as his mother tried to make him feed.

Jia finally lay with her head on her mother's lap and listened to the baby's shallow breathing. Someone shouted in agony from the far end of the tunnel. She saw a soldier push the teacher against the wall and pick up his suitcase and tip it upside down. When the teacher stepped forward, the soldier jabbed him with the butt of his rifle and brought the weapon up and pressed the barrel under his chin. The teacher snapped back his head and his eyeglasses fell off. Jia looked at her mother, who only shook her head and told Jia to mind her own business and go to sleep. They all needed to rest, she said.

Jia said: "Tell me the story of the tiger."

"I've told you that fairytale a hundred times," her mother said. "It's for children younger than you."

"I like the story, please?"

Her mother began as she did every folk tale. She sighed dramatically as if gathering herself for a lengthy and profound lecture, and said: "In the time long ago when animals smoked their pipes...a ferocious tiger from high in the mountains of Gwongwan-do walked into a village one night while the people were sleeping. He did this because he wanted to eat someone's cow. The hungry tiger did not know that another thief, a human, was also prowling among the village houses at the exact same time so that he could also steal the very same cow. As the tiger crept through the darkness he could hear a baby crying somewhere, so he wisely decided to crouch down in the shadows and wait until the child went back to sleep. The tiger was very hungry, but he was also very smart and patient. When he finally crawled closer to the house, he heard the mother tell the screaming baby that if it did not stop crying a tiger would come and eat it. But the baby continued to cry. Then the mother gave the child some ripe persimmon fruit to eat and with this the infant quickly stopped its fussing and settled to sleep in its mother's arms. The tiger was very surprised at this. How could such a thing as a simple persimmon fruit be more convincing and powerful than the threat of being eaten by a fearsome tiger? A persimmon tree must be very powerful, the tiger thought."

Jia's mother stroked her forehead and rocked her in her arms. "From that day forward, we have always used the wood of the persimmon tree to protect our most valuable possessions. We make our strongest house doors out of it to keep away the hungry tiger at night. All tigers today know its power and strength. Now it's time to go to sleep, child. I've told you the silly story. We have to walk a long way tomorrow and we don't know what will happen to us in the days to come. None of us knows how long this journey will take or what we will find at its end."

Jia's mother reached over to the *jige*. She took out the carved persimmon wood box and showed Jia the family ancestor book.

"I want you to see this," she said. "I've never showed it to you. You're old enough now to understand. In this box is everything that is dear to us."

Her mother touched the brass clasp that held together the book's ancient pages, some of the older imitation vellum sheets so faded that you could barely read the bold Hangul script. She opened the *jokbo* and pointed to her great-grandfather's own name written phonetically using old fashion Chinese tone marks.

"Your brother's name is also here and it will be his duty to keep the book safe when your father and I are gone," her mother said. "Your name will be written one day, along with the names of your children. Promise that you will keep the *jokbo* safe until Hyeon is old enough to know what to do with it. Do you promise?"

Jia watched her mother wrap the book in its cloth and return it to the box.

When they woke at dawn the soldiers were once again shouting at the teacher. Now they were shaking the notebook in his face as they held him up against the tunnel wall. He raised his hands as they spun him around and searched his pockets. When he tried to resist, they kicked aside the open suitcase and began taking out more books and tossing everything into the dirty stream that flowed through the tunnel. They tied the teacher's hands behind his back and pushed him out of sight.

Jia's father pulled her close and pressed her face into the crook of his arm when they heard more screaming.

CHAPTER 20

"Syngman Rhee high-tailed it south, the old coward," the American Sergeant said. "And that's after he shot people he already had in jail because he thought they were commies. Truman and old Mac think he's a swell guy. He's a coward. This mess is his fault. And I don't give a pass to Mac, either. I don't think he knew what was cooking. He was too busy living fancy in Tokyo, and now we got us this crazy shitstorm."

The Sergeant tipped back his helmet and blew smoke sideways from his mouth. He fished matches from his pocket and lit the Corporal's cigarette and watched as the younger soldier inhaled and swung aside the short M3 machine gun that was strapped to his shoulder. The Corporal nodded, as if he just wanted the conversation to end. They'd told him to stand guard and watch over the hundreds of nervous-looking refugees and keep everybody in line, and this made him uneasy. They told him to be on the lookout for suspicious characters, and now here was this old grunt from another unit, whose name he didn't even know, yapping non-stop about things the Corporal hardly understood.

"How do you know this stuff?" The Corporal said. "It's mumbo jumbo to me. I just do what they tell me."

"Keep my ears open, that's how I know," the older soldier said. "Bird Colonel took me up in his spotter plane last week and I saw the whole circus from two thousand feet. Incheon, Seoul all the way down to Daegu, we followed the railroad to see where those damn Bolshevik tanks were headed. You can bet old uncle Joe Stalin is behind this. The Russians are watching everything. Haven't seen it like this since France in forty-four and they didn't have refugees to get in the way. These North Koreans, now they got themselves those good Russian tanks. Same ones that rolled over Berlin. Probably a shitload of commie China gear from that runt, Mao. That's what happens when nobody's watching the store and Uncle Sam sure wasn't watching, yes sir. Old MacArthur fell asleep on this one. Fell asleep at the wheel, plain and simple."

The Corporal had been told to stop any of refugees who wanted to leave the tunnel. He'd been instructed to be on the lookout for sketchy luggage or anything that might resemble a radio or transmission device. These people were hiding old school hand-crank radios, he'd been told. Mothers with babies with radios stuffed in those baggy skirts so they could call in the American positions. Now the whole miserable bunch was gathered up at the tunnel entrance, families with screaming children, and some of them poked their heads out and nervously studied the sky. Nobody wanted to be trapped in the crowded tunnel. It was like they expected to be let loose at any moment so they could continue down the road to Busan, which is where everybody had been told to go. The Corporal knew otherwise. He'd already received his instructions. It was off the record, something that just sifted down through the chain of command. But he'd certainly received his orders. Nobody, not one refugee in this bunch, was going anywhere.

Both soldiers watched as aircraft formed a black V on the horizon, dropped altitude, and made their slow approach toward the viaduct. The two lead planes, F-82 Twin Mustangs, yawed slightly before veering away and descending toward the horizon. The other eight planes in the squadron now flew directly overhead, sending the refugees who'd gathered at the entrance surging back into the chaos of the tunnel. The Sergeant and the Corporal watched the Mustangs dip their wings into a wide turn.

"They'll be back," the Sergeant said.

He pointed to a woman carrying a child who was being chased into the tunnel by one of the South Korean troops.

"I wish my Lieutenant would tell us what to do with these people," the Corporal said. "They don't know it, but there's no place for them to go anymore. We got word that this was the end of the line. No way they'll make it to Busan, anyway. The train don't run anymore and the tracks are off limits to civilians. How many of them do you think there are?"

"It don't matter how many there are," the Sergeant said. "They've been dropping those leaflets, so everybody's been warned. There's spies in there, you can be sure of it. These people are slowing down the whole damn regiment. Babysitting was never part of the plan. We can't move jack shit on that road south with these people on it. No supplies. None of our own tanks, if we had them, and we don't."

The Sergeant dropped his smoke and watched it burn. "That son of a bitch Rhee, I read that he told everybody he was in it for the long haul. Like a Captain who stays with the sinking ship, that kind of horseshit. I'm cavalry, old school –– Garryowen and kill the damn Indians, you know? But when I read that the old man up and skedaddled, somebody who with a straight face tells his people he's staying to fight and he turns and runs...that kind of clown riles me. He's on Uncle Sam's payroll, for godsake."

The soldiers watched as the South Korean troops started waving their arms. Somebody shouted through a megaphone for the refugees to stand and assemble outside the tunnel, where people were already being searched with their hands in the air.

"I watched our own twenty-fourth infantry, green kids with weapons from the last war, fight up near Seoul. Might have been Osan, not sure. Just teenagers with not enough ammo and no training. We had no air support. They didn't even think of that, do you believe it? I don't recall everything exactly, so much has happened in the last few weeks. But it was no contest at all. They had five hundred men that hightailed it south like spooked cats. They came at us like a hot knife through butter, those North Koreans. Nobody expected that at all."

They watched another wave of aircraft, this time slow flying Air Force P51s, whose .30 cal machine guns were designed for ground strafing. The Sergeant kicked at the dirt and shook his head.

"Those up there? They should have brought the Air Force boys to Seoul right away," he said. "Would have saved a bunch of people when Rhee told his troops to TNT the Han River bridge. Could have bought some time. Could have shipped trained units from Japan. Rhee's men never told the civilians about the bridge demo, so guess what? There's four-thousand of those poor people, men and women and kids, walking across when it happens. And whammy! A thousand dead and the rest hanging on for dear life while that old man Rhee is down in Jeju drinking tea and asking Washington for more money. And we're paying the bastard cash to be a first class coward while his whole 4th Division gets knocked around by the North. What a shit show. I bet not one person back home knows what's going on over here. And now we're running scared while some old men in Washington sit around with their pencils and notebooks figuring out what to do. I didn't live through the Hürtgen Forest in forty-four just to get kicked around by some third-rate commie Army."

The Sergeant watched a group of refugees milling around in the tunnel, picking up their things and looking like they might want to make a run for it. The P51s were getting closer. There was a deep rumbling as the six planes banked into another V shape to begin their final approach.

"These poor saps," the Sergeant said.

CHAPTER 21

This time it was a tall American soldier with a cigarette dangling from his mouth and she watched him calmly drag the teacher away by his feet as if he were a doll.

It had rained, and the small man's upturned hands and hair were caked with mud. His shoes were gone and the white shirt was bloody, one sleeve torn off as if someone had cut it with a knife. The soldier withdrew the pistol from his holster, and in the same smooth and uninterrupted movement, he aimed and fired. The blood spouted from the side of the teacher's head as he lay slumped with his eyes open against the tunnel wall. The soldier took a puff on his cigarette, turned and walked away.

Jia heard the audible groan from those refugees who were close enough to see what had happened and then her mother reached with one hand and pulled her back into the tunnel. The bombs began falling. The Americans ran with their rucksacks bouncing, shouting and waving their weapons at the refugees who were still camped outside along the stream.

Those inside began to shout. Some tried to run. Other armed men appeared at both ends of the tunnel, where they stood pointing their rifles at those who were huddled against the cement walls with nowhere else to run. The soldiers began shooting. Some people again tried to escape, but more men with rifles were waiting and they too began firing until the confused swarm of people began to rush from one end of the tunnel to the other, back and forth. Each time they turned to change direction there were fewer of them left standing, until the refugees who remained alive just sat and watched as the soldiers stepped carefully among the dead as if tallying their work. Jia stood shivering in absolute terror as she watched three women who'd tried to run get shot in quick succession while their families screamed after them.

She turned and tried to find her mother in the chaos of the smoking tunnel. Jia searched for her father and finally saw the back of the familiar straw hat. He was rocking back and forth on his knees, alone in the mud next to the dirty stream, stooping and methodically lifting his cupped hands to his face like someone engaged in prayer. Someone conducting a ceremony. He stooped forward and again sat up straight, just as she'd seen him do when they visited the temple shrine in the village. She heard more shots fired from every direction and struggled ahead through the crowd of running people. The airplanes were shooting at the refugees who'd tried to escape from the tunnel. Jia finally crawled up behind her father and touched his shoulder as he kept trying to drink from his hands. Bowing and lifting the water to his mouth. Again and again, he raised his elbows as if he were now attempting desperately to splash himself. And then he spoke with a strangely shallow gurgling that sounded nothing at all like his true voice.

"The water won't stay," he said. "It keeps spilling."

He continued his rocking as he tried to scoop up the water. His shirt was soaked black and when he again brought his hands to his mouth, Jia saw the gouts of bright red arterial blood flowing from between his fingers.

"It keeps falling out," he said in that nearly indecipherable and froggy voice as Jia once more watched him try to drink.

"Oh, I'm so thirsty," he said.

Suddenly, he gave a long and heart-wrenching moan, his voice rattling, his shoulders suddenly trembling as if he were shivering from the cold.

Jia reached around and tried to turn his head but her hand fell into a gaping wet hole. The side of her father's jaw was completely gone, as if something had reached to his otherwise untouched face and simply torn it away. The gouged red chunk of hanging flesh revealed the exposed protruding white bones of his cheek. When he tried again to drink, the water slobbered through what nubby broken teeth still hung from his red gums. Her father seemed not to realize any of this as he continued to rock on his knees, breathing heavily and with great effort, apparently painless as he tried to splash water onto the ruins of his face.

"So thirsty," he said.

The straw hat slipped from his head into the stream and quickly floated away. When he turned to look at Jia, his eyes were pressed tightly shut. He exhaled with a violent final shudder, spraying her with blood as he fell into his daughter's arms. She cried out. She could not sense where her own feet might be at that moment, or if she'd truly just watched her father die. Jia felt as if she might suddenly float away with the entire world in tow. All she'd ever known and loved now seemed as if it were being taken away piece by piece. Nothing felt real at all as she combed her fingers frantically through her father's bloody hair and stroked the familiar bald spot on top of his head. In death, he now seemed so very small and fragile as the very last of him shuddered and then lay still.

The rifle shots grew louder. Jia crawled to the wood *jige* carrier and took the canvas sack that contained the ancestor book and their clothing and she looped the drawstring over her shoulder and stood and shouted for her mother. People were shoving past her and when she looked back toward where she'd last seen her father, he was gone. More soldiers had begun shooting again from where they stood at the tunnel opening. She was quickly knocked down by someone and covered with the sudden crushing force of another body, and another, until she lay pinned beneath a terrible smothering weight that took her breath away. She could hear the muffled pandemonium above her and felt other bodies falling as she tried to gulp air in the small space she'd made between her crossed arms. The only other sounds now were the constant, nearly muted bursts of rifle fire and the shrieking screams of those who continued to die around her.

In the hours to come she lay buried in complete and suffocating darkness. She tried to take tiny sips of air, her cheek pressed against the wet and stinking crook of someone's arm. The hem of another woman's foul-smelling skirt was snagged around her head like a shawl. When she tried to move her trapped legs, her feet went numb and another great shifting burden pressed down, as if more bodies had been piled on her from above. She felt something tug and snap in her hip, but when she cried out her tiny voice was lost in the confining darkness. A rancid, sticky mucus trickled down through the mass of legs and arms. She gagged and tried to turn her head, but she could not and so continued to take her small sips of air. When she tried to scream it sounded like her own voice was very far away. She closed her mouth and finally jerked herself onto her side. There was a small space now, and so she twisted one leg loose, then the other. She sensed the cooler air on her foot as she finally crawled and pushed her shoulders free from the pile of entwined dead bodies. She pulled herself along through the tangle of arms and stiffened legs, a foul gummy moisture on everything she touched, until she could bear it no longer and fell back exhausted. It was so very hot. She held on tightly to the bag she'd looped across her shoulder.

She rested. The dead lay entangled everywhere around her, seemingly posed as if armatured by some careful and gruesome sculptor so as not to appear the same. She moved from one corpse to another, stopped for a few moments, then pushed forward with all her strength toward where she thought she saw the dimly lit tunnel opening. There was smoke everywhere and the tunnel was filled with the echoing moans of those who were still alive. She shouted her mother's name. A burst of more shooting erupted from no known direction, but Jia ignored everything now as she aimed herself toward the light.

They found each other in the morning, next to the railroad bridge in a smoking ruin of burned trees. She'd never seen her mother looking so miserable, almost unrecognizable, the baby swaddled across her back, her brother Hyeon clutching her torn and filthy dress as they both came crawling from a bomb crater where they'd spent the night. Smoke poured from the tunnel and Hyeon, suddenly animated and crying loudly, stumbled ahead on his injured leg and kissed his sister on the cheek. Her mother held her close as Jia sobbed and tried to describe what had happened to her father.

The soldiers strolled back and forth inside the tunnel with their rifles unslung. They patrolled the mounds of uncountable dead, stepping over twisted bodies, examining things as if inspecting a shipment of carelessly arranged inventory. A stinking gray haze drifted over everything. A refugee holding a shirt against his bleeding mouth stood bent and sobbing next to a pile of someone's belongings that had been set afire by the soldiers.

They walked hidden in the trees along the road. More bodies lay where they'd been shot in a ditch and Jia watched an infant crawl and try to nurse on its dead mother. They heard the rumble of more planes pass overhead and watched them disappear over the horizon. In the distance, flashes of light and the deep thumping of more bombs falling further up the valley. The persistent crack of rifle fire continued all day and seemed to follow them as they headed south. There were still refugees walking, this time only haggard stragglers who'd somehow survived the slaughter at the tunnel.

Jia's mother gave them dry cornmeal to chew and when she pulled the blanket from Ji-Yeong's face her brother's eyes were shut tightly. A white crust of rime had formed around his mouth, as if someone had dusted his lips with baking flour. His smooth and pale porcelain cheeks seemed oddly radiant, his chubby baby fists clenched at his side as if caught in some final gesture of defiant resolution. He wore an odd baffled look. In death, the tiny child seemed diminished, a more delicate version of what had already been so small and fragile. Her mother did not cry at all. She only wore a heavy woebegone look of complete and hopeless dejection as she murmured to herself and continued down the road with the baby in her arms.

When they finally found a place to rest, Jia touched Ji-Yeong's closed eyelids as if her fingertips might contain some witchy magic that could bring her baby brother back to life. Her mother wrapped the child in a torn quilt they'd found and she carried the body in her arms for miles until she saw the proper mountains to the left and to the right which would signify good luck and remembrance.

Jia soaked a rag in a farm pond and as they washed the tiny body her mother calmly spoke to her son and said she was sorry that they could not have the village shaman perform a proper *kut* ceremony. She apologized for allowing him to die in such a meaningless and dishonorable way. She said it had not been his fate to grow old and have a family of his own, and for this she was truly sorry. She explained to Jia that it had been her brother's destiny to end his short life in just such a manner, at this exact time and place, and that no one would have been able to alter such a foretelling. His fate must be embraced, she said. Her mother gently stroked the baby's forehead with her finger and said she regretted she could not place coins on his little eyes or cotton in his ears, or a spoon of rice in his mouth. The prescribed traditions were now impossible. This too, her mother said, had been ordained beforehand. She said it was now their duty to remember where he'd been buried so that it could be recorded in the ancestor book in the correct manner. And so they dug the wholly improper grave and scooped out a patch of grass which they placed on top of the burial mound. They marked the spot with four stacked flat stones to signify balance, tranquility, wellness and peace.

After standing silent for a time, Jia's mother finally cried out and fell to her knees and bowed sobbing in front of her son's gravestones to ask for his forgiveness.

CHAPTER 22

There was the rich, moist scent of rain. The familiar summer heaviness of the coming monsoon season filled the air and rows of birds were perched in the trees everywhere. A thick white vapor hung swaying like a veil inches above the black asphalt road. The exhausted refugees walked and hauled their loaded carts through this clammy fog with their feet detached as if they themselves were becoming invisible to the world. Disappearing slowly with each weary step. Forgotten ghosts of those who'd traveled this same path before, all of it a prophecy of what was to come in the days ahead.

Jia watched a bleeding shoeless man in torn clothes standing in the open, apart from everyone, trying to read the burned pages of a newspaper he'd found snagged on a bush. He glanced forlorn at the sky and finally tossed the blackened sheets away as if what news he'd been told didn't matter after all. As if he'd just been reminded of how powerless he was to change anything, and to wish otherwise would be a waste of time. He wiped one eye with the heel of his hand and turned and quickly continued alone down the road.

Jia thought that Hyeon's foot was broken, the black toes swollen, his ankle cocked to one side. It was impossible for him to walk, so they'd been carrying the boy between them in a sling made from a rice sack. The burlap bag was crusted with food and when they stopped, Jia tried to wash it upstream of where they'd last seen any dead bodies. Her mother wondered aloud if this world and those living in it would ever be clean again.

Jia tried to remember her little stone house with its thatched roof, but she could not. She tried to recall the smell of the *ondol* charcoal burning in winter beneath the floor of their kitchen, but she could not. It was as if the memories of her short time on earth might have been devised from a life not her own, and now they seemed to be fading away one by one. She'd lost possession of her brief past. Her filthy hair smelled terrible and still contained her father's dried blood. She'd only been able to arrange his hands across his chest before the soldiers started shooting again and she was swallowed by the screaming crowd. She'd never had time to light three incense sticks and say a prayer. It haunted her that he'd been abandoned in such an awful state. Without the shaman to perform an intercession to account for his violent and unexpected death, her father's poor soul would now be lost. He would become a wandering spirit, inconsolable and rootless forever in the void of death. He would remain adrift if the place of his burial could not be recorded in the ancestor book.

Hyeon had lost his shirt and his bare feet swung from ragged trousers. They'd abandoned much of their belongings at the tunnel. Her brother now wore a cap his mother had made from scraps. Her mother took off her own headscarf and gave it to Jia and told her to tuck her long hair away while they walked on the road. She said there would now be bad men everywhere and that war allowed such dissolute people to prosper at the expense of those who were unaware of such evil. Little girls and women were especially in peril, she said in a formal and calm voice that Jia thought sounded very strange. Her mother told her to rub dirt on her cheeks so she would not look so pretty.

Jia had also hurt herself in the tunnel and she now walked with a limp. Something had been yanked painfully out of place in her hip. They followed the railroad tracks at night to avoid the straggling soldiers who had been detached from their units. These were the most criminal kind of people, her mother said, for they heeded no rules and had no leaders. At dawn they stopped at a deserted farm where Jia stepped over a half eaten rooster that lay among hundreds of other featherless and burned chickens scattered about the barnyard as if they'd been dropped cooked from the sky. The farm was only a collection of mud huts with straw roofs, where a flock of crazed ducks ran back and forth across the courtyard. Her mother caught one by its feet and quickly wrung its neck and they roasted the meat behind a wall so their fire would not be seen from the road.

There were no other animals and they washed themselves in a pond where they made tea from a bag of leaves they'd found in someone's abandoned suitcase. Her mother found bowls in the house along with stale biscuits and a box of rice flour. They slept among giant clay kimchee urns and farm tools in the burned barn and finally drank from a lidded cistern where they washed Hyeon's mangled foot with fresh water. They changed his bandage. The boy's shin was grotesquely swollen, his face now hot and red with a fever. They scraped bits of chaffed corn and dried oats from an animal trough and her mother ground this with a stone and made cold mush for her son to eat. Jia was finally able to clean her father's blood from her hair.

They walked on. For days they traveled south until more convoys of troops arrived in their trucks and tanks, arresting and scattering what refugees remained on the road. There was constant shooting at night. The airplanes returned and they listened to the steady volley of artillery beyond the flashing horizon. The hollow thunder of the constant bombing at night became commonplace.

At a crumbled railroad depot whose ruins were still smoking, they covered themselves with empty canvas mail sacks and slept off the wet ground in a two-wheel luggage trolley. That night, as they scouted the tracks ahead to see if tomorrow's route would be safe, they came upon a barricade of furniture and crates behind which Jia saw soldiers encamped with their cookfires glowing. They ran into the forest. She heard shots fired behind them and her mother pulled Jia into a ditch, where they lay while the North and South Korean soldiers battled each other. The sky brightened and there came the strange metal pinging vibration of a mortar tube discharging. Seconds later, a blast lifted clods of dirt and whole tree limbs above the railroad tracks. They ducked their heads and shielded Hyeon with their own bodies. There was now nowhere at all to run. Jia curled herself into a ball beside her mother and clasped her hands behind her head as she felt the percussions shake the ground. It continued like this for hours. A section of railroad tracks lay twisted and smoking after another big explosion. When the shooting paused, her mother sat up blinking and covered in dirt. Hyeon seemed to be sleeping, and after Jia felt his cheeks with her hand she told her mother the fever might have gotten better.

"He feels cooler," she said.

Her mother gave the slightest smile, as if she was reluctant to show hope. She kissed her son's forehead and gently massaged his shoulders and nodded.

"It seems so," she said. "But we should stay here until the shooting stops. They won't see where we are if we don't show ourselves. Don't stand up. Maybe tomorrow we can find another way."

She pointed to the forest behind them, the bushy trees with their full summer leaves now covered in dust from the explosions.

"If the planes come too close, we will run into the trees," she said. "Maybe into the mountains to find a better road south. We should walk with other people now. Traveling alone isn't safe. Maybe there's a village in the mountains. The train tracks are too dangerous."

Jia lay in the grassy ditch for hours, her arm hooked across her mother's leg as if to make certain that she was still there. As if to grasp what little might remain of the known world of a little girl. She now felt incidental to everything around her, an irrelevant bug in the grass that could be blown away by the wind at any moment. Life seemed altogether temporary and trivial, as unimportant as the weeds she'd once uprooted with her feet in their rice paddy back home. The steady clatter of rifle fire was getting closer, although the rhythmic steadiness of its sound was somehow comforting and so she finally fell asleep.

Jia woke in the night thinking that she had felt her mother shudder. Perhaps she'd been dreaming and had trembled in her sleep. She lay completely still in the dark and Jia decided it was good that her mother was finally getting her rest. It was silent, the night very clear and warm. A half moon floated behind a silvery white cloud in the sky just as it had always done at home. She heard the insects and the tree frogs croaking as if nothing at all had happened. As if there was truly no war or soldiers fighting. Jia was not sure that she might not actually be in her own bed listening to the crickets outside her window, and so she reached out and touched her mother's oddly cold bare leg and drifted into a deep sleep.

When she opened her eyes in the cool morning dusk the world lay silent. The trees shook and hissed in a slight breeze that carried with it the smell of burning wood. A haze hung above the barricade on the tracks where the soldiers had been shooting at each other for much of the night. Hyeon was moaning from where he lay spooned against his mother. Jia squatted and looked up and down the dark railroad tracks and saw that the soldiers were finally gone. There were no planes in the sky. No refugees anywhere, only the mournful sound of a cow lowing from someone's distant barnyard.

When she reached to cover Hyeon with his quilt Jia saw the round dark stain in the center of her mother's back, no bigger than a thumbprint. It was still wet. The white cloth scarf that her mother had tied around her hair just yesterday had come undone and her beautiful long black braids hung loosely across one shoulder, the very ends soaked and matted with blood. Her clasped hands were composed against her stomach and the expression on her face was serene, though she now lay twisted to one side as if something had forced her to roll over during the night. Eyes closed, she wore her look of calm affirmation as if death had not at all been remarkable or unexpected. As if the end had been gratefully painless and sudden, despite what she'd heard of such things.

Jia felt instantly breathless and fell screaming onto her mother's body. She sobbed for so long that it seemed as if she might empty herself. As if the worst of the many horrors she'd imagined during these past weeks had finally come true.

She kissed her mother. Over and over, she kissed and hugged and petted her mother's cold arm until both their faces were wet with Jia's tears.

Hyeon remained asleep. She heard the approaching rifle fire somewhere in the distance and so she walked sobbing to the village station house alone and emptied the luggage trolley in which they'd slept the day before. She knotted a pouch into her brother's blanket and half-dragged him across the tracks, and when she lay him in the cart his open eyes fluttered and he looked from side to side before falling back to sleep. Jia took one of the canvas mail sacks and shook out the envelopes and small packages and took the ancestor book and put that at the bottom of the bag. She gathered their few utensils and one of her mother's blouses. Socks and rags for Hyeon's bandages.

Matches and a folding knife from the pocket of her mother's skirt. She gathered the bowls and what food and dried tea that remained in a cloth pouch fastened with a drawstring. Everything in the world she now owned lay in the luggage trolley with her brother.

She heard the gunfire coming closer from the direction of the railroad tracks.

Jia pressed her face for the last time into her mother's long hair and it smelled like firesmoke and the faint scent of what they'd managed to eat the night before. She gently kissed her cheek and it felt like wax. She covered her with a blanket she'd found in the station house. It bothered Jia terribly that her mother's curled up legs would not stay straight. She looked down at the faintly outlined shape of the face beneath the blanket shroud and several times whispered her goodbyes before she finally cried out, "...eomma...eomma, I don't know what to do. Please tell me what I should do."

Jia saw more soldiers with rifles walking along the railroad tracks. She ran to the train station. Showing in the puddles of dried blood were the footsteps of those who'd already passed through the waiting room that day. Behind the brass ticket cage she found a metal drinking cup. A soaked and moldy cardboard suitcase left on a bench gave her a pair of child's socks and a summer jacket that she wrapped around a kitchen knife and spoon, and all of this she dropped into the mail sack. In a small office on the floor behind a desk that had been splintered by bullets lay a dead woman covered with fallen plaster. She was staring up at the spinning ceiling fan. It smelled awful in the room, the sweet metallic reek of blood, and Jia held her arm across her mouth as she gathered more things before she finally could stand it no longer and ran outside.

She pulled the cart by its long yoke handle along a path behind the station that seemed to lead away from the railroad tacks, into the mountains where her mother said they should go. The gunfire seemed to be getting closer and she heard a lone plane flying overhead. There were bodies everywhere now, feet sticking out from bushes. People lay slumped where they'd fallen, their arms crossed jointless in their laps like dolls. A chewing cow with a bell around its neck stood in the middle of the path and stared at her before trotting off into the forest. A man swung dead from a clothesline post hung with freshly laundered trousers he would never wear again.

She met a family encamped in the woods who said they'd walked for three weeks from Seoul, their numbers reduced by half when they were strafed by aircraft during the bombing of Kumi near the Nakdong River. Two girls Jia's age helped her pull the cart that next day and they said they'd heard that the only hope for anyone was to get to Busan, where the remaining government troops could protect them.

The next village was not much more than a row of smoking craters filled with more rubble. Loose farm animals roaming wild-eyed. A whole orchard lay black and wasted from the bombing, as if someone had taken a torch to its fruit trees. Only stone foundations and charred brick chimneys remained to mark where houses had once stood. Squawking chickens and ducks walked everywhere.

Jia and her brother rested on a clean mattress that sat miraculously untouched at the bottom of one of the craters. Someone from the encamped refugees brought her a bowl of salted cabbage and pieces of grilled *sanjeok* on a skewer. Also a clay pot filled with fresh water. It was her first true meal since her mother had killed the ducks. Such a luxury, she thought. Hyeon was silent and gloomy as he tried to chew the meat and when he asked where their mother and father were, Jia forced a smile and said they'd been separated and that they would all soon meet in the safety of the city. Hyeon cried out when Jia peeled the stinking bandage from his foot. She told her brother to look away and try to be brave as she tried to clean the infected wound. The scabby gash on his ankle had torn open and become inflamed. A bone protruded from the spongy white flesh, and dark veins were visible beneath where the skin on his foot had turned blue. A clear resinous fluid seeped from the wound and his entire leg now felt burning hot. A red stripe wiggled along beneath the skin of Hyeon's shin as if someone had dragged a bead of paint with a finger. Her brother could not bear to have Jia touch his leg, and when she tried to drip clean water into the wound he shrieked and swung his fist and said he wanted to see his mother.

"You're stupid. You don't know what you're doing," he said.

"We have to find a doctor," Jia said and pleaded with him as she held the dripping rag in her hand. "I have to clean it. You have to be brave."

"Get away!" he shouted and turned and buried his face and began to sob.

Jia waited until he was asleep before she walked through the camp asking if there was a doctor among the refugees. Nothing but shaking heads and shrugs, everyone with their own concerns as they looked at her with suspicion. Someone said to take Hyeon to the stream above the village and put his foot in the icy mountain water, but of course her brother could not walk and she could not carry him that far. When she described Hyeon's condition to one man he nodded and said he was sorry but it was a sign that the leg might already be putrid.

Someone who was wrapping a child's hand with gauze gave Jia a waxed paper envelope filled with disinfectant powder. She made a paste in her palm with the clean water and when she tried to put it on Hyeon's wound he swung his arm and knocked her hand away. Jia shouted at him and began to cry while he held up his shaking fist and told his sister that he hated her. Hated her more than anyone in the world.

"The only thing you know how to do is hurt me!"

Hyeon's glassy eyes twitched when he spoke. His speech was slurred and he seemed groggy, his phlegmy voice deep and congested as if he'd suddenly caught a chest cold. He began coughing, the white spittle sticking like paste at the corners of his mouth. She touched his forehead with her hand as she'd seen her mother do and it was burning. Her brother's hot breath came in short labored gulps. He finally wheezed deeply before settling into an uneasy sleep in which he constantly jerked his legs and opened and closed his mouth as if he wasn't getting enough air.

That night Jia heard approaching footsteps from beyond the glow of the fire she'd made from sticks and paper scraps. When she turned, there was a lantern flame swinging toward her in the dark. Trembling, she reached for their kitchen knife and held it against her back. An old woman's face appeared behind the yellow lamp light, a goblin dressed in a tall hat and billowing *hanbok*. The dark pleated skirt was elaborately decorated with hanging strings of beads and colored scarves that flared wildly as the woman stepped forward like someone who'd just appeared on a theater stage. She studied Jia's miserable stick fire and the pot of water boiling in its coals. Hyeon lay curled up and groaning with his bandaged foot sticking out from beneath the quilt.

"They told me the boy was sick," the woman said.

She squatted and looked sternly at Jia. She held up the lantern. "Girl, where is your mother and father?"

"They're coming back," Jia lied and pointed over her shoulder. "They'll be here soon. They went to get water. I'm not supposed to talk to strangers."

The woman nodded and seemed as if she might smile. She glanced at the two-wheeled luggage cart and its meager cargo. She looked at where Jia had emptied the contents of the mail sack. The single wooden bowl from which she and Hyeon had shared their meal. The pile of rags and the dirty quilt she'd wrapped around her sleeping brother. Jia's shoes were untied and the woman saw that she'd used the laces to bind the boy's rag bandage.

"No. You're alone," the woman said and swung the lamp. "Can I sit? You don't have to lie to me. I won't hurt you."

She pulled off her rucksack and sat with her legs folded crosswise beneath the long skirt. Jia noticed that the woman's ankles were wrapped in puttees, something she had never seen before and it reminded her of bandages. The toes of her tooled leather shoes were upturned like the footwear of a forest fairy from a nursery fable. Her belt was bright yellow and the baggy blouse she wore over the wide skirt was contained within a tight vest embroidered with strange symbols and Hangul incantations that Jia could not read or understand. In the glow of the fire the woman's ancient walnut face was severely creased and her tall hat seemed fastened to her head with another brightly colored scarf. Her enormous shiny ear rings dangled from beneath her long white hair in the firelight.

She had never before been this close to a Mudang. The frightening old soothsayer and shaman in her own village was someone none of the children wanted to approach or speak to and so she was always avoided. Mudangs kept to themselves and Jia had never really heard one speak except during the trance ritual of a *kut*, in which the shaman's dancing and chanting were used to invite happiness and repel certain spiritual evils. Jia stared wide-eyed as the woman opened her rucksack and unwrapped a cloth filled with dried noodles. She handed this and a few small soup onions and a cucumber to Jia.

"Let me show you how to cook this for the boy," the Mudang said. "You can put that knife away now."

"I know how to do that," Jia said and took the food.

"Child, then you don't need my help. That's good," the old woman said and grinned. Two of her front teeth were gold and they gleamed in the light from the fire.

"That's good. These days I'm afraid the young ones will have no time to grow up properly or to learn new things. To do, is to learn. You will have much to do in the terrible days to come."

The Mudang reached into one of her enormous vest pockets and took out a tiny stoppered bottle. "Put this on the boy's foot," she said. "Tonight and in the morning and again the same way tomorrow until it's completely gone. I'll come by before the others leave and give you something else, and you can tell me what your plans are."

"My plans," Jia said.

"You can't stay here."

The old woman slowly got to her feet and spread her hands. "As for me, this is my village," she said. "I don't think I'll go anywhere. That's my plan. But you, child, you can't stay. They can come and do what they want with me, but this is my village. I suppose it would be best for you and the boy to remain until he gets well, but that is something I cannot advise in these awful times. With dangerous people everywhere. You should go with the others, find a family to travel with. Nobody who comes from the North from now on can be trusted, do you understand? They will all be equally dangerous. Above all, the soldiers. Make sure you use the medicine on the boy tonight."

She turned and walked off without another word. Jia watched the soft disconnected glow of the retreating lantern until it finally disappeared and everything was quiet once again, the only sound the snapping of the burning sticks as she added more wood to her little fire.

She boiled water and tried to wake Hyeon and force him to eat the noodles, but he only coughed and chattered nonsense and pushed her hand away. She rubbed the salve from the bottle on his foot and when he tried to kick her hand she finally shouted for him to stop and emptied the rest of the foul-smelling medicine directly onto the wound. He struggled, but she held down his leg and told him to behave in the same voice she'd heard her mother use hundreds of times when she scolded her children.

That night Jia watched the distant flashes and dreamed that she and her mother were walking through their peaceful village, the lovely white cranes stepping daintily in their long-legged haughty manner through the brown water of the rice field.

In the morning she woke in the dark in a cool drizzling rain. She heard the kitten long before she saw it hopping up and down in the shadows as she lay where they'd slept on the quilt in the cart.

The skinny creature seemed to weigh hardly anything as it jumped sideways and arched its back and pranced off with its tail raised, only to return and rub itself against Jia's foot. She stroked the tiny bony face with one finger and the kitten gave a squeaky yowl and leaped past her onto the cart, where it sat licking itself, one extended leg contorted to the side as if this very spot had already been a special place to make itself at home. Jia's father had always said that cats were useless and should not be kept as playthings but only used to catch mice. They could find their own food, he said. Cats and dogs should not be fed just for the pleasure of seeing them eat. They should never live in the house. On a farm there was no such thing as a pet, he said. Animals must always work.

She offered the kitten a ball of cold sticky rice. It sniffed and licked the rice and sat chewing with its head bowed between its paws and stared at Jia with its curled tail switching.

"Goyangi," she said. "There's nothing more for you to eat, *nabi*."

She was petting the cat in her lap and whispering to it softly when the Mudang returned.

The old lady looked more ancient in the early morning light, grandmotherly in a way, less frightening. Her voice seemed softer and when she smiled the corners of her creased eyes turned up sharply and a burst of more wrinkles stretched across her brown cheeks. At home her friends said that the fingers of a Mudang could magically turn into sharp knives, and it was in this way that they cut the throats of chickens used for sacrifice to the spirits of the forest. All Mudang could fly by merely lifting their arms. If they took out their chimes of little bells and shook them over your head they could cast a hex on you and your entire family that would continue for generations. The curse could last a thousand years, for the life of a Mudang had no end and its spirit would merely die and return again and again for eternity. Nothing could escape the fate of a Mudang's curse or the power of one of their cures.

The old shaman now grinned and looked up at the overcast morning sky, the hills beyond the abandoned village in silhouette as if they'd been cut out of paper.

"The dawn still comes even if the rooster dies," the Mudang said. She watched the kitten leap from Jia's lap and run off into the woods.

The old woman shook her head. She leaned and spat. "Those creatures are bad luck. You should hope that one day it runs away."

She reached into her pack and handed Jia a sheathed knife with an intricately carved bone handle. Jia took the heavy blade, which was as long as her arm.

"I want you to take that with you," the Mudang said. "It's very sharp. It's not for cooking, understand? Take very good care of it so that it takes care of you."

Her eyes got bleary and seemed unfocused as she studied Jia closely and then looked over at where Hyeon lay sleeping. She reached out and gently brushed aside Jia's hair.

"Once, I had a young one just like you. A very long time ago. So long it hardly seems real anymore. The Japanese took her from me. Yes, such a very long time ago. You remind me of her. You've made me remember things I thought I'd long forgotten. I'm not sure if that's good or bad, but you've put them in my head now forever. The body stores its wounds and memories like water."

It had stopped raining. The old woman looked up at the brightening sky and cleared her throat as if she wanted to purposely shift her thoughts elsewhere. She forced a smile and took Jia's hand. The Mudang wore a bracelet hung with little charms. Each of her long bony fingers were decorated with tattooed symbols and dotted circles that seemed to extend along her wrist and up beneath the sleeve of her blouse. The Mudang had a smell to her, a rich earthy odor, the scent of freshly cut gass. The forest, Jia thought. She'd never met anyone who smelled like the forest.

The Mudang turned over Jia's hand and traced her finger across the palm to the top of her small thumb, and she nodded as if satisfied with what she'd found. As if what she'd deciphered from the map was satisfactory.

"Good. Now close your hand. Tight like this," the old woman said and made a fist. She took Jia's clasped fingers into her own two bony hands and pressed them against her warm lap.

She looked over at the knife where it lay. She muttered a soft incantation during which she squeezed Jia's small fist and then seemed to shiver briefly as if suddenly overcome by a chill.

"Don't worry," the Mudang said and stared at the knife she'd given Jia. "When the time comes, you'll know how to use that in the way it was intended. Until then, always keep it close to you. Honor the knife. It will be used at the proper time in the proper way. But keep it safe, understand?"

Jia noticed the image of the tiger stitched onto the Mudang's sleeve, the animal's exaggerated long yellow trail trailing up toward her shoulder. When the old woman took out another of her little flasks they both turned and listened as Hyeon woke and began to speak some half-dream gibberish before collapsing exhausted onto the quilt.

The Mudang put the salve onto her brother's raw wound, the blistered foot now horribly swollen, the nails on his toes replaced by blackened knobs where the bone had begun to break through the putrefied skin. The red stripe on Hyeon's leg was now much darker. A single vein on the boy's throat pulsed violently. The old lady lifted Hyeon's head and touched his sweaty cheek. The Mudang now blew hoarsely onto the child's face through her cupped hands, a long and exaggerated exhalation that she repeated several times before closing her own eyes again. The old woman then began to chant in a wholly altered voice that was deeper, like a man's reedy baritone. She recited some strange rhyme with a steady cadence and fell into a brief trance. She swayed from side to side with her eyes closed, her lips still moving.

Jia did not see the Mudang take anything from her pocket or the rucksack, but suddenly the old woman was awake and holding a writing brush in her hand. There was an ink bottle balanced on her knee as she began to paint flowing Hangul characters on a long and narrow scroll that seemed to have also appeared out of nowhere. When she was finished she lay the tube of paper aside and told Jia to wait for it to dry.

"Take this charm for yourself," she said and nodded at the scroll. "Keep it safe along with the knife."

"Can you bless my brother?"

"I cannot," the Mudang quickly said with some sadness as if she'd expected just such a question. "I cannot do any more for the poor boy. This is for you only, I'm sorry."

The old woman said to come close. She held her hands together and quickly blew on Jia's forehead. Her jewelry rattled as she passed her hand in a circle across Jia's stomach and her hip and held it there in the manner of a benediction. She stood and turned to leave. Again, that rich smell of grass and earth as she shook out her baggy dress and composed herself.

"Why don't you walk with the others?" Jia said. "To Busan. With me."

"I won't leave this place," the Mudang said. "They can try to do what they want with me when they get here. They don't know it, but I will write their names in red. I will not leave. This is my home. The ancestors are here. Everything I know is in this place and if I leave, the chain will be broken. All will be broken and scattered and it can never be repaired again."

"But they'll hurt you," Jia said.

"Child, you talk like such an old lady. I think you were born already grown up," the Mudang said and laughed. "Remember what I said about the rooster. It will all be fine, but you will have to be patient, child. It will be your most valuable lesson in this world, to learn patience and wait for fate to arrive at its appointed time."

She smiled and swung the hem of her billowy skirt as if there might be something to shake away. As if she might at that moment rise and fly off into the sky. She lifted her arm with its swinging medallions and delicate chains, and she said, "Travel well, child. You've been licked by the tiger, and so your life may have many seasons. Longer in its seasons than you could ever imagine."

***

Jia carried the purring kitten with its head poking from the knotted shirt she'd found hanging on a clothesline. She decided not to give the cat a name. It might be taken from her like everything else in the world and it would be worse if it had a name.

She pulled on a pair of boy's pants she'd found, and with scissors from one of the abandoned houses she cut her hair. She pulled Hyeon in the cart and continued south.

Jia hid the Mudang's knife next to the ancestor book at the bottom of her bag, the scroll wrapped and tied around its scabbard. Where the Mudang had passed her hand across her stomach, Jia now felt a bloated soreness, as if she'd eaten spoiled food. When the Mudang had blessed her she'd felt immediately light-headed. Meanwhile, her sore hip had gotten better, though she continued to walk with a limp.

After traveling all day, she followed a long line of refugees across a broken bridge made from floating pontoons the Americans had tried to blow up during their retreat. She slept that night with others in the wreckage of a bombed-out factory near Waegwan. She heard babies crying and people shuffling in and out of the enormous, roofless building. The gunfire grew louder as they got closer to where the fiercest fighting had begun near Busan.

Her brother's foot was worse and he could no longer move his other leg. It was as if the fate of both limbs depended on the health of the other. He shivered violently in his sleep, though he now burned with another, hotter fever. In his dreams he called out his father's name and pleaded with his mother to bring him fresh cold water to drink from the village well. When Jia once again asked if someone knew a doctor, they only shook their heads and stepped away from the terrible smell of Hyeon's rotting foot. Everyone in the group walked constantly as if there was no other point to life than to put one foot before the other. The truth was, no one truly had anywhere to go.

She was feeding the Mudang's onion soup to Hyeon when her brother's mouth trembled and convulsively clamped down onto the spoon. He gave a weary moan, and when it seemed as if he might finally say something, the boy only arched his back and stiffened into another violent clonic spasm. When the seizure passed, his eyelids fluttered as if they'd been pasted shut to avoid seeing what might now come. And then he lay suddenly draped loosely across Jia's lap with his arms outstretched, still and soundless, his emaciated body for the first time peacefully composed within the folds of the warm quilt. His little boy's face looked so relaxed, the feverish red cheeks now paled into a bashful blush that gave him a glowing radiance, a false countenance of health. And though Jia thought this could not possibly be true and that it might all be part of someone else's separate nightmare, this is how her brother remained while she held him dead and rocking in her arms.

One of the refugees said he would stand as the funeral *sangju* and helped her dig the grave. The man showed Jia how to wash Hyeon's body and he wore a makeshift armband to signify his respect as an invited guest of the family. There was no true and clean cotton to be found anywhere, so they twisted scraps of cloth into the boy's ears. Uncooked rice in his mouth for when he reached the afterlife. They stacked more stones.

When the shooting began again, the kitten without a name leaped from the cart and ran off and she never saw it again.

In the years to come she would often think of that day when it felt as if her heart would dry up and blow away; when it seemed as if she'd been destined to love nothing and nothing in the world would ever love her in return. Kim Jia-Soon felt swallowed and helpless.

Someone gave her a cap and she wore it low to cover her face. She took a better pair of boy's trousers from a broken shop window and in the weeks ahead, with the dirty mail sack hanging from her shoulder, she must have looked like another wandering troll lost in the war's wasteland. She slept in ditches where her fire would not be seen at night. She spent the long rainy monsoon summer days hiding in the ruins of other nameless villages. The dead and sick lying everywhere no longer surprised her, and as she got closer to Busan there were more and more refugees pushing bicycles and struggling along the crowded road with their loaded baskets on their heads. Pulling their rickety wheeled carts, these were the final survivors. Whole herds of cows and people hazing ducks and chickens with their sticks. Even the children being carried in military trucks had gray hair from the pale dust that covered everything.

She felt safer when she cooked and ate alone. When she reached Kimhae, Jia crossed the river with the others, crawling along the collapsed bridge pilings as she'd been shown by her father. Uncounted days passed until she finally arrived in the city, which had been transformed into a vast encampment of shanties and tents. Jia had never seen such a frightening place, where 140,000 troops had now gathered to make their final stand against the invading North Korean Army.

The giant ships that rocked at anchor at Busan looked like islands. She slept in alleys under tipped wooden crates and waited in line for food that soldiers handed her on metal plates. At the wharf she joined other orphaned children, who each evening picked through a filthy smoking trash yard where they sorted things that might be sold on the streets of the city. In an alley behind a military kitchen they picked through piles of the unopened tins that contained American soldier food. Wrapped chocolates and biscuits and jars of lovely sweet jam that she'd never tasted before. She marveled that such delicious food could have been tossed away, uneaten.

She was walking along the government pier, inspecting trash cans, hoping to find something to replace her worn shoes, when a military jeep flying a blue United Nations flag pulled up behind her. The two soldiers gave her something to eat and took her to a field with canvas tents arranged in rows where a nurse gave her fresh clothes and pointed to a galvanized steel basin with a curtain hung on a rope for privacy. She didn't know what to do with the can of powdered soap she'd been given, so she sprinkled it into the warm tub water and truly washed herself for the first time since she and her family had been chased from their home so long ago.

They took her to a large room filled with cots and baby cribs. There was a stack of toys in the corner, fuzzy stuffed little bears and dolls, and one of the round-eyed American women with a white hat gave her a chocolate candy bar. That evening she sat with the others at a long table where the tallest man she'd ever seen stood with his hands clasped as he bowed his head and spoke in Korean. He said that no one could touch their food until they were finished praying. The tall man flipped through the pages of his black book and asked all the children to thank God in His glory for their salvation.

From that day on, when the Pastor Man found her with little food or hope in sight, she thought he'd truly been sent by the unfamiliar and foreign god he'd spoken of. By whatever heavenly concordance of salvation had up until now been beyond her ability to understand. It was like breathing sweet air after being smothered, something beyond mere comfort or pleasure. This was finally peace and safety and the embrace of another human being who she felt would not harm anyone. There was now glorious magic, a vibrancy, in the realization that she could sleep without dreams or fear. That she would not wake in the night and wonder where she was or who might be shooting at her. She could finally mourn her dear parents and brothers. For Jia, a calm and peaceful appetite for the world had miraculously returned. It was all she could do not to run up and kiss the Pastor Man's hand each evening as he stood like some heavenly temple angel with his book and prayed softly for what she thought was surely no one else but her.

Days later, she was sitting alone on her bed in the orphanage, the pleasant smell of food drifting down the hallway. Dishes clattering and people laughing. She listened to the shouts of other children, who came rushing into the dormitory from a playground filled with things Jia had never seen before; where they tossed balls back and forth and stood in a circle and sang songs while holding hands. She was given a long flowery skirt to wear by the Pastor Man's wife, herself dressed identically with her hair gathered into a high bun on her head. Her blouse buttoned demurely, her heavy shoes more like a man's boots. The heavy silver cross swinging from her neck caught the gleam from the saucer light fixtures that hung from the dormitory ceiling.

Brother Caleb's wife stood for a moment smiling down at Jia and then sat at the end of the bed and folded her hands in her lap. She had a strange Korean accent and spoke in the old- fashioned way of a grandmother.

"You're a long skinny thing, aren't you? And so pretty," she said and gently patted Jia's foot. "We'll have to fatten you up and get you strong. There's much work to be done here for the Lord."

When she smiled, Sister Sarah's white teeth gleamed. She had round blue eyes and her dark hair had a raven's wing of gray running up the middle. She asked Jia how she could have slept so long with all the morning clatter and laughter from the children.

"The guns made noise, too," Jia said. "I can sleep anywhere."

"There are no guns here," Sister Sarah said and brought out her arms as if she were embracing all the other children in the room. All the children in the world.

"You don't have to worry about that sort of thing anymore. Not here. This is your family now and these are your brothers and sisters. Now, it's time to get up and get busy with the Lord's labors," she said and pointed to the broom leaning against the foot of the bed. "We all do our part here. Myself, Brother Caleb, all of us do God's work every day without question."

Jia took the broom and swept between the infant cribs that were lined against the wall of the dormitory. One of the babies looked up at her from behind arms so thin they seemed made from the bones of a bird, the infant's giant blinking eyes deeply set in its starved elfin face. The tiny heart pounding behind paper-thin skin stretched over its delicate ribs. She reached into the crib and the child grasped her finger with its tiny hand, hardly any strength in its grip. The baby smiled and Jia felt a sudden pang of sorrow as she remembered her own baby brother's happy round face. The way he kicked his little feet from where he hung swaddled on his mother's back.

When she finished, Jia stood at the wall flicking the light switch on and off. She stared at the hanging ceiling lamps that were shaped like tea cup saucers, never having seen such a wonder in all her life. She had once lived in a world lit by candles and oil lamps and wicks flickering from glass lanterns.

The next day the Pastor Man stood on a table with his zippered black book and asked all the children to stand and hold hands and pray. Sister Sarah assembled those orphans separately who were sick and they were marched past Brother Caleb one by one. He put his hand on their heads and closed his eyes and blessed them all, and as he touched certain children his arm twitched intensely toward the ceiling as if pulled from above by a string. As if drawn toward heaven by God Himself. This is when Sarah cried out excitedly, jumping slightly, and clapped her hands and asked everyone to do the same. She said the spirit of the Lord had just entered the room and was doing His work through her blessed husband.

"Say hallelujah!" she shouted.

And Kim Jia-Soon, with her eyes tightly closed, put her hands together and said, "Hallelujah."

PART THREE

Spring 1968
The DMZ

"Energy never dies. It will not be destroyed.
It goes somewhere else. All that ever was, still is."
– Private First Class Yevgeny Lee

CHAPTER 23

He'd been cleared to carry a weapon and continued to work as a driver for General Yardley, but they placed him on restricted duty.

He knew his shoulder ached too much to disassemble and clean the M14, and he didn't know if he could hold a pistol in the firing position. When he got tired in the afternoon he walked canted to one side like a movie mummy monster shuffling in its bandages.

With his half-ass work schedule, he could have easily loafed his time away at the hooch, but Profar knew he'd just spend his days getting high and watching the girls at the Water Dragon Club. The Robideaux Guard Post was the safest place to have a conversation with Lee, and they now had much to talk about. Both soldiers felt that they were being watched.

Somebody at the USO library told First Sergeant Bingham that Profar had been an English major in school and now had plenty of time on his hands, so Yardley's G2 resource officer volunteered him out of the blue to teach a three-day class on any book of his choice.

The students were senior ROK officers who wanted to brush up on their English language skills. The G2 said to consider it as a personal favor to General Yardley, who'd made sure that Profar was still assigned as his part-time driver, which meant that he would continue to collect his hazardous duty pay. Profar chose *Huckleberry Finn*, and just like that, a dozen paperback copies arrived promptly the next day by special courier from Seoul.

The top Korean officer, a bird Colonel with a bulldog neck who looked like he could hold his own as a professional wrestler, caught on to the book's plot right away and said Huck, who he called "Hook," wanted to emancipate himself in the same way that Jim, his pal on the raft, wanted to free himself from slavery. The Korean Colonel wore the battalion patch of the 707th Infantry, the white tiger battalion, the Korean Army's most elite special forces unit.

"And so they both say society is not always correct, no?" The Colonel asked Profar during the class and looked round the room, very pleased with himself.

"And you must run from what is wrong and seek to walk on the correct path of life, yes?" he said

"Yes, sir," Profar said. "You nailed it, sir. That's a bullseye."

"Nailed? What kind of eye?"

"Yes, sir. You got it right. You hit the target. It means you got it correct. Very good, sir," Profar said and spent most of that hour explaining the book's wide range of American slang and colloquial phrases. He told the beefy and dangerous-looking special forces Colonel with the Al Capone scar running down his cheek that it might not be useful to use certain words that appeared in the book, such as "bodkin" or "jabbering palaver," during a routine conversation.

"It's an old fashion way to talk, sir," he said. "I'd take whatever Mark Twain has to say with a grain of salt, anyway. He liked to kid around."

"Salt," the Colonel said.

"Yes, sir," Profar said. "Don't take him seriously. The guy who wrote the book."

Nobody in the class needed to be told that the Mississippi River was a symbol for freedom. They easily related to the idea of the Mississippi's resemblance to their own Imjin River and the dragon of Korean folklore. Profar let the class run with this theme, since he'd never thought of it himself.

These hardened soldiers liked the book's kindhearted and generous Widow Douglas, who they called *halmoni,* because she reminded the Korean officers of a stern country granny who enforced harsh rules but had good intentions. They joked she was like a lady Confucius, someone who provided the guideposts of life. The classes were held in a sandbagged artillery bunker. Everybody sat on green metal folding chairs. The dirt floor was covered with a canvas tarp that showed black burn marks from ejected 105 mm shell casings.

When he wasn't teaching proper American literature or driving the General, Profar continued to loiter at the hooch in the Ville. He was in limbo. He told Lee about seeing Remo at the barracks and his friend said that Jia had been asking every day if anybody knew what was up with her wealthy MIA yeobo. She just wouldn't give up hope. Remo still owed payments to Choi, both for Jia's rent and her monthly contract.

"This is her last chance," Lee said again. "There's no future for somebody like her."

They sat on the steps watching the mamasan clean her laundry. The water pipe was gushing and she took out a soaked and soapy skirt and started pushing it across the washboard. They wondered why she just didn't pay somebody to do her cleaning. Everybody knew the old lady was the richest woman in the Ville. She ran Choi's operation and had a key to his office. She carried those keys on a lanyard everywhere she went and they chimed like bells when she walked. The mamasan was always locking or unlocking something, scurrying around, ducking in and out of the big wooden doors that led to the alley. It reminded Profar of a bell mare. He remembered his grandmother's farm in Minnesota and how there was always a mare who wore a big bell around her neck and she was the one the other horses would follow each day into the pasture. The bell mare wasn't any smarter than the other horses, but she had the bell and so they followed her dutifully.

All the girls liked the mamasan, who's teeth seemed shockingly white when she smiled. She was the buffer between Choi and the rest of the world. None of the girls wanted to have personal contact with their pimp. The mysterious Mrs. Yoshida knew each of their life stories and how much money they owed on their employment contract. If one of them misbehaved, she never had a problem interceding with the boss. But she also protected the girls from the GIs when things got rough and made sure they didn't miss the required clinic appointments. Mrs. Yoshida knew the local Korean National Police and the useful clerks at the provincial judicial office, so things got taken care of. She knew the Army CID civilian employees at

Division HQ, and so many problems of a criminal nature were often quietly resolved. You rarely saw Choi at the club, and if you did he was sitting at the cash register behind the bar counting money or slapping buttons on his mechanical calculator. If you saw him in the courtyard talking to the mamasan or one of the girls, then something was serious. He only showed up when there was trouble. Otherwise, it was Mrs. Yoshida who kept things under control in the Water Dragon universe, walking back and forth, working and stooping, her plastic flip-flops clacking on the courtyard stones and that ring of keys chiming like a bell. She was the bell mare.

"You ever meet him?" Profar said.

"The pimp?" Lee said. "He asked once if I could get something from the PX. Had a big grin on his face, like this was supposed to be a privilege for me. To be his pal, you know. I said shit no, so now he ignores me. He strikes me as just another alley thief. Just like the kids who steal stuff off the supply truck tailgate when it stops at the MP checkpoint. Dresses nice and talks good English and all, but he's just a thug who rents out his slave girls for quickies."

If they saw Choi at night it was when he was standing in his favorite corner behind the bar so he could watch the girls do his work. He had an office next to the club and always parked his black Mercedes in the alley, blocking the door. They said when the car was parked like that, he was counting his cash.

The girls acted differently when Choi was at the club. There was a tense vibe. Everybody got busier and stopped talking and they walked faster and carried their drink trays with a sense of urgency.

"If God had a heart," Lee said in that tone of voice he used when he wanted to sound grandly eloquent. "He would not be divine because his heart would be broken if he saw what happens here."

"The hell does that mean?" Profar said.

"You know what I told Jia the first time she asked about you in the hospital?"

"That I was handsome?" Profar said.

"I told her you lost both legs and that your pecker may have been cut off in the ambush."

"You're repeating yourself again. And she said?"

"She called me a freaky stoner," Lee said. "The mamma was walking by and started laughing. She never laughs. The old girl swung her grocery bag at me. Said I would never amount to anything in this world and that my corrupt ways were a disgrace to my ancestors."

Lee stared off into the middle distance, like he was revving up for another speech about a former life.

"What I said happened with her in Busan, that wasn't half the story," he said. "The preacher she hooked up with was getting UN money for his orphanage. There was no way for the government to take care of orphan kids and babies in those days. The streets were filled with homeless children, so the Army sent them to the missionaries. Guy's name was Brother Caleb. They found Jia starving and dressed in rags. He gave her food and that's all she wrote. Jia referred to him as her uncle. The missionaries baptized her in a bath tub and said her new name would be Julia. They taught her English."

"If she was so safe, why did she leave?" Profar said.

"The pastor put her to work on the street, fluttering those eyes at horny soldiers so they'd buy stupid trinkets from her with their magical dollars, which was better than gold in those days. Korean script was worthless after the war. It was all about GI money and candy bars and getting aboard the United Nations gravy train.

"But the orphanage and preaching the Lord's word wasn't enough for Brother Caleb and his wife," Lee said. "They branched out and made their kids hand-write letters to overseas donors who were asked to sponsor one of the orphans. Meanwhile, the UN money keeps flowing in by the barrel. Turns out, Brother Caleb was skimming from his all-cash operation and sending money to a PO Box in the states. More dough found its way into certain congressional campaign coffers and the pockets of lobbyists who were part of the financial daisy chain created to rebuild the Korean economy. It all worked fine until the 8th Army Inspector General gets word that the good and benevolent Brother Caleb has been hitching free Air Force cargo flights to Tokyo, where he kept a swanky bachelor pad in the Shinjuku nightclub district. There's the beachfront house in Thailand, too. By this time, Caleb was wearing a white robe and sandals and calling himself

"The Messenger," through which all godly guidance flowed. He predicted the end of the world and said only members of his church would be granted a heavenly one-way ticket for the coming Rapture. The End Times. There were rumors about private spiritual healing sessions for his prettiest girls, who he'd take on weekend trips to Tokyo. That's when the whole jackpot came crashing down.

"When they finally arrested the pastor, Jia got the stinky end of the whole mess and they put her in jail, along with her cult buddies. She found out the details about Brother Caleb years later when she read about it in the papers."

Lee stretched out his hands. "Enter Mr. Choi Il-Seong, the pimp," he said. "But I'll tell you that story later."

"And she told you all this?"

"Once she got going, it didn't stop. It's not like I asked questions. We were talking about the ambush and the hospital and off she went. She asked about my family in Chicago and she said she wished she could see her mom and dad again."

They sat watching the girls in the courtyard. Food smells drifted from the mamasan's porch where she was cooking on her hot plate. There was a hunk of meat lying on a cutting board and Mrs. Yoshida whacked at it with an enormous cleaver. Lee said he wouldn't want to piss the old lady off, by the look of how she handled a blade.

"Look at those arms," he said. "She's one tough cookie."

They watched the mamasan make short work of the meat. She gathered some of the pieces and started frying them up.

"She was telling the truth, Eddie," Lee said. "About her past. I believe every word. She's got no reason to make stuff up."

Lee explained that when Jia first met Remo he was just another customer. Choi had been pressuring her to land a good quality yeobo, somebody with real cash. At the time Remo was a notorious tipper. He started dressing nice when he came to the Ville. Brought gifts. Kodak film for the girls and then signed on with Choi and told Jia that if the stars lined up, maybe he could take her home.

"Why Remo?" Profar said.

"There were Majors and Colonels waiting, true. But Remo had solid money," Lee said. "I had a bottle of officers' club Chardonnay, so we got crocked. I told her about my dad and mom's store and growing up and what happened to them in the war and one thing led to another. Her family was wiped out. She was on the road alone, a little girl. That's when she asked about you and if you were okay."

"How do I know this isn't all in your head?" Profar said. "You were drunk."

"I know what I heard, Eddie," Lee said. "She asked how old you were and where you came from in the states. She said you had tranquility, *ahnjong*."

"Shove it."

"A liar hides his lies in the truth," Lee said.

"What?"

"You know what I mean," Lee said. "Let me tell you something else, Eddie. Choi killed her baby."

Profar listened as Mrs. Yoshida tuned in a Korean station on her radio. Wistful music drifted across the courtyard.

"I don't know if it was his or not. She clammed up," Lee said. "She went where all the girls get sent when they get knocked up. Outside of town, to that clinic with the barbed wire where the girls get their shots. Not far from the old Japanese cemetery where they bury poor people and foreigners. That's where the business girls who don't have anybody get put in the ground. They call the clinic the Zoo because everybody walks around like a zombie, they're so drugged up. God knows what else goes on in there on top of the penicillin shots. The Koreans run it, but Uncle Sam writes the checks. I got the feeling that the deal is that the clinic makes sure the girls can't have kids again after they get discharged. She had that look, you know. Like they tried to do something else to her in that place."

They watched Mrs. Yoshida haul out another chunk of meat. She sliced off the fat and put that aside on a plate and raised the cleaver and made short, surgical work of the beef. The sound was thunderous.

Lee explained how Choi had found her sitting apart from the others at the police station in Busan. This was after Brother Caleb got busted. Of course, the pimp had spotted her right away. It was Choi Il-Seong's job to be on the lookout for beautiful young girls, and this one was absolutely dazzling. She was sitting apart from the others, hands folded in her lap and long legs crossed, wearing some sort of old-fashioned western skirt that came to her ankles. Just stunning. Even so young, she must have emanated her own light.

They'd been selling their trinkets on the pier, lined up at the wharf like a gauntlet of buskers and peddlers. Jia was hawking charms and bracelets, things to pin on someone's cap, logoed hats and beanies displayed on a poster board that she held and waved at the passing sailors. Smiling. Batting those cat eyes. She'd been told by Sister Sarah to smile at the sailors. She was wearing her long dress, hair gathered into a bun. All of them were dressed in spinster shoes and braided hair. The police were waiting when Brother Caleb showed up driving his school bus to take the cult girls back to the orphanage. Jia watched them cuff his hands while he smiled and proffered his heavenly blessings on the police officers. A criminal benediction from His Holiness, the pope of thieves.

Jia was 16 years old and once again she was alone and had no one.

CHAPTER 24

Next day, the Korean civilian secretary at Bingham's office handed Profar his revised set of orders, formally assigning him to General Yardley's official security detail. When he walked in, Bingham was eating from a mess hall tray. With his mouth full, he pointed at a chair. There was music playing, AFN's Top 40 countdown, and Bingham stood chewing and turned the radio off.

"You look like you have questions," Bingham said. He wiped his mouth with a paper napkin. The place smelled like noodles.

Profar held up the papers. "I thought I was restricted."

Bingham said: "Per instruction from the G3. I know what the clinic said. This is just a paperwork thing. The old man himself mentioned you. You got a rave reviews about your English language abilities from those ROK officers you had in that class. Yardley found out and said he needs somebody to organize his JSA notes and write up reports that somebody can actually understand. This is his way of making sure nobody assigns you elsewhere. Said the last guy was illiterate and Yardley doesn't know how to type. So there you have it. You're the luckiest GI I know."

"What about the driving?"

"On-call," Bingham said. "For when they have a meeting with our North Korean friends. Perez put in a good word. And I vouched for you, for what it's worth."

"We just met," Profar said.

"You didn't flap your mouth," Bingham said. "The tube."

"The catheter?"

"Nobody needs to know about that."

"Everybody knows about the dick tube," Profar said.

***

The Joint Security Area T-2 conference building reminded Profar of the basement TV room at home in Duluth, where his mother groomed the nappy shag rug every Saturday with a garden rake.

She'd plugged in the new color Zenith console the night before he had to report to the Army recruiting center and he and his brother celebrated their new technology by watching the Johnny Carson Show. Profar stayed up late and drank beers on the patio, where his mom talked about World War Two. She got weepy and had a brief crying jag when she remembered how good his dad smelled in his uniform the day she kissed him goodby at the old train station on Freemont Avenue. She sipped her glass of wine with tears in her eyes and for the first time watched Profar light a cigarette without griping about the satanic evils of tobacco.

Today, the JSA walls and the yellowish fluorescent ceiling lights made the conference area feel gloomy and sad, like a bus station waiting room. The foam ceiling panels muffled every sound, so the place always seemed smaller than it really was.

There were far too many people in the room. Glum MPs, equally glum North Korean soldiers standing at attention, the armed ROK guards at the doorway wearing white gloves. The ceiling fans buzzed annoyingly. Everywhere you looked someone was writing on a notepad or pointing to a sheet of paper. The scuffed Linoleum floor was marked with cigarette burns. People were coughing, clearing their throats, and Yardley's translator seemed to be having trouble adjusting the General's headset and microphone. From outside, one of the Malinois guard dogs started barking and the North Korean officer who was Yardley's counterpart took long drags on his Soviet Laika cigarette. The giant hats the North Korean officers wore looked like bakery cake forms.

General Yardley walked noticeably stiff-legged from the men's room and winced when he took his seat at the table that divided the conference room in half. A white line split the table itself in two, as if prepped for some exotic variety of ping-pong. The North Koreans took their place opposite the row of American and ROK negotiators. Easels stood everywhere, each displaying maps and charts with arrows pointing to photos of the captured Navy ship, the USS Viator.

Yardley squinted over his reading glasses and nodded at Profar, who switched off the room lights. Somebody turned on the 8 mm film projector. The flickering image showed the ship's crew being marched past the bollards of their docked ship somewhere in Pyongyang. The sailors looked haggard, some with their arms in slings or wearing bandages. The film ended with a camera pan of a room packed with surveillance equipment and radar screens. The North Korean General switched on the light on his table pedestal, took a drag on his cigarette, and started shouting as he read from a red three-ring binder.

Profar flicked the lights on and crossed the room to his seat next to Perez, who watched Yardley gulp water while the North Korean officer carried on with his theatrics. The General adjusted his earpiece and shuffled papers and opened and closed a notebook embossed with the 8th Army logo. He covered his gooseneck microphone with one hand and said something to his G2 officer.

The USS Viator had been seized only days after North Korean infiltrators tried to assassinate the Korean President at his home in Seoul. One of the easels near Yardley displayed a poster with the headline, "North Korean Adventurism" and showed the dead communist assassins arranged side-by-side on a tarp.

By this time there had already been a dozen meetings to discuss the Viator incident and its imprisoned sailors. Today, the North Koreans presented the ship's navigational logs.

"The US must accept these facts," the North Korean General shouted, "They must apologize for its crimes and denounce them for the ears of the world. If you will sign this document, perhaps we can proceed with negotiations."

He handed a single sheet of paper to Yardley's G2 and leaned in his chair and folded his arms. The American General took another long drink.

"You are advised that the United States reserves the right to ask for compensation under international law," Yardley said as he peered over his glasses.

"...and that its vessel was captured in international waters well outside the recognized twelve-mile limit, and as such requires that your government return our property as well as apologize for your illegal action."

The North Korean General smirked. He looked over at one of his colleagues.

"A mad dog barks at the moon," he said. "This is what we say when such things are told with the disrespect that you now show. The hooligan Americans do not surprise me, and I disregard your age and your rank when I hear such things spoken by the American General. The American war maniac devil President Johnson, who worked for the criminal Kennedy who is now dead in hell, has mislead his people with these lies. This, of course, is typical of all capitalist dogs, so I am not surprised."

"I propose a recess while we study your document," Yardley said. He took another drink.

"I accept you request for recess," the North Korean General said. He stood and made a bee-line for the men's room while Yardley filled his large glass.

When they resumed, the North Korean officer squared his documents on the podium and glared at Yardley.

"And now on the important subject we must speak about again," the North Korean said and adjusted his wobbling mic.

"Let me remind you once again of what happened. At twelve-fifteen hundred hours on January 23 your Navy vessel committed the crude and aggressive act of illegally infiltrating into the coastal waters of our country an armed spy ship of the US imperialist aggressor that was equipped with war weapons and espionage tools. Our brave vessels returned the fire of your piratical gang of war sailors and spy criminals. Here we are, at the sixteenth meeting between our two sides and you have not admitted to anything. Not one thing. You have not signed. You have not agreed. You have only acted like stupid and ignorant people. To sign the documents that we have given you is the only basis for a settlement of this matter."

Yardley interrupted. He lifted his finger in a particularly lazy manner that he knew would annoy the North Korean General. "Did you know, sir, that according to your report that you yourself stated that the ship's log of our vessel indicated that the USS Viator was fixed at thirty-two miles inland? Thirty-two miles, sir. That's what you're claiming?"

The officer waved his hand dismissively and said, "Your comments are petty stratagems. They are not true. I will look into this matter."

"What I say is as true as rain. Look at the report. The proof is in the pudding," Yardley said. The North Korean General looked puzzled as he listened to the translation.

Yardley sipped from his glass, and said: "If there is nothing further, I recommend we end today's unproductive meeting and remind the Democratic People's Republic of Korea that it is the turn of the United States to request and convene the next session. You will be informed of our preference later this week. Thank you."

The General pulled at his trouser leg to make sure the urine bag and the Foley catheter were secured. He gathered his papers and nodded at Profar, who came and took the General's briefcase and walked ahead down the aisle behind one of the MPs, who cleared the way to the exit door. Outside, the General said a few words to one of the wire service reporters and posed for a *Stars and Stripes* photo beneath the T-2 building sign. The General called over Manny Perez and the two of them headed to the conference area restroom. Profar pulled the jeep into the narrow space between the two buildings in order to block the courtyard entrance and waited for the General and Perez to complete their business in the restroom.

CHAPTER 25

At the hooch, he stared at the wet blotches on the wallpapered ceiling where the rats were running back and forth like they were playing a relay game.

Profar could see where their feet shook the hanging light fixture. He wondered how big they were. Like rabbits, actually. That big. Like big fat bunny rabbits with long rat tails and big rat teeth with four-inch long whiskers. They were up there every night, not six feet from where he lay sleeping on the bed. If you thought about the rats too much it got very creepy, because you knew there were ways they could come down at night. Come down and chew your lips off if they wanted. He'd had food that went missing and he knew what stole it.

Lee said that if you didn't wash your hands or brush your teeth after you ate and then went to sleep, the rats would come up and lick whatever body parts smelled like food. If you had crumbs on your shirt, they'd eat the shirt. That was just Lee's bullshit, but it made you think.

While the roof rabbits competed for track and field trophies, Profar had the idle memory of watching Flash Gordon on TV when he was a kid. Lee was sitting reading a paperback with his feet propped on a chair. His cigarette burned in a tea cup saucer. The hooch door was open because the heated floor was making everything too hot, so Profar peeled off the green sweater his mother had sent him from Duluth. The ugliest sweater he'd ever seen, but he felt bad that she'd worked so hard on it, so he wore it out of guilt and loyalty. It was pretty warm, though.

"I liked the Clay People," Profar said.

Lee didn't look away from his book, which was titled, *I've Been Down So Long It Looks Like Up To Me*. He said his favorite Flash Gordon character was Ming the Merciless.

"Emperor of Mongo," he said. "One tough son of a bitch. Loved the eyebrows."

"He lusted after Flash's girl, the lovely Dale Arden," Profar said.

"Ah, the shapely Dale Arden in those rodeo boots," Lee said.

The rats seemed to have bunched up at the far end of the ceiling and he could see the thin plywood visibly bend from their combined weight. He heard their squeaks. Profar imagined them gathered together in the dark of the ceiling, deciding what game to play next. What the rules would be, what coveted prize should be awarded. He decided that if he were a rat, that's where he would live. In the space beneath the corrugated sheets that covered all the hooches, where it was warm and safe, not ten feet from a reliable food source. From Profar's ceiling, it wasn't that far to the kitchen at the Water Dragon Club.

The Clay People could melt into the stone walls of their caves to escape their enemies. They were kind and gentle and never bothered anybody. Profar told Lee that he pretended to dissolve into the dining room wall at home when he was a kid, just like the clay people. His mom said he was nuts, though she'd made his Flash Gordon Halloween costume from a pair of long underwear.

"Flash's gun didn't shoot far," Lee said, flipping a page in his book.

"It spit," Profar said. "The bullets spit two feet. I never believed that part. I didn't believe the space ships, either. You could see the string. Seemed like they were made from the same tinfoil my mom wrapped my lunch in."

"Dale had a nice ass," Lee said. "Even for back in the day, it was nice."

The rats started walking around aimlessly across the ceiling and their squeaking sounded louder, like they were upset about something. Kind of cute, the squeaks, but if you remembered they were fat ugly rats who ate trash from the stinking garbage barrel out in the alley, it sounded sinister. Maybe they were plotting something for later. Profar hoped he wouldn't have to use the outhouse squat toilet in the middle of the night. The rats hung out in the byeonso.

Profar wondered about the tiger in the DMZ, patrolling its territory. One of the ambush patrols had found the half-eaten carcass of a wild boar floating in the river and everybody figured a bear had killed it. Profar didn't think so.

"Sooner or later we have to say something to somebody," Profar said.

Lee closed his book and listened to the scrabbling claw sounds as the rats charged across the ceiling like some rodent cavalry.

"I suppose we do," he said.

"We might get shit because we waited this long," Profar said.

"They'd give us shit no matter what we did," Lee said.

Somebody swung open the alley door and they sat up straight and stared at the flickering police lights. There was a ruckus of stomping boots and shouting. When they reached the alley, a standing crowd of GIs and bar girls were staring somberly toward the Water Dragon Club's rear entrance.

The dead body sat propped up against a brick wall next to one of the communal byeonsos. She was wearing a single unlaced white sneaker on the wrong foot as if the killer might have done something as a hurried afterthought. Or a cruel joke. Lee recognized her as Mae Wong, a new girl in the club who'd been learning the ropes as a drink hostess. He said she'd been recruited by Choi from Daegu and went by the working name of Tammy, one of a half dozen other Tammys employed at the Water Dragon Club.

Her short black hair was neatly teased into a tight bouffant and she wore a black velvet choke collar fastened with a rhinestone clasp that now shone brightly in the gleam of the flashing police lights. But for the broken bottle of OB beer that had been jammed halfway into her mouth, her alert open eyes made it appear as if she were studying the handle of the twelve-inch Army K-bar blade that protruded dead center from her crotch. Her other shoe lay a few feet away next to Mae Wong's sparkly white clutch purse, the kind of dainty costume accessory somebody would wear to a high school prom. The purse was open and a lipstick and a makeup mirror had fallen out. On the black alley stones lay a pink hair barrette. Someone had crushed a burning cigarette onto the middle of Mae Wong's forehead. Like she'd been cruelly anointed. The half-moon imprint of a large shoe heel was clearly visible on her bruised and bloody cheek.

Two MPs with twelve-gauge riot shotguns slung across their backs were stretching yellow barrier tape across the alley and a KNP officer held out his arms as he tried to haze away a group of screaming girls who'd been trying to get closer to Mae Wong's body. More angry bar girls were shouting and waving at a row of Korean police with batons who stood guard behind the yellow barrier tape.

Two plainclothes Korean detectives stepped out from the club's alley door escorting a handcuffed GI dressed in civies and wearing sunglasses. The front of the soldier's shirt was torn and he appeared to be staggering drunk. He was blabbering something, then started laughing hysterically. As they shoved him toward the armored police wagon, the GI looked at where they'd stretched Mae Wong out on a gurney sheet and he started crying and shouting out her formal Korean name. Shouting like he was apologizing for something, pleading perhaps, but doing it in such a crazed manner that you knew there must be much more to the story.

They loaded the dead girl into the ambulance and the vehicle seemed to be in no hurry as it crept down the dark alley with its red tail lights blinking.

Lee walked up to a group of girls and asked them a question but they turned and folded their arms as if on cue and walked away.

"What's with that?" Profar said when they were back inside the hooch.

"I don't think they feel warm and fuzzy about us people right now. About GIs," he said. "Tammy was a very sweet girl."

CHAPTER 26

The mamasan was standing in the courtyard at a large butcher block table next to the communal water faucet. Profar lifted his hand in greeting, but she ignored him.

The beef hindquarter lay on a plank that was covered with a towel. She raised the cleaver above her head and swung it down on the raw meat with surprising force and speed. She did this again and again in quick succession, sometimes trimming things expertly with a filet knife, until she had the stacks of butchered flank and hip and tenderloin cuts neatly separated and set aside in a plastic basin filled with ice. She covered the basin with another towel and stood there and wiped her hands. The mamasan stropped the enormous cleaver against her leather apron, sharpening it further on a whetstone as she glared icily at Profar and stepped out into the alley.

He'd expected something altogether different when he walked into Choi's office. The place seemed too tidy. There was the western sofa with its puffy feminine pillows. The fake leather recliner positioned beside a Philco console TV on which sat English and Korean language newspapers. *Life Magazine* with Jane Fonda dressed in a leather pantsuit on the front cover. Two stereo speakers were mounted on shelves at opposite corners of the ceiling and there were framed tourist photos of the Empire State Building and the Golden Gate Bridge hanging above one another on the wall behind Choi's lacquered desk. A coffee table book about Disneyland lay on a side table that held an oddly lifelike Japanese Geisha doll lamp stand. There was a breakfast nook with a fridge and a four-slice toaster straight out of Ozzie & Harriet's TV kitchen.

Choi sat relaxed with a green banker's lamp at his elbow and an abacus and hand-cranked adding machine side-by-side as if meant to confirm each other's calculations. He stepped from behind the desk and shook a smoke from a pack of American cigarettes. The wall safe and its locked brass cage was something from the Nineteenth Century. It didn't surprise Profar that the chain and pendant behind Choi's shirt collar was gold. Shiny pimp jewelry. And there was the pimp ring, too. All properly pimpy, this bordello honcho in his red room where one entire wall was hung with citations and an award of from the American Korean Chamber of Commerce. No pictures of people.

Choi offered Eddie Profar a chair.

"Tell me something about yourself," the pimp said as if this was a job interview.

Profar remained standing. His ribs ached. He tried to straighten up.

"I don't see how it matters. If I sit," he said.

"As you wish," Choi said. "Tell me what state you are from. I've traveled in your country.

"Minnesota."

"Very difficult to pronounce. Like Mississippi and Connecticut," Choi said.

"Is that right," Profar said.

Yevgeny Lee, the oracle of village gossip, said that Choi had spent time stateside in a student exchange program that offered Korean nationals a two-year junior college scholarship. He'd lived with an Army officer's family somewhere in Indiana where the military trained its accountants.

"Can I ask your rank?" Choi said. Profar told him he was an E4.

"If you were a Corporal you would have said so. You must be a Specialist. A clerical rank, no?"

Profar said, "I'm not a clerk. I just spent three months in a hospital because I got blown up by a land mine. I'm not a clerk."

Choi gave a twisted smile. "I was told that you are a driver. For the division commander, of all people. The General himself. A privileged position for a clerk."

"If you say so," Profar said. "What's that got to do with anything?"

"Because you are the one who asked to see me," Choi said. "I like to know who I'm talking to. I wasn't aware of your existence until Mrs. Yoshida told me you wanted an appointment. You are a tenant, a customer...so it's only polite that I see you. The soldiers here don't ordinarily ask to speak with me. That, and because you are the General's driver, so there is some courtesy involved."

"Courtesy?" Profar said.

"And yet you stand here and speak with a tone that some would consider to be rude," Choi said. "Are you a rude clerk, Specialist Profar? You are in my country and in my workplace and I see before me a very young man who seems impatient, although it is my time that is being used. The time of a businessman. I have business to do, I hope you understand."

"It's about Miss Kim," Profar began. "And I know all about what kind of business you're involved in."

"In my culture it is proper to use the formal name when speaking of someone in the third person, did you know that?"

"I didn't," Profar said.

"If you throw a stone from a hill in Korea chances are it will strike a Kim a Lee or a Park, did you also not know that? Exactly which *Miss Kim* do you refer to? I have many Kims in my employment. Can I ask your age?"

"How old I am doesn't matter," Profar said.

"So, you do not know her true name."

"I know her name. It's Jia," Profar said.

"Her proper name that should be spoken in the proper way. She is Kim Jia-Soon. Now you know. Mrs. Yoshida informed me of your concerns."

"I'll keep that in mind," Profar said. "About how to say somebody's name."

"How can I help you today?" Choi said. He tugged at the sleeve of his white shirt and glanced at his watch.

"I want to do Miss Kim, Kim Jia-Soon...a favor without her knowing about it," Profar said. "She owes money. They all owe you money."

"They? More insults," Choi said and looked away and flicked something off the corner of his neatly organized desk with one finger. "The Specialist E4 chauffeur clerk warrior has more insults."

"I'd like to pay her rent for a month," Profar said. "I know you made her move from her other place and I know all about Remo and that he stopped paying her yeobo fees and everything."

"And everything. What would that mean? Everything," Choi said.

"The marriage school classes," Profar said. He tried to not scratch where the wound on his belly itched like crazy. He felt the bandage around his ribs start to slide down his chest. He was sweating.

"There's the paperwork fees," he said. "Remo's other fees. I'm told he promised to cash out her debt. And now he backed off and she's broke. That's what I wanted to talk about. I'd like to help her out."

"Is there anything else of such a private nature that you wish to know about me, Specialist Profar? Such a bold presumption from the young chauffeur. That he would expect me to share business details with a stranger. He insults me in my own office about sensitive employee matters and claims he knows everything. You know nothing. Your friend, the soldier Remo, he also knows nothing. None of you know anything of what happens here. It is illegal in my country to hold an employee in debt apart from a legitimate business reimbursement, you should know that. And it is illegal for a foreigner to become involved in any promissory agreement, regardless of it satisfying such a debt or not."

Profar said. "I just want to do her a favor, is all."

There was a clamor outside followed by shouting and the clatter of pots and pans dropping in the alley. Choi bounced from his chair and leaned out the door. The room was overheated and Profar guessed they still had the charcoal floor warmer blasting, so the brief gust of cool air was a relief. He was starting to feel sick. Choi chattered something in that guttural, hissing way Koreans had when they were very pissed off. A woman's voice answered softly. Apologies seemed to be spoken and more murmured voices came from the alley. He thought he recognized the mamasan's voice. Choi mumbled to himself as he stepped behind his desk and pulled down the sleeves of his white shirt. The gold chain flickered in the light and he pushed the jewelry aside and smiled.

"What brings on this sudden interest in my employee Kim Jia-Soon? I've known her since she was a child, so perhaps I may be sentimental toward her. Protective, you might say. Can I assume you would like your own arrangement? To be her yeobo, perhaps? Just ask her. She knows the procedure quite well. She is a professional. This is no secret and it's all very proper and legal and sanctioned by the authorities. But you must know this or you would not be here. I sense that you have, as they say in your country, done your homework."

"I'm not interested in the yeobo thing," Profar said. "It's just doing a favor. There are a few of us who want to do her a favor until she gets on her feet and so I'd like to know what it would cost. One month. What would that cost to buy her some time?"

Choi rolled his eyes. "Now, you are a liar. A lying young naive clerk Specialist. But that's not my concern. If you wish to be her hero, a hero to someone who would have sex of every imaginable description with a depraved street vagrant if such a vagrant possessed twenty American dollars, that is your concern. It is not my concern. The answer is no."

"I didn't ask the question yet," Profar said.

"I know the question. You are not the first to ask it. You think you are, but you are not."

Choi wrote on a pad of paper and shoved this across the desk for Profar to read.

He smoothed the front of his shirt with his hand and stood. He faced the wall photo of the Grand Canyon as if searching for inspiration. As if preparing for a lengthy and serious speech. He stepped to the sofa and sat, and though Profar now wished he could also get off his feet he instead leaned against the wall and read the note. His chest ached and everything seemed to itch all at once. He was starting to sweat like crazy and he knew Choi had noticed. He hoped he wouldn't get dizzy and keel over. His stomach churned.

"That's how much it would cost?" he said. "You're out of your fucking mind."

"Such language from the young American clerk soldier," Choi said and wagged his finger.

"Specialist Profar," he said. "I've always known that out there, out beyond that door where you and thirty-five thousand American soldiers do their work...that there really exists no actual military. Not in the true sense of the word. Not in the common military sense. Only a very small number of you are actual soldiers who carry and shoot their weapons. You carry pens and use typewriters and place sheets of paper in file cabinets. You are retail shoppers of merchandise, a garrison of buyers of curios and drugs and embroidered silk jackets and of course the services of whores. Always the whores. Simple-minded young bordello patrons and fornicators of limited taste and discretion is what you really are. But you are not a military force. You are all sex buyers extraordinaire and cheap wine drinkers and spoiled teenagers who carouse madly while their one million North Korean colleagues remain quite serious and alert about their duties not two miles beyond a barrier that only has the stopping power of a backyard fence. Do you actually think the young North Koreans behave as you do? With the same privilege and depravity? Do you think the North Korean soldier goes on leave in Tokyo or Bangkok? He does not. Where we are now, in this province alone, ten-thousand sex workers have been registered each year since nineteen-fifty-three. Each woman has been told that it is her patriotic duty to do what she does, which is to boost morale of the US soldiers. To boost your morale, Specialist Profar."

Choi brushed something from the top of his shoe and inspected his hand. "What I see in this country, Specialist Profar, is a political chess game, nothing more. A commercial trade agreement legitimized by your own government's Mutual Defense Treaty that was signed when the armistice was signed. I have never myself seen a real American Army other than those who fought and died in the true war long ago. The great invasion route not far from here, through which Mongols and the Japanese once traveled to occupy my country, is now a place where American men play baseball and sit at tables making pottery to pass the time. They play volleyball like women. They collect souvenirs to send home to their wives while they sleep with their yeobos and sell PX blue jeans at great profit to our street thieves."

Choi watched Profar stretch and reposition himself. He suggested once again that he sit down, but Profar shrugged.

"I was younger than you when the war began," Choi said. "Though my family was from the South, I was conscripted one day while walking down the street in Jingae. I felt I was twice your age when the war ended three years later because of what I witnessed. Much of my family remained trapped in the North. I doubt if I will see any of them again. They may have died, I don't know. We Koreans are accustomed to uncertainty. We have a strong belief in fate. That first summer when your B29s dropped bombs on a ship filled with refugees in Yeosu harbor, that is when I knew it was no longer possible for me to be a young man. Or to put my faith in governments. Our own leaders, Rhee himself included, murdered their own people. Soldiers from the North executed us, as did those from the South. Destroyed thousands of peasant refugees as if they were insects. Innocent people who didn't know the difference between a communist and a cow. This is when all the young people in this country ceased to be children.

"I can go on, of course, with my history lesson. I had not planned to talk so much. I sense that you now look down your western nose at me. I should explain that the entertainment business arrangement we enjoy here—the clubs, the girls, businessmen like myself, that it was entirely created by your military. You can read the official agreements yourself. Were it not for this establishment here, these girls and myself, the entire country would be swallowed in poverty. But that's not why you came here, for a political lesson, although I am happy to help with your education. A Colonel, the commander of an entire regiment, once asked the same question you are about to ask, so go on. Let the file clerk ask his question."

"When this Colonel asked, did you answer?" Profar said.

"Money was the answer, of course, and now you also have a number," Choi said and tipped his head as if remembering something. "Do you know what GDP is, Specialist Profar?"

"You're changing the subject again."

"It's all the same subject," Choi said and spread his arms. "The girl Kim Jia-Soon, this entire village, the Army and this divided country, yourself, it's all the same subject. They are indistinguishable, you understand? What you see here...not just myself and my employees, but thousands more up along the road from here to Seoul, this represents three percent of the entire Gross Domestic Product—the monetary value of the goods and services, of this entire nation. This service we provide, this export of a natural resource, is all we have since the war ended. It is our national treasure. These young women. Since two million civilians were killed in the war and all of our industry destroyed, this has been our cash crop, so to speak. As important as rice. Or fish from the sea. This business of entertainment workers and the service they provide for the pleasure of your gallant United States Army."

"When you talk about money. You mean the kind of money Remo has," Profar said. "The Colonel you talk about didn't have his kind of money, did he?"

"Of course not," Choi said.

"This is more than you told Remo," Profar said. "Not even that rich son of a bitch has that kind of cash. He wouldn't be allowed to make a transaction like that as a soldier and he sure couldn't cash the check in this country. You're bullshitting me. You wouldn't have let her go. It's all smoke and mirrors."

"Apparently you are correct," Choi said. "For I have already been so informed by the soldier Remo himself. He says that he can no longer pay the required fees. We shook hands."

"Does Jia know any of this?"

"She will learn everything in time," Choi said. "It is not my role to counsel her about personal money matters. She has a long-standing legal debt to repay and a contract to honor and that is all I can concern myself with. Contracts are taken seriously in this country, especially this one. In any case, your gesture of charity would change nothing. She would be the first to say this. I have known Kim Jia-Soon for a very long time. She is a realist. All Koreans who survived the war are realists. I think I have already told you too much."

As if it had been an afterthought, Choi turned in his chair and looked at the photo of Disneyland hanging on the wall. "No Korean could have dreamed up such a fantasy. Only Americans are capable of inventing such an impractical fairyland world. Take Vietnam."

"I'm not here to talk about Vietnam," Profar said.

"You are also fighting that war because of your fantasies," Choi said. "And you are losing to a former pastry chef and his self-taught amateur military commander. The same former grammar school teacher who defeated the French. The Viet Cong, unlike the Americans, are not burdened by fantasies."

"You never answered my question," Profar said. "You won't ever let her go, will you?"

Choi did not answer. He leaned and pointed at the photo of the Disneyland castle.

"Americans live in a world of magic fairies and heroes on horseback who rescue innocent people from harm. To you people, all of life is black-and-white, good and evil. Nothing is gray. And here I am in a room with one of those heroes preparing to rescue another damsel in distress. Do you understand?"

"What I understand is that you don't have employees. You have merchandise. Like slaves. Jia is your merchandise. Just like the stuff in this room that came straight from the PX in Yongsan. All of it goods traded for more goods."

"Three percent of GDP, Specialist Edward Profar. Three percent," Choi said. "You speak as if I am the only villain in your fairytale. As if I thought up this entire system by myself, when it was your own government that devised everything. You think I am the pimp, however it is Washington, DC where the pimping begins. The one wearing the black hat is not me. The entire republic of Korea participates in this commercial enterprise. As does the KNP. Along with your military. As I said, your soldiers are not soldiers. They are consumers of regulated and carefully priced merchandise. Only a very few truly protect us. The others only buy the services of whores and count the days until they will return home."

Choi lifted the granite ashtray on his desk and held it at eye level. "Every stone has a violent past," he said. "It's a saying my father once told me. In this country we are accustomed to things that are unfair and brutal. We have learned never to be surprised. When the Japanese were driven from our land we were not surprised when the Americans came, which promised more of the same. Just another occupier, you see? And it is you, Specialist Profar, and people like you who continue to do this."

"I don't know what you're talking about."

"I am not talking about stones, Specialist Clerk Profar," Choi said. "As far as your damsel is concerned, she must continue her life here as it is. All will remain the same. This is without question. She knows this and she will not be surprised. Koreans know how to embrace their fate. Do you know of Nietzsche, Specialist Profar?"

"Who?"

"The philosopher," Choi said and waved his hand dismissively. "It doesn't matter. Your effort, though you believe it to be noble, will only bring the damsel trouble and you will be to blame for what might happen next. Stop meddling, Specialist Profar. Your own country has already done enough meddling in our affairs."

"I'm not finished with this," Profar said.

"Again, I am not surprised," Choi said. "You are a dog pulling on a toy. You will never get the toy, do you understand? This toy never belonged to you and it is I who have always owned it. We are just playing a silly game here."

Through Choi's open doorway Profar could see the rain falling through sunshine, rainbow weather.

The pimp kept talking. He spoke of Korea's history, how the 38th parallel itself was like a fissure in a bone, separating families forever because a clerk just like Profar had once decided it must be so. He said this rupture of Korean genealogy would take centuries to repair. Choi's own grandmother, he said, had told him she would one day meet him in the world of the dead after the Americans were finally gone.

"Take your own civil war," Choi said. "Kinsmen, brother fighting against brother. It is the same with us. Your politicians in Washington, sitting at a table with a map, did this when they separated our country with a pencil line, like someone cutting a loaf of bread and with as much thought. Do you understand at all what I've been telling you? Have I wasted my time?"

"You're just screwing around with me."

Choi shook his head sadly: "Of course you do not. And this is a problem. You do not understand that we are one nation and two states. We are two unfinished nations made so by an unfinished war that has turned us into incomplete human beings. Jia, your damsel, is herself unfinished and you would like to make her whole and complete. A noble cause, of course, but this is impossible. You are trying to be a gallant and improbable savior just as your country tried to be a humanitarian when it said it was saving Korea from itself after the world war. You thought the Japanese were the villains, but you yourself were villains of a different stripe. And now you come here to beg for Jia's freedom as if she lived in a jail. As if I were her jailer and had the power to bequeath such freedom."

"You do," Profar said. "And she's in jail."

Choi tore a sheet of paper from the accounting journal on his desk and crumpled it into a ball. He lit the paper with his Zippo and watched the flame catch and rise into white smoke.

"*Soji*," Choi said. "Do you know what that word means, Specialist Eddie? It's not the name of the liquor you drink at my club."

Choi didn't wait for Profar's answer. "*Soji* is the burning of paper on which the names of spirits are written. In this case the spirits of family members. There are three million pieces of *soji* paper in our recent history. Three million dead. As you Americans say, you are in water over your head. Go home when your tour here is over. Go to Minnesota. What a wonderful sounding name that is. Think what you will, I actually thank you for your service because you are a naive and innocent boy. But do not meddle further into what does not concern you. Abandon your quest, Specialist Clerk Profar. No good will come of it. What you consider to be love is actually an affliction. A disease for which there is often no cure."

CHAPTER 27

Next night at the Water Dragon Club they had one of their special shows.

Sometimes, it was a new band or a famously nimble stripper from one of the city clubs in Itaewon. There were jugglers and acrobats, Jiu Jitsu demonstrations. Once, a female sword swallower. They'd recently brought a woman from Osan who arrived wearing a *hanbok* dress, her hair bound up in the old courtesan style, and she played music on a pear-shaped Korean lute. After the performance, during which she recited Joseon Dynasty poetry, she took off her little slipper and passed it around for tips. When the GIs started pawing at her fancy dress, her ornate belt came undone and she grabbed her lute and stumbled screaming out the alley door.

Tonight's act was a magician who performed illusions like catching a live 5.65 mm bullet in his teeth and the standard guillotine stunt in which he'd call up a club girl as a volunteer and slice her in half with a samurai sword. The magician wore a tuxedo and a top hat. The Table of Death, the old needle-through-the-arm routine, several impalement stunts and a levitation trick were part of his repertoire.

Manny Perez was sitting at the bar drinking Soju while the magician set up his gear on the stage behind the dance floor. Lee and Profar joined him and turned their stools. There was sparse applause when the recorded intro music started playing and then a single spotlight turned on and the magician doffed his hat and walked onstage into a pool of light.

Perez raised his glass and pointed. "This was before you fellas got here, but last year this guy tried something new," he said. "Brought a monkey. One of those little organ grinder monkeys. Had it dressed in a bow tie and a diaper. Cute little shoes on his feet. The fur on his head was combed and parted in the middle, like he'd used Brylcreem. The monkey kept scratching his nuts and smiling at the audience. I remember those little pointy teeth. I learned later that when a monkey scratches its balls it's mad at you."

"I do that when somebody's bullshitting me," Lee said and pawed his crotch.

A strong soup smell drifted from the kitchen. Lee waved to one of the girls as she walked across the dance floor carrying her tray of drinks. She threw him a kiss and handed a beer to the magician. The club was packed and noisy as usual and though the ceiling glitter ball wasn't spinning it had caught the spotlight's beam and so the entire dance floor was covered in polka dots.

Perez said: "So, the monkey's job was to bring out props for the magician, like a little assistant. He wore a top hat. He carried this little wand that he kept trying to chew. And the whole time he's scratching himself like crazy. So, the magician was getting ready to release one of those white doves from a silver pan when the monkey all of a sudden jumps off the stage and hops on the bar and starts running back and forth. He's screaming the whole time with his hands up in the air, like he's pissed off about something. He grabs peanuts from a bowl and knocks somebody's drink from their hand. Guys tried to catch him, but that little bastard was pretty light on his feet. Then the monkey stops and stares at the backbar shelf where they keep the pricey booze. The good stuff nobody can afford. For some reason, there's a pile of condoms sitting up there and the next thing you know the monkey's tearing open a pack of military-issue Trojans with his teeth. He waves the thing in the air, pulls it over his head like it's a swim cap. His hair is greased up good, so he yanks the Trojan down over his eyes, then his nose and then snaps it over the bottom of his little chin and sits there like it just dawned on him what a dumbass thing he'd just done. His face is squished flat inside the condom like a bank robber with a nylon stocking over his head. He tries to open his mouth and scream, but no dice. You could hear the little squeaky monkey voice. It was awful to look at, let me tell you. He's trying to scream and he somersaults and starts clawing at his face with both hands, clawing away at it, all the time twisting and flopping around on the floor. He starts to wet his diaper. Then he shits. He's never getting that thing off, that's for sure. So he goes batshit crazy and now he's really scratching his nuts and he runs around with his arms held over his head, all the time squeaking in that monkey voice, until he finally jumps back onto the stage, grabs his throat with both hands and just keels over and drops dead right in the middle of the spotlight like this was a part of the magician's act the whole time.

"Well, everybody in the club went quiet. You could hear a pin drop. A few of the guys clapped. The magician just walked over and grabbed the monkey by the tail and carried him off behind the curtain and came out and started the show like nothing had happened. Didn't say a word."

Lee tipped forward and snorted into his hand. He dropped his forehead onto the bar top, bumped it up and down, and started laughing. Profar just grinned and swigged his soda water while Perez raised his Soju in a toast.

"Rest in peace, little fella," he said. "The show must go on."

Profar finished his drink and went to the hooch and dozed off while he read a book. When he woke he smelled something cooking outside.

He watched her through the half-drawn paper window shade as she squatted next to the hotplate on her porch and poured something from a pot she'd filled from the courtyard faucet. He could hear water boiling. She stirred it with a wooden spoon and sat on her heels and watched the steam rise in the cool of the night. She pulled a blanket around herself with one hand. Her long black hair flowed from her wool cap down across one shoulder and when she looked up at the night sky Profar saw she was crying. Her face was shiny. Her bare knees were pressed together and she seemed pale and ghostly in the glow of the courtyard lamp. He was surprised that he hadn't seen her selling drinks at the club that night. Profar wondered if she was thinking about Remo. Or anybody else at all. They had officially canceled all yeobo marriage classes at camp because of Cobb's death, and he knew that even if they started up again that Jia would not have time to finish the mandatory course. She couldn't pay for anything, anyway. Without the classes, no matter what Remo would have done, she could not get the waiver for her papers to leave Korea for America. It would take a bureaucratic miracle, a magical windfall of perfectly aligned paperwork signed by the right people.

She stood with the blanket draped like a cape across her shoulders and began to sweep the porch steps. Profar stood away from the window. He felt like an idiot, spying like this.

He stepped outside and tried to look surprised. She fastened her robe and smiled. A demure, shy grin with her eyes downcast.

"Big rain maybe tonight," he said and she looked at the sky like she knew he'd had no idea what to say to her.

"You go on duty?" she said.

He sat and laced his shoes. "Not on the fence. At least for now," he said.

"Helelleh, he say you still sick," she said. "He tell me about how you both get bombed. We all worried you was dead, you and Helelleh."

Her glowing smile seemed to reach beyond her face. She was so beautiful standing there in her ratty robe, long tangled hair clipped in place with a single barrette. She clutched the robe with one hand, her painted fingernails chipped, and she stepped closer. She smelled faintly of whatever noodles she'd been cooking.

"I see light on when I come home," she said.

"Couldn't sleep," Profar said. "I'm like an old man, everything hurts. And those guys who run across the roof." He fluttered his fingers. "The rats," he said.

She laughed. "Jwi," she said. "Imo, she always try to kill with poison. Always they come back. Too many jwi in this place."

"Mrs. Yoshida should get a cat," Profar said.

Jia shook her head and came closer, "Imo, she don't like the cats."

"Either do the jwi," Profar said. "That's kind of the point of having a cat."

"She from old Korea times," Jia said. "Old time people from war days say cat is taksan bad luck. You own cat and nothing ever be lucky in life."

He scooted over and she sat next to him on the porch steps and when their knees touched she moved aside and stared at where her pot sat steaming. Her necklace caught the light and sparkled against her skin.

"You know Remo, yes?"

Here it comes, he thought. He nodded.

"We're not pals."

She looked away and crossed her arms. "You tell him Jia ask one more time that he please come to village, okay? A favor for me, okay? He will know why I ask."

"Sure. I'll do that."

That night the rain drummed against the doors of the hooch. He watched her go to work dressed in her bar clothes. She held a poncho over her head and ran in her heels across the courtyard. The club closed early because it was the middle of the week. When she came back she helped the mamasan carry a basket of laundry to the old ringer machine. He watched them talk and remembered that Lee told him they spoke in the same country dialect. Farm girls, both of them, though Mrs. Yoshida's mixed Korean and Japanese family had been prosperous rice merchants since before World War Two.

While they stood under the porch awning Jia wiped her eye like she was crying. The rain pounded the corrugated roof and Profar thought the mamasan didn't at all seem sympathetic to whatever was troubling Jia. Instead, she turned away and started loading laundry into the round barrel of the courtyard washing machine.

Profar couldn't sleep because of his back. His leg was going numb again. The damp cold didn't help, and so he tried stretching himself flat on the warm tile floor. The heat from the *ondol* felt good. Jia's lights stayed on for most of the night. She came outside once wearing the robe again and stood holding an umbrella, looking up at the rain. She smoked a cigarette. In the glowing lamplight, even her shadow seemed beautiful.

He listened to the rattle of claws against the ceiling, like someone had spilled a bag of frozen peas. The animals would occasionally stop and fight and squeal and then resume their aimless running. It went like this all night long. Those rats were always in hurry. He hardly slept.

"Jwi," he said out loud and tried to remember how her voice sounded when she'd said it. "Jwi."

Lee hated the rats. He just knew they'd come down one night and chew on his toes. He'd heard of such things happening in the winter during the war when soldiers slept outside in the ruins of a village. Profar had only once seen a rat. It was long and lean and gray and he'd caught it sniffing an empty bowl on the table where they ate. It rose on its hind feet and stared at Profar and ran straight up the wall into a hole he never knew was there. Ran up like it had suckers on its feet.

He fell asleep thinking about the North Korean soldiers who lay dead and rotting in the tunnel and he wondered if the tiger had ever returned to feed. The dead soldiers were from the North, but he still felt bad for them.

CHAPTER 28

The typed note said to report to the east gate motor pool where a drowsy Corporal behind the wire cage handed him the keys to one of General Yardley's three official vehicles, this one a shiny late model jeep with a new canvas rag top and intact seat cushions.

The other vehicle Profar usually drove to Panmunjom was a standard Ford quarter-ton rig with the M60 swivel mount in front of the jump seat nobody ever used. The old man liked to present a gritty infantry persona in front of his well tailored North Korean counterparts, so he often opted for a topless standard issue patrol jeep instead of the new M151 Profar now drove off the motor pool parking lot. Yardley liked to wear his field fatigues and camo helmet to the Joint Security Area until the US Ambassador complained that he looked too much like a common eleven-bravo ground pounder instead of the international diplomat he was now supposed to be. The captured boat and General Yardley were front page news around the world. Reuters, UPI and AP had made him a celebrity. He received teletype messages each morning from the White House.

Today, Profar wasn't driving the General to the JSA.

This time Yardley was wearing his standard Class A uniform, seven rows of chest salad on display above his left jacket pocket as they drove to the camp USO recreation center, where a mandatory assembly had been announced concerning an "important mission topic."

MPs stood guard at the entrance. The General's silver paratrooper badge sparkled as he stepped behind the speaker's podium. He shuffled his notes, put on his reading glasses. He adjusted the combat infantry badge pinned above his rows of award ribbons. Among his decorations, the Silver Star he received for valor as a platoon First Lieutenant at the Battle of Desolation Ridge in the Mundung-ni Valley during the Korean War. From the back of the room where Profar sat, Yardley's two shoulder stars twinkled in the stage lights.

Yardley flashed his trademark Teddy Roosevelt grin and folded his hands before him like a church preacher ready to spew fire and brimstone to his flock. He nodded to somebody in the front row and shuffled his notes.

"Gentlemen, gentlemen," he said as the room darkened. He pointed at the large projection screen on the wall behind him.

"Let me get to the point. Hell, I won't even tell a joke, although you might think what I'm about to discuss is worth a laugh. I assure you this is not the case at all. I'm here to speak about serious business that affects each of you."

The Kodachrome slide of a sandbagged DMZ outpost surrounded by coils of barbed wire appeared on the screen. The image dissolved into a closeup of a soldier taking aim across the 38th Parallel buffer zone with his M14 rifle. The General turned, and with his clicker device quickly cycled through a series of other photos that showed American soldiers in various modes of combat. Shots of mortar blasts. The swinging legs of a low-flying Huey helicopter door gunner above the Imjin River. The final wide-angle shot of dead North Korean infiltrators and their captured arsenal displayed like a battlefield still life.

"These, as you all know, are the familiar images of what continues to be a slow-burning conflict here in South Korea," he said. "We are still at war, as you've noticed. The enemy continues to kill our men. He continues to infiltrate and murder. A communist agent brutally assassinated one of our own NCOs just recently. It's been busy here. With the conflict in Vietnam, those people in the North think they can catch us with our shorts down. They think we're not paying attention. There are many foes, many forms of the enemy in a war, and they come in various shapes. It's no different up here on the DMZ."

The room was dark but for the red emergency exit lights at either end of the stage where Yardley, now illuminated by a single spotlight, raised his hand in a flourish and pointed at the screen.

"Gentlemen, meet another enemy," he said with a little extra vinegar in his voice.

At first, the color illustration of the fifteen-foot-long penis, rendered in spectacular medical detail, resembled a pale, eel-like sea creature hanging upside down from a hook. A fisherman's catch at a boat dock weight scale in Key West, perhaps. A new species of finless shark with the mouth of a sea lamprey. Maybe a dolphin without flippers or an alien space creature. There was an audible groan from the audience, along with nervous chuckling and side glances, and then a slow crescendo of snickering that soon turned into laughter and loud applause. Yardley himself seemed surprised by the clapping. He raised and lowered his arms and asked for silence.

Her looked at the screen. "Now, now. Please, please," he said. "I thought that would get your attention. That's some pizzle, am I right? An all-American love hose in its complete and utterly naked and honest glory, a splendor to be proud of. Something..." and now the General lowered his voice and growled.

"Something to protect at all cost," he said.

"Did you hear me? Are you looking at this? This, your fine American love pipe. The future fruit of our glorious nation and that which should not lightly be plucked from the tree of life. Gentlemen, this whale of a penis on the screen behind me is the golden wellspring of your progeny, the seed-maker of future generations of Americans. Your sons and daughters. Those you now risk your life for. Gentlemen, the United States Army did not send your young healthy asses six thousand miles across the sea just so you could endanger God's good work. Are you listening to me? This is the Lord's precious and perfectly engineered manhood. The blessed and healthy American treasure that swings gloriously on every gallant warrior in this room."

They now applauded mightily. They whistled, some of the soldiers standing with fists raised and shouting out their agreement, and then they clapped and whistled louder as Yardley clicked his clicker and pointed.

It was a photo of the giant billboard sign that every soldier at camp walked past each day:"Danger! You Are Now Entering a Venereal Disease Zone!"

"You are all familiar with this, I'm sure," Yardley said, his face eerily illuminated by the podium light. Like somebody with a flashlight telling ghost stories.

"And you might, perhaps, wonder why I have referred to your masculine member as the enemy. Let me explain further."

General Yardley turned a few pages. Click. A montage of official-looking documents appeared on the screen, along with the photo of a pretty Korean woman smiling from behind a bar top at a saloon. She was dressed wholesomely in a white blouse with a bow tie.

"First I must remind everyone that we, all of us, operate under specific laws as guests in this country. One of those rules, number one-thirty-four of the Uniform Code of Military Justice prohibits—and I quote, 'the pandering, prostitution and solicitation of another in order to engage in an act of prostitution.' Another law, also important, concerns the so-called 'purchase of a night off' of a licensed hospitality and entertainment employee in order to obtain the exclusive company of a bar worker. You all know exactly what I'm talking about. You also should know that it is illegal to purchase the remainder of a specific type of contract between a Korean national and his or her employee. You also know what I'm talking about in this regard. I won't go into any more details. I am not a lawyer. I'm a soldier just like you. If you don't understand what I just said, please take one of the brochures located at the exit doors as you leave the building tonight. Read it carefully. Read it twice. Those who violate any of these regulations can and will be prosecuted under Article Ninety-Two for failure to obey a direct order. Am I being clear so far, gentlemen? Bullshit is not my game, so I want to make all of this clear. Am I being clear? I just gave everybody a specific order. All righty, then. Let us proceed."

Yardley pointed at what many soldiers at camp referred to as the Clap Sign. "Many of you have had your photo taken in front of this billboard so you could have a souvenir of your Korea tour. That's okay. I also have a sense of humor. I understand. Some of you men have sent your photo home to friends and family. You've walked by it a hundred times on your way to the village where, and I don't blame you here, you engage in a little fun. Let off some steam. Have a few well-earned drinks. And of course, dance with a pretty girl. This is often a dangerous job you have, protecting the frontier of freedom and keeping the world safe from crazy Bolsheviks and commies and followers of that chubby Chinese fruitcake, Chairman Mao. That's all normal. You are red-blooded American men and American men like to enjoy themselves. You have needs. I understand. The United States Army understands. The Korean government understands. That's why each and every licensed hostess at every drinking establishment is required to carry an identification card that certifies that she has been properly examined by a medical professional. Penicillin, gentlemen, in our business is as important as bullets.

"Often, that's just not enough. People get careless." Yardley said. "Things are overlooked. Sometimes this happens with warriors like you."

The screen suddenly brightened with a closeup photograph of an actual penis suffering the first and primary stage of syphilis. The organ resembled a drooping red and blotchy serpent speckled with dark lumps and weeping canker sores. The next slide showed the same penis coming at the audience head-on, like the grotesque face of a charging, eyeless alien with giant floppy and hairy round ears—something toothless with its vertical pale and swollen lips dripping fluid from a mouth that itself was overwhelmed with more frightening sores and ulcers.

There came a collective groan from the audience and immediate silence as the slide rapidly changed to more views of the same horrifying penis. This time there was background music, a brooding horror film soundtrack that swelled into a crescendo as the photos turned more gruesome.

Someone in the audience shouted "Awe, Jesus! Awe, sweet almighty God!"

"Is this what you want, gentlemen? And that's only the early stages," Yardley said. "After everything heals up and you think you're okay, Act Two does a number on your insides. You get rashes. Your hair falls out and everything starts hurting. It's like you're a hundred years old. After that, and this can take many years, your brain starts to go. Things get whacky and you begin to lose control of your muscles. They call it the *tertiary* stage and by this time, god damn it men, by this time it's just too late. You're a vegetable. Nothing more than a cabbage. You might be only thirty years old but you can't even get up and take a piss. You're wearing diapers and drooling. Your young, beautiful wife has to wipe your ass."

The General looked out across the darkened room. The entire front row of soldiers sat slouched forward in their metal folding chairs, many of them with their heads in their hands. Others stared blankly up at the screen, where Yardley continued clicking his clicker to show the entire range of skin rashes and throat sores and bald bleeding heads that were the result of untreated syphilis. A few soldiers stood and staggered toward the door, where the MPs quickly escorted them back to their seats.

He wasn't finished. Yardley's clicker went click. Click. Click.

"I want you to keeping looking up here, men. I want you to ask yourself if this…if *this* unholy and monstrous THING up there is what you want to bring home to your dear innocent wives and girl friends. I want you to consider that not only will venereal disease kill you, it will kill slowly over many years, blinding you along the way until it finally eats your brain and leaves you sitting in a hospital bed slobbering like a deranged idiot, not knowing your own name, all because at one time when you were young you didn't think of the consequences before you started enjoying yourself. That time in the Republic of Korea while on duty on the dangerous DMZ, when you allowed your pecker to do the thinking for you. Gentlemen, is THIS what you want?"

Yardley turned and clicked and the looming penis image faded slowly into a beautiful color aerial photo of the green DMZ and the winding Imjin River. Profar could barely see it from where he stood at the back of the room, but in the corner of the photo, sitting on top of a hill, was the square speck of Robideaux Guard Post. He could almost see the ring of sandbags encircling the little shack.

"Okay, that's enough," Yardley said. "I think I made my point. I also believe we all know why we are on this important mission here in this country," he said and pointed to the next image on the screen as it changed abruptly to a map of Korea.

"Up and down this stretch of real estate, up and down the DMZ, from 1953 until now, seven-thousand communists have infiltrated into this country. They came to kill us with bombs and land mines. They came to cut our throats and shoot us. To poison the water and sabotage Korea's development. To cause fear and havoc. Our own First Sergeant Cobb, your beloved Top, as you all know, was one of their many victims. These same infiltrators have at their disposal the ability to throw thousands of rounds of artillery in our direction in one minute. That's sixty-seconds, gentlemen. And you and I are at the center of the enemy's bull's eye. We are the tip of the defensive spear. We will be the first to fight and we will be the first to die."

There was sparse applause and a few cheers as the map on the screen dissolved into an American flag that unfurled and waved gently. Military marching band music played.

"None of this matters," Yardley said. "Our ability to protect Korea and the western world against the resources of the communists will not matter if we become a military force of sick peckers. Of diseased penises. You see, if you allow your swinging manhood to think for you then the enemy won't need artillery. They won't need rifles and land mines to defeat us. They won't need infiltrators and three-hundred-thousand well-trained troops on full alert to destroy us. They won't need to crawl across the ice of the Imjin River at night in order to plant land mines in the middle of the god damn night like they did when they recently tried to kill your fellow warriors Specialist Four Edward Profar and Private First Class Yevgeny Lee."

Yardley shaded his eyes against the spotlight and squinted out into the crowd. "Profar, where the hell are you?"

Eddie Profar, startled when he heard his name, looked around sheepishly and raised his hand and quickly sat down. A few soldiers clapped and one of the MPs standing by the rear door looked at him and nodded approvingly.

"And so, gentlemen," Yardley said, closing his three-ring binder. "Those are the simple facts. Your very manhood is at the front line of the world's united war against Marxism and those Bolshevik morons in Moscow. Let that sink in and try to remember what I've said today. Keep yourself strong and healthy. That is all. Carry on."

The lights came on. There was the immediate sound of hundreds of shuffling boots. Yardley stepped from behind the podium and turned on a perfect pivot and saluted the American flag that still waved on the projection screen.

Profar was already standing next to the jeep when the General walked out looking at his wristwatch and hopped into the passenger seat.

"And now I get to visit with my pals up at the JSA," he said sourly. "How did I do?"

"Yes, sir. Very good, sir," Profar said. "I think they liked it."

"Did you like it?"

"I understand what you're saying, sir. About staying healthy, I mean." Profar lifted his hand off the wheel and acknowledged the saluting guard as they drove through the camp gate. Another vehicle with the customary four armed MPs followed behind as both jeeps raced up the highway.

"Can I ask you a question, sir?"

"Roger that," Yardley said.

Two soldiers walking on the shoulder of the road turned and snapped to attention and saluted when they noticed the General's red pennant flag. Yardley lifted his hand halfway to his face and tipped his head.

"The part about buying a contract, sir," Profar said. "I didn't understand that." The General seemed preoccupied with a document he'd just pulled from his briefcase. He studied the paper as he spoke.

"Well, it's against the law for a foreigner to pay out a bar girl's contract with her employer. Even asking for it is a no-no. If you get reported, it's deep shit," Yardley said. "It's that simple. This isn't our country so we can't poke our nose in every god damn thing. Some of these business girls have gotten themselves into a deep financial hole with their employers and the Army doesn't want its troops to get involved in such legal issues. There's a whole set of different rules for us soldiers. The mission here is complicated enough. Why do you want to know?"

"No special reason, sir," Profar said. "I just never heard of that, the part about the contract. Thank you, sir."

"Where did you live in Duluth?" Yardley said.

"East End, sir."

"I grew up near the bay," Yardley said. "I never meet somebody from there."

"Yes, sir. Kind of odd, all the people you've known in the Army."

"I've not been back in many years," Yardley said, looking out across a flooded rice field as they climbed the hill toward Panmunjom. Profar could see the big fake North Korean structure they were building behind the JSA compound. It looked like a movie prop even from this distance.

"I have fond memories of Duluth," Yardley said.

The road here twisted between low barren hills. Profar could see the security detail in his rear-view mirror, the mounted M60 barrel bouncing stiffly up and down. The MP in the back, one hand steadying the weapon as he stared off toward the trees where the JSA finally came into view. They passed two checkpoints where the jeep slowed to a crawl before proceeding along a fence topped with razor wire.

"Colonel Jackson the G3 advised that I shouldn't put the dick picture up on the screen. I think it made all the difference. It was hard to ignore, I'll tell you that. There's some show biz involved in this, I suppose. At some point you just have to say it the way it is." Yardley said and grinned. "I think it made an impression, that big ugly thing up there on the screen. Scared the hell out of me when I first saw it, I'll tell you."

"Yes, sir," Profar said and grinned and kept looking straight ahead. "I think you hit a nerve. I think the guys appreciated that."

"Duluth," Yardley said. "Hardly anybody is ever from Duluth. Nobody famous ever came from Duluth."

"There was Bob Dylan, sir," Profar said. "He was born in Duluth."

They stopped at the final checkpoint where a foreign military officer in a blue United Nations helmet shouldered his rifle and snapped a crisp salute. The General took his briefcase from between his feet and stepped out of the jeep and turned to Profar.

"That doesn't count. He's a god damn Bolshevik, Profar," Yardley said. "Everybody knows that."

CHAPTER 29

That night, you could tell by the way the MPs stood bunched in small groups with their weapons unslung that something unusual was happening in the Ville. The Korean police at the main gate were carrying nightsticks. There was an uneasy vibe in the air, like the smell of ozone after a storm.

Lee and Profar took the sidewalk route from camp to the Ville. It had rained all day and the narrow alley was a sloppy mess. The rain had finally stopped after gusting sideways all afternoon. As they crossed the street, Lee pointed to somebody handing out cardboard signs to a group of sour-looking club girls who'd stepped outside in their work clothes.

The club was half empty. The weekend house band stood on stage tuning their guitars, making sound checks. The drummer practiced spinning his sticks while his bandmates watched and cracked jokes. Mrs. Yoshida stood behind the bar with her arms folded, listening to a group of girls who seemed upset about something.

They sat at their tall stools and Lee nodded at one of the drink hostesses. She was holding her empty tray at her side, swaying with her eyes closed as one of the guitarists hummed into his mic.

"That's Ha-Joon," Lee said. "She goes by Katie."

She had an oddly elegant big-boned peasant face, something suited for a painting by the Dutch masters. Her hair was piled with no great care on top of her head and she wore a plain black pleated skirt and a white blouse, like a school uniform. No heels. Her perfectly proportioned body seemed strangely foreign to such an ordinary face. She closed her eyes and began to shuffle across the floor as she danced with her invisible partner. The guitar player kept strumming and humming. The drummer began a slow beat on the snare with his brushes as Katie wrapped herself in her own arms and began to sway beneath the spinning glitter ball. She occasionally glanced over at the leering GIs who watched her intently from where they'd started lining up at the bar. Somebody whistled and Katie smiled and winked as she continued her one-woman performance.

"She caught her fish," Lee said as they watched somebody in uniform walk out and reach for Katie's hand. They began to dance. After a short conversation, during which he whispered into her ear, the soldier stepped away and headed for the door. Katie stood there looking confused and the mamasan walked over and handed her a towel and they both went behind the bar and started pouring drinks.

"Maybe her price was too high," Profar said.

Lee grabbed his peanuts and started talking about Flash Gordon and Ming the Merciless and if the lovely Dale Arden actually deserved to wear that crown during her trip to Mars.

"Technically, she wasn't a queen of anything," Profar said.

"Hollywood," Lee said. "The crap they do. Take Custer's Last Stand, for example."

"Don't tell me you were there," Profar said.

"I wish," Lee said. "I never get to go down in glory. When I die, it's always some dumbass way."

The dance floor got crowded and Katie made her way across the room with her loaded drink tray. She stood chatting at a booth and when one GI began rubbing her back she jerked away and bumped him playfully with her elbow.

"Sweet girl," Lee said. "If you get up close she's got that face, though. Smallpox. I suppose from when she was a kid. Lots of people got it after the war. Otherwise, a beauty. She's just a matchmaker. Never takes somebody out back, just gets them drinking and all happy and turns things over to one of her pals. I think the other girls watch over her because of the face. They make sure nobody steps over the line. The old lady doesn't let people get rough with any of her ladies. You don't want to get on the bad side with that woman, no sir. She's like Mickey Mantle with that meat cleaver."

When Katie walked past, Profar saw the cut lip and the bruise on her jaw where the makeup had rubbed away. She smiled without turning her head and took the empty tray behind the bar. Lee set down his beer and said he had to use the byeonso.

"I think they shrunk my bladder at the hospital," he said and grabbed more nuts and quick-stepped through the rubber kitchen door.

When he came back Lee said: "There's people out there with torches."

"Like a fire torch?"

"Like what the villagers had when they walked up to the castle looking for Dr. Frankenstein. That kind of torch."

"Maybe it's a party," Profar said.

"Well, they invited MPs with rifles," Lee said.

They watched a young Korean man sit in the shadows at the end of the bar. It was unusual for a local to be seen in a camp town club, unless he was a bouncer or a cook. It was frowned upon by the police, since this part of the village was set aside as a tourist entertainment district for GIs only.

The young man was neatly dressed in a white shirt and blue pants. Lee guessed his age at about sixteen. He looked nervous and didn't seem to know what to do with his hands as he sat watching the girls and soldiers mix it up on the dance floor. Mrs. Yoshida looked out from the kitchen door and was giving the boy a once-over when a girl brought him a Pepsi and a napkin. The mamasan stood and watched.

The boy shook a cigarette from a nearly empty pack and looked over at Lee.

"His hand's shaking," Lee said.

The boy lit his smoke and tapped the ash into one of the club's cheap little tin ashtrays. He sipped his soda pop.

"Maybe he's here to get laid. Kind of jumpy about it, you know?"

"None of them would touch him. It's not legal to do that kind of business with a Korean. Maybe at one of the clubs in Itaewon over in the big city, not out here."

They studied the boy while Lee chewed his peanuts and lifted his hand in greeting to a group of loud GIs who'd taken their seats at one of the tables where you could order food until seven o'clock. The Korean teenager kept looking around, watching the girls. He smoked and crushed the butt a little too violently into the ashtray. He lit another cigarette.

A group of girls came through the alley door. They hung their jackets in one of the lockers outside the kitchen and one by one walked out and started dancing with each other. That's how it usually began: they danced and squirmed, preliminary foreplay for the leering GIs. The band jumped into their first cover song of the evening.

Just then, Katie stepped from the kitchen carrying a tray of steaming noodle bowls. She walked to a table where one of the GIs slid his hand along her bare leg. He started rubbing Katie's thigh up and down. She squirmed away expertly back into the crowd and headed for the bar. Somebody at the table whistled and Katie raised her middle finger over her shoulder without looking back and vanished into the kitchen.

The skittish teenager had been watching all this and you could tell something was getting him terribly agitated. He kept looking at his folded hands and then he'd glance at the ceiling, like he was thinking something over. His lips were moving. When the mamasan came out and took her place at the cash register to tally receipts, the boy leaned across the bar top and began to shout something at Katie, who was now headed to the same table of GIs with her loaded tray. He kept pointing at her and shouting, slamming his fist on the bar.

Mrs. Yoshida was snapping rubber bands onto rolls of currency as she listened to what the boy was saying. She turned and watched Katie, who was now staring at the boy with a worried look on her face. And then it seemed like she'd just seen a ghost. Katie held the empty tray at her side and looked at the floor with her shoulders slumped as if she'd just been caught doing something very wrong. Her face flushed red with a heartsick look of sudden shame and disappointment. The boy stood and held his stiffened fists at his side and shouted Katie's formal Korean name and that's when Mrs. Yoshida suddenly stopped what she was doing and beckoned to someone at the far end of the dance floor.

"Oh, boy. It's his sister," Lee said. "I think we got trouble here."

"What did he say?"

"Well, let me see if I got this right," Lee said. "He called her a *kijichon* whore garbage slut. He said she was as filthy and useless as the bottom of his shoe. A disgrace. A rutting vile barn animal, a sex-crazed sow. He said she wasn't worthy of her ancestral name. He said he'd come here to bring honor to his family and all the shamed ancestors."

The mamasan and the boy began to argue. He tried to push past her. She took his arm to lead him away. Katie stood surrounded by a few of the girls who tried to escort her into the back room. And then the brother, who was jumping up and down as he revved himself up, finally shoved the mamasan aside and headed straight for his sister. He looked half-crazy.

It happened very quickly. Profar and Lee hopped off their stools just as the brother ran past and caught up with Katie. She turned and covered her face with her elbows as he snatched the back of her apron and yanked her off her feet. When one of the other girls stepped forward, the brother smacked her. A few GIs were shouting at the boy when the club bouncer, a beefy off-duty KNP patrolman, appeared out of the shadows and performed a perfect horizontal shoulder tackle that sent both bodies sliding across the length of the waxed parquet dance floor.

With the ceiling glitter ball showering them with happy dots of light, the boy and the bouncer lay entwined and grunting in each other's arms like a pair of altogether disoriented and drunken lovers. They lay this way locked in each other's grip for quite some time. The much smaller teen seemed surprisingly strong but was totally smothered by the bouncer's size and weight.

Suddenly, the bouncer cried out in an unlikely high voice and rolled sideways. He doubled over with both hands gripping his stomach. Profar saw the dark blood seeping out from between the man's fingers. The brother raised himself on one knee, the long kitchen knife still in his hand, and looked back where Katie was now being pushed into the kitchen by her friends. The brother called out and ran toward her with the knife raised above his head, shouting curses that Lee said called for his sister's death and journey to Hell. He cried out after her with a rehearsed formality and said she must now die because such is always the fate of a common whore who peddles her body to the American occupiers for the cost of a carton of cigarettes. He said she had dishonored her entire family for generations to come and for that she must now suffer a just punishment. Lee translated this just as the brother caught up with his sister and wrapped her hair around his fist and began smacking her face with the blunt handle of the knife. Katie screamed out as her brother ripped away the front of her bloody blouse and turned to shout that now everyone could see the vile nakedness of his whoring and shameless sister, and for this they must all now also witness her death.

Mrs. Yoshida had already disappeared into the kitchen. When she came out behind the bar she was holding something heavy in her hand. The smoking hot pan was dripping grease as if it had just been pulled from the griddle. Katie's brother was standing with the knife raised high and he hardly knew enough to defend himself as the mamasan walked up from behind and without expression swung the pan in a roundhouse arc and brought it down on the boy's head. His glasses went flying. Some of the cooking grease in the pan formed an oily aerosol nimbus around his head, and when Katie tried to reach over to her brother she was immediately pulled away by her friends and dragged screaming into the kitchen. The mamasan stood nonplussed with the eighteen-inch cast-iron skillet swinging at her side, the boy sprawled with a halo of blood pooling across the polka dotted dance floor.

Lee and Profar watched the MPs wrap a bar towel around Katie's brother's head. When he seemed to come to his senses they lifted him by the armpits and hauled him off to a chair. They could hear Katie screaming out her brother's name from the kitchen. Mrs. Yoshida was behind the bar, organizing another batch of receipts.

Lee and Profar stepped outside where they smoked and watched another line of GIs form at the front door of the Water Dragon Club. The band began to play. A black KNP van pulled up and two policemen appeared holding Katie's handcuffed brother by his arms, the blood-soaked towel wrapped around his bleeding skull like a turban.

"Nice swing she's got, the mamasan," Lee said and stepped on his cigarette. "Just about took his head off."

"I never saw that before," Profar said.

"I don't know why it doesn't happen more," Lee said. "These girls have a complicated life. They send money home to the farm. They lie about working in a restaurant or in an office. Choi lets them visit their families. He knows they'll come back. He knows how to find them if they don't. Katie probably has her own deal with Choi, even though she doesn't work the back rooms. Sooner or later, all their families find out what their little girl has been up to. These women will never be forgiven for what they did, even though they're saving Korea's ass with the money they make for the government."

Lee said he would spend the night at camp so he could get some sleep before his shift at Robideaux the next morning.

"You on duty with General Pee Pee Pants?" he said.

"Yeah, I think I'll crash here tonight."

"Join me?" Lee said and took two freshly rolled stubbies from his shirt pocket.

CHAPTER 30

They finished and sat in a blue haze on the steps and then smoked cigars from Lee's stash of Padróns. It was drizzling softly and the courtyard doorways were in shadow but for the glow of the lamp in Mrs. Yoshida's window.

"The woman of mystery, is she married?" Profar said.

"Hubby died in the war," Lee said. "She's half Japanese and so was he. Usually, that's not a good combination in this country. Still, I hear her family was well-off."

Blue light flickered from the mamasan's TV. Music drifted through the open doorway.

"She's a riddle," Lee said. "Might have been a working girl herself at one time. When I ask, they change the subject."

A bass guitar thumped from the building across the alley. The cool air was heavy and damp so Lee's smoke hung in the air as he coughed and puffed and tried to blow rings at the toe of his boot. He studied the cigar's perfect gray ash.

"I was thinking about the retreat to Smolensk in 1812."

Profar turned away and bit his cigar. "Here we go."

"I never know when it comes, Eddie boy," Lee said. "When it hits I just have to talk. It helps me keep my bearings. This stuff can't be allowed to stay in my head."

Lee had that faraway look, like he might physically drift away.

"Kutuzov, the son of a bitch, circled around and surprised everybody. We fought at Krasny and that's where a cossack cut my leg to the bone with his sword. It never really healed. I didn't see him coming. Nobody ever saw a cossack coming. It was November, cold like you wouldn't believe, none of us had real boots. I had parade shoes from when we marched through Paris and they were wrapped in rags. The bastard Bonaparte didn't plan for the Russian winter. Here we were, outnumbered three to one and their troops were totally comfortable in the cold. We were jealous of their furry hats and long coats. They had real clothes, they had food and we had nothing but Napoleon's speeches about the glories of France. How all of Europe was threatening us. How we needed to defend ourselves here on some God forsaken steppe halfway to Asia. The glory, he always talked about the glory. Can you imagine him using that word in such a time? We wanted to go to Minsk for supplies but heard the French had already fallen, just completely collapsed. It seemed hopeless. Napoleon's famous luck showed up and he made a diversion move to the south. The Russian fools fell for it. That crazy Corsican pulled another rabbit from his hat. We were able to cross the river on pontoon bridges. In war, the trick is always to keep moving. I don't care how sophisticated we are today, the Army that stands still gets the shit kicked out of it. Those who stand still are destroyed and Napoleon always knew that."

"Couldn't have been colder than Korea," Profar said.

"Correct, Edward," Lee said. He took a puff and blew at his boot.

Profar hoped this was the last of it, but sadly it was not. It began to rain harder and Lee got a second wind.

"We'd already marched five hundred miles in freezing weather," he said. "Such suffering. Napoleon was a psycho to put his men through that torture, but of course he always thought of himself first. In the end, every life was dispensable for the sake of the cause and the cause was whatever Napoleon wanted it to be. The sadness and misery of others was unimportant. The killer of thousands, he was. That prick finally deserted us to go to to Paris in his comfy carriage. Only twenty-thousand were left standing after fifty-one days of battle. A band of starving boys stumbling across that Russian wilderness in their rags like beggars, the snowdrifts as high as a house. Every night we heard the wolves howling beyond our fires. A shabby Army of homeless vagrants. The Russians must have been laughing. My boy,

Eddie...that was the worst of all my lives. Worse than Babylon, where I had to watch Alexander die."

Whenever Lee said, *my boy,* it usually meant the story would continue.

Profar looked over at Jia's hooch. Her plastic slippers sat outside the door on a rug decorated with dragons.

"My boy," Lee said. "Tsar Alexander, to his credit, refused to believe the myth of Napoleon. He wasn't like the Austrians and the Prussians. Mr. Romanov considered Bonaparte just another lucky man and luck eventually runs out for everyone."

Lee shook his head and said he had no regrets. "Bonaparte had some assets," he said. "He could spark the worst of patriotism in a way that would make you blush. Those men, me included, loved their little fat psychopath dearly. It's a good example of why you should always mistrust charisma. Charisma is dangerous. Our anger at Napoleon was almost always surpassed by a greater love. The rascal had us hypnotized. He killed us and we loved every minute."

Lee was caught in mid-sentence when they heard the commotion in the alley. People were running past the courtyard door, the sound of a wailing police siren and the rhythmic stomping of feet out on the street. A chorus of chanting voices rose up like cries of disappointment at a sports stadium. By the time Profar snubbed his cigar and ran outside a crowd had already formed and so they both followed it down the block to the MSR.

Hundreds of shouting women stood in the steady drizzle shaking their signs in front of the camp gate. Their glowing torches, diesel-soaked rags on sticks, cast flickering shadows against the walls of the MP shack, where soldiers had already set up wooden saw horses as traffic barriers. Lee and Profar pushed their way to the front of the surging protesters who had already formed a long line along the highway.

The simple unpainted wooden coffin was draped in a white sheet, a single Hangul text character drawn with red on its side. Mae-Wong's name was spelled in bold block English letters on several of the signs that were being shaken in front of the MPs, who stood at the gate entrance with their shouldered M14s. The procession was followed by rows of more torch bearers marching in step, their faces painted completely white like a cadre of frowning phantoms, also chanting oaths like medieval church worshippers carrying the corpse of their incorruptible saint to its holy crypt.

Profar recognized one of the bar girls from the Brooklyn Aces Club and she and someone else were holding a banner that said, "Justice Now for Sister Mae-Wong!"

A school bus filled with more bar hostesses from a neighboring camp town arrived. Like visiting conventioneers, the women stepped off and each was handed a sign as they too gathered in the street that had now been blocked from traffic by two parked Korean police vans.

The girls started chanting General Yardley's name. Somebody rang a cow bell and a few marchers began to blow whistles and stomp their feet as the call for Yardley's appearance grew louder. Suddenly, a row of MPs began sweeping the protesters with their flashlights. The Korean cops were taking photos. From somewhere in the crowd drums began to drum and after a while the persistent beat fell into rhythm with the stomping feet and the waving signs and the hysterical shouts of Mae-Wong's name.

A deuce-and-a-half arrived filled with military police wearing their DMZ arm bands. The MPs jumped off the truck carrying four-barrel tear gas launchers. They formed ranks and crept toward the crowd. Somebody shouted a command through a megaphone and the soldiers strapped on their riot masks and stood at attention behind the yellow saw horse barrier. A girl with her long wet hair blowing stepped out from the crowd in her high heels and floozy bordello skirt and stood silently in the middle of the MSR holding up a giant portrait of Mae-Wong's smiling face. She raised her fist and began screaming, "Justice. Justice. Justice!"

The chanting, now fully synced with the drums and joined by the shouts of village shop owners and their customers from across the street, grew louder as everyone called out the General's name, "YahdLEE! YahdLEE!"

A Huey helicopter, its bay door sprung and the .50 cal with its hanging ammo belt clearly visible, made its treetop approach along the street and banked to hover above the camp. Its searchlight shined down on the protesters. The rain swirled violently in the aircraft's rotor wash. The crowd faced the blast of wind, fists raised and shaking. Another row of MPs holding riot shields appeared and stood with their batons held low in two hands so they could push the surging women away from the gate.

General Yardley's hardtop civilian vehicle appeared with an escort of patrol jeeps that quickly parked diagonally behind the pole gate, their own red lights flashing and sirens blaring. The General stepped from his car dressed in a rubber green poncho and field cap and he rather nimbly hopped onto the vehicle's hood and raised his arms. He nodded and waved at the crowd and pointed at a row of bar girls who were screaming angrily and jumping up and down with their signs. Somebody handed the General a bullhorn.

"Go home," he said, his tinny voice barely recognizable in the noise. "This won't fix anything. Please go home. It's time to go home."

The General stood and stretched his arms again as he pleaded for order.

"Please, I think…" he managed to say before ducking his head to avoid something tossed from the crowd. Vegetables. A melon came flying. Fruit taken from one of the market stands across the street sailed through the air and potatoes bounced off the hood of Yardley's car.

When he tried to speak again the shouting only grew louder, the crowd surged closer and more tossed objects flew through the air. The closest row of protesters began jumping up and down, shaking their Mae Wong picture posters and banners and screaming for justice for their fallen sister. Revenge for their murdered friend. From somewhere else came a man's scratchy voice through another megaphone, his amplified Korean profanities calling for the American occupier Yardley himself to be dragged off to prison. To be expelled like the cloven-footed Japanese devils and the Russian monkey communists from the North, he said.

With more trash flying through the air, General Yardley ducked away as an MP wearing a flak vest stepped up and guided the General off the hood of the vehicle. A great cheer lifted from the street as Yardley retreated into his car and was driven away.

Beneath their umbrellas and jackets held above their heads against the falling rain, everyone began to sing softly. It was some gentle Korean lullaby that Lee said he did not recognize. The torch-bearers carrying Mae Wong's coffin swayed their sad cargo back and forth as they sang their mournful song, the crowd now tightly compressed as the protesters faced the guarding MPs and began to sing louder.

The next edition of the *Warrior* newspaper did not mention the protest at all, though Profar had watched its reporter take plenty of photos. He had expected *Stars and Stripes* to report the event. Predictably, they did not. The local Korean newspaper ran a photo with a brief caption that said the incident had been the work of restaurant waitresses who had been protesting for a wage hike. Mae Wong's coffin, the torches and the signs or Yardley's appearance were never mentioned. Instead, there was a splashy front page feature in that week's *Warrior* that celebrated the first anniversary of the new men's barracks building. Another story appeared about a Korean tailor in the village who had donated the award shawl to be worn by that year's 1968 Miss DMZ Beauty Pageant winner.

Mae Wong's suspected killer, confined at the camp stockade according to the protocols of the US - Korea Status of Forces Agreement, was finally processed out of the country under an emergency family leave and grievance order. He'd never been detained or questioned by the local Korean police. Somebody in Yardley's office told Profar that the soldier was dishonorably discharged and was being temporarily detained while awaiting charges at the federal prison at Fort Leavenworth, Kansas.

CHAPTER 31

Profar's duty schedule gave him plenty of time off. He spent most days at the hooch until it was his turn to drive the old man to Panmunjom.

The NoKos wanted more meetings, which meant that they were in a hurry to get something resolved. They'd asked Yardley to sign another statement admitting that the *USS Viator* had sailed into North Korean waters on a spy mission, another example of the American devil President Lyndon Johnson's attempt to meddle into the honorable affairs of the Democratic People's Republic of Korea. They said the sole purpose of delaying negotiations was to take away attention from the American military's spectacular military failure during the Tet holiday attacks on the city of Hue by their gallant North Vietnam brothers-in-arms.

Yardley refused to sign anything. He again demanded the release of the captured crew, whose whereabouts remained unknown and whose fate was getting serious international attention.

The *Warrior* newspaper was usually filled with Army-speak stories about training exercises, staff promotions, grip-and-grin photos of Koreans shaking hands with smiling Americans, and features about the military partnership between the ROK and US military along the 150-mile-long DMZ. Lately, as instructed by General Yardley's public information officer, the weekly 36-page newspaper was packed with tips on how to avoid VD in all of its sinister forms, along with hints on how to refrain from socializing with women in the village who might potentially infect you with a number of varieties of other sexually transmitted diseases. There were charts and drawings and scientific bell curves illustrating that week's 8th Army STD infection rate, along with a directory of medical terms and photos illustrating the gruesome consequences of gonorrhea, herpes, syphilis and related ailments. There was also a list of symptoms you should watch for in your girlfriend, at which time it was your duty to inform the dispensary's community relations health specialist. The newspaper's sports section included sidebars on how to identify the characteristics of chlamydia along with facts and figures about soldierly genitalia hygiene.

That week's *Warrior* had a photo of the General himself looking stern as he pointed his finger at his North Korean counterpart. An ambush patrol had captured two infiltrators floating across the Imjin River in another fake deadfall raft. In the newspaper photo, Yardley was sitting next to a large photo showing their captured weapons. They'd also discovered three northern spies who'd been working for months as Korean camp domestic employees, one of them a popular houseboy who spoke perfect English and worked at the camp's artillery barracks. Loaded grenades, a rigged mortar round attached to a flashlight battery detonation device and a radio transmitter were found in his foot locker.

Manny Perez said he was afraid that Richie Kraus, the *Warrior* editor, had gotten wind of Yardley's pee bag and that if word got out everybody would think it was Perez who couldn't keep mum. Profar knew the truth, of course. Most everybody but the North Koreans already knew about the General's famous catheter and his new superman ability to drink gallons of water without ever getting up from his chair at Panmunjom.

Mae Wong was buried following the customary three-day waiting period. The cemetery reserved for unidentified indigents and those without family was located outside the village next to the US Army's non-organic burn pit. The former Japanese cemetery had also once been used to bury refugees during the war and was now managed by a loosely organized group of local entertainment workers. Provincial officials seemed to have no interest in what happened at the cemetery or who was buried there.

Since it wasn't practical to keep Mae Wong's body at her rented hooch during the waiting period, the police, for sanitary reasons, had wanted to store the corpse at the Soyosan Health Center, the Zoo. The girls at the Water Dragon Club were outraged, so they pooled money and paid for the body to be taken to a missionary chapel that offered Christian burial services for a fee.

Profar watched Richie Kraus standing under a tree with a group of girls who were already gussied up for work. Their heavy makeup and teased hair seemed out of place in the bright sunshine. Kraus tried to take pictures, but the girls ducked and shook their hands and scattered like they were being attacked by wasps.

The procession followed Mae Wong's unpainted coffin to the grave site, the body inside wrapped in its customary seven-layer shroud. A hired mourner dressed in a white jacket and baggy ceremonial trousers sang a Korean dirge in a peculiar low and throaty voice as he led the small gathering up the hill from the MSR. When they got to where the hole had been dug beforehand by the coffin bearers, six men who'd been recruited from the village, they symbolically lowered and raised the bier three times before it was placed at the edge of the grave. There were other rituals that should have been followed. In Mae Wong's case, nobody knew the name of her ancestral village or the whereabouts of her family and so they hoped that her soul would proceed unimpeded to the afterlife, despite the hasty and abbreviated ceremony.

There was no eulogy. There were no relatives to witness the burial. Those few people on-hand merely bowed twice in the direction of the coffin as it was lowered by cloth straps whose ends were then tossed to lie on the coffin cover in a precise and long established manner that was directed by the professional mourner.

There were officially about 400 bodies buried at the cemetery, mostly sex workers and anonymous paupers. The cemetery also contained North Korean and Chinese soldiers who had been killed in post-truce skirmishes as well as unidentified infiltrators who'd died while crossing the DMZ. This is where they brought them, since the North Koreans hardly ever wanted their dead spies to be returned. Those graves, unlike the others, were courteously situated so they faced due north. Profar learned this from Kraus and he immediately thought about the bodies that were still rotting away after all these months in the tunnel near Robideaux.

This section of the cemetery had uneven scattered grass mounds that ran up the hillside, most of the sites marked with a number on a small cement post. Some of the markers had Korean text etched into a metal plate fastened onto a cement tile. The plates that were fully marked showed abbreviated narratives of the life that had been lived, the proper clan lineage and the name of the deceased's ancestral village. None of the bar girls buried here had such markers and most were grouped as randomly numbered stones around the base of a tree or a small obelisk that had no inscription at all. Some had faded wooden Christian crosses. It all looked like an abandoned country garden with neglected patches of weeds and dead grass where something might have once grown but now lay ignored and forgotten. There were fences around rectangles of dirt and shallow, unmarked depressions in the soil. A sadness hung over everything.

Richie Kraus kept taking his pictures.

"You think they'll actually put that in the paper?" Profar said.

"No chance," Kraus said. "I might try to give it to *Stars and Stripes,* but they'll ignore me. Things get more political and goofy the closer you get to the main office in Tokyo. I go there every two weeks to lay out the paper at the print shop and lately all I get is hush-hush notes about anything that doesn't make the brass look good. It's just the way things are. Vietnam is a total shit show since that Tet battle and they've cut the budget for Korea big time. You guys know that. We're on a shoestring at the paper. It's just me and a clerk and another reporter. Used to have a staff of six. Now there's no money to buy film and chemicals for the dark room. I had to beg to get a jeep today to drive us out here. That thing the other night about the dead girl, whatshername, doesn't make anybody look good. Hell, I might just sneak home the film when I rotate next month. I've had it with this circus. I'm glad they didn't send my ass to Vietnam, but Korea is a special flavor of horseshit."

"I heard what happened to the psycho who stabbed the girl," Profar said.

"There was no way they were keeping him in-country," Kraus said. "Should have hung him by the nuts for what he did. You can bet old man Yardley made this vaporize so it couldn't become a bigger issue. They didn't want him talking to anybody, so Eighth Army put a PIO flak on the flight back to The World, just in case. The man kills somebody and now he has his own PR agent. Read what the law says about a soldier committing a crime in Korea. You'll be amused. I don't have any feelings about these hookers, one way or another. I just don't. I stay away from them. I got a girl back home and I don't want my dick to melt off. But that wasn't right, what he did."

Somebody from the missionary house stood dressed in his church vestment at Mae Wong's grave and read from the Bible. A few girls remained with their heads bowed, though most had walked away and were waiting at the bottom of the hill to catch the bus to town.

"Yardley has that much clout?" Profar said.

"Everything he says and does is being watched by the State Department," Kraus said. "The White House gets a transcript of every meeting. It's got LBJs fingerprints all over it. Yeah, the old man has a whole shitload of clout these days. I hear they're close to an agreement, but Yardley needs something dramatic. He needs a Big Thing, something that makes a splash. Something with drama that the Pentagon can grab and shove up that North Korean General's ass. He needs something to push the commies over the edge. The old man is God at the JSA. If you want any favors done, now that you're his driver, right now he might just be the best known General in the United States Army. This is what makes careers. That thing with the piss bag so he could embarrass the Northies, that's not what's going to help him put this thing over the edge. Drama. They need something dramatic. A rabbit out of the hat. They need a Big Fucking Thing."

"You know about the catheter?" Profar said.

"Brother Eddie, everybody knows about the old man's pee-pee tube. He's a damn hero,"

Kraus walked off to interview the missionary where two men were tossing dirt into Mae Wong's grave.

Jia was standing alone in front of a flowering tree above where they'd put Mae Wong to rest. There was a nice view across the valley from here. She'd already spotted Profar and he raised his hand and started walking up the hill. He watched her wipe her eye with the heel of her hand. Her smile seemed forced. She held an empty glass vase. The small mound where she'd put flowers in a stone cup was marked with a numbered cement post. Other similar markers were scattered randomly nearby. It seemed like just another weedy forgotten patch of dirt in the cemetery nobody really cared about.

"Finish what you were doing, I'm sorry," Profar said. "I came here with a friend." He pointed at where Richie Kraus was interviewing the professional mourner.

Where Jia had been kneeling next to one of the grave markers there stood a pail of water and another potted plant.

"He my baby," she said.

She took the pail and spilled water on the little mound. She scooped the wet dirt and pressed the blooming flower into the soil and patted everything with the side of her foot. She stood and pushed away the hair blowing across her face. Her eyes were glassy. Everything was silent up here, just the shaking leafy trees and the distant whine of traffic from the highway.

"He die before he born," she said. "Kim Hyun-Woo. I give him same name as my father. Not Korean custom to name little boy after grandfather. I do, anyway, for honor. He die long time ago in war, my father. When I was a little girl."

She sighed. "Nothing I can do now about my baby boy. Nothing I can do."

Staring at the stone post, she spoke with sober detachment about the child whose face she'd never seen or touched. How the doctor had reluctantly shown her what there was to show and this was what was now buried at her feet. There was nothing more to be done. She told Profar that life carries on whether we participate in the journey or not.

The leaning pear tree that shaded the grave seemed to be the tallest and oldest in the cemetery and where its enormous roots had broken to the surface the little marker post had begun to tilt.

Kraus whistled up at Profar from the bottom of the hill and waved from where he'd parked his jeep.

Profar looked at Jia. "I didn't mean to interrupt."

She touched his shoulder and when her hand slid down along his arm she laced her fingers into his and squeezed his hand.

She picked up the empty pot. He carried the pail and they walked down the hill together. She brushed against him when she lost her balance and he held the small of her back with his open hand. They briefly looked at each other and while she held his gaze, Jia's long dark hair blew away from her perfect unsmiling face. Profar could smell incense in the air.

When they got to the jeep she squeezed his hand again and kept walking. Profar had almost offered her a ride in the jeep, but realized that civilians were not allowed in military vehicles. She sat alone on the bus stop bench with her hands folded in her lap.

"I've seen that one. The girl you were talking to," Kraus said as they drove past Jia and Profar waved. She didn't notice him.

"She's something. What a looker."

Profar snapped. "Let's just go."

"She your yeobo or something? Shit, man. Sorry, I didn't know…"

"She's not. Just go on now. Go."

CHAPTER 32

At the Water Dragon Club that night he sat in a corner at a table whose wire legs were bolted for safety to the floor. He took two pills from his shirt and swallowed them with one long gulp from his glass of soda water. One of the girls stepped out of the dark and set a bowl of peanuts on the table and walked away. Thirsty customers are good customers and he knew she'd return soon.

The house band finished their tuning and sound checks and began to play. Profar felt the throb of the bass through the bottoms of his shoes as he rested his aching head in one hand. Every day it was something. Today his skull was pounding.

He thought about the cemetery. He knew the song the band was playing very well and when the Korean singer started singing, Profar couldn't understand the words at all. People began to dance. Two identically dressed girls with matching hairstyles and the same flourish to their eye makeup walked past and simultaneously gave him a come-hither look, like this was a practiced routine. Profar shrugged and shook his head. The tallest girl leaned and winked and blew him a kiss across her open palm. Both girls held hands and started dancing with each other. They looked over at Profar. Their spiked shoe heels were so high he wondered how they could possibly walk.

Jia stepped out of nowhere and stood frowning with one hand on her hip. She looked him over like she was ready to give him a scolding.

"You no dance no more?" she said. "Lee your friend he dance all the time. Like crazy man he dance up and down. I never see Eddie dance."

She was dressed in a tight silver skirt with a slit that revealed her bare hip. She took a stool from another table and sat down. Her long hair spilled over her strapless shoulder and her perfume smelled fruity and sweet. She crossed her legs and leaned and stared at him intently with her chin in her hand. She batted her lashes. It was the first time he'd noticed the faint scar below her eye, a half-moon welt that was covered by her makeup.

"My dancing days are done," Profar said and raised his soda water in a mocking toast. "A lot of things are done and gone with me. Doc said to take it easy. I can't even drink booze for a year. No wine, no beer."

"You too skinny," she said. "I make food for you sometime. You no like club girls no more?" she pointed to the crowded dance floor.

"I like them good enough," Profar said. He sipped his drink because he didn't know what else to say. "It's no big deal. I'll be fine."

She leaned closer. The scar was like a faint frown and was more visible when she smiled.

"Maybe soon everything number one, okay?" She said softly.

Profar lifted his glass in a toast.

"You funny boy," she said and turned to watch the dance floor.

The slight glitter in her eyelashes caught the light and Profar studied the silhouette of her bowed and slender neck as her pale hand with its swinging silver bracelet once more pushed aside her dark hair.

They watched while two GIs led their partners across the dance floor. One of the soldiers took a tissue and blew his nose and looked at his hand before he pulled his girl close and started swaying to the music. The girl he was dancing with looked away as if she was embarrassed.

Jia shook her head. "No Korea man clean nose in front of woman like that," she said. "You watch now. No girl who see this come for more dancing with him tonight. Just sell drinks to him, no kissy and no quickie time in hooch. He dirty man, blow nose like that and then touch her."

Profar took the laminated food card from the chrome rack that held salt and pepper shakers and hot sauce. There were color photos of noodle bowls and chopped vegetables. Platters of steaks. He thought about Mrs. Yoshida swinging her giant cleaver in the courtyard, the serious look on her face when she chopped the meat.

Jia nodded toward the dance floor. "See man over there? He wave at girl. Not nice to ask person to come with finger like that. Not polite. Very bad, and only do that with little child. Do with grown up person and you make taksan insult."

She frowned and made a show of grabbing the menu he'd been reading and she dropped it back into its wire holder. She stood and took his hand and led him out on the dance floor like someone guiding a child gently across a busy street. He felt like a clumsy oaf. Eddie Profar didn't really like to dance at all.

Profar saw Mrs. Yoshida watching them from her stool next to the cash register. She was bundling rolls of money, as always. Jia pressed against him and whispered in his ear. She smelled like soap and perfume, a pleasant heat to her breath.

"You worried to dance with me?" she said.

"I'm worried you'll take advantage of a poor cripple."

"You funny boy. I no understand what you joke, that's okay," she said. "Now you dance with Jia."

The smooth slippery satin fabric of her skimpy skirt stretched across her slim hard waist beneath his hand. In her heels she was very tall. He could almost look directly into her eyes. As she pressed against him, her long shape busty and lean, he guided her to an empty corner and in the bright flickering light she squinted with those dark feline eyes and lay her cheek gently against his shoulder. He hoped she wouldn't hear his pounding heart as he moved his hand across her hip. The band was playing something slow. He felt as if his feet had detached and were drifting away.

"I would have bought a real drink," he said. "You didn't have to dance with me just to make me buy a drink."

"I know. Lee already tell me that doctor say drink make you sick. I don't want to make you sick, Eddie."

"I would have still bought one," Profar said. "I didn't say I'd drink it. Does my friend Lee tell you everything?"

She ignored him. "Who your whole family name?" she said. "I know Eddie, but who your family name?"

When she couldn't pronounce it they both laughed.

"You can call me whatever you want," he said.

"Where your name come from?"

"My name?"

"We know in Korea who family people are from the old times," Jia said. "We know what village and what time life start and how old. In Korea, baby is already one year old when born. Always we know the names of ancestors and when they born and die. Everything we write in family book."

"We didn't have a family book," Profar said. "They were farmers, that's all I know. Grew corn and had cows and horses. It's just a name."

"You know my name?"

Profar said it and she smiled. "How come you're not a Debbie or Kitty or a Sally, like everybody else?"

One of the girls walked by and said something to Jia, who looked annoyed and pushed her away with one hand. She gave Profar a sisterly kiss on the cheek.

"What's that for?"

"You can call me any name, too," she said.

"How about Peggy Sue?" he said. "Like in the Buddy Holly song."

"Who she, this Peggy?"

"Just a girl in a song," Profar said. "Is that okay?"

She laughed and touched his shoulder. "Peggy Sue just fine. Between me and you, our secret only. I try to remember Peggy Sue."

She leaned into him with her bare shoulder, her palm and cheek pressed against his chest. She toyed with his shirt button. Opened it and closed it.

"You come my hooch in one hour, okay?"

"I told you," Profar said. "Doc says to watch it. I don't feel that great, anyway."

"Not what you think. You come in one hour and I cook for you," she said. "Give you tea, make you feel better. You look skinny sick, so I cook, okay? Nothing more. I don't play trick on you, I promise."

Before she walked away, she said: "One hour, my house. I be Eddie's *noona* tonight, like big sister. Not no business girl. Peggy Sue cook for Eddie and make him fat."

He sat for a while and watched them dance. He could study them as they moved in that crazy red saloon light all night long. The soldier who'd snorted impolitely into his tissue now sat looking lost by himself at the bar, taking self-conscious sips of beer and trying to look relaxed. He probably wondered why nobody would come within a few feet of him. After a while he wiped his mouth with his hand and stood and walked out.

Profar looked at his watch and headed to the door. The mamasan, wearing her wash woman apron, nodded at him without smiling as she counted her money and wrote in her ledger book.

CHAPTER 33

In the old stories from north of the Amur River deep in the Siberian Taiga, she was known as an otherworldly shapeshifter and wilderness wraith destined to always wander, a mythical and rootless sojourner who was fated to never know a true home.

She was required to kill something large each week to stay alive in winter, and when she ate it could mean devouring thirty pounds of meat at a single feeding. She was a shadow stalker, a patient and audacious assassin who could only chase her prey at top speed for a very short distance. She'd been taught her bold hunting ways early in life after watching her mother pull her immense five-inch-wide forepaws over the stern of a fishing boat on the Razdolaya River north of Vladivostok.

The force of her powerful bite was 1,000 pounds per square inch, though she needed only a tenth of that strength to crush the throat of a human being. Slightly more for a full-grown deer. She could easily lift and drag away a 1,200 lb. carcass and the swipe force of her dinner plate-size paw could knock a galloping horse off its feet.

She would often adjust her daily hunting schedule to the habits of her wily prey, and she once killed a fox only to leave it lay as bait with which to lure something larger and more worthwhile to eat. When she attacked she did not simply charge, she combusted. She exploded into a ferocious, kinetically charged ball of ochre fur that could launch her heavy bulk instantly into a running ten-foot stride at thirty-miles-per hour through a foot of snow. She could jump twenty vertical feet from a dead squat.

A neuronal mirror behind her richly layered eyes reflected the slightest incoming light twice, and so the interconnected synapses and glial cells of her retinas glowed white and green at night in the shine of a full moon. When they absorbed the artificial rays of a flashlight or an electric lamp, they burned scarlet red like embers in a fire.

In total darkness, she could see six times better than a human and each eye's field of vision overlapped the other to form a binocular, three-dimensional image. The wide row of dense nerve cells in the center of each eye allowed her to track the distant shape of a running deer on a moonless night. She could recognize the colors green, red and blue. Her hind paws, with their blunt toes, were rounder than those of a male and by the age of two years they'd already reached their maximum width and promised that she would likely one day weigh at least five hundred pounds. A full seventy percent of her adult body weight would be solid muscle.

She had twenty times fewer bulbous nerve endings on her tongue than a human, so she did not care at all how her food tasted.

The long white whiskers on her muzzle, structured more like pipe straws than true hairs, could detect the slightest change in barometric air pressure. Similar, shorter bristles situated in tufts above her eyes and on her cheeks and the front of each foreleg had their own sensory advantage during a hunt. It was told in those same ancient legends of the Amur River Valley that a tiger closes its eyes during the final seconds of an attack so that it might see you better.

It took a year of walking for the tiger to reach Gyeonggi Province, where one day she saw a fisherman in a boat pushing upstream with a pole through the shallows of the Imjin River. It was early fall. Hidden in the tall shoreline reeds with her paws outstretched in the sand, she studied the man and let his scent whisk across the special scent organ on the roof of her open mouth as the boat drifted by in the current. She watched him drop his stone anchor and cast his net and when he was finished she patiently followed the man as he pushed himself with the pole closer and closer to shore. By this time she had not eaten for days and the wound on her hip had made chasing food very difficult.

She'd already wandered south these many months as a solitary nomad, following the convenient food source of other rivers until she reached the two-mile wide Korean DMZ, where the military barrier terminated in a lush coastal forest on the shore of the Sea of Japan. This was familiar terrain that reminded her of her first home in Siberia. And so this is where she remained until winter came and she was forced to roam further inland. After she'd hunted the protected, game-rich barrier zone along the Imjin, with its deer-like Goral goats and fat wild boar, she had the instinctive sense that she might have finally arrived at a new home.

Her mother's forepaw had been shattered by a poacher s twelve-gauge shotgun two years before, when both tigers were discovered feeding on bait inside a deadfall trap in the arboreal forest of Russia s Primorye wilderness. It was deep winter when the yearling cub, also wounded when the same load of military buckshot ricocheted into her hip, and its mother then escaped into the snowy taiga outside of Vladivostok near the China frontier.

In that first painful week they walked a surprising distance, thirty miles a day, along a tributary of the Amur until they could finally smell the sea at the North Korea border. Here they rested. For weeks, they managed to scavenge food along a beach, where they watched from a distance as an entire company of infantry troops from the garrison at Wonson completed a maritime training exercise. Men in parkas carrying weapons swarmed across the sand. Boats landed in the crashing surf. They grew accustomed to the noise of rifle fire at night. The soldiers' glowing cookfires brought strange and confusing smells.

The men were packing their gear into their trucks at dusk when the two tigers discovered that such creatures might be the slowest and most convenient prey they'd ever encountered. They could barely run. It was better than chasing deer or avoiding a wild boar's swinging tusks or eating low-calorie scraps of carrion, although that was what had kept them alive that entire winter.

Waiting for the soldiers to return, they scavenged seal bones and dead gulls and salmon with hooked jaws that lay staring side-eyed from the beach sand. An old smokehouse next to a hunter s empty tarpaper shack provided leftovers of rotted and desiccated deer meat. The cub chewed on a bear rug torn from the wall outside the cabin. When it smelled something high in a tree it managed to pull itself to the raised platform, where it clawed off a leather door hinge to reach the enticing cache of frozen fish inside. Enough to feed on for a week.

For the month after that, in the wet late winter coastal weather, a stormy time when game was always scarce, they hunted the occasional rabbit or wandering boar that might be feeding on what was left of that fall's crop of pine nuts that still lay buried under the snow.

The clumsy North Korean humans never returned to the beach.

When the mother died from her wounds that spring, the cub lay with its head on her tail for days until it finally limped away on its swollen hip in search of something to eat. It killed a hibernating bear and carried away its twin cubs.

The only direction it knew to go was south, the bearing from which the soldiers on the beach had come. The direction toward which her mother had walked. She was now lured by something powerful, as if the northern winds that blew across the sea from her birthplace in the Primorye Krai was showing her the way to another, better territory.

For the next six months the cub traveled along the seashore, occasionally wandering inland for several miles, always returning to follow the magnetic lure of water, scavenging mostly, until it came to the outskirts of a city where it lay and waited and then killed a horse and a soldier in a wagon who'd been hauling trash to a garbage pit. It had learned to recognize the uniform of a soldier. And then she continued her ceaseless walking, this endless and irresistible urge to meander. She wandered until she reached the boggy headwaters of the Namdae River and from there once again turned south.

By January she'd finally traveled far beyond the salt scent of the ocean, past anything that had ever been familiar to her. She followed the Korean seaward highlands to where the peninsula bowed inland along the 38th parallel. From here she walked west through the lush green forest preserve that had largely been artificially created by the Korean War, until she reached the famous serpentine loop of the Imjin, the River Dragon.

And here, with a new and unfamiliar territorial sensation stirring within her, she stopped and began to watch for trespassers.

CHAPTER 34

Her hooch had two windows and a double sliding door decorated with painted persimmon flowers whose bright colors had faded long ago.

Everything stood in rows and stacks, a study in orderliness. There were posters aligned on the walls: a *Ladies Home Journal* ad for Breck Shampoo with a blond in a pageboy doo smiling at herself in a hand mirror. The other was a page from the Sears and Roebuck catalog showing a woman admiring her new shoes that said, *Flats are for Fun.*

The airy room had a sultry look, candles burning on shelves where cosmetics sat arranged by size and shape, like apothecary inventory. A stack of American fashion magazines next to a bowl of cookies that smelled like mint.

On a green footlocker in the corner she'd set aside Remo's things: a shaving kit, jeans folded over civilian shoes, his shirts and a brand new Nikkormat camera still in its PX box. Everything looked like it had been placed there in order to be picked up at some later date. Maybe she still had hope.

Next to the neatly made sleeping mat was a low table with a hot plate, a wash basin. Pearlescent bottles of face makeup and eye shadow sticks arranged before a mirror like artists' tools. He didn't know what to make of this exotic lair of a woman whose present life he could not imagine, and whose history was even more unthinkable. The *Ladies Home Journal* on the nightstand, its page bookmarked, seemed set aside like a text meant for further study. In the corner, a Philco television, something Remo had certainly purchased for her.

Jia stepped from the little storage room next to the hooch. Hardly anyone except the mamasan had a multi-room apartment and it looked like Jia had the best of the two. She'd changed into a tee shirt and jeans. Without makeup, she seemed younger. She asked Profar again about the ambush and he turned and lifted his shirt.

"Say hello to Frankenstein," he said.

She stared at the ugly row of raised welts.

"You no work at DMZ no more?" she said.

"I'd rather be up there than driving."

She told him that Lee had already explained his new job. "Helelleh, he sick, too. Down there. Everybody know he sick too much and they no touchy." She wagged her finger. "Lee, he like little clown brother. Always making jokes. Everybody like Helelleh."

She crossed the room to scoop cups of rice into a Sunbeam cooker that still wore its PX label. He smelled something peppery and she told him it wouldn't take long to finish the meal she'd been cooking, and so he waited cross-legged on the floor.

He watched her take sliced meat from a covered plate and mix it with the rice. She scooped something finely chopped and sprinkled it on the rice, along with spices taken from a shelf lined with jars and labeled tins. The room was filled with the food steam and it smelled wonderful. While Jia waited for something to finish warming on the hot plate, she stepped into the store room and returned with a cold soda that she poured into a glass decorated with a black-and-white military unit logo. The division logo and its slogan.

She moved back and forth across the room with a practiced grace. A peculiar smoothness of balance with which she carried her things. That slight limp she had when she walked fast. He wondered why on earth she was cooking like this for him. Why was he was getting such attention? He knew nothing could come of it, and if she touched him nothing would likely come of that. He certainly had no money. He wondered now why he'd bothered with his clumsy and childish visit with Choi. Nothing would come of that as well.

"You relax," she said. "I finish soon."

He watched her like an infatuated school boy, for the moment hopelessly in love with the effortless, unconscious poise of her every movement. She served the meal as if she'd planned the order in which it should be eaten. The noodles first, followed by little bowls of chopped vegetables and the meat mixed with the rice and another darker rice that seemed sticky and was stacked in balls in a bowl decorated with silhouettes of birds. She brought a spoon and a fork, but Profar instead took the sticks with their wood-burned dragon markings. Jia watched as he loaded his empty plate with the food and began to eat.

"I like to watch you eat," she said.

"You're not hungry?"

"I already do," she said and smiled. "I watch you eat now. Okay?"

"Okay."

She sat with her long legs folded and pointed at the red rice cakes and the sliced grilled meat soaked in sesame sauce that tasted like garlic. She made sure he took both kinds of kimchee and explained that one wasn't very spicy because she knew Americans sometimes didn't like things too hot. Profar felt like he was performing for someone as he ate and swallowed and nodded. He wiped his chin with the folded wet cloth she'd set aside. He said that it all tasted great. Like nothing he'd ever eaten before. She set down a plate heaped with spicy bean sprouts and then another with cucumbers loaded with a red sauce and spinach and also peeled radishes sliced so thin they were transparent. She mixed this with tiny potatoes. The smallest potatoes he'd ever seen, marble sized, that could fit into a teaspoon. Profar wondered how she'd done all this on a simple hot plate in this tiny room, and when he saw how much food would be left over he said: "You made enough for a party."

"Ajima, she eat some. My friends, too. Everybody like when I cook. No worry. You take to camp for Helelleh? I see him eat always dry noodles from mess hall bags like you. You both too skinny. This better than mess hall, yes?"

"Much better, yes," he said. He spoke with his mouth full and she laughed. The giggle of a young girl.

"Now I make you tea," she said. "Tea like medicine. Best tea in village. My province where I was born is where Korea grow first tea in old times."

She cleared everything away. He watched her arrange two cups without their saucers next to a tray as she kneeled beside the low table. She poured hot water from a brass pot into one of two bowls. She whispered and called it the 'cooling bowl,' and she smiled and arranged things again to make certain all was placed in some ordained order that was a mystery to Profar. She touched everything with both hands, precisely, as if it were an anointment and looked off to the side as she poured the water again into the second bowl, adding the tea slowly, again cradling the bowl with one hand. Theatrical in every detail, he thought. Like something that should be performed on a stage in front of an audience. Then he realized he was the audience.

"Ginger root with honey," she said. "Good for stomach. Good after food."

She turned her face coyly and poured his cup and filled her own and carefully placed the delicate white saucers beneath each cup.

"Remo, he no like when I do the tea," she said. "He laugh and say it take too long. He always in a hurry, hurry. Always *balli, balli*. I say life is too fast so we do the tea in no hurry to make life last longer. He not understand."

Profar also did not understand, but he lied and nodded. She handed him his cup. She seemed to enjoy that he did not slurp the tea but sipped it carefully while looking at her over the rim of his cup. He watched her gaze into her own cup as she drank and he did so as well. They finished the tea in silence, the only sound the rain dripping softly outside in the courtyard.

He felt he might have wolfed down his food and slurped the tea. He felt like a big oaf sitting at the low table with his legs folded while she sat there as naturally elegant as ever, totally at ease in her world.

She took his empty cup. She cleared the bowls from the tray and turned and carried everything to the wash basin on the table where the hot plate sat plugged into the wall.

"Tea taste good?"

"The food was great and everything was perfect."

Each day this got more complicated. She kept looking at him, studying him. He sensed she might want him to stay, but he took his jacket and stared dumbly at the floor and thanked her again for the fine dinner. His tongue was tied.

He hadn't seen it before, but the strange knife that lay wrapped in a paper scroll on the wall shelf seemed to have been set apart from everything else in the room. Like a shrine for something meant to be used in a ceremony. Nothing else sat close to it but a burning candle on a glass tea saucer. The decorated sheath, the carved bone handle with its brass knob, something that seemed like it might be too heavy for her to carry. She saw him staring at it, but he decided not to ask what it was.

"Somebody give it to me as gift a long time ago," she said. "To protect me. Maybe it's magic, I don't know. Maybe if you believe something is magic, it will be magic and have power."

It was warm, the heat rising from the floor. The candles flickered in their red jars. The cool humid breeze blew through the doorway. The smell from the meal he'd just eaten filled the room, and he thought he shouldn't say anything further and so he nodded and stepped toward the door and mumbled, "Thank you again for the fine dinner. This was a nice surprise."

Without a sound, she stepped up from behind and when he turned she slipped her cool smooth hands beneath his shirt against his skin and then wrapped her lovely arms around him.

CHAPTER 35

The North Korean General pulled down the brim of his enormous bundt cake bakery hat like he expected things to get windy.

"America the bold gangster is the unchanged arch criminal and toothless wolf and the principal enemy of the DPRK," he shouted. "Just as our Marshall Kim Il-Sung's great-great -great-grandfather defeated the imperialist US monkeys in the year 1866, so will we devour the same Satan before he poisons our people with more lies."

He sighed thoughtfully. "You will be ashes when we make a small pile out of your buildings in Washington from our bombs and missiles that fall like rain upon America."

General Yardley cupped his earphones and listened to the translation. The North Korean leaned across the conference table.

The translator's measured voice was monotone: "Now, it is up to the America to choose whether it should exist or not. We offer this generous proposal to you. As our great leader has said when he promised to push himself up from American depredations: We will make fruits cascade down and their sweet aroma fill the air on the sea of apple trees at the foot of Chol Pass!"

Yardley covered the mic and whispered to his G-2 officer, "What the hell is this twerp talking about?"

The North Korean took off his reading glasses and glared at the American General.

"Miracles can only accrue in our country, not yours," he said. "I pray for the longevity of our great leader and comrade Kim Il-Sung. I also pray for the crazy American Satan leader Johnson, the murderous devil with a tail Johnson, so that he may fail in his prosecution of the peoples of Vietnam. Our comrades. You dirty fellows are clowns and monkeys for thinking we will bend to your threats because you are traitors for all ages and the source of all evil in this world."

Profar and Manny Perez sat in their metal folding chairs. There were the usual photos of the USS Viator and aerial maps of the DMZ. One of the easels showed a photo collage of a recent ambush near Robideaux that had killed three soldiers and a United Nations liaison. The headline said: REDS SLAY 4 IN DMZ NIGHT RAID.

Every discussion, each introduction of a new visual aid, took twice as long during these sessions. The American translator was often interrupted by the North Koreans for 'twisting the words' of their chief negotiator, Lieutenant General Kang Reyung-So, who was also the operations officer for the Deputy Marshal of the DPRK in Pyongyang, North Korea's second highest military official. The translation dispute put a hold on further negotiations while the JSA's liaison team re-phrased the statement to the satisfaction of General Kang's staff. The transcript and its addenda then had to be entered into the official record by vote.

Profar whispered to Perez: "Do they always go on and on like this?"

"You wouldn't believe what they call us," Perez said. "One of their Colonels said the old man was a fat monkey bastard. Yardley didn't blink. He just drank more water. They were having one of their drinking battles that day. Finally the other guy calls a break and high-tails it to the head. The junior officers can't piss until Kang takes a leak and that's when it gets interesting. There's a urinal hierarchy. You can see them cross their legs. Yardley must slam a gallon at these meetings. They almost knock each other down trying to get to the damn toilet. I can't understand why they haven't figured it out. Everybody knows about Yardley's bag."

The North Korean stood and shouted: "I will not let Satan speak to me this way!"

Lee had asked Profar to listen for obscene words. He said the NoKos used profanity better than their southern brothers. The North Korean junior officers sitting in rows behind their General often joined in on the accusations like a repeating chorus.

He heard this phrase today: *Mi-Chin-Nyeon*. This was easy to remember because it sounded like *My Chin is Neon*, so he wrote that down and showed it to Perez.

"Ah, *you crazy bastard*," Perez said. "One of my favorites. The old guy says *ji-Ral* a lot. They say it loosely means, *bullshit*."

Profar looked at the *Stars and Stripes* in his lap. There was a story about a night ambush on the same road where he and Lee got banged up. They found the three-quarter-ton truck with bullet holes in the windshield. The two scouts, on their way to a routine patrol, were dead. After a brief firefight, another squad repelled and killed the infiltrators. There were seven empty ammunition clips lying in a ditch next to the road along with their spent 7.62 mm Soviet cartridges. The pictures showed the wet blood blotch on the driver's seat and the Colt pistol in the dirt in the middle of the road. They had the pictures mounted on one of the easels.

It got dark outside. The room dimmed, and while both sides shuffled papers and made notes about the official transcript changes, Profar listened to the steady thumping of rain on the roof. Building T-2 looked like the other structures. Same dull blue paint and fake wood wall panels. Yardley tossed back another glass of water.

The General opened the conversation with his official report of the DMZ ambush, the fifteenth such incursion that year, calling it "a disgusting violation" of the armistice agreement that would not go unanswered.

"I want to tell you, Kang," Yardley said, avoiding the use of the North Korean's military rank. "The clear evidence here, like the evidence in all the previous violations, is overwhelming. No amount of insults against the United States can change that fact. With that said and entered into the record, I wish at this time to return to the purpose of the meeting today and that is the criminal boarding and capture of the USS Viator and its crew in international waters that took place several months ago. I repeat at this time our conditions for satisfaction, and these are that your regime return the vessel and its crew as well as apologize to the government of the United States for this illegal action. Furthermore, we remind you that the United

States reserves the right to ask for compensation under international law regarding the illegal capture and theft of its property."

General Kang smiled as the American gulped his water.

"We have a saying. The empty wagon makes the loudest noise," Kang said. "I pity you who is forced to behave like a hooligan, to disregard your age and honor to do the bidding of the war maniac Johnson for the sake of bread and dollars to keep your miserable life safe. You probably served the dog devil Kennedy who is now in Hell, a corpse with a hole in his head. If you want to escape his same fate do not act like the devil, like all the American Satans in this room."

Kang read from his stack of papers. "On January 23 you committed the crude and aggressive act of infiltrating the armed ship in discussion, the imperialist vessel Violator..."

"Let me stop you right there, General Kang," Yardley said. "It's *Viator*, not *Violator*. Do not use that word. It is the wrong word."

Kang didn't look up. He listened to the translation.

He said: "...the spy ship that was equipped with aggressive weapons and materials of espionage for the purpose of making evil intentions of the United States against the Democratic People's Republic of Korea and its brave and honorable leader. For this reason our brave vessels fired upon the pirate ship in discussion to stop such criminal acts in our coastal waters which were designed to worsen tensions in the region and make another war of bloody aggression."

Kang held up one finger and listed his government's demands. "First, the United States must apologize and admit that it intruded into our waters and it must assure the Democratic People's Republic of Korea in writing this will never happen again."

Yardley countered: "I will investigate any reasonable allegations and before you continue I must say that I will not be diverted by your bombastic tactics and childish insults. I propose a recess."

"I accept your proposal for recess," Kang said. He looked at his own pitcher of water. Yardley took a drink and instructed his assistant to hand over the USS Viator's navigation log in response to North Korea's continued claim that the vessel had strayed illegally into its coastal waters.

"I repeat that the United States must admit, apologize and assure. The three A's, as you would say. This should be easy for even you to remember," Kang said.

When they adjourned, Perez turned to Profar. "Kang pretty much gives that same speech every week."

"This wasn't really a meeting, was it?" Profar said.

"First, the old man and the other guy insult each other," Perez said. "They make faces. They give each other something to sign. Then they say they're going to recess. What it really means is that everybody goes home. This has been going on for sixteen years."

"The dick tube, does he put it in himself?"

"Now he does," Perez said. "We had to go to a room over in T-3 the first week because he couldn't do it right. Kept falling out and his pants would be wet and he'd walk sideways to his chair so nobody would see it."

"Couldn't do it right?"

Perez watched to see if Yardley was finished talking to a Sergeant Major wearing a blue UN helmet.

"You have to insert the tube until the pee starts coming out, and then it's about two inches past that. He'd always stop pushing because it would sting a little and he'd panic," Perez said. "I told him to use gel and that he'd get used to it. Everybody gets used to it."

"He's okay with it now?"

"I think he wants me to hang around in case something goes wrong," Perez said. "He wants me here with my full kit, like I'm going to do surgery on him or something. The official reason I'm here is that last year one of the South Korean translators got a heart attack. That was his excuse, to have me around for staff safety. It's really to take care of his weiner hose."

"Cushy job," Profar said.

"Almost as cushy as yours," Perez said. "Hey, listen. I heard somebody up the road from Robideaux saw weird tracks."

"What kind of tracks?" Profar said.

Perez nodded to General Yardley, who'd picked up his brief case and was walking toward the two MPs guarding the side exit door.

"Probably a bear," Perez said. "You guys are always telling ghost stories."

Profar parked the jeep between the two corrugated metal buildings and waited for the General.

Two days later Yardley received a phone call from the US Embassy in Seoul about the latest demand from the North Koreans. "The White House doesn't want this," the intelligence attaché said. "The boss said he wants something better, and fast."

CHAPTER 36

"Manny says he can tell when the old man is taking a whiz," Profar said. "He looks at the ceiling and swallows. It can't feel natural, going in your pants. He drank a swimming pool yesterday, gallons. The Korean guy went to the head four times. Might be why he got so mad. Yardley's under a shitload of pressure, I'm not sure he has anything. It's a stalemate. Things are jumpy up there."

"You'd be proud," Lee said. "I didn't get hammered all week. They shot a scout at the hot springs. Said the muzzle fire came from our side of the shore, which is weird. Means they got through the fence and circled behind our guys."

The GP shack door was open, a breeze blowing from where they'd been burning trash along the service road. A sour sewer stink. There used to be cricket and frog sounds from the bushes and trees below Robideaux. Everything within a hundred meters was dead now, the river willows raked away by the dozers.

"I've been thinking. We should go back," Profar said.

"The tunnel," Lee said and lit his cigarette. "Every few days one of us says that, but we don't actually do anything, do we?" He opened the fire door on the cold diesel stove and tossed in his match.

"You can't let them stay there."

"Any one of them would have cut our throats in a heartbeat," Lee said and tried to blow a smoke ring but all he managed was a white blob that floated through the open door. "Why the sudden love of humanity?"

"I don't want this hanging over my head," Profar said.

"It's already hanging over your head," Lee said. "They'll ask why we waited so long. Too late to fix it now. Our irresponsible fuckery has fornicated us, my friend."

"We'll say we we'd already told Cobb," Profar said. "That thing with his yeobo spooked us. We got scared and the ambush put us out of commission. They'll put two and two together."

"The Army never puts two and two together. They'll say we're soldiers. We're not supposed to get scared," Lee said. "They'll lock our asses up in the stockade and we'll get court marshaled and then you'll really have something hanging over your head. We're too deep now to tell anybody anything. It's time to let sleeping commies lie."

"It's out there," Profar said. "That thing can kill one of our guys the same way it killed those Northies. Let that sink in."

"I think it just hunts people in the winter because it's easy. Maybe it went back where it came from. Maybe it likes the taste of North Koreans. Maybe that's it, Eddie. We just don't taste that good."

"Next time our guys do an ambush patrol at night, maybe it's waiting for them and so it's our fault," Profar said.

"So you want to tell Bingham?" Lee said. "He's more lifer GI Joe than Cobb. The last time we told somebody they tried to kill us, remember?"

Profar said: "Maybe we should see if it came back."

"You're serious?"

Profar nodded. "If there's no sign of it, we'll shut up. I'll know when I see tracks. I'll know."

Lee opened the stove door, took a final drag, and tossed in the cigarette.

"Just say when, Daniel Boone."

"I'll go myself," Profar said. "I'll say I was the one who found the NoKos and you won't get into trouble. They already don't like you. I'll say you were out walking patrol like a good boy and I saw the tracks and I followed them to the tunnel and you'll be out of the picture. I don't mind."

"That's a lot of lies to keep track of, Edward," Lee said. "Maybe we should take the bodies downriver."

"They'll know," Lee said. "They'll send stuff to the lab in Seoul."

"People die in the Imjin all the time. In a week they'll be at the bottom of the bay at Incheon."

They lit cigarettes, as if smoking might provide wisdom. There was no sound but the breeze creaking the plywood door on its hinges.

Profar stepped outside and used the piss pipe. He didn't feel like walking to the latrine. When he returned, Lee had pulled on his mud boots. He had that look, like he was about to launch into another monologue.

"We don't have time for time travel, brother," Profar said. He looked at his watch.

"This reminds me of Borodino," he said.

Profar sighed. "Borrow what?"

"Borodino. The Russia campaign."

"Not now."

"It was my last campaign before I got killed. I wasn't much older than I am now."

They slung their weapons. Profar hitched his .45 holster and tightened the belt outside his jacket. They stepped outside and headed along the slippery clay trail below Robideaux. The Imjin was running high, piles of deadfall racing past in the current. Whole tree trunks bobbed and turned violently in the channel of the river.

"Generals and conquerors, they're grifters and crooks," Lee said. "They said MacArthur was larger than life, but he was a sick freak. Like all the other self-absorbed freaky psycho generals. Napoleon, Alexander, Genghis, give me a name and I'll show you somebody who killed people because he had something up his ass about changing the world. I know. I was there with two of them, Alexander and Bonaparte. Don't give me that look."

Profar said, "Wrap it up."

They walked along the stone outcrop above the river until they found the path leading to the tunnel.

"Napoleon was the worst," Lee said. "Generals fight when they've got nothing to lose. The soldier fights when he has everything on the line."

"You're starting to repeat yourself."

They mucked through dead undergrowth. Everything green here had been denuded. There were striped orange barrels of defoliant stacked along the highway and they'd begun to leak. The colorless liquid would not freeze in winter, no matter how cold it got, and the stockpile had begin to leak. The empty barrels were supposed to be hauled away, but the helicopters never came. Today, the chemical smelled like musty laundry.

The river curved in an oxbow through the broken cliffs, and it was behind a collapsed rock shelf that they'd found the cave that winter. The DMZ's two-decade accumulation of trash metal since the war had altered plant life up and down the barrier fence. Like the battlefields of Verdun and Belleau Wood, this place was a bonanza of discarded copper and steel and their countless offspring ingredients. There were strange patches of oxidized red dirt and rock where tons of wartime metal and nitric explosives had been buried in the disturbed soil. The DMZ plants had evolved to accommodate this rich accumulation, and some things that thrived here grew nowhere else on the planet.

They stood back-to-back with their rifles raised. "You remember which way?" Lee said.

There were animal tracks post-holed into the mud. A chaos of hoof marks showed where a boar had grazed on willow shoots along the beach. The explosion of tracks were like the indentations of a broomstick, along with furrows where the animals had rutted in the mud. There was the track of a bear that had wandered down from the cliff to feed on miserably tiny fish whose white bones now lay scattered on the dark sand. Here the shore was a dense stretch of shrubbery. Nobody ever patrolled here because of the wetlands and the mud.

"It took a nap right here," Profar said.

He pointed to the flattened reeds where the bear had rested with its paws outstretched in the sand. Lee said he couldn't see anything. Profar traced the hind foot drag mark.

"Bears waddle when they walk. When it got up, it zig-zagged," he said. Lee stood aiming his rifle down the trail.

"Then it climbed up there," Profar said. "Probably used that trail behind the shack and we never knew it. There's still those Korean pine trees where they didn't spray and everything around here eats pine nuts. The deer, the wild pigs. That bear."

The mud got deeper. There was another collection of tracks, older scuffs and pug marks that disappeared when they reached hard clay.

"Did you smell that?" Lee said.

The wind changed direction and the odor was suddenly gone. Profar saw the enormous rock that had shielded the tunnel opening they'd seen by moonlight that winter night. The reek hit Profar in the face as if the odor had solid form and shape, a touchable stench that seemed like it would penetrate his skin.

Lee said, "Now I don't want to go in."

A mist hung above the trail. The river had risen further up the shoreline. They high-stepped through the weeds and pulled themselves up the side of the cliff. Kudzu vines everywhere, dead and matted like hair. They'd been here twice now, and each time it had looked different. They took out their flashlights. Birds flew past, little swallows. Lee thought it was bats and he jumped. Profar unsnapped his holster and when Lee saw this he did the same. They stood in the entrance and listened while their eyes got used to the dark. When Profar coughed, the echo bounced along the length of the tunnel.

They saw the bodies immediately. They'd been dragged closer to the entrance since the visit with Cobb. Each wet shape was partly clothed and lay next to the other, the three North Koreans face-down. The backside of each concave neck was jellied with a gummy mucilage of flesh and hair.

"It undressed them," Lee said.

The convective breeze whistled through the cave. In the corner lay the soldiers' furry winter caps, a shredded quilt jacket. Something that looked like a chewed boot. Canvas straps and empty pistol belts. Everything lay mottled into unrecognizable piles like filthy laundry. The tiger had done all of this.

Lee said, "None of this seems real."

"It hasn't been here for a while," Profar said and pointed at the degraded pug marks. Five claws on the front, four on the hind feet, one of which was skewed sideways as if the animal had slipped in the clay.

"That's good," Lee said. "I don't want to see it."

"I know what a bear weighs with a track like this. I don't know what cats weigh. Males are bigger. That's big for any cat."

He examined the cleanest track opposite where the tiger had slipped. "It's hurt. Something's wrong with the hind foot. It didn't slip. It walks that way all the time."

"God almighty does it stink," Lee said. "Don't tell me any more details, Eddie."

One faceless body lay beside a wood crate. The bodies tossed off a terrible smell and the swallow nests had their own odor and there was the heavy musk scent where the tiger had stopped and peed on the crate. The birds flew back and forth, squawking each time Profar and Lee moved or spoke. Lee shined his light and the birds blinked down from their nests and pruned their feathers.

"What are you doing?" Lee said.

Profar stooped and poked his finger into a shirt pocket and pulled out something wrapped in waxed paper.

"Should have done this the last time," he said.

The map was readable. In the soldier's trouser pocket he found laminated photos. A Russian equipment repair manual. Lee turned his head and fished through the jacket of another soldier and took out more documents. He held up the filthy papers.

"Something else for insurance," Profar said and jammed everything into his ammo pouch. "I want to prove that we were here in case somebody gets any ideas. I don't trust any of them."

"You mean Bingham?"

"In case he wants to take the credit and then it's just our jackass word against an E8 lifer Sergeant," Profar said. "We're nobody, once the Army gets hold of this information. We need collateral. Once the big guys get involved, they'll try to make us disappear."

"That smell," Lee said.

"It marked its territory," Profar said.

"Could it get across the river in summer?"

"It knows where to cross," Profar said. "They swim. Maybe it never went north. Maybe it's been doing this for a long time, staying on our side in summer and hunting on the ice when it's cold. They like the water."

"Let's stay here until the fog burns off," Lee said.

They sat outside with their rifles on their knees, watching the river.

"Seems like a lot of trouble to cross over just to pee," Lee said.

"I don't think it cares much about trouble," Profar said.

"Romance," Lee said. "I think it cares about romance. You think it has a mate?"

"Where would it find a mate?"

"There can't just be one of them," Lee said.

Lee hunted in his pockets for a cigarette. "I'm sorry I said that."

"Wouldn't matter," Profar said. "It has better eyes than us. It can smell everything. We can't see or hear or smell anything at all."

A dark patch appeared on the foreshortened horizon. The hills grew darker and when it cleared and they could get their bearings Profar checked the magazine of his M14 and told Lee to do the same.

"We're getting the new sixteen," Lee said.

"I'll believe it when I see it," Profar said.

"Let's get the hell out of here," Lee said. "I'm spooked. If that river gets higher we'll have to go through the bushes."

Profar was already walking ahead through the thinning mist, the M14 unslung and held at-the-ready as he studied the cliff and glanced at Lee. He started to clamber down the slope of loose rock, slipping and holding onto the bushes.

"It stinks like sulfur," Lee said and followed.

When they reached the beach Profar sniffed. "The hot springs," he said. "We're downwind."

"Some guys brought girls to the springs for a skinny dip one night," Lee said. "They almost got smoked when a patrol squad heard them splashing around. It was foggy like this and they all came walking out jay bird naked with their hands up."

Pale sunlight broke through a cloud and lit the turbulent river. When both soldiers were within sight of the guard post they stopped in their tracks and stood listening.

There came from no known direction a deep murmur, a susurration, like the sudden loud rustle of voluminous fabric followed by a deep bass rumble. Almost a drum roll. It wasn't so much a growl as it was a slow clanking of iron sprockets, more like machinery than something alive. Profar felt his legs wobble.

And then came the deepest and loudest roar either of them had ever heard. And so they ran.

CHAPTER 37

They stumbled into the shack and turned and stood with their rifles leveled and aimed.

She could have easily caught them. When Profar looked over his shoulder as they sprinted up the steps she was trotting along loosely, looking from side to side, the floppy primordial belly pouch wobbling back and forth. She was hardly a dozen meters behind them before they managed to reach the guard post.

And now her enormous shape filled the open doorway.

She sat canted against the malformed hip and her green eyes caught the natural window light as the sun came out from behind another cloud above the river. Her forefeet remained demurely aligned side-by-side like those of a dancer about to leap. The black tail tip raised and twitching, the rise of one shoulder blade sharply lifting the hide on her back. She swung her enormous head from side to side, the single black spot visible on each round ear.

It was quiet enough inside the tiny shack so that they could hear each other's heavy breathing.

The tiger's muscled shoulders flinched as it dropped its jaw and licked itself. It raised and held one forepaw suspended and licked once more and briefly narrowed its eyes like a giant house cat sitting on a rug, supremely composed and confident.

She moaned. This was not a cat's purr. It was a phlegmy rumble, a vibration that traveled through the floor. Profar had never heard such a sound and the hairs on his arm prickled as he tried to decide what to do. To shoot? He hardly knew he was holding the M14. He didn't really know where he was or that Lee had already begun to raise his weapon and take aim at the tiger.

Profar now felt as if he'd stepped over an invisible line that separated truth from what had only been imagined. Reality informed his worst fear. There was nothing that could have prepared him for any of this.

She opened her mouth and yawned and the putrid reek of her breath in such a confined space was overpowering. A wind gusted through the door and lifted orange fur from the animal's oddly contorted and scarred hip. The long tail, itself like some living thing independent of the tiger, curled and twitched as if the animal might itself be unsure of what to do.

With a much softer growl the stubby ears suddenly flattened. The tiger opened its mouth again and Profar saw the long funnel of its pink tongue. The yellow teeth. The terrible, shaking roar that came next rose up from the floor of the shack and did not seem to belong to the animal itself.

Lee fired.

When the smoke cleared, she was no longer there. The door swung wildly on one broken hinge.

"Why did you do that?"

"It was coming," Lee said.

"It wasn't coming," Profar said. "It was sitting. Looking at us. Why did you shoot?"

"Jesus, Eddie. That thing was coming," Lee said. "You wanted to wait? For what? Did you see the ears? You're the hunter. You know what that means."

"It had all morning to kill us," Profar said. "You think it wasn't watching the whole time we were out there? It could have caught us, easy. Did you hit it?"

"I don't know," Lee said. "I don't know how I could miss."

"Well, it's gone," Profar said. His ears were ringing. "And we have to go find it."

"Find it?" Lee said.

"You can't leave that thing out there, wounded," Profar said.

There was blood on the floor. They crept down the steps with their weapons raised. Outside, he saw where one hind paw had sunk into the clay and Profar studied where the tail had brushed sideways like a dustpan broom at the moment the tiger had leaped in the direction of the river. There was another larger splash of blood, a starburst. The forepaw prints were misshapen to show where the animal had jumped into the bushes along the trail.

"It's hurt." Profar said. "We have to get it."

"Get it?" Lee turned on a complete pivot with his rifle lowered. "I don't want to get it. I want to get out of here."

Profar studied the tracks and guessed that she'd leaped five or six meters from the trail into the bushes, and that's where they now had to walk.

"There's a village down the road," Profar said. "People working in their fields. You'll be here tonight and there's Fletcher in the morning. All that other stuff we talked about, it doesn't matter now."

"Let's call it in," Lee said. Profar walked backwards and followed.

"And this time, we'll tell them what?" Profar said.

Lee walked with his rifle raised. They'd poured gravel on the path because each spring the melting snow would form ruts as water ran downhill to the river. In spring the ruts would freeze and thaw and by summer they'd be forced to bring a front end loader and grade more dirt to repair the damage. Today, as the morning grew warmer, the rainwater was rushing in a steady stream. Lee quickly went inside the shack and returned with the spotting scope. He glassed the beach up and down.

"You think it went back?" he said.

"Back where?" Profar said.

"Wherever it lives,"

"I told you. There's nothing to go back to," Profar said. "This is where it lives. You and me are unwelcome guests."

They decided to go inside, where Lee stood at the window with the scope and watched the shore while they discussed how to word the report about the tunnel that Profar said he should write. They would keep all the details of what they said in a safe place and enter an abbreviated version into the duty log that would be handed over to Bingham.

Profar held his wristwatch up to the light. "Who's on shift in the morning?"

"Carlow," Lee said.

They sat and watched. A flock of cranes lifted from the reeds on the far shore. The birds circled with their long stick legs dangling and disappeared over a North Korean hill.

"They told me you talked to Choi," Lee said. "That's dangerous, my friend. He's got the law on his side."

Profar pushed the plunger on the diesel stove. There was still fuel in the pan and the smell filled the room.

"I just wanted to help," Profar said.

"If you want to do that, your money isn't the answer, Edward."

"You told me money was the only answer."

"I have some advice," Lee said.

Profar crossed the room and tried to close the broken door. He fiddled with the bent latch. He tipped the M14 and shook the weapon to feel if he had a full magazine. You could tell by the weight and balance of the rifle. They sometimes used a couple of tracers in their loads to keep tally, but he was pretty sure it was all live rounds in there.

They kept their eyes on the window. The stacked sand bags outside were soaking wet and water dripped from the corrugated roof onto the porch. There was an empty machine gun plate on the railing outside next to a rusting metal folding chair. There was grass growing on the perimeter wall and somebody had jammed a girlie magazine between the sandbags.

"You think we scared it off?" Lee said.

"No," Profar said.

"Eddie, around here, there's only one thing more powerful than money."

"What's that, Einstein?" Profar said. "I can't believe we're talking about this right now."

"I have to talk. If I sit here and it's quiet like this, I'll just worry," Lee said.

"So, talk," Profar said.

"Eddie, the biggest baddest thing in the Army is politics. "

"Choi has the KNP in his pocket," Profar said. "He knows the judges. He sends the Quartermaster a birthday cake every year. He's friends with the Lutherans, the Buddhists. His name is on a plaque on the wall at the Methodist food bank. He's about as well greased as anybody in this town."

"You've got Yardley's ear," Lee said. "He's your Minnesota bro, you said that yourself. You spend hours every week with a damn two-star General. Nobody on his staff has that kind of access. And for some reason he's all chatty with you, a lousy Spec. 4 driver with a busted gut and broken ribs. Right now, with that shit with the boat and the talks at Panmunjom, Yardley is the only guy who can squeeze Choi's nuts. He's got political mojo."

They sat in silence, the wind gusting outside. More birds squawking overhead. At this time of year, when the seasons changed, all the birds and the animals seemed to be on the move along the DMZ.

"Eddie," Lee finally said. "Why don't you ask Yardley to do you a favor? Ask him to suggest to Choi that he release Jia from her debts, and then ask the good General to pull strings at the embassy in Seoul to give her a visa waiver. A one-way TWA ticket to Seattle would be appreciated."

Profar stared at Lee. "Are you high?"

"Straight as a pencil," Lee said. "Now, you ready to hear the rest of my suggestion or you just want to keep staring out that window? That thing's not coming back. Hell, maybe I killed it."

"You just made it angry."

Lee sat next to the furnace and kept his eyes on the door.

"Yardley is desperate," Lee said. "He's got nothing to show at Panmunjom except those charts and stupid diagrams. Right now, it's headline news everywhere. Pictures of poor navy guys in prison. Pictures of them looking sad and skinny. It's a PR nightmare. Yardley wants his third star so bad he can taste it, but unless he delivers at Panmunjom he's headed home in disgrace. You see where I'm going, Edward? What did we just do today?"

"You want me to tell Yardley about the tunnel?" Profar said.

"If Yardley can surprise those people with pictures of dead soldiers who were caught infiltrating through a secret invasion tunnel, those commies will have instant diarrhea."

"You're loaded."

"The maps, Eddie. The maps and whatever else is on those papers we took from the bodies."

"And the pictures we took with Cobb, yeah," Profar said. "Still in the box under your bunk?"

"A buddy at the signal office," Lee said. "He won't know what he's looking at. He can make prints. Those people take autopsy pics for the CID. He's seen everything."

"What made you think of this?" Profar said.

"It's a gift," Lee said. "You'll have to take care of the details. My work here is done."

"The North won't want this public," Profar said. "They'll want to turn it into a PR thing for their side, just like Yardley does. All the NoKos care about is saving face for their glorious leader, Mr. Kim."

Lee joked that he might just track Jia down in the states when his hitch ended and take her to meet the folks in Chicago. Profar said no woman would be stupid enough to take up with a former failed soldier who fought for Napoleon.

Tandem Hueys now flew their daily recon route above the river. They watched the aircraft tip and turn downstream.

They did not hear the creaking weight on the steps. By the time they heard the door bang on its broken hinge, it was already too late.

The door burst open with such force that the damp outdoor air rushed into the room as if a vacuum had been released on a rubber seal. The tiger's sheer bulk again overwhelmed the tiny space.

When Private First Class Yevgeny Lee reached for his weapon, the tiger tracked his hand with her slitted eyes as if she'd not expected such a foolish maneuver. Her tail snapped sideways and swung with a metronome cadence. She narrowed her eyes and made that throaty, chuffing sound. When the tiger glanced at Lee, who now stood and stepped away from where his M14 remained on the bench, she snarled and showed her teeth.

Profar hardly had time to blink before there came the sudden explosion of fur. The wood floor creaked like someone had tipped over a heavy piece of furniture. His reflex was to raise his arms and windmill backwards, and as he did he felt the tiger push him aside as if he were weightless. The receding bottoms of Lee's muddy boots appeared upside down beneath the tiger's forelegs as the animal easily dragged him away. Lee's cap fell off and Profar could see that his friend's fake pink plastic ear was now missing. There was a red blotch on the floor connected to a long streak of more blood that led outside through the doorway. The tiger's musky funk lingered. Lee had remained entirely mute during the attack. Not a scream, just the sound of his boots bouncing along the floor, one arm reaching up to embrace the tiger's neck as if Lee was afraid be might be dropped.

Profar ran outside and blindly fired. He saw the four smashed tracks in the clay at the bottom of the steps. He went inside and took the flashlight and grabbed two twenty-round magazines and shoved the ammo in his jacket pocket. He couldn't catch his breath. He leaned against the sandbag wall outside and tried to think. The tracks were headed toward the river. He crab-walked through the wet shrubbery and in the shine of his light he saw where the tiger had rested. There was a patch of gouged dirt and the drag marks where it seemed Lee had struggled and might have tried to crawl away. Lee was not dead.

Profar thought he should have taken the radio and called for help right away. Stupid. He was stupid. He thought to return to the shack but knew there might be a chance he could catch up with Lee. He studied the skew of the pug marks of the foot opposite the tiger's damaged hip. The animal was in no hurry. He saw another squirt of blood. Lee's or the tiger's? Maybe it was here that the animal had noticed that Lee was still alive. Maybe it had finally killed him. Crushed his skull with those six-inch incisors. Profar's mind raced. He tried not to walk too quickly through the brushy trees that now made the trail a perfect ambush spot. And then there appeared at his feet a straight and worn path that aimed itself to the unexpected opening in the soil. Here the pug marks ended. Clumps of hair clung to the bushes.

Profar stood immobilized by the weight of his own boots and considered the consequence of crawling down into the shoulder-wide hole at his feet. He felt the updraft of damp air, a dank and sweetly rotten smell rising from where the tiger had dragged his friend.

It was the air shaft they'd seen when they first walked through the tunnel. He'd had no idea it might be this close to the guard post. The tiger had been coming and going this way all along, less than a hundred meters from their shack, using the same path that led past the guard post outhouse.

He held the flashlight in his mouth and squatted. He aimed the rifle into the hole at his feet. No sound down there but a hollow dripping and a splash where he'd kicked dirt with his boot. A draft vented up and he smelled the odor of the tiger. He took hold of a dangling tree root and lowered himself with the M14 slung across his shoulder.

In the flicker of his light the wet stone tunnel walls glistened. He remembered the broken crates piled everywhere and the wires hanging from the ceiling. The narrow gauge rails bowing away into the dark. He saw the grooved pick marks and blasting bores, the clay floor with its plank walkway now covered by flowing water. On the wall were the braces and fittings for what might have been a future pipe to circulate air down from the hole he'd just climbed through. He'd seen this all before, never imagining that it had been dug so close to the path that connected all the river guard posts.

He gripped the light beneath the rifle and panned the tunnel. He took the roll of electrical tape from his cleaning kit and fastened the flashlight to the M14's wooden fore stock. Just beyond the bend ahead lay what was left of the North Koreans. He wondered if that thing would be waiting for him. He cringed when he stepped on something soft, but saw it was a pile of empty sacks. Loose stones clattered and splashed into a puddle somewhere in the dark beyond the bright reach of his light. The sound echoed twice and then all was quiet but for the hiss of his own labored breathing.

As he walked crouched with the M14, his light reflected on twin metal locker handles and he jerked away and stumbled. They'd looked like slitted eyes.

Something very large stepped out of the dark.

She sat with her white whiskers incandescent in the glow of the flashlight, her eyes scarlet, and regarded Profar with almost snobbish indifference. As if his visit had been expected and he was not all what she'd hoped for. She made that odd chuffing sound, not threatening at all. It sounded like a polite greeting. She stretched one paw and stepped forward from the shadows. She stared at him with that enormous head held high, both spoon-shaped ears swiveled forward. The tiger's shoulders came to the height of Profar's waist, its jaws higher. Her overpowering odor filled the space between them and when she raised and lowered her tail Profar thought it might signify a final countdown to something.

"Lee?"

His echoing voice sounded pitifully small, an octave too high, the tone of a little boy asking if there were monsters under his bed.

"It's Eddie," he said.

When he shouted Lee's name again her ears instantly flattened. She lowered her muzzle and released a throaty moan and then that familiar sustained growl. Her lips curled as Profar lifted the M14 and took aim, the eyes now a brighter red in the flashlight's beam. He thought of switching the rifle to full automatic, but knew it would be too hard to control and he'd only make things worse with all those ricochetting rounds. If Lee lay anywhere nearby, he might just shoot him too.

"Hey, pal," he said. "Buddy, you there?"

Lee's weak voice quavered from somewhere in the dark directly behind the tiger. Profar steadied the brass buckle of the rifle's canvas strap around his fist and he fired.

The tiger had been standing ten meters away and had already covered half that distance before Profar managed to pull the trigger and fall away to avoid the charging animal. She swiped at him with one paw, tearing the laces from Profar's boot with enough force to send him cartwheeling into the wall. He rolled and accidentally squeezed off two shots that pinged loudly off the rock ceiling. He fired continuously at where he'd last seen the tiger until the magazine was empty. He squinted through the smoke and bits of falling rock with the rifle across his chest and clawed at his ammunition pouch. He snapped in the new magazine and struck the end with the heel of his hand. He secured the M14 strap around his forearm and walked aiming his .45 with his free hand.

"Lee? Where are you, brother."

The tiger was gone. She'd run outside.

He studied the divot where the leaping animal had landed in the soft clay and pivoted. He ran in the opposite direction and shouted Lee's name.

Yevgeny Lee lay with his arms folded across his chest. The front of his jacket and shirt were torn completely away. There was a round puncture mark on the side of his bare chest that sucked air each time Lee tried to take a breath. The frothy hole was leaking something pink and phlegmy and it contracted and opened, expelling a snotty foam with each of Lee struggling gasps. Lee closed his eyes tightly with great concentration and held his mouth open, panting. There was a second beveled wound in the center of his chest where broken bone tented the skin alongside a pair of deep claw marks. The tiger's bite had penetrated nearly the entire depth of Lee's chest, snapping one rib whose sharp protruding end now moved each time Lee tried to inhale.

Profar tried to hide his own panic. "Don't move. Just don't move. You'll be all right. You'll be all right."

Lee turned away and blinked and closed his eyes.

"It's gone," Profar said. "Don't worry, you'll be okay. It ran away. That thing ran away."

Profar took his K-bar and cut the quilted insert from Lee's torn jacket sleeve. He folded a cotton scrap it into a square and pressed this against the other bleeding lesion on Lee's neck. He still had the roll of electrical tap he'd used to fasten the flashlight and he tore off a long strip with his teeth and strapped it across Lee's throat until it seemed the worst of the bleeding had stopped. Lee's scalp had been peeled away and now hung over his ear like a carelessly fitted toupee. Profar folded the flap of skin and hair back onto the raw skull and apologized as Lee screamed out in pain and lifted his knees. There were tears in his eyes.

Lee's chest heaved and he began to cough, a slobber on his lips. Profar took the knife and cut away the bloody shirt. The pink foam oozed in and out of the wound and Profar tried to remember what he'd been told about sucking chest injuries but he'd long forgotten what to do. The vein on Lee's neck pulsed violently and his eyes opened wide each time he tried to take a rattling breath. The hole in his chest kept whistling and then it suddenly stopped. Lee convulsed and arched his back. His lips darkened.

Profar slapped his jacket pockets and when he found the ballpoint pen he pulled out the clear ink tube and little spring with his teeth. He blew air through the hollow plastic barrel. He cut the pointed end of the pen barrel at a sharp slant to make it wider and pried out the end cap and once more blew through it. He wiped the sticky mucus from the wound and pushed the point of the pen barrel alongside the broken rib that seemed like it wanted to puncture the skin. He took a guess as to how deep he should push the hollow three-inch tube into the wound. He then tried to make a seal with his palm around the puncture and immediately he heard the release of air as Lee gratefully took a deep breath. His eyes opened wide. The color came back to his lips. Another slow gasp came and this was followed by a noisy wheeze until Lee seemed to fall into a steady rhythm of controlled breathing. Lee stared up at nothing in particular, a lost and questioning look. The pen barrel wobbled from his bleeding chest.

Profar didn't know the purpose of what he had just done or if he'd remembered how to do it properly, though it didn't seem like he'd had much time to come up with something else. Lee was in great pain and Profar took his hand and squeezed it. He knew what he'd done was just temporary.

"I'm sorry I hurt you," Profar said.

Lee's eyes fluttered and closed tightly as he took another careful breath. Profar pressed his hand against the base of the pen barrel and took more tape and tried to fasten his freakish medical contraption against Lee's chest. He wasn't sure he'd sealed the pneumothorax, but Lee closed his mouth and now seemed able to breathe through his nose as the upright pen barrel wobbled slowly back and forth in the wound. The puncture on Lee's throat began to seep blood through the bandage and Profar cut more cotton and tore off another length of tape.

"Brother, I have to go and call on the radio. I'll be back, all right? You hear me? I'll bring the med kit. There's drugs in the med kit. I'll put something on the cuts and you'll feel better. I promise."

Profar took Lee's hand and held it firmly against the wound on his chest. He tried to remember what he'd been taught about using a morphine ampule with a chest injury.

"I know it hurts bad, pal. You can't go to sleep. Okay?" Profar said. "Don't let go of this and don't go to sleep. Keep your hand right here and hold it straight, understand? I'll bring the meds. I'll be back before you know it."

He squirmed up through the tunnel ventilation hole and imagined that the tiger could be waiting for him at the top. It could be waiting for him at the shack. He unslung the rifle and with one hand fired once and waited before he pulled himself through the hole. His chest was pounding and when he stood to run he felt something snap in his hip and the pain shot like an electrical jolt down the length of his leg. Jesus, not now, he thought. He held the rifle in both hands and spun around and fired as he jumped up the outpost steps. He tore the first aid box from the wall and grabbed a smoke grenade from the metal ordnance locker. He called for the medevac on the field radio. He made his way back, not caring if he met the tiger on the trail, and when he saw Lee's prone shape he fired his rifle toward the tunnel entrance at nothing in particular.

Private First Class Yevgeny Lee lay staring at the ceiling with his eyes wide open. Dirty water dripped down on his face. He'd pulled the makeshift intercostal pleural drain tube from the hole in his chest and it now rested in his outstretched hand, along with the cotton bandage he'd torn off his lacerated neck. There was a deep raw claw mark on his upturned palm, like a stigmata, though it was no longer bleeding.

"Oh, Jesus," Profar moaned. "Why did you do that? No. No. No. Why did you do that?"

He knew the medics could not be allowed to see the tunnel.

He wondered about the tiger, but it was too late for that. He took Lee by his feet and hauled him outside away from the tunnel entrance. He rested and tried to gather his thoughts and then dragged Lee to the beach. He felt like he was in a terrible fever dream and half wished that he would just go crazy and be done with it. Or that the tiger would appear and do everybody a favor and kill him, too. The rain had stopped and after a while he heard the thudding chop of the helicopter rotors and when he looked up there were only the gray clouds above the gray river. Another flying parade of cranes drifted across the sky, their squawks fading. He tossed the purple smoke grenade toward the beach to mark his location.

And then he smelled the odor.

She sat with her tail raised and twitching as before. She looked away toward the sound of the approaching medevac Huey and studied Profar with those penetrating green and white eyes. He switched the M14 to full auto and fired wildly. He aimed a single shot and missed. How could he miss? The tiger ignored this completely as if she'd expected his poor aim and was not at all startled by the noise. She looked at him without flinching. Her tail bobbed up and down.

"You," Profar said.

He fumbled with the canvas ammo pouch and dropped his last magazine and watched it bounce away. He took out the .45 and chambered a round. The Huey came into view as it fell into a descending hover above the beach, the rotor wash blowing stones and water sideways. When everything cleared, Profar thought to fire the pistol but the tiger was already gone, vanished into the billowing grenade smoke like some magical forest beast in a fairytale book.

CHAPTER 38

He woke shivering with chills in the sleepless night and lay there in the dark staring at the ceiling. He felt worse that morning and knew something else was wrong with his insides. He'd whacked up his back climbing through that hole in the tunnel and now he had little feeling in his foot.

"You still have sutures inside," the doctor said. "They can take six months to dissolve. Don't expect things to get better right away. Your chart says you had all those infections. They should have just sent you home."

"Yes, sir," Profar said. "I keep doing what they say and the next guy tells me something different. Meanwhile, I'm still here."

The doctor handed him more paperwork and sent him on his way with two bottles of new pills.

The JAG office sent an investigator after Profar told the medevac crew that they'd run into a bear while on duty at the guard post.

"You figure it out," he told the officer who was taking notes furiously during the questioning. "My friend died and you're asking me biology questions. I feel like barfing. Do you want me to barf? It was a bear. Write that down because that's what I'm saying."

He knew the rain would have washed away the tracks by now. He still needed to talk to Bingham. Everything was different now. The only thing he could eat was scrambled eggs and toast at the mess hall. He drank milk when he took his pills. The doctor said the low-grade fever would go away, but it didn't. Yardley's office told him to take the week off.

Nobody was eager to let out the word that some dangerous creature might be prowling the DMZ, so they turned the investigation over to the

Korean police, who hired a wildlife researcher from Seoul. Lee's wounds were officially identified as those inflicted by an Asiatic black bear. Bingham and a ROK investigator were present when they questioned Profar. The Korean officer said he recognized Profar from when he taught the Huckleberry Finn class.

The KNP investigator, who wondered out loud why he'd been called to a casualty debriefing that involved animals, said he'd have to consult with one of the local village elders who'd had hunting experience along the river.

Bingham ordered Profar to move his things into the central barracks. He would not be authorized to carry weapons until further notice. That day, the swelling below his ribs got worse. There was a hard knot growing under the skin. When he went to the toilet and looked, everything was the wrong color. They took more blood at the dispensary. When he went to the barracks and swallowed one of the new pills he was out like a light and woke in the middle of the next day feeling more tired than when he'd gone to sleep. His head seemed foggy and he felt stupid and couldn't think straight. He tried to write a letter home and froze in the middle of a sentence when he couldn't remember his brother's name.

When he knocked on Bingham's door, the Sergeant was wearing flip-flops over his green socks, his dogs tags dangling and his cropped hair wet like he'd just stepped out of the shower.

"Well, if it isn't Gunga Din, king of the jungle," Bingham said. "I thought they told you to lay low until things get sorted out?"

"It's another infection. That's what they say when they don't know. I need to tell you something, Sarge."

Bingham pulled on his starched fatigues. His empty holster lay on the cot and Profar noticed for the first time that the Sergeant's single window overlooked the basketball court outside the barracks building. From here, he had a nice view of the very top of Soyosan Mountain rising in a blue haze above the valley miles away. There was a legend about a Buddhist monk who once lived in a temple on the mountain and who had abandoned his vows after falling in love with a beautiful Korean princess. His blind and thoughtless infatuation with a woman had made him lose everything. He'd shacked up with somebody from another world and got screwed twice for doing it.

"I don't know what you're up to," Bingham said. "Every time you come and see me, my life gets more complicated."

The Sergeant struggled with his starched shirt. "That was weird shit you talked yesterday," he said. "I suppose the lab geniuses will sort things out."

"It's about to get weirder," Profar said.

"It won't surprise me," Bingham said. "I think you and Lee dreamed something up. Maybe mistakes were made. The animal bullshit doesn't add up. For one thing, there's an ammo magazine missing. You boys signed for four and three were returned to the ordnance locker. You told them yesterday how many rounds you fired. I had them check where Lee got picked up. Nothing. Just the spent cartridges. In the report you said you fired one burst on semi and this animal you talk about, it got Lee. None of that adds up. He couldn't have gone anywhere with those injuries. What were you doing at the GP, anyway?"

"Where did they take him?"

"PFC Lee? In a cooler behind Gate Two. Then it's off to Yongsan for the autopsy," Bingham said.

"There's something else," Profar said.

"I just knew it."

"Let me talk, Sarge. Then you can ask all the questions you want."

Bingham buttoned his troublesome shirt. He crossed the room and sat. He flipped his hand at Profar and told him to get on with it.

Profar tried to speak with confidence and Bingham never interrupted. He just sat and looked at his clasped hands and got up and stood at the window.

Profar explained about the dead soldier on the ice that winter night. How they'd been high. He described the three North Koreans in the tunnel and how Cobb said it was a storage bunker the North Koreans were planning to use as a warehouse for a planned invasion. A place to store supplies for when they got their act together. Cobb had told them that he was sure there were other tunnels under the DMZ, but that they'd not been found. It was a matter of time. And now, against all odds, these two dope-smoking grunt Army jokers had done it.

"That's when Cobb told his girl," Profar said.

"The yeobo," Bingham said. "He told his yeobo about this tunnel."

Profar nodded. "Roger that. And somebody knew we were coming down the supply road that night and that's why we got ambushed."

"Bullshit," Bingham said. "How would they know?"

"The yeobo thought it would be Cobb driving that way. It was us instead. We had the same jeep. Her plan was to kill Cobb."

Bingham said. "Take me there and I'll decide what's true."

Profar handed Bingham the envelope with the photographs and a sample of the documents they'd retrieved from the dead bodies.

"I have to see it myself," Bingham said and looked at the pictures. "How do I know these are legit?"

"I've got negatives, and I've got other papers," Profar said. "I'm never going back to that place. Here's what I want, and if I get it I'll tell you where the tunnel is and give you the rest of the stuff."

Profar told Bingham what he wanted for Jia.

Bingham said. "You expect me to tell a two-star General to do that? Cook the books and arrange for a foreign national to evade the laws of this country, not to mentioned the Armed Forces Agreement, and at the same time to falsify immigration papers with the involvement of the US Embassy? You been smoking weed, Profar?"

Bingham seemed to have a fascination for his window. He again looked in the direction of Mount Soyosan.

"To forge exit papers. To give a plane ticket and cash to a prostitute?" he said. "Under the table money to be delivered to a damn pimp? Just so you can get a hooker sent to the United States?"

"That's not what it is," Profar said.

"I'm not a moron," Bingham said. "This is my second tour in this country. Profar, these girls are not members of the junior varsity high school volleyball team. They know how to play the GI game."

"Her name's Jia," Profar said.

"Whatever." Bingham waved his hand. "Get your young ass out of here. You're not feeling well and they gave you a lot of pills. You seem like a good kid and I already know you're a damn good solider, so consider that your saving grace. Get out. We never had this conversation."

"That's the deal," Profar said. "If you don't take it, I'm not telling you where the tunnel is or where those dead Koreans are and Yardley won't have shit this week when he bargains with the NoKos. If you ignore this, I'll talk to the newspapers and everybody gets embarrassed. You'll put me in the stockade, but by that time the story is out and Yardley and you and the embassy and yeah, the White House, look like stupid shits. Like dummies who didn't see an invasion tunnel being dug right under their noses. You'll never get those sailors out of North Korea."

Bingham folded his arms and looked at the floor, deep in thought. He gave a slight nod.

"I'm giving you a chance to use this information like you see fit. Nobody needs to know about the tunnel except the North Koreans. As far as the world is concerned, there were just a few infiltrators shot that night and they had nothing to do with the tunnel. Let things die down for a while. The Northies will call the dead soldier heroes, because that's what they always do. It's a PR dream. A way for them to save face. And you and the old man can pretend like you made a great deal for the return of those navy guys. I'm giving the General a chance to tell Washington that he's finally got an agreement that the North Korean's can't refuse."

"How do you know Yardley isn't already close to a deal?"

"I've been in that room," Profar said. "The Northies will wear us down."

Profar stood and pressed one hand to his side. His ribs were exploding. He pointed to the photos on Bingham's desk and hoped his heart would stop pounding.

"I've got better pictures that show everything. Unless I get what I want, I know somebody who can get them published."

The muscle in Bingham's cheek twitched. He glared at Profar.

"Why would the North care about those bodies?"

"Saving face. Kim Il-Sung would lose face. When that happens, people get shot."

Profar now said, "Here's what I think. The General says that unless the sailors are released he'll give the information to the world in a way that will only flatter the US. He'll say that it was the North Korean leader's incompetence that made the discovery possible. They won't stand for that. General Kang will never let that happen, because Kim will have him shot for letting things get out of control. Without my information, Yardley never gets a third star and he heads home with his tail between his legs. Tell him that his humble Spec. Four jeep driver is the only hope for a deal at Panmunjom."

"So your girl gets her visa and ticket?"

"Her name is Jia. Her contract with Choi disappears."

Bingham said. "That's an illegal financial transaction."

"I want her to have cash when she gets to the states."

"He'll bust me down to buck Sergeant," Bingham said: "There's too many loose legal ends."

"The Army juices people all the time." Profar said. "It bribes truck drivers who deliver booze to the officer's club. It lets the ROKs steal diesel fuel. Consider it overhead."

Profar nodded at the photos in Bingham's hand. "That box in the picture," he said. "TNT fuse chargers. A shitload stacked to the ceiling. The old man would thank you for catching this little project before things got serious. You'd get all the credit. Tell him you persuaded me to spill the beans."

Bingham squared the photos in his hands like he was stacking a deck of cards. "I'll show it to him. If he doesn't think it's bogus, expect to take us out there yourself."

"I'm not going back there," Profar said. "How long does a visa take?"

"If this is real, time won't matter. Somebody picks up a phone, it's done."

"Once Choi has his money," Profar said. "Once she's on her way, you'll get the other maps and pictures."

Profar worried all that night. Without Lee, this scheme was based on his word alone and a few underexposed photos that could have been taken anywhere. He hoped they'd see the propaganda value of the maps. If somebody wanted to get rid of him, Bingham would surely know how to make him disappear. He doubted that they could find the tunnel on their own.

When he walked into the dispensary for another follow-up, he waited for an hour before he was told to pee in a bottle and then they tested his blood again and he waited. The doctor, another Captain who noticed that Profar was clutching his side, pointed at an exam table covered with butcher paper and told him to sit and take off his shirt.

"Looks like you're headed home," he said. "But first you're going to the 122nd Evac in Seoul. Your liver is a disaster. I'm recommending immediate discharge. I don't even want you to wait to get processed at Kimpo. You should have been sent home months ago."

"Sir?" Profar said. The doctor handed him an envelope and read the results of his last blood panel.

"Not sure why they ever let you loose down in Busan. You've got serious problems that can't be fixed here. You'll need to see somebody who can make more sense of this. It says you were authorized to carry a weapon?"

"Yes, sir," Profar said. "I'm on the CG's security detail."

The doctor handed Profar his x-rays.

"Show them these," he said. "One of those vertebrae got really screwed up. And they put you on a train? Even driving that jeep wasn't doing you any favors. Why were you at the DMZ?"

Profar shrugged. "My friend was there. They let me draw a weapon."

"You really shouldn't be carrying more than five pounds."

"They've been sloppy with the regs lately," Profar said.

"Damn Army," the doctor said. He signed another document and handed it to Profar.

"Yes, sir," Profar said. "The damn Army."

CHAPTER 39

Late the next afternoon, Bingham didn't even turn around when Profar knocked and walked into the office. The Sergeant had Profar's medical file on his desk and he was looking out the window again.

"You have your deal," he said. "He about fell on his ass when he saw the pictures. Said he recognized the Chinese blasting cap boxes. He called you 'that Duluth boy' and told me to have drawings made from the photos. There's an emergency JSA session in two days. Nobody else will be attending but Yardley and two embassy people. Nothing in writing. He thinks they'll bite, if what you say about those other documents you have is true. I'll take him to the tunnel myself."

"Nobody gets the other maps until I know she's on her way," Profar said.

"Understood," Bingham said. "We're on a tight timeline. No guarantees."

Profar handed the Sergeant the directions. He'd walked along the river enough times to know the exact distances, and so he described the rocks, the beach, the kudzu that hung across the tunnel opening. He'd made no plans if the tiger decided to show up. He described the air shaft opening into the tunnel.

"The NoKos will have twenty-four hours," Bingham said. "Then the sailors walk free and we hand over three bodies. Yardley agrees with you that they'll be called heroes. He knows they'll put on a show to make Kim Il-Sung look good. That's always behind everything, to make the Big Guy look like a genius. In return, we're admitting that the Viator made a navigational error. They get to keep the ship. They want to say they whupped the United States Navy in a sea battle."

The final documents were hidden in plain sight in a cellophane pill pouch stuck under a sand bag at the Robideaux Guard Post. He figured the first thing they'd do is search his bunk at the barracks and his hooch, so he'd accounted for that.

"And if they don't bite?" Profar said.

"Then we put on our own show to explain how the inept Kim Il-Sung bungled their invasion tunnel. They won't let that happen."

"Jia gets on a plane first," Profar said. "Choi's money and the contract gets settled beforehand. Nobody gets the other papers until she's in the air. If the Army screws with me, I'll make everybody look like an absolute dick. I will."

Bingham nodded. "All our asses are hanging out there on this one. Based on that tunnel's dimensions, and if those maps you have show the other tunnel locations, our engineers say they could push across five thousand troops an hour. Tell your girl she needs to be at the MP gate at eighteen-hundred hours on Thursday."

"Choi isn't easy to deal with," Profar said.

"You leave the pimp up to us," Bingham said. "But she has to get her debt officially released. The embassy doesn't want any part of that. It would leave a paper trail. Choi will know we can't acknowledge the money he's getting. Should we be worried about that?"

***

When he knew the cash had been delivered, he told her everything. He saw the bruise on her cheek. She explained that Choi had been angry that two armed MPs had come to stand outside his office door while an American wearing a suit instructed him in no uncertain terms what was expected to happen. He said the Americans insulted him.

"He is dangerous," Jia said. "He knows how to play games. He has played these games his whole life."

She told Profar that it was foolish for him to become involved in her fortunes, good or bad.

"That you are a soldier does not matter. He fears nobody. He will not sign no papers. He will take the American dollars because he knows they will never admit to giving him the money."

She fell into his arms, and this time it was her heart that was beating against his chest. She trembled as he held her close and kissed her hair. He was enraged when he saw the long red swelling along her jaw.

"He say this is my fault. He say I tell you to come see him. He calls me trouble-maker. He say Jia is old tired *changnyeo* who now good only for cleaning GI toilets. He say he put me in Zoo house and this time I never come back."

"He won't do that," Profar said.

"He make insurance on all working girls so when they die before they pay contract he make money anyway," Jia said. "All men like Choi have insurance on bar girls if they die."

He gave her the bus ticket to Seoul. Someone from the embassy would be waiting for her. She would have to get her signed contract endorsed by the local KNP so she could receive her travel stamp.

Profar gave her an envelope. "They wrote everything down for you. Do exactly what it says. I can't be involved anymore."

"He crazy mad at me, so he never sign. He lose face if he sign, money or not. He lose honor."

"He can buy plenty of honor with that money," Profar said.

She touched his face. "You sweet, nice boy," she said. "You don't know men like this. Honor is more important than money for Korea man. More important than life."

CHAPTER 40

She stood for the longest time in the alley outside his office door, working up the courage to knock, and thought about the first time she'd met Choi Il-Seong so long ago.

He seemed very nice, well groomed, his shoes shined and his language so polished she thought he might be a school teacher. He stopped in front of the jail cell door that day in Busan and smiled. He walked down the hallway and spoke to one of the KNP patrolmen, who came and unlocked the door and said she could visit with her guest for a few minutes while they finished the paperwork charging her and her friends with vagrancy and the public sale of commercial products without a license.

Choi handed Jia a white card and introduced himself and said he owned a local restaurant and tourist entertainment establishment. He said he had many acquaintances in the police department and that all three district court judges were close friends. His family had lived in Busan for generations; she could ask anyone. Since the Joseon kings and queens, he said. Jia had no idea what king and queens he was talking about. She had never seen someone's business card.

He asked where she was from. Jia lied and said she was born in Seoul and was a student and he shook his head and said, no, her accent had given her away. She was not from any city. He asked if she spoke English.

"The pastor man taught me," she said.

"Your pastor. The criminal?"

Jia said. "They were from California America."

"California America, that's very sweet. You are very sweet and pretty," he said.

He wore a double braided gold chain. She'd never seen shiny shoes like his before and he smelled of cologne. Jia had never heard of a man who wore perfume or seen one who combed his hair that way except in the American magazines she saw displayed in the street stalls of Busan. He touched the top of his slicked head while Jia explained that she hadn't known what she was doing was illegal. He took out a cigarette and lit it gracefully with a match that he sparked by scraping it against the bars of the cell door. He blew the smoke and waved it away with his hand.

"Your pastor. This man who sent you here. He's now in trouble. Very much trouble. You won't be seeing him again," Choi said. "I need someone like you. A lovely young polite lady who speaks English and who has manners. Maybe I can arrange something." He pointed down the hallway. "I have friends here. I'll speak to someone."

"I don't know you," Jia said.

"You would be paid," he said. "You would not be selling cheap shirts off a street corner like a peasant. You are not a waif. You would have nice clothes, a clean place to live. It's your luck that I happened to see you tonight. It's fate that I am here. You believe in fate, don't you? I'll keep you safe."

"What would I be paid to do?" she said.

Jia remembered that this is when Choi took a long look at her. His eyes wandered down her legs that showed from under the frumpy floral skirt that Brother Caleb had forced all the girls in his cult wear.

When she was packing her few belonging and getting ready to leave with Choi, he spotted the long blade, the Mudang's knife that she always carried with her when she was on the street.

"What's that?" Choi said.

"To protect myself," Jia said.

"I will protect you from now on," Choi said.

When she finally knocked and walked in, he looked up from his desk and shook his head when he saw the papers Jia was holding in her hand. He started lecturing her.

"I took you from nothing. You were begging in an alley while that fornicating pastor had his hand down your pants," Choi said. "I expected you to come today."

He sneered at the papers she dropped on his desk. Choi's cigarette lay smoking in the glass ashtray. Jia stood with her arms folded and looked away, trying her best not to fall apart. Choi had always terrified her. That's what he would want now, to watch her crumble before him like a weakling. The office was silent. The rain pounded incessantly on the metal roof. Choi took his cigarette and she watched the smoke coil in the humid air. The wall safe within reach of the desk stood open and when he saw her look at it he swung the heavy steel door shut.

"And you gave me a better life? This life?" she said.

"You already have your money. That's all you ever wanted. Let me go. Sign it. You said yourself that I'm of no use to you anymore."

From his desk Choi took out the bundle of American currency, wrapped fifty-dollar bills, and dropped it on top of Jia's employment contract. He reached and touched one of the safe's gleaming brass handles.

"The Americans brought me this," he said. "I suppose you already know. There's much more, of course. Enough to fill a suitcase. More than you're worth, really. You would not believe how much money someone thinks you are worth. Honestly, it surprised me. I did not expect to be paid in American dollars. Can you believe such a fortunate thing? Now, where would a woman of your meager resources obtain such funds? I never knew you had such influence."

"I don't know anything about where the money came from, Choi Il-Seong."

"Someone who has your interests in mind," Choi said. "Perhaps the brave warrior chauffeur office clerk Profar, is that who I should thank for these funds? I had no idea that a Specialist Four made such a generous salary. That sickly worthless naive boy? He has nothing. Just as you have nothing."

Choi set the money in the ashtray and tore away the wrapper. He waved his lighter with a slow flourish and touched the currency and watched it catch and burn.

"I have just destroyed what it costs to keep your miserable slut stomach filled with food for a year, do you know that?" he said. "That's what I think of the money from your hero, the sickly office clerk Profar. The chauffeur. Your other gallant yeobo, the soldier Remo, once told me he would pay for your freedom. We both now know that was a lie. They all lie when they make this promise. Never in my many years has one of them actually done what they said they would do in the name of love. Your man of God, the pervert and rapist Bible swindler, Brother Caleb, should have taught you that much. I think I should wait to see where this money came from and perhaps we can then have a proper conversation. Now I am curious."

"There's no time for that, Choi Il-Seong," Jia said. "You know there's no time for that. Now keep the money and let me go."

The money curled and turned black in the tray, bits of ash lifting and floating across the room in the breeze that came through the open doorway where a small rug was beginning to get soaked from the blowing rain. Outside it thundered softly. Choi grinned and poked at the burning bills with his pen and watched what was left of the money catch fire and rise into a flickering blue flame. He smiled and leaned in his chair.

"There's no time for that," Jia said. "Please sign it now, Choi Il-Seong. You have what you want, now give me my freedom. Please, it doesn't matter where the money came from."

Choi composed his hands on the desk and shook his head in disapproval like a parent refusing a pleading child.

"What a mistake I made with you," he said.

Choi looked up as Mrs. Yoshida suddenly stepped out of the rain and paused in the open doorway with her wet hair dripping, a flash of lightning briefly illuminating the dimly lit room. The sky behind her turned pale and there came the rumble of loud thunder. She wiped her face with her sleeve and walked up and stood defiantly next to Jia. She wore a green military poncho draped across her shoulders and stood there with her hands behind her back. She hissed angrily.

"The contract. Give it to her, Choi Il-Seong," she said.

She touched Jia's arm. "Give it to her now. You have all the money in the world. You have enough contracts and you have the promise of many more. This one is no longer of any use to you. Let her go. She can't wait while you tease her with your cruel talk."

When Choi stood, Mrs. Yoshida gently pushed Jia aside and nodded at the desk.

"We will not leave until you sign the paper," she said.

Another volley of thunder rumbled outside. Rain splashed onto the rug. The office lights flickered.

Choi stepped from behind the desk and took Mrs. Yoshida's by the shoulders and pushed her aside. As she stumbled, he reached and caught her by the hair and began to slap the back of her head until she finally fell to her knees. He now used his fist. Jia jumped on Choi's back, but he easily shook her away and stood over Mrs. Yoshida, who stared up at him from her knees with one hand held to her bleeding mouth.

"You miserable old *ban-jjokbari,*" Choi said. "You filthy useless dried-up wash woman! What do you know about who is useful to me and who is not? It is you who are of no use to me. You're no better than the other Japanese half-breeds who never belonged in my country. Maybe the *zainichi* should go back where she belongs. You are the one who I pay and feed, and in return for what? Such loyalty? Now get out, you pitiful old woman. I will deal with you later."

Mrs. Yoshida caught Jia's gaze and nodded sternly at her, and then stood and staggered into the alley.

The pile of money he'd burned continued to smoke. Choi pushed the ashtray aside. He spoke slowly, his voice all but drowned by the loud downpour of rain outside.

"You should be grateful," he said. "You were as good as dead and I gave you life, or do you not remember this? I gave you safety. You were invisible until I found you sitting in that filthy Busan jail. And this is what you do in return?"

"Sign the paper," Jia said.

Choi looked away as if he were speaking to someone else. "And still she insults me," he said.

Choi unbuckled his belt and pulled it free. He took Jia by the hair.

"Children who disobey must be punished," he shouted. "Children who refuse to learn their lessons must be punished."

She tried to pull free as he lashed her bare legs with the belt. Choi twisted her hair in his fist and as she windmilled her arms they both lost their balance and tumbled to the floor, where Choi got to his knees and straddled her and began to claw at her clothes. He slapped her and began to drag Jia screaming across the floor to the little bedroom where he sometimes slept.

Choi Il-Seong never noticed Mrs. Yoshida standing in the doorway with her wet gray hair spilled across one shoulder, her torn clothes dripping. She held the long knife that she'd retrieved from Jia's room, the Mudang's blade, at her side; the knife that Jia had once received as protection so long ago. The blade's white bone handle with its carved tiger face was clearly visible. She took one long step forward and waved Jia to the side and stood with the blade pointed down at the pimp.

"*Jjokbari*, put that thing away before you hurt yourself," Choi said and tried to stand, but Mrs. Yoshida kicked his shoulder and sent him back to the floor. Choi's eyes darted around the room.

Jia snatched together the front of her torn blouse and stepped away just as Mrs. Yoshida nodded toward the desk and shook the Mudang's knife. Choi reached out and the mamasan quickly swept the long blade.

"Sit over there," she said.

Choi sat at the desk and clutched his bleeding hand. Mrs. Yoshida stepped behind him and pushed the wheeled chair forward and pressed the blade of the knife against Choi's neck. She pressed it firmly and was surprised how very sharp it was. A thin bead of blood rose at Choi's throat and began to drip onto the desk.

"I've butchered pigs much larger than you," she said. "I know where this knife needs to go. I know all the spaces between the bones. I could do this with my eyes closed. Do not test me, Choi Il-Seong."

She wedged the dull backside of the knife between two of Choi's vertebrae and pushed until he winced and cried out.

"See? One more twist with the sharp side and you will never take a step again. It will not hurt," Mrs. Yoshida said. "Keep your hands on the desk," she said. "The next time there will be no warning. If you move, the knife will move," she said. "Where is it? The contract."

Jia pushed the papers in front of Choi.

Mrs. Yoshida shoved aside the ashtray with its pile of burned money and took the pen from where it lay on the desk.

"Nothing will be signed today," Choi said.

He sat hunched while Mrs. Yoshida leaned her weight onto Choi's shoulder and watched the drops of blood soak the fabric of his white shirt.

"He knows I can sign his name, anyway," she said. "I do it for other things. They won't know. Nobody will know. I know where his papers are and I know where he keeps his money."

"I'll tell them it was a forgery," Choi said. "You can't get away with this."

"And I will tell them about the bribes," Mrs. Yoshida said. "About the taxes you have not paid. The money you have in that wall. You already know this. Now sign it."

When the pimp Choi suddenly leaped to his feet and pushed Mrs. Yoshida away, the old woman fell and struck her head against the steel door of the wall safe. As Choi stood looking down at her, Jia picked up the Mudang's knife and shouted at the pimp.

"Don't you touch her, you miserable bastard,"

The heavy blade now felt suddenly lighter and seemed to pulse in her hand with a life of its own and when Choi growled maniacally and stepped toward her, she swung it effortlessly because the Mudang's knife now weighed hardly anything at all and seemed to move as if another much stronger hand was guiding it.

CHAPTER 41

Manny Perez called in a few favors at Mortuary Affairs.

"They told me you could have ten minutes," the medic said and unlatched the steel door on one of three Quonset huts that sat end-to-end behind the camp clinic.

Profar didn't know this place existed. Nobody knew this place existed. It was where they kept dead North Korean infiltrators and GI suicides and those who'd died under questionable circumstances. Lee was headed to Seoul for his autopsy.

Inside, the white tile walls were glaringly bright. It reminded Profar of a subway station restroom, a long windowless half-cylinder building with double stacked rows of numbered latched doors on the far wall. Oversized lights blazing in their wire baskets. A rattling metal ceiling grate blew cold air and a gutter pipe ran down the center of the cement floor to a drain hole where Profar could hear an incessant trickling.

Manny Perez yanked open one of the stainless steel doors and out rolled Private First Class Yevgeny Lee on rubber casters, feet-first, as if his draped white shape was floating on air. Profar could recognize the shrouded outline of his friend's face beneath the sheet.

"He looks smaller," Profar mumbled as Perez pulled away the sheet.

"They all do," the medic said. "The fat guys look thinner. The tall guys look shorter."

They stared at the body. Perez took Lee's fake ear from his pocket. He twisted the prosthetic onto the clip on the side of Lee's head.

"They found it on the floor in the shack," Perez said. "It's only right that we put it back, don't you think?"

The round and doughy hole in his chest, where Profar had stuck the ballpoint pen, looked like a tiny moon crater.

"I don't know if I helped him with that," he said. "I didn't know what else to do."

"It's not like people carry around a thoracostomy needle in their pocket. Or chest patches," Perez said and pulled down the sheet to reveal the lumps along the side of Lee's chest. "You did your best."

Perez looked at his watch and walked away. "Don't beat yourself up about it. He didn't have a chance. The lights are automatic. Just push him in and shut the door."

From here Lee would be delivered to the casualty operations officer at 8th Army in Yongsan. He'd depart Korea from Kimpo, where a few months ago they'd held in absentia memorial services for the two sailors who'd been killed during the capture of the USS Viator. Profar had seen the photo in *Stars and Stripes*. From there, Lee would travel in the cargo bay of a TWA charter flight filled with happy soldiers who themselves were also headed to their families after completing the standard thirteen-month hitch in Korea. After a stop at Yokota Air Base in Japan it was a right turn across the Pacific and a straight shot to Tacoma, Washington and Fort Lewis, where he and his band mates from Duluth had spent their last weeks together before being shipped off for deployment. Profar imagined Lee's flight landing at O'Hare in Chicago, where his parents would accompany their boy for the twenty-minute drive on the Kennedy Expressway to the Lawrence Avenue exit, where his parents' grocery store stood on a corner below the walk-up apartment where Lee had spent his childhood. Maybe the funeral would be traditional Korean, maybe his mother would insist on a Russian Orthodox service. He knew Lee would not have cared.

Since he'd officially been killed in a combat zone while on hazardous duty, there was a question on how to categorize Lee's death. Things would have been easy had he died in a traditional firefight. Now, the complex paperwork alone might delay the body's return to the US by a week. Profar was certain that his friend would have found this final bureaucratic circus terribly amusing. A symbolic and highly gratifying FUBAR, he would have said. And then he would have continued with a half-hour jag on the clerical bungling he'd witnessed in Napoleon's Grand Armée in 1812. Or the chaos that ensued after Alexander the Great's death in Babylon in 324 BC.

The briny disinfectant smell lifted off the corpse. Lee looked like he was all bones. Just so skinny. And the big feet; he would have joked about his own big feet. A wet sponge, the square brown kind that you'd use to wash a car, lay next to his face on the stainless steel table. A pool of something like coagulated toothpaste next to it, a pair of used surgical gloves crumpled up next to that, as if it had all been left behind in haste after they'd washed the body to get it ready for shipment. The bloodless finger-sized puncture wound next to his windpipe was there, bruised black and still scabbed. It was hard to believe the tiger's jaws could open wide enough to make such a wound. Perez had told him that the tooth that had punctured Lee's right lung had penetrated the thickest part of the sternum. The flimsy pen barrel Profar had used might not have had the proper reach to release the pressure in the chest cavity for very long.

"Hey, bud," Profar said. His whisper echoed off the tile walls. "It was me who wanted to go back to that place. It wasn't you. I'm sorry."

Lee's dark wet hair was combed. His head rested on a rubber wedge that made it seem like his friend was gazing lazily off to the side.

Profar felt strange that he'd just spoken to a dead man. The room, except for the slight dripping sound, was so quiet that he could hear himself breathe. Lee's arms lay at his side and his dark fingernails were shiny like they'd been painted with polish, but he knew this meant something else. Perez had explained it. The toes were that way too, and Profar remembered that they'd wiped the body with temporary embalming liquid for the long truck ride to Seoul. It was summer and it was hot and humid.

Profar spoke again: "Bye, brother. Come see me some day."

Manny Perez poked his head through the door. "The CID boys still have custody of the body and they'll be headed here soon. It wouldn't be kosher if they saw that I let you in here. Sorry."

"Did they tell his parents?"

"Oh, they know by now," Perez said. "Red Cross does that right away. I don't know if they sent somebody to the house, but there's always a telegram. I've seen the telegrams. Two sentences is all. Bam, bam, thank you ma'm, your boy is dead. Stop. Pretty lousy way to find out your kid is gone."

"Maybe he'll get a medal," Profar said.

"A medal."

"He should get some kind of medal for his folks to have."

"Yeah, for his parents," Perez said. "That would be nice. It was really the same as getting shot. Worse, actually. Wouldn't be the way anybody would want to go. It's no different than getting wasted in a firefight. They should for sure give him a medal."

Profar tucked the sheet neatly around the body and made sure the very top was straight and properly aligned across his face. He pushed the wheeled shelf into the wall until all you could see were the bottoms of Lee's pure white bare dead feet standing stiff and straight with the chain of his dog tag swinging from one toe.

CHAPTER 42

With her hand shaking, she gave the bus driver the ticket and showed her red health certificate, confirming that she'd received her shots that month. The civilian driver glanced at the ID card and shrugged.

"What do I want with that?" he said. "I can't let you ride without the pass from the police."

She showed the stamped and translated note from the local KNP medical officer authorizing her to travel on the MSR. The driver tipped the card toward the dashboard lights and studied it as if it were the first time he'd seen such a thing. He squinted at Jia's photo and nodded. General Yardley himself had pressured the police to issue the order that no bar girl employed in the special entertainment district was allowed to leave the camp town zone using public transportation without the approval of local law enforcement.

She sat with the small suitcase on her lap and watched the village recede in the dawn darkness. She felt an unexpected sentimentality for this place that had caused her so much sadness and from which she'd longed to escape these many years. Why the sudden nostalgia, she couldn't explain. She tried to ignore the flood of memories. She recalled how Choi Il-Seong had forced her to swallow the secobarbitol pills so she would be relaxed on her first night with a GI, a disgusting man whose hair smelled like sour milk and who'd asked her to do things to him that had frightened her. He spoke to her constantly in a rapid, gibbering English she could not understand. She'd kept her eyes closed, and when the man with his greasy stinking hair and sweaty cold hands was finally finished he dressed and gave her a quick kiss on the cheek and rushed from the hooch without closing the door. While she was frantically cleaning herself and brushing her teeth and rinsing her mouth, she couldn't take her eyes off the crumpled twenty- dollar bill he'd tossed on the bedside table. Choi had told her she would get used to it.

And then in a brief flash she now recalled when she first became the soldier Remo's yeobo. They'd already moved into their hooch and he'd made his passionate promises about marriage, about coming home with him to begin a new life. She'd taught him a playful and well-known bawdy drinking song with Korean obscenities and when he sang this out loud while he was drunk one night at the Water Dragon Club the other girls began to laugh and point at him. And so he beat her that night with his belt in full view of his friends. After the MPs came and took Remo to camp, Choi woke her in the middle of the night and shouted that she shouldn't play tricks like that again and that she must apologize to the soldier she'd shamed and embarrassed.

With the ticket stub gripped in her hand, Jia read the instructions on the envelope she'd tucked down the front of her blouse. She began to have doubts that any of this was real. She had for days felt that Profar's improbable scheme might unravel at any moment, but then he'd put his arms around her and explained everything and how this was her only hope. He seemed different from the others. He'd promised that he would find her once she arrived in the states, though she had no faith that fate might not conspire against her.

The bus pulled in front of Gate 2. GIs dressed in uniform boarded and gave Jia a knowing glance as they shuffled down the aisle with their duffle bags and took their seats. There were a few chuckles and one of the soldiers turned and smiled at her. Jia looked away. Civilian employees wearing their laminated ID cards, houseboys and janitors and the evening shift cooks who worked at the twenty-four-hour mess hall—they boarded and sat and spoke softly in Korean as they looked at Jia without expression.

As the bus turned onto the highway, she watched a man with a broom sweep that night's empty beer bottles and paper trash into a pile on the sidewalk in front of his small shop. When they drove past the cement tank traps and artillery bunkers that slanted from both sides of the road at the edge of the village, Jia recognized the large building behind the barbed wire fence. There was a brightly lit sentry booth with a guard standing outside. A pair of mercury lamps illuminated the long driveway that led up to the Soyosan Health Center, where Jia had been forced to stay after Choi Il-Seong first brought her to the village from Busan. She was pregnant at the time, a sixteen-year-old girl about to experience yet another terror in her short and horror-filled life.

Jia watched the building's ominous silhouette smear past the dark bus window, her own phantom reflection hardly recognizable. She forced herself to stare ahead at the promising glow of the coming sunrise on the horizon.

She nodded off into a sour and disturbed sleep.

In the familiar, repeating dream she lay shivering in a cold room, a bare light on a cord swinging in its shadow from the ceiling. Enormous cockroaches rattled across the floor and vanished beneath the stinking bed that hung from the wall on chains like a shelf. The grinning nurse with red eyes standing in the doorway said, "I have something for you," and she placed a wrapped box on the bed. The nurse took a paper cup from her tray and told Jia she must now drink her medicine, and so Jia obediently did. Her stomach burned and when she heard a noise and looked outside, the bathroom door had burst open and flooded the hallway with a river of sewage. Her roommate was a girl with bruised cheeks, her gown soaked with blood, front teeth missing. From where she lay, the girl watched Jia examine the parcel and said, "Hide that. They steal everything here," and she folded her arms and turned to the wall and began to sob.

In that freezing room Jia stepped into her slippers and went into the stinking hallway. The bathroom door was shut again and she heard a soft grunting inside, and when the woman stepped out she avoided Jia's gaze and walked away clutching her belly. There was a basin filled with blood in the corner and the floor next to the squat toilet was enameled with frost. The naked babies lay scattered in pieces and when Jia tried to see their faces someone from the hallway shouted, "You shouldn't look. Please don't look." There were posters on the wall that proclaimed, *The Labor of Your Work Honors Us All.*

In the same dream that had repeated itself now for years, Jia shrieked and ran to her room, where she found her own mother sitting on the bed. She wore her familiar white head scarf and soberly handed Jia a package wrapped with a bow as if it were a gift. She heard thumping. When Jia assembled the pieces of the baby boy inside the box the infant pumped its little legs and smiled up at her. Jia turned to her mother and said, "What should I do?"

"Pick up the little baby and ask what he wants," her mother said. "Don't look at his face."

"Don't look at its face?"

"No, you mustn't look at the little boy's face."

There was a letter in the box. "It's from the baby's mother," Jia said. "She wants me to ask why her little boy died."

"Talk to the little baby," her mother said. "Go ahead. Don't be afraid. It's only a baby."

Jia asked the question and turned away, ashamed.

Her mother asked what the baby had said but when Jia tried to speak her mother was already dead.

Jia said: "The baby said to tell his mother he was sorry, but that it had not been the correct time for him to be born and that everything would be all right and he would return at another time."

Jia tried to light a match to look at the baby's face but the infant blew out the flame and closed its eyes and it too died with a tiny exhalation of breath as if it had finally been allowed to rest.

She woke in her seat on the bus with a scream. The startled driver was staring at her, shaking her shoulder.

"Wake up. We're at your stop, understand? Wake up."

She took the suitcase and reached into her blouse to make sure the hidden envelope was still there. She pushed past the driver, stepped off the bus and was surrounded by honking street traffic and the bright lights of the Yongsan garrison.

At the USO booth she handed the older lady sitting behind the desk another envelope. The unsmiling woman wore a long skirt with a smiley-face name tag pinned to a sweater that was buttoned to her chin. She regarded Jia suspiciously, held up the envelope and said that this had nothing to do with her and she would have to find an MP. Jia sat clutching her suitcase, and when she saw two men in suits walking quickly toward her she felt her face flush with heat. She followed the men into a small room behind the booth, where the USO woman got up from behind her desk and hurried away.

An hour later she was introduced to two men in uniform, one of them a Korean who said he was from the Embassy and that he would accompany her to the airport. He handed Jia a document and examined her signature and folded the paper into his jacket pocket. He said one of his colleagues would meet her at the airport in Tacoma with further instructions. She had no idea of where Tacoma was, but she nodded.

"And the document?" he asked.

Jia had been holding this envelope during the entire journey that morning and it was wet from the rain and smudged from her constant fiddling. She asked if it was possible to please have a copy of the signed papers and the man shook his head sadly and said that she could not. He spoke formally and said his instructions had been to only obtain these certain papers and attest to their receipt and that it would further be examined by other authorities in order to ascertain their final legitimacy. She took out the promissory note with its notarized blue provincial district court stamp. On it were Choi's scratchy signature and the Hangul characters designating Mrs. Yoshida as a witnessing attestor to the document's legal acquittance. There was a further note at the bottom of the last page under Choi's second signature signifying that all Jia's debts had been satisfied in full and that she was henceforth absolved of all future manner of promissory as outlined in the statutes of Gyeonggi Province, Republic of South Korea.

She watched while the man examined the watermark and embossed notary stamp. The embassy man nodded and handed Jia her one-way ticket to Tacoma, Washington.

"Someone will meet you," he said. "At the customs office. They will be expecting you. Good luck. Are you carrying anything on your person that we should know about? Your ticket has a diplomatic endorsement so you won't be subject to a standard customs inspection, but we'd like to know."

Jia lied and said she did not.

He turned and nodded at the MP. The three of them walked to the boarding area where people were gathered at the large window that overlooked the runway. Outside, they had red rope strung across the tarmac and a red carpet led from the terminal building to a waiting Pan Am 747. There was a long banner attached to the side of the mobile passenger boarding stairs that now began to creep toward the aircraft. There was a large crowd of people. Newspaper reporters stood by with their cameras.

When her flight was announced she showed her boarding pass to the attendant, who pronounced Jia's full and complete name slowly and with great courtesy as she welcomed her aboard.

She'd never been on an airplane and she was nervous. When the aircraft began to taxi to its take-off position she closed her eyes and gripped both armrests. For a moment she thought the sudden, explosive rumbling of the engines might mean something was wrong and that the plane would at any moment tear apart. She felt a flutter in her stomach on take-off and it was as if she were weightless and was herself floating in air. She expected at any moment to wake up from another dream.

From her seat Jia looked down at the green corrugated landscape and watched a farmer walking behind his ox in a bare field alongside the airport runway. The slightest trace of the summer's barley crop, she thought. The faint young shoots casting the field in pale green, a favorite memory from her childhood. The plane flew very low and as it tipped its wing to turn, she could easily see the hooves of the farmer's ox kicking up the rich black turf. The farmer, reins looped across his shoulders and his hands on the twin posts of the antique plow, was dressed in his baggy white work pants and rubber boots. He wore a floppy straw hat and this reminded her of her father and the memory of him working the fields in their village so long ago. She remembered how pleasant it was to walk through the water when she was a little girl, the thick paddy mud warm on her bare feet. She remembered the cranes flying and the smell of the persimmon trees and she thought she might begin to cry.

She felt a flutter in her stomach as the aircraft suddenly dropped its wing and circled in a wide arc as it gained altitude and turned east over the city.

She watched sunlight flicker across the distant black tidal flats of Incheon Bay and then the wide Han River appeared below as it curved through the endless hazy sprawl of Seoul.

She'd once felt open-hearted about the world and its people and had welcomed the unfolding glow of each day's beginning, but that had ended long ago when the war took away her childhood. Today, when she finally stepped aboard the plane, she felt the baggage of her history fall away piece by piece. For so long, the world had seemed stark with only sharp edges. Nothing soft about anything, each day without promise or hope. But not on this day. Not in this moment.

She was so tired. She closed her eyes and saw the faces of her brothers: Hyeon smiling over his shoulder as he walked beside her parents, who were wearing the clothes they'd died in. Her mother's beautiful long hair bound by the white scarf; baby brother Ji-Yeong's little face peering from where he hung swaddled on his mother's back. Her father with his floppy hat, bent beneath the weight of the wooden *jige* that sagged heavily with all their belongings on the day they'd been chased from their home forever by the war. And then they faded away.

She rested her hand on the lumpy hem of her jacket, where Mrs. Yoshida had sewn the pouch filled with American dollars. The very funds Eddie Profar had arranged to be delivered to Choi Il-Seong, and for which the pimp no longer had any use.

Jia slept in her seat with a familiar ache in her heart as the plane lifted through clouds that now reached toward the perfect blue horizon.

CHAPTER 43

Profar looked up at the blustery sky and wondered where she was at that moment.

The rain itself seemed wetter when the summer monsoon finally arrived with a great windy downpour that sent the sidewalk vendors and noodle sellers running for cover beneath their canvas awnings. There were no more calm spring drizzles or cool nights where Profar slept with the hooch door open so he could listen to the saloon drunks make their ruckus as they headed to camp through the alley behind the Water Dragon Club.

Now, it was the daily cloudbursts of pounding warm rain that flooded the alley byeonso and turned the shallow river that ran through the village into a whitewater torrent. Something you could ride in a canoe. The bar girls carried their umbrellas everywhere as they ducked in and out of doorways in their high heels and skimpy bordello skirts. GIs stood in line outside the club beneath their rubber ponchos like patient ticket holders to a music concert, the MPs in their long black slickers standing by and looking dangerous, like disapproving chaperones.

Nobody had seen Choi Il-Seong for two days now, and there was a rumor that the Water Dragon Club owner had mysteriously left town and that Mrs. Yoshida had moved her things into his office and was now in charge of everything. Choi's new black Mercedes 280SL ragtop had been moved down the street, where it sat locked and parked outside one of his other village properties. Someone said they'd seen Mrs. Yoshida sitting at Choi's desk well into the night, signing documents and paper-clipping them together and putting everything into individual envelopes.

They ordered Profar to Yongsan for more tests. He thought they would have taken enough of his blood by now. He waited on the bus bench beneath the front gate awning for the night shuttle to Seoul, where he would stay at the 8th Army transient barracks for the early morning appointment at the 121st Evacuation Hospital.

He watched that night's party crowd walk past the MP checkpoint. You could pretty much flash any piece of paper at the MPs and they'd wave you through. There was more rain, of course. It would stay that way for the next month. The colored neon saloon lights across the street flashed their blurry reds and yellows on the wet asphalt of the MSR. A happy, colorful light show. A few girls who Profar recognized stood smoking hunched beneath their umbrellas in a doorway. Their lipsticked faces were lit theatrically by the glow of a pink sign shaped like a naked dancer in stiletto heels. Cathouse neon art. He could hear their laughter. One of them held out her arm and shot a middle finger at a shouting GI across the street and they all burst into giggles and ran down the street. Loud music pounded and thumped from every doorway.

The rain stopped abruptly as if a faucet had been turned off. Everything stood wet and dripping, the street steaming as the vendors assembled their tents and tabletop grills in preparation for another night of commerce in the Ville.

The next morning after his tests a doctor wearing Captain's bars came with his clipboard and gravely told Profar to sit. He had good news, he said.

"You're going home."

"Sir?"

"Home," the Captain said. "A three-month early out. I already called your admin NCO and explained everything."

"They've told me that before," Profar said.

"This time it's for real. Your Top wants you to call him," the Captain said. "We can't treat you here and sending you to Japan for another evaluation would be a waste of time and delay your discharge. And so you qualify for a medical early out. I could have the paperwork done in Yongsan and send you to Kimpo today, but they took over a whole charter flight for those sailors from the ship."

"The ship," Profar said.

"The one the North Koreans captured last winter," the Captain said as he wrote on his clipboard. "The USS Viator. You read the papers?"

"Not lately. I know all about the boat."

"Well, that was the front page today," the Captain said. "They agreed on something at Panmunjom. A last-minute deal. Those boys are headed home just like you, but they got priority with the transportation. Airport is bound to be a circus with all the press coming in. You can either stay here for a couple of days or head to your unit. You probably want to get your gear."

"Yes, sir," Profar said.

"Okay. Done," the Captain said. "I'm guessing they put you on a transport flight straight to Fort Lewis. Not as comfy as a commercial charter, but quicker. You'll be in a hurry to get home, I'm sure."

"Yes, sir."

"If you have personals back at your unit you can forward it. Maybe ask a buddy."

"I don't have anything, sir," Profar said. "They can just toss it all."

"Nothing sentimental? Souvenirs, that sort of thing?"

"I had a dog once," Profar said. "I kept his collar. It would be nice to take that home. Maybe when I call my Sarge. I don't really have anything I want from there."

"What kind of dog?"

"Shepherd," Profar said.

"That's rare in this country," the doctor said. "A rough life here for dogs. I wouldn't pick this place if I was a dog. They seem to end up on somebody's menu. I only eat the vegetables when I go to town."

He walked Profar to the door. "Make sure you take the meds. Start them right away and get the prescription filled stateside before they process you out. I don't know how the VA works these days, but it's free if you get the meds from the base pharmacy at Fort Lewis before you get processed. I gave you enough for three months."

The Captain handed Profar his envelope. A nurse gave him two pills and water in a paper cup.

"Sir? What did they say about the deal?" Profar said. "In the papers, what did they say about the deal with the North Koreans?"

"Said we made them an offer and the North Koreans seemed very pleased. They're never ever happy about anything, but in the picture I saw your CG and a Korean guy smiling. Everybody seemed happy. No details. They never give the details on these things and when they do it's not the truth. It's nice to see those boys safe. Who cares about the details, right?"

***

After he picked up his travel orders from the garrison TMO desk, he put everything he owned in his duffle bag. It was funny how quick the Army could get rid of you when it wanted to.

He used half the money he had in the world for a taxi to the airport instead of bouncing around in a bus through the rat maze streets of Seoul. The cab was a dented Fiat with squeaky brakes and a clothes hanger radio antenna. The smiling driver had a single front gold tooth that gleamed in the rear-view mirror as they zig-zagged through the city. The neighborhoods in Seoul still had crumbled buildings from the war, whole blocks of structures leaning to one side like they'd been blown over in a wind. There were construction sites everywhere, but mostly it was old bombed houses and the craters and deep battle trenches that had never been filled, all of it overgrown with weeds or used as a garbage dump. Somebody was always burning something in an alley in Seoul. There were smoking tire fires everywhere, along with piles of flaming power line posts. As the taxi made a shortcut, Profar saw men sitting in a circle and tinkering with lawnmower motors. That was the other thing about Seoul: people everywhere fixing stuff and cutting up scrap metal. Sitting on curbs with a screwdriver or a hammer, their entire world in a hurried state of repair. Something being re-shaped and pounded everywhere. Nobody ever said that Koreans didn't know how to work. Profar felt he would forever have a sweet spot in his heart for these people.

He watched a pack of skinny dogs race from the alley, chased by a surprisingly nimble old lady with a broom in her hands. What breeds of dog you saw were of questionable pedigree, oddly colored curs missing tails or ears, walking with a sideways waddle. They were seasoned and wary refugees themselves, like many of their owners had once been. This was a land with no time or sympathy for pets. Everything and everybody was on their own.

Early in his tour he'd bought his puppy from Mr. Yun, who owned the embroidery shop across from the main MP gate. He'd just been assigned his cot at the Quonset hut and the NCO there also had a dog so Profar kept the shepherd pup on a chain outside during the day. They fed it mess hall scraps and it drank water from an ammo can. Tex had a white blaze shaped like the Lone Star State on his forehead and a curled black tail with a white tip that he carried high like he had an attitude about the world in General. Like he had Chow or Husky in the family tree, which meant that he was born to wander. At night after work and when they weren't loitering at the club, Profar and Lee sometimes tossed a Frisbee to the dog as it ran across the helicopter landing pad behind the Quonset hut. Tex had cost Profar ten bucks in American greenbacks and he was pretty sure he was high when he bought the dog and snuck him through the MP gate in the hood of his parka.

"People here have better things to do than feed a house pet," Lee once said. "Koreans think we're nuts the way we treat animals that don't earn their keep."

A few weeks later, the dog slipped free from his collar and when Profar went to the village that weekend he saw the pelt in the food market nailed to a wall next to a pile of clay *onggi* kitchen pots. White tip on the tail. The map of Texas on the forehead. Profar bought the hide for twenty bucks and him and Lee buried it under a pile of stacked stones next to the helo landing pad.

At Kimpo he stood at the window overlooking the cargo taxiway and watched a line of newly arrived soldiers in uniform walk toward the terminal carrying their duffle bags on their shoulders. They looked jaunty in their new boots and starched fatigues, fresh from AIT school. The Korean stewardesses in their tight powder blue skirts and berets stood smiling and giving little Asian bows from the bottom of the boarding stairway. Some of the GIs were wearing the bewildered look of someone just awakened from a nap as they were hurried into the waiting bus. One of the flight attendants held up a sign that said *Welcome to the Land of the Morning Calm*. Another waved the cardboard cut-out of a grinning cartoon tiger. A happy greeting from tiger land.

It was another hour until his flight. He fretted about Jia. He was sure he'd never see her again. He didn't know at this moment if what he'd done had been stupid. None of it now seemed real at all.

He found a seat in the boarding area and picked up a newspaper from a plastic chair. The giant headline said, "They're Free!" There was a picture of the USS Viator crew standing in a row behind a speaker's podium on the tarmac at the San Diego airport. The sailors seemed to be taking turns shaking hands with a Navy admiral, and a large banner hanging from the fuselage of the commercial aircraft behind them said, "Welcome Home Heroes!"

He'd tried to phone Bingham that morning. There was no answer. They were starting to line up at the boarding gate and Profar shook out coins from his pocket and found a pay phone and dialed up the NCO office at camp. When Bingham picked up, there was a long pause and he could hear the Sergeant take a deep breath. There was background chatter of somebody talking and laughing in the barracks office.

"Sarge?" Profar listened to Bingham give another deep sigh and then the Sergeant spoke in a hushed voice that sounded like he might be covering the phone receiver with this hand.

"Where are you?" he said.

"Did the rest of it go okay?" Profar said.

"I asked you a question. Where are you?"

"Kimpo. Ready to get on the plane. They said they called you. They're shipping me home."

"They sent a TelEx to the company CO. Did you know they were giving you an emergency medical discharge?"

"Not until my tests came back," Profar said. "I figured they'd keep you up to speed. Did the thing we talked about go okay?"

"Well, they didn't keep me up to speed," Bingham said. "And the G2 is on my ass for not keeping track of you. When does your plane leave?"

"They're getting ready to board."

"Well, get on it," Bingham said. "I can't explain much right now, just get on that flight pronto. Understand?"

"You can't just say that and not tell me what's going on. What happened to her?"

"It all went okay. We appreciate you trusting us," Bingham said. "I mean, getting the documents to us and the map before she was actually on the plane. Everything would have been impossible otherwise. She's somewhere over the Pacific right now. But there might be a hitch on your end."

"A hitch."

"Eddie..." Bingham lowered his voice.

Two MPs walked into the boarding area and stood there looking around and then one of them took off at a brisk pace down the hallway. The other soldier looked at his watch and kept his eye on the crowd as it assembled into a line next to the ticket counter.

"Jesus, Sarge," Profar said. "What kind of hitch?"

"They can't find Choi. Apparently, before he disappeared he lodged a formal complaint with the KNP and the 8th Army Provost Office and said you tried to bribe him into altering a legally binding agreement between him and one of his employees. He must really dislike you, Profar. Nobody counted on him doing that. Nobody thought he would go to all that trouble after we gave him the cash."

"He's pretending he didn't get the money and that it was me who tried to pay him off? That doesn't make sense."

"Because this whole deal is off the books," Bingham said. "Nothing's written down. This thing has been verbal. Officially it never happened and there's no way the embassy or the CG's people are going to admit it ever happened. The cash, I mean. There's no trail. If they find you, Eddie, nobody here is going to know your name. You understand? Not one son of a bitch will admit to being part of this deal. Now that the negotiations with the North Koreans are history and all the right people got their pictures taken, nobody is going to give a shit about Specialist fucking Four Eddie Profar. If Choi ever shows up, all he has to do is swear under oath that an American soldier attempted to bribe him. And he'll turn over some token cash and keep the rest. That's the end of it. That's the end of you. The powers that be can't risk you talking about what happened with that tunnel and the girl. Only a few people know the real story. Nobody will take your side in this."

"You don't know where Choi is?"

"Gone. Like smoke. The Korean cops aren't talking. They need to cover their asses, too," Bingham said.

Somebody behind the ticket counter spoke through a hand mic and instructed the first twenty soldiers to board the aircraft. Outside the window, the Air Force cargo aircraft's giant wings looked like they were a mile long and Profar could see GIs heading toward the boarding steps.

"I'm sorry, Eddie," Bingham said. "They want you in for questioning. I'm doing you a favor here. Get on that plane and there's a chance if you get out of Korean air space they won't pursue it further. Right now they don't know where you are. I didn't tell them. But they'll track you down through the hospital and your doctor and then all bets are off."

"Why are they doing this? Why do they even care about me?"

"After that protest at camp with Yardley and the case with the murdered Korean girl in the Ville, there's no tolerance for anything that looks like the Army is favoring a soldier who might have broken a law. They think you broke the law. Choi said you broke the law and it made all the alarm bells go off. They'll make an example of you, Eddie."

"What if I go to the papers?"

"Look, I think it might blow away once the PR cycle is runs its course. You won't go to the papers. You know why? They'll just find your girl and bring her back to Korea. Do you want that? They'll track her down. Unless she's real smart, they'll track her down. They have all the time and money in the world for stuff like that."

"Choi was a crook. Not just a pimp," Profar said. "She's smart enough, Sarge. She's smart enough to disappear."

"Okay. Agreed," Bingham said. "Choi's manager, some lady who runs that club, she gave the cops all kinds of dirt on him. Turned over his records. He's the biggest slicky boy black marketeer in the province. He might not be back in town anytime soon. That would be in your favor, of course.

Hopefully, he took Uncle Sam's cash and he's in Bangkok right now living the good life on our dime."

"Just get on that plane," Bingham said again. "I don't want you sitting in the Yongsan cooler for a month while they sort this out. We both better hope Choi doesn't show up. That's your saving grace, if he doesn't show up. I have to go now, Eddie. Good luck. Get on that plane right now."

CHAPTER 44

The women stood assembled in a circle with their hands clasped before them like reluctant penitents showing up for a church sacrament nobody wanted to attend.

They turned and watched as Mrs. Yoshida and another girl from the River Dragon Club stepped forward with little ceremony and let the small box they were carrying tumble into the grave. Mrs. Yoshida looked around as if not knowing what to do next. She nodded at someone, who picked up a shovel and tossed a few clods of dirt onto the tiny coffin. Everybody wondered out loud how the pimp Choi Il-Seong's body could have fit into such a small container, but of course most of them already knew.

The miniature coffin, fashioned from scrap wood and seemingly made in haste by someone who might have never before held a hammer, had been brought from the village in the trunk of a taxi. The driver himself had carried the box up the hill from where he'd parked his cab along the MSR, thinking perhaps that this might be the remains of just another poor unknown soul who was being buried at the town's seldom-visited pauper graveyard.

After a while, the women each filed past where they'd just buried what remained of Choi Il-Seong and one by one put a match to their individual promissory notes and tossed the burning sheets into the smoking grave. One of them angrily kicked dirt onto the box with her foot and shouted a profanity as she tore up her document and tossed the fluttering scraps of paper over her shoulder. Some of the burning pieces curled and lifted from the grave and blew away across the cemetery. Without a word or another glance the women turned and walked off, some with their arms around one another. A few were laughing. They were dressed plainly today, nothing sparkly, no short sequined skirts or teased up hair or makeup on their faces. They always seemed younger when you saw them away from the glitter ball lights at the River Dragon Club. Today they were just cemetery visitors on a sunny spring day, properly saying goodby to an acquaintance who'd died. Mrs. Yoshida stood by the grave and looked at the sky and closed her eyes.

Fifteen miles away at Panmunjom there was another funeral. Each of the three little coffins was wrapped in white linen like a holiday gift and situated with great care on a draped table that stood in the gravel walkway between the T-2 and T-3 conference buildings at the Joint Security Area. The coffins contained the remains of the three North Korean soldiers that had been retrieved from what was now officially known on classified US Army documents as Imjin Incursion Tunnel Number One. Each coffin was labeled with two calligraphic Hangul symbols signifying that its contents should be considered eternally revered. North Korea's 6th Light Infantry Division military band stood nearby on the gravel pathway playing martial music that soundly overly boisterous and celebratory for such a serious occasion. They performed while marching in step where they stood in the gravel, as if they were getting ready to announce the start of a sporting event. The musicians were dressed in their regimental T-64 tank uniforms, each wearing a holstered sidearm, and they stood close enough together so that their large formal dress hats nearly touched as they played their music. The tuba players were positioned only inches from where they could have easily stepped across the demarcation line into South Korea.

When the song was over the bass and tenor drum players performed a loud and swelling roll, after which three ROK color guards from the South wearing white gloves walked in a dirge two-step up to the table that displayed the remains. They bowed slowly in unison. Each South Korean soldier lifted one of the boxes and walked somberly to the center of the walkway, where a strip of raised concrete marked the demarcation line between the two nations. The boxes weighed only a few pounds and each trooper held his individual coffin straight-armed and handed it to his counterpart in North Korea. Those three men were dressed in white naval uniforms and they each turned on a perfect pivot and marched off briskly as the band kicked in with a mournful funeral requiem, something decidedly Western. Maybe Chopin or Mendelssohn. They carried the boxes toward the grandiose North Korean pavilion they were constructing behind the humble JSA conference structures.

The marching band dutifully followed the soldiers and their boxed heroes up the marble stairs.

CHAPTER 45

In the long years ahead he hunted for her everywhere. He wrote letters he knew she would never read.

For a time, he lived near Tacoma in a cabin and drove a Corvair three-speed that wobbled dangerously whenever he raced along the river road to his job at a factory that made rubber kitchen appliance gaskets. He drove a taxi in the city and took GI Bill night classes at a junior college with a view of the bay. There was another job driving a fork lift at the NAPA warehouse, where he picked heavy car parts off the shelves. And another as a janitor at an aircraft fabrication plant in Puyallup.

He'd found out earlier that she'd worked as a cashier at the Fort Lewis commissary, and might have lived somewhere near the harbor. When he mentioned her name to the manager at the all-night restaurant the woman glared at him like he was a pervert and walked away.

When they finally sent him his transcripts from the University of Minnesota in Duluth, he took the Corvair and his monthly VA disability pension and headed to Colorado. He swapped the car in Boise for an old Ford truck with a camper top and hired on for two weeks as a highway flagman at a construction site in Rawlins, Wyoming.

And then for many years, following obscure information that almost always brought him to a dead end—beyond the countless odd jobs and aimless travel and occasional trips home to visit his brother in Minnesota, she just vanished. Not a trace of Miss Jia Kim, which is what Profar assumed she might now be calling herself in America. Her tracks had all but vanished.

A collection service he'd paid for a few days' work said they found someone with her name and possible matching background on a list of tenants who lived in a North Side Chicago apartment building. Profar wondered if Yevgeny Lee had told her about the Korean community on Lawrence Avenue. And so one winter on his way to visit his brother for Christmas in Duluth he took a bus to Chicago, where he spent the night on a bench in the Greyhound station on Randolph Street and took a room at a fleabag motel near Albany Park.

The entire city block where the Lee family corner grocery store was once located had been razed to make room for a strip mall with an enormous Asian supermarket. There was an outdoor holiday fair on the day he took the CTA to the Pulaski Road station. With its smoking barbecue grills and piles of Korean food, the noisy place sounded and smelled like the weekend market in the Ville. There were, of course, dozens of Lees in the local phone book. He wanted to tell them about their son and how he'd been there when he died, but Yevgeny Lee's mother and father had also turned to vapor and vanished. The address he'd been given for the apartment building where he hoped Jia might have lived turned out to be a fire station.

He continued to write the letters, thinking that if he put his thoughts on paper that his memories might be set free to live elsewhere. He was getting weary of his endless recollections and he wanted what he'd written to have a life beyond his own, even if his letters ended up in the trash.

His brother helped him land a union card to work the final two months of shipping season that winter as a stevedore unloading freight at the Port Authority pier in Duluth. He then bought a junky car and wandered for a few aimless months through the Dakotas, working indoor construction jobs until spring, when he finally found work as a trucker hauling lumber between Rapid City and Grand Junction, Colorado.

He was goosing his thirteen-speed semi along a seven-percent grade west of the Eisenhower Tunnel one day, tapping gears down to sixth so that all the Jake brake cylinders would kick in, his air compression inhibitors clacking loudly, when the truck jack-knifed and sent 5,000 board feet of lumber onto I-70. Ski season traffic was tied up for twelve hours.

After he lost that job he took on a seasonal contract cleaning picnic sites and pit toilet bathrooms in the Pike National Forest. It allowed him time to fish and hunt and they gave him a free summer campsite twenty minutes outside of Colorado Springs.

Two winters later found him living at the old Cliff House Hotel on Cannon Avenue just blocks from the cog railway in Manitou that took tourists to the top of Pikes Peak. He would walk between the track timbers up the steep incline steps in the off-season just to clear his busy head; three hours up and three hours down, not the safest thing to do for somebody with a weak ticker and a bad knee, but the physical effort cleared his thoughts and helped him sleep.

At the hotel Profar worked as a general fix-it man. They gave him a basement room that was a few minutes walk to the bus that took him to the VA Hospital, where they looked him over every few months to see if the parts he'd damaged in Korea were still working. Each year they'd find something else wrong with him. First, it was his hearing. Then more grim news about his back and knee. The heart started stuttering and getting out of whack during his second decade out of the Army and they decided that the worsening atrial fibrillation and the weakened valve might have been affected by the defoliant they'd sprayed up and down the DMZ in 1968. The stuff they'd stored in leaking barrels a mile down the road from the Robideaux guard post shack. They upped his monthly disability check, gave him pills to thin his blood and told him he'd be okay as long as he stopped drinking and smoking or exerting himself too much.

One spring years later, he made his way south to the San Luis Valley where he again found work at an RV campground in Monte Vista, where he was the oldest part-time seasonal worker employed at the Rio Grande National Forest. The rangers at the park called him Pops.

By now, he'd become the habitual traveler. An aimless, untraceable sojourner seemingly carried by the wind to all points of the compass.

That year, he watched the migrating cranes as they came drifting into the valley at night by the thousands. The silhouetted birds with their long necks extended looked like strange pterodactyls from another epoch as they flew overhead beneath a vast dome of stars. Studying the dark shapes pass overhead from where he lay in the bed of his truck, the Sangre de Cristos in silhouette in the distance, the squawking creatures reminded him of the cranes flying above the Imjin River on a winter night in Korea. He felt as if he were recollecting the life of a total stranger.

He then spent the years crossing southern Colorado through Gunnison, Salida and Buena Vista, where he hired on as a fly fishing boat guide and cooked picnic meals for tourists on the banks of the Arkansas River. A dude ranch in Fountain hired him to lead packhorse trips up Cheyenne Mountain for the wealthy guests staying at the Broadmoor Hotel in Colorado Springs.

His last year in the mountains, after the VA doctor warned him he should live at a lower altitude because of his heart, he bought an old retired buckskin roping horse and stabled it for free in exchange for fencing a five-acre pasture for a rancher near the Garden of the Gods. On late afternoons he'd ride bareback across Highway 24 up a trail to watch the sun set behind Pikes Peak.

Profar trotted the sleepy old horse through Manitou Springs one freezing New Year's Eve, his saddlebag filled with cold beers, not a cop in sight. When he spurred the animal through the door of a saloon and raised his drink, a hundred cheering drunkards turned and wished him well. He was tipsy, cock-eyed as he waved and slurred a greeting to honking traffic. He stopped the horse in the falling snow in the dark and raised his beer in a toast to the future. The same hopeful, solitary tribute he'd made to himself so often these many years.

He called his brother that night, fully drunk and slurring his words, talking gibberish. His brother reminded Profar that the doctors had told him to lay off the booze.

Profar asked why he'd never been able to gain traction in his own life.

"You've been interested in too many things, Eddie. Maybe you spread yourself too thin."

After a long silence, his brother then said, "Why don't you just come home, Eddie? We've got room at the house. The kids always liked you. They always loved your stories. Hell, everybody likes Uncle Eddie's stories. You could live at the cabin, if you want. We never go there because the kids can't get a signal for their damn phones. It's quiet with no people, Eddie. Just like you like it. We're both not getting younger, you know. You'd be close to the family. I always hate to think of you out there alone."

"I have a dog," Profar said. "He's not much. He's a mutt. His name is Tex."

"There's plenty people in town who still know you," his brother said. "How come you name all your dogs Tex?"

"Like who do I know up there?"

"Jimmy Lewis, for one," his brother said. "From your old band, back in the day. You've known Jimmy since middle school. Other people, too. They ask about you all the time. You're like some wandering minstrel on the road to adventure. People ask me all the time what you're up to, where you're going next. Nobody can ever find out where you live."

Profar told his brother his life had come to nothing. He'd dawdled time away, somebody who'd never held a real job. Close to flat broke most of the time. If it wasn't for his Army disability pension, he'd be living on the street. He wasn't much more than a common drifter, a tramp who never stayed with a woman for long before he'd find something wrong and get restless all over again. He wondered what their mother would have thought.

"I don't know where these years went," Profar said. "You were right. I never found just one thing to be good at. One thing to love. I didn't leave any tracks, anywhere. It's like I walked on water, and not in the good way."

"If you see your tracks laid out in front of you, Eddie...it's not your path," his brother said. "Uncle used to preach that, remember? After dad died, he always said that and we'd laugh and look at each like he was nuts. I was always jealous that he took you to that island."

"You were too little," Profar said. "You always hated the woods, anyway."

"I know, but I still got mad about it."

On his way to Duluth he stopped in Chicago, everything he owned that mattered jammed into his old Army duffle bag with his name and rank still stenciled on it. He took along the dog. He'd found a directory of graves for the Korean section of a cemetery in the city and Yevgeny Lee's name was on the list.

He stayed in a cheap hotel on the North Side that accepted pets and drove to Lee's childhood neighborhood, where he ate lunch at a restaurant that served the same kimchee and spicy beef soup he remembered from his meal that week they'd sprung him loose from the hospital in Busan. There was a banged up pay telephone mounted on a wall inside the restaurant. There was a directory hanging from a hook whose cover was filled entirely with Korean script. The boy behind the counter brought his coffee.

"I never saw anybody use that thing," the boy said. "I don't know if it even works. People have cell phones, you know."

He crossed the room. He opened the phone book and laughed and told the boy he was looking for somebody named Kim.

"Mister, you know how many Kims live around here? Like, zillions. My uncle owns this place and half the people who work here are Kims."

He took the book and thumbed through the Kim pages. He dragged his finger down past the long columns of tiny six-point text until the Kang surnames began. He raced back up the list to the final dozen Kims and rubbed his eyes when he saw it.

Kim, Peggy Sue.

He swept one hand across his face as if wiping away a heavy drowsiness. He stared at the name and gulped his coffee. He tore out the page and walked to his hotel, thinking of what he should say to her. He sat looking at the phone for a long time before he finally dialed.

"Jia?"

The cadence and inflection of the slightly husky voice on the recorded message was so very familiar. As if time had never passed after all these decades. Her accent had almost disappeared and she spoke with a brisk confidence, all business. He tried to imagine what she looked like.

Profar spoke haltingly, stammering as he tried to hide his excitement and surprise. He carried on a bit too long about how good it was to hear her voice and apologized repeatedly for bursting unannounced into her life. He said he'd been searching for her all these years and immediately knew that he now sounded like a stalking degenerate, a desperate and unwelcome stranger from the past. A loser calling out of the blue, someone whose name she may have very well forgotten. He told her the name of his hotel and said he didn't own a cell phone and asked if she might have time to see him. Only to say hello, he said. Nothing more than that. Just a few moments for old times' sake.

"Please call," he finally said in a voice that sounded as if he were pleading.

"I knew it was you when I saw that name. I just knew."

When he hung up, he realized that she might be married now with a husband. He was thinking of calling again to apologize when he felt the sharp, stabbing pain race across his shoulder and decided that he'd just walked too much that day. Leave it alone, he said. Don't bother her again. It's good to know she'd made a new life, so be satisfied with that. There was never any hope of getting together, anyway. It had all been just another one of his fantasies. He opened and closed his numb hand and felt the icy tingle race up his arm and settle in his shoulder.

He sat for a long time on the edge of the threadbare bed in that shabby room, petting the dog. He felt overwhelmed by so many things as he looked down at his feet and put his head in his hands.

He thought he should call Duluth, but then felt dizzy and knew it would just make his brother worry if he sounded weird on the phone. He hated when people he loved worried about him. He'd already said that he would stay an extra day in Chicago so he could visit Lee's grave. They'd joked about the lousy motel he was staying at and Profar said Kerouac always preferred the charm of flophouses because they seemed more real and honest. Like a pair of worn jeans you could trust. Maybe he was just suspicious of the swanky side of life, he told his brother. He couldn't afford anything else, anyway.

He thought of bringing her flowers, but decided this also might be too much. He'd just seem like a decrepit former suitor showing up in the doorway.

He shaved and put on his best shirt. He wrote down her Beverly Boulevard address and decided he would lay down and take a short nap. He was so tired. His heart was pounding and all that walking had left him gasping and light-headed. It took him forever these days to catch his breath. He had so much to think about. He went to the bathroom and splashed water on his face and stared at himself in the mirror.

And then the phone rang. He nearly tripped answering it.

"Jia?"

A long silence, during which he heard someone young laughing in the background and then the yowl of a cat.

"Who is this?" It sounded like her, though it wasn't.

"Pardon me. I'm sorry,"

"Who is this?"

"I was looking for Miss Kim Jia-Soon. Thanks for calling back. I appreciate it very much."

"Who wants to know?"

"I'm sorry," Profar said. "I'm an old friend of hers. I'm sorry to bother you, really I am. Your voice. You sound just like her. I got this number from the phone book."

"What phone book?"

"I apologize, I thought I explained..."

"Mom doesn't live here anymore," the woman said in the careful way you speak when you're not quite sure you haven't given someone too much information.

"You never said who you were."

"You sound like her," Profar said.

Profar could hear the echo of his own hurried breathing in the phone receiver. He looked down at the worn rug. His numb hand began to shake and so he sat on it.

"Sorry again," he said. "It's just that...your voice. It sounds so much like her."

"And you knew my mother, how? This is strange, you understand that, don't you? Calling up like this. I thought it might have something to do with her estate. She changed her name legally a long time ago. Never told me why, but everybody called her Peggy. Nobody called her that old name."

"Jia," Profar said. "We knew each other in Korea. Her estate?"

The woman's voice grew somber: "Mom passed away last month. We're getting ready to rent her condo. We just never changed the voice mail. She still gets calls. I don't know why I'm telling this to a stranger."

"Her condo," Profar said.

"She owned the whole building, actually. We're renting out her unit. I'm not usually here. We were cleaning up when you called."

Profar's chest tightened. It felt like someone was shoving a cement block against his ribs.

"You could be some crook for all I know, a weirdo. I should probably hang up."

"I wouldn't blame you," Profar said. "A stranger calling out of the blue. I wouldn't blame you at all. Can I ask you a question? Did your parents live there for a long time? I had another friend in that neighborhood. I was looking for him, too. I'm so sorry about your mom."

"I never knew my dad," she said. "That was mom's idea, her name. Peggy Sue. She was always afraid somebody would come and send her back to the old country. You're not going to ask if you can come over, are you? That would be really strange. I'm afraid that's not going to happen, mister. Even though you've got me very curious. It's not a good idea for you to come over. I'm sure you understand."

"Of course," Profar said. "I just can't get over how much your voice sounds like her. She was a wonderful woman. I'm so sorry. We were friends, you know."

Profar felt his voice quavering. His dry throat tightened.

"People always said that," the woman said. "That she was sweet and nice. She had a lot of friends. Maybe you did know her after all."

"It was a long time ago. In Korea, of course."

"She never talked at all about Korea, except for the war. And it was just little stuff, no details at all. I think she wanted to start from scratch when she came here. She never liked to talk about the past, ever."

"Can I ask your name?"

"I'm not comfortable with that, mister," the woman said. "Not at all. I see what you're doing. Next thing, you'll want to come over for a visit. She named me after her mom, that's all I'll say. I have my grandmother's name. I think I've talked to you too much already. I don't mean to sound rude, but you have to be careful these days. People play tricks."

Profar told her his name again and where he was staying and said, "Your mom had a scar right under her eye. The tiniest scar, a little half-moon.

When she smiled you could really see it if she wasn't wearing makeup. She had a slight limp, too. When she walked fast, you'd notice. She was self-conscious about the scar. She said the limp was from when she was a little girl, in the war."

"I better go now," the woman said after a long uncomfortable pause, during which Profar could hear her blow her nose and sniffle. Her voice thickened.

"How did you know about the scar? This is so strange, mister. How did you know? I have to go now. I'm very sorry."

"I'm glad you called me back," Profar said. "I don't want to make you uncomfortable. Best wishes to you. I'm sorry about your mom. She was special to me."

But she'd already hung up.

He vaguely recalled staring at the phone and sitting on the bed with his hands in his lap, totally exhausted.

The last thing he remembered from what remained of the earthly world was being hypnotized by his own image in the bathroom mirror at that decrepit hotel, strings of lank wet hair across his sweating cold forehead.

The phone had started ringing again after he'd hung up, yet he didn't have the strength to walk a few feet and reach for it. It kept ringing and ringing.

His old heart came to life inside his chest like a pair of stomping feet, the angry rhythm all out of whack, a constant and confused fluttering, like the sustained vibration of a small motor. A faint growl instead if a true heartbeat. He tried to take the few steps to where the phone continued to ring persistently on the table. He suddenly weighed a thousand pounds, his feet impossible to lift. The ashen pallor of his face in the mirror seemed welcoming. He was now staring at the True Eddie. The Final Version of Eddie Profar. A wormy twitch crept across his cheek and he suddenly had the sense that the world would now be forever unrecognizable. As foreign as another person's dream. He opened his mouth to shout, but what came forth was the voice of someone speaking under water, a desperate gargle instead of words. His head felt like it might explode.

He wobbled in the tilting room as if he were on roller skates as he desperately gripped the sink basin with both hands. The pain in his chest and head now thundered as he crashed to the floor, the world falling away beneath his feet as the telephone rang and rang and he realized that Jia's daughter was calling him.

EPILOGUE

They continued to assemble at his bed each morning in small deputations, like visiting delegates who'd come to bid farewell.

They lifted his blue hand from where it rested wrapped in tubes and tape at his side. As they paid their respects, he'd inhale and wonder why he didn't smell his dog. The little shit wouldn't know what was going on, but they could have brought the dog.

He had no idea of where he was, though he'd heard a ship's horn one night. He wondered how he'd arrived here from the motel.

With his supernatural snout he could now smell all the way to the nurse's station, where each evening one of them ate strawberry yogurt. The scrape of the plastic spoon, the lingering fruity scent. He took a whiff of someone's shampoo as her hair ends trailed across his cheek. The mint on another's breath. There were the children, their feet scuffling, and they smelled like candy and milk. What fun it would be to just sit up, open his eyes and start jabbering like nothing had happened.

His head now calmed down. It was always a problem, putting a lid on his busy brain. He became suddenly interested in the numbness of his distant ghost feet. The entire world and all it contained now ended at his feet. His dead toes, heavy and thick down there. He could feel it when somebody touched his hand. He could hear them mumble, like they were afraid to wake him. If they only knew. He could smell the nurse who came to wipe his face with the cold towel. Then the people would touch him and whisper more greetings. His brother would sit at the edge of the bed and talk to him like he expected a full conversation to ensue. Like he expected Eddie to answer.

Who were the others? His brother was the first to arrive in the morning and he would try to squeeze Eddie's hand back to life. He had his special sound when he sat. Someone else had been coming lately and he could feel the wedding ring on her finger as she stroked his arm and smoothed the bedsheet across his chest. There was a familiar feel to the delicate bones of her hand. She smelled wonderful and he thought he'd once heard her sob when she touched him.

At the end of the day the sound of all their fading footsteps in the hallway broke his heart.

He lately had the feeling he was standing alone in an abandoned house. The kitchen drawers were pulled open, peeling paper on the moldy walls. The smell of wet carpet. Garden weeds trying to crawl through the broken windows, nature taking everything back.

It was always too warm or too hot in the room. He thought he might have a tube somewhere for what little food they now gave him. The hose in his throat tasted bitter when he tried to swallow. Profar was peeing warmly into his bag when somebody came up to the bed and held his hand. A stranger who he'd never smelled before.

"Eddie, it's me."

The room turned ice cold and the hand would not let go.

"You were awfully hard to find, old pal," the voice said. "It's your turn now."

The visitor patted Profar's hand and squeezed it.

"Relax, Edward. It no big deal, the way it happens. See you around."

He fell asleep listening to the man's shoes creak where he imagined the door might be, as if he'd turned around for one last look. He woke from a clamorous dream filled with strangers whose expressions seemed to demand that he know them.

When everyone was gone that night, a nurse who smelled like hairspray lifted his arm and tugged the pee tube before it had a chance to empty. He felt embarrassed as he lay there naked as she wiped him and changed his gown. She did not put the tube back.

The medicine cart rattled and something icy stung his wrist as the nurse poked him with another needle and left the room and squeaked down the hallway. All the machines on the wall above his head were now silent. Those people who remained in the room were sobbing. He was overcome by a pleasant numbness.

Oblivion came like the crack of a whip.

He'd existed now for so long in a constant state of imminence and looming threat, first dying and then resurrected. He'd wished often that it would just be over, but when it finally came there was no gentle fade from life to death, no stepping over a certain line or barrier. It arrived as a sudden thunder with him being lifted assuredly into a dreamy void. He felt himself dissolve, suddenly overwhelmed by an unexplainable love for all the world and everyone in it as he drifted from here to there into the depths of an unfamiliar darkness. All silent now and filled with odors so rich and true it made him swoon.

And just as suddenly, he was also no longer alone.

She lay next to him with her massive forepaws outstretched, the snow powdering in the thick ruff of fur at her throat. The river ice was blown bare in patches and the stars burned overhead. It was the first full moon of the lunar calendar, the January *ohgiil*, signifying hope for a season of prosperity and good fortune.

She chuffed softly, a greeting, and turned to lick his shoulder with her rough sandpaper tongue and he looked up and studied the bright moon as he'd so long remembered it shining above the frozen Imjin River. He had come back to begin another journey.

In tandem, they turned and watched the two approaching shapes casting their cones of yellow light as they walked from the far side of the river. The soldiers' breaths steamed in the thirty-below air as the brightly silhouetted shapes moved across the featureless snow, their flashlights swinging like lanterns. Behind them, brighter lamps were shining from the DMZ fence.

The tigers looked away, as if they knew their eyes would glow scarlet in the beams of the flashlights. The soldiers' boots crunched.

The female tiger stood and shook off the snow and walked away, her hind foot twisted slightly sideways from her wounded hip as she trotted and joined the male, who bounded effortlessly forward in ten-foot leaps and began to run. They tucked their shoulders and flattened their ears, their strides perfectly matched, hind paws falling precisely into the track of the forepaw print as they settled into an easy loping gait that took them beyond the reach of the soldiers' sweeping lights.

As they ran, she opened her jaws and without a sound bit him gently with her six-inch teeth, a lovable gnawing of the loose pouch of skin at his throat. He leaped and pivoted on his hind legs as their enormous bodies rose and tumbled in the snow, and he answered with his own snarling bite as she twisted and growled in his powerful clasp. They wrestled. She moaned. She clawed and swiped at him with theatrical anger and then they stood together and rubbed against each other and continued their romantic moonlight game.

Ahead, the illuminated snow showed the looping serpent shape that had given the Imjin River its ancient name. The tigers continued to brush and bounce against each other teasingly, their heavy breaths turning to falling frost in the cold, as they ran beyond the reach of the powerful DMZ barrier lamps. Far behind them, the two soldiers with their rifles continued to walk slowly and flicker their flashlights back and forth across the crystalline expanse of the frozen river.

As they ran, the female turned and looked squarely into his eyes. She leaped ahead and began to run faster, inviting him to follow.

At that moment, as he roared and playfully pretended that he could not catch her, he was certain that the purest words require no provenance or reason. That they come from where they were first formed, carried across the world by a wind reborn in the heart of the one who said those words before they were thought. And as such, became the unspoken and everlasting truth.

Now that they'd claimed each other after all this time, and he'd returned to start anew, he realized they could run forever and never leave the bounds of their newly found home, and that all who would intrude from this moment on would simply pay the cost of trespassing.

- THE END -

OTHER BOOKS BY GOJAN NIKOLICH

The Gopher King: A Dark Comedy (2020)

Hallucinogenic. Meditative. Depressing. Intelligent. Poetic. Layered. And, most certainly, literate...Just know, the writing alone will leave you breathless."
–Joel R. Dennstedt, *Readers 'Favorite Reviews*

"...like a mashup of *Platoon* and *Gremlins* scripted by William S. Burroughs...his prose is entrancing."
–*Kirkus Reviews*

"They say we read non-fiction for facts but for truth we read novels, a thought that came to me often as I enjoyed this book."
–Tim Butcher, *NYT* Best-Selling author of
The Trigger: Hunting the Assassin Who Brought the World to War

...a verbal portrait of PTSD suitable for hanging in any VA hospital...
I highly recommend putting a velveteen gopher on the desk of every VA shrink."
–Charles Templeton, Vietnam Veterans of America

"...a fascinating and extremely thought-provoking romp through the fantastic and the fatalistic."
–Bridgett Harris, *The Colorado Springs Independent*

...intense, disturbing and laugh-out-loud funny,
The Gopher King" might leave you a little shell-shocked, but in a good way."
–Scott Miller, *The Vail Daily*

Ashes in Venice: A Vengeance Thriller (2022)

Intelligent, complex, polished and fiendishly entertaining...
Gojan Nikolich is an author you ll be glad you found."
–**Steve Quaid,** *Indies Today*

"... unique, twisted and ingenious. A not-to-be-missed thriller that will have
you cheering for the bad guy as it blends a troubled cop with a vigilante
murderer."
–***Sublime Reviews***

Unpredictable, brilliantly crafted and deliriously unhinged
...Nikolich s word craft is nothing short of jaw-dropping."
–***BestThrillers.com***

A tightly wound and brilliantly constructed psychological thriller
...A stunning procedural from an author to watch."
–***The Prairies Book Review / Canada***

"A hauntingly clever story...fast-paced and intricately detailed."
–***The BookLife Prize***

ABOUT THE AUTHOR

Gojan Nikolich is a former newspaper reporter, editor and public relations agency executive. He and his wife once owned a 100-year-old weekly newspaper in Colorado and his writing has appeared in the Chicago Tribune, Chicago Sun-Times and Pacific Stars & Stripes, Tokyo. He reported regularly for WGN and WBBM radio in Chicago.

Nikolich's novel, *Ashes in Venice*, was chosen Best Psychological Thriller of 2022 by BestThrillers.com.

"...his prose is entrancing," *Kirkus Reviews* said of his award-winning Vietnam War dark comedy, *The Gopher King*.

He graduated with B.A. and M.A. degrees in English Literature from DePaul University and served as a decorated US Army Sergeant with both the 2nd and 4th Infantry divisions.

OTHER TITLES BY GOJAN NIKOLICH

NOTE FROM GOJAN NIKOLICH

Word-of-mouth is crucial for any author to succeed. If you enjoyed *Tiger Season*, please leave a review online—anywhere you are able. Even if it's just a sentence or two. It would make all the difference and would be very much appreciated.

Thanks!
Gojan Nikolich

We hope you enjoyed reading this title from:

www.blackrosewriting.com

Subscribe to our mailing list – *The Rosevine* – and receive **FREE** books, daily deals, and stay current with news about upcoming releases and our hottest authors.
Scan the QR code below to sign up.

Already a subscriber? Please accept a sincere thank you for being a fan of Black Rose Writing authors.

View other Black Rose Writing titles at www.blackrosewriting.com/books and use promo code **PRINT** to receive a **20% discount** when purchasing.

www.ingramcontent.com/pod-product-compliance
Lightning Source LLC
Chambersburg PA
CBHW051435190726
48289CB00001B/193